THE STELLAR QUEST

A Novel by

Paul Alexander Fichera

ALSO BY PAUL A. FICHERA

www.PaulFichera.com

Your Inner You

A women's lingerie company mails Keir Adrian Travaglini a catalogue invite addressed not to him but to Keira Travaglini. His girlfriend thinks it's hilarious, and starts purchasing items using Keir's mistaken name and his address. Keira wins a contest, a whirlwind extravaganza through the main tourist cities of Europe. "Keira" wins the contest; not "Keir." It sort of gets complicated from that point on.

Angie's Revenge: A Tale of Many Lifetimes

A newly married thirty-something woman discovers one night she's meant for way more than merely cooking and cleaning … and other wifey things.

Yesterday's Child: An Adventure Through Time

A gifted high school student discovers he can astral travel to the future where he learns humanity's ultimate fate; it falls on him to make it not happen.

Aiden, You've Been Very Bad

"I know what he did, Tracy," Ann Marcella said. "And how many times he's done it. And you're in no condition to go back out there looking like your cat just died."

Ann extended her hand and told her. "Aiden's been cheating on you, hasn't he? And you just found out from your best friend? ... I can help." Ann reached into her purse and handed the girl a business card:

GET EVEN, LTD.
"Don't risk Jail, he's not worth it.
We'll handle it."

Kayelle's Return: A Sci-Fi at Christmastime

The Nazca Plain in fact stood as a curious strip of land the Inca Indians had used as a painter's canvas upon which they had scribbled twisted patterns and lines into the hard red desert rock. From the ground the lines were meaningless, and as roads went nowhere. Yet from the air they formed patterns and shapes: a condor, a fish, a spider, a monkey. They were believed to have been etched by the Inca themselves, for their gods who they hoped would see them.

Crossing Cassandra: Some Folks Just Shouldn't be Messed With

A playboy is offered the "best sex" of his life by a woman who offers him her daughter's phone number. He's terrible when it comes to his lack of respect for the female gender. And the woman, herself, as gorgeous as she is, has no interest in him. Will he take the bait? We'll see.

DEDICATION

Dedicated to those
Who see tomorrow and ask,
How soon?

And to Kathryn and Dan.
Friends who were a
Great help in getting me to finally
Get these books out there.

And Norbert,
Who thought the Stellar Quest was good
A long time ago.

TABLE OF CONTENTS

INTRODUCTION

In *The Stellar Quest*, 25th Century Terrans (Earth-based humans) do not live on the land anymore. Those lucky enough to be on Earth at all, live within "island cities," structures of metal and crystal, rising like giant mushrooms above the plains of Earth. For all intent and purposes these cities are like their floating counterparts (the space cities), adrift above the Earth, Moon, Mars and Venus. They remain as detached from Earth's soil and as self-sufficient as the cities humanity has erected in the darkness of the night sky. The Earth has begun the road back to healing after the great abuse foisted upon it by humanity in centuries past (and this despite the insistence of a few back then that no such thing by mankind's hand had happened) and life beyond the Island Cities is livable again. The majority of the human race now knew better than to ever again trust itself to take up residence on the surface. It is a dangerous place for humans, who by this point have the good sense to remain content to live in the comfort of their above and below ground sealed cities.

Paul Alexander Fichera
June, 2015

BEYOND PLUTO

-1-

December 25, 2410.

A radio telescope array on Ceres (the largest at 785 kilometers of the asteroids in the belt between Mars and Jupiter), its antennae aimed skyward, listened to the sounds of the galaxy. Then it spoke. Perhaps someone out there would hear and one day answer. Calling and listening, one then the other, the array was like a lone wolf on a lone peak, howling into the wilderness in search of another. For four hundred years the search for intelligent life beyond the solar system had been undertaken by the human race, conducted under various project headings upon every planet, asteroid and outpost where the opportunity for a more accessible window to the universe was accorded. Except for one possible response received almost a century before, the results had been mostly disappointing. Whatever life existed, if it existed at all, amid the stars beyond Earth's sun, no real evidence of its presence had ever been uncovered.

Still, the hope remained.

-2-

In the eternal darkness beyond Pluto, and so far distant that only the pinprick light of the Sun could be spotted in the night behind them, the crew of the starship *Stellar Quest* bid farewell, perhaps forever, to the home solar system of the Planet Earth, and continued on for Eighty-two Eridani, a star twenty light years from Earth. The first attempt ever to reach another solar system, the *Stellar Quest* began it journey in the autumn of A.D. 2410. Evidence suggested planets might inhabit the Eighty-two Eridani system, and if so in about twenty years the *Stellar Quest* hoped to make planet fall upon one of them. The voyage had been undertaken in response to that very same radio transmission received a century before. The signal had originated in Eighty-two Eridani.

Captain Mitchel S. Katill, ship commander, as he studied the dark emptiness before him, was unsure which he dreaded more: finding nothing upon arrival, not even a world to set down upon, or meeting a whole new civilization with not one ancestral link to humanity.

The ship could not survive a return trip to Earth, not without new provisions mined from the Eighty-two Eridani system. What faced his crew ahead then, was death or the unknown.

He couldn't decide which was worse.

***

Mitchel was topside on the bridge that hour, and he was alone, absently monitoring the consoles and information stations the Bridge Crew worked in the course of the mission. There were eight other crewmembers aboard *Stellar Quest* beside him, all below and already asleep in their suspended animation chambers. He was procrastinating; he would join them in cryogenic slumber directly. It wasn't as if they or even Mitch needed to remain awake. The ship was on course, and being run entirely by the flight program. There was nothing to do until the *Stellar Quest* completed its journey across the Interstellar night twenty-three years hence than to sleep and await the voyage's end.

They'd left the home solar system behind more than a month ago; all that lay ahead was empty space; a million stars were out there in humanity's Milky Way galaxy alone, but they were so far away, it was downright foolish to even contemplate someday setting sail for them. Space warps and wormholes, while exciting prospects, and good fantasy, were concepts way too impractical and exotic for anyone to give serious thought to . . . at least in this time of Mitch's lifespan. Eighty-two Eridani on the other hand was relatively close (20 light years) as distances in space went. The ship was presently moving at its cruising speed: ninety percent light speed.

Which was funny. Pluto lay only five hours out beyond Earth at one-hundred percent light speed. It had taken the *Stellar Quest* most of a week to reach it, its diminutive snowball presence— so pathetic a one as to a long time ago be demoted from a planet to a lowly asteroid— had shown itself quite unimpressively in the viewport ahead. And then nothing, a star-strewn vastness had lain ahead that was a sobering reminder of just how alone in the universe the eight of them really were.

And to even achieve that familiar "space travel" look in the forward viewports, like in all the age-old science fiction stories, meant using imaging compensators to correct for the image distortions created by their high-speed travel. Without it, a "rainbow/starbow" had begun to overtake the stars and slowly consume the night skies as the vessel accelerated out of the home solar system to past twenty percent light speed. All forward windows had revealed that the stars directly ahead were beginning to turn blue. Each hour, as the ship's speed increased, that circle of color expanded, while the stars directly in the center of the infestation slowly disappeared. All rearward screens, meanwhile, showed a similar effect only in red. It was the Doppler Effect, red-shifting the stars the ship accelerated away from, and blue-shifting those that lay ahead. Gradually, the two colors had spread across the heavens until they met.

At ninety percent light speed, only a narrow starbow (a band of seemingly compressed stars, some red hued, and the rest blue) now

11

encircled the ship directly along its mid-section. The forward stars were gone, so too the rearward. Those ahead had had their light frequencies shifted beyond visible blue, while those to the rear had passed infrared. It was as if the ship sailed amid a vast black nothingness, and it was at those times (when the distortion compensator algorithm was not being utilized) when Mitch wanted to just turn the forward screens off. Either way there was nothing worth seeing out there anyway.

The mission would be one-way; it was just too impractical to seriously expect the *Stellar Quest* to return to Earth, once a settlement in Eighty-two Eridani had successfully been begun. Should no settlement— no compatible world to Earth's— be found, and no hope of adopting the star system as a residence for humans, then of course the crew would make journey for home. But in all cases the bad news was always that another twenty plus years would pass until they returned. Half a century of time would pass since their original Earth departure at the very least. Everyone they once knew would either be dead or near to it. The crew— even had they not preserved their bodies in cryogenic sleep for the long haul— would not have aged near as much as their counterparts on Earth had they remained awake, because of the effect of *Time Dilation*. As the *Stellar Quest* reached its point nine zero cruising speed, time aboard ship had begun to slow. Mitch knew this, intellectually, but consciously he had no measure of its effect. Even the chronometers moved at what seemed normal time, but one hour aboard ship now represented almost two and a half hours back on Earth.

A shame. Aboard ship, the twenty-three year long voyage would only age them ten years. But what would have been the point of it?

Might as well stop putting it off, he decided.

He worked his way to the lower decks, back near Engineering and briefly regarded the sleeping stances of the four men and four women who served under him on this endeavor. He smiled and nodded to the present situation.

"Time to do it," he said to no one in particular, not even a sentient computer with vocal address to wish him a pleasant sleep. And then entering his own hibernaculum (sleep chamber), he allowed the robotics to install the necessary connections and fluids to sustain him over the next Ten (Twenty-Three?) years.

Soon, he was under and gone from the world of conscious thought. His only last thought was the hope that this endeavor to find a home in a distant solar system would not be one for naught.

PART ONE:
THE HAGERTONS

CHAPTER ONE

Saturday, October 25, 2415

Frida and Jeffrey Hagerton, age thirteen and nine, were in Frida's bedroom in the island city of New Allentown in the Blue Mountains of eastern Pennsylvania. They were within Frida's manger shaped "bed," adrift in its anti-grav floatation system, just seemingly floating in midair about a foot or so above the hard bottom of the trough-shaped sleep chamber. The two Hagerton kids were two of the city's newest additions. As had been the standard practice for many generations by this point in the new and 25th century, new additions were only allowed when room opened up within the island cities.

Frida and Jeffrey appeared to be day-dreaming as they floated in veritable zero G inside Frida's bed, but they weren't in actuality. They were "virtual reality" travelling. The tiny, skeletal headsets atop their heads were called *Neural Sensory Imagizers*. A small deck on Frida's nightstand, transmitted sensory data to the headsets which in turn distributed it to the five sensory centers of the human brain.

The two were just now completing an hour long walk through the caverns of Luray in the Blue Ridge Mountains just east of the once land-based town of Luray, Virginia. After an hour of threading past stalactites and stalagmites, columns, draperies, flow stones and elevated walkways meters above in some cases the cavern floor, they were now about to ascend the entry stairway, hewn out of the limestone rock, up to where the gift shop, reception area and adjacent automotive museum of the old facility once resided.

That was all gone now, even the hedgerow maze that once existed on the grounds to entertain and frustrate those souls courageous enough to try to work their way around the false turns and dead ends to make it to the center and then back out again. All long gone. Now what only existed was but a tiny cedar-wood cabin, a facade actually, butted up against the old cave entrance. No one actually came here anymore, not without special permission. A force field in fact guarded the entrance, and would only be lowered when the proper access permits were proffered.

Not that Frida and Jeffrey had need of such things; they weren't really there. They had accessed a neural-transmitted touring site that allowed them to visit and peruse the caverns without ever setting foot on the grounds. A tiny, floating sensor sphere crystal which resembled your average size soap bubble— both in size and behavior— was dispatched from its storage nook in the cedar-wood cabin and sent down into the caverns, wafting through the air, propelled by its internal gravity-defying drive. Latticed and layered with organic sensors, it recorded the surroundings, read the images, sounds, the feel of the place, smells and even tastes. All five of the senses human bodies used to interpret the world around them, were replicated in the tiny sphere, as it wandered the caverns, the data transmitted to its distant "clients." It was like actually being there. The deck unit on Frida's nightstand even added her and Jeffrey's imagined presence in the caverns to the simulation. All they need do was open their eyes and be aware of each other.

Upon the bed, Frida's waist-length blond hair fringed her high cheek bones and forehead. She wore a short purple skirt with a burgundy-red sweater and matching tights. Jeffrey, meanwhile, dark-haired, wore a dark brown pullover and denim-blue trousers.

It was autumn, the summer months were long gone, and the two— apropos for the season— dressed accordingly. As well, in fact, for exploring famous caves, like Luray, at this time of year (even if the experience wouldn't really affect them physically, seeing as they weren't really there). The chill of the damp, dark cavern hung all around them, nevertheless, as if it were all very real, and their bodies reacted accordingly. Frida could feel the cavern's chilled air gamely attempt to penetrate her tights and shoes and numb her toes. She'd been splashed more than a dozen times since entering the cave by all the seepage from the surface ground water, dripping off the stalactites and the ceiling, plipping, splashing and dampening the surface rock they walked upon.

The cave entrance was over ten meters above. Though they could have floated upward, like ghosts (which is what the Sensor Sphere was doing), they tasked the data stream's realism simulation by climbing. Once at the top and in the facade cedar-wood cabin, they opened the exterior door and squinted what they imagined were their real eyes as they entered the sun lit autumn wilderness beyond. The Blue Ridge Mountains, to the east, were tree-lined in rich autumn colors, as a deep, blue sky and fluffy white clouds hung above the entire scene.

"Hey, you two!" they suddenly heard. Keith Hagerton, their father, appeared all at once before them. He had entered Frida's bedroom. The kids saw him. The neural circuits of the Sensor Sphere transmission added Keith's form to the simulation.

In her mind, Frida instructed the simulation to shut down. Her bedroom solidified before her and Jeffrey.

"Yeah, Dad?" she replied.

"Your mother called," Keith said of Kimberly Hagerton. "Your mom's invited us to a picnic lunch in one of the terrace parks topside."

***

The three Hagertons exited their family "residence" in the city and began the walk up the corridor for the nearest "turbo lift" to the city top terrace. In moments, the four were topside and from the transparent, protective bubble up here came the gorgeous expanse of Berks County and the Blue Mountains of Pennsylvania. Kimberly Hagerton met up with her family, left the quaint, specialty stores in the shopping district and the now fully reunited family strode off to a grassy, tree-laden picnic area, where they lunched on fruits and vegetables, mainly corn on the cob, potatoes, green beans and some vegetable concoction that was meant to look like a hot dog on a wheat bun. It was way better for one than the real thing ever was.

***

After lunch, Frida and Jeffrey were over near an edge of the protective bubble, and were just gazing out at the countryside. Keith approached them both.

"Is that New Jersey over there?" Frida asked her father, pointing to the far eastern horizon.

"What's left of it," he said. "This far north it's all mostly bogs and submerged forests today. The Atlantic pretty much washed most of the cities that used to be there a hundred years ago away and most of south Jersey with it."

"What was it like?" mused Frida, wistfully. She glanced to her father then.

Keith shrugged. "It was a place to call home once," he said. "Many did. It was one of the most crowded places to call home in the whole United States. All I can tell you is what I've seen in the archives, Friddy. If you're curious, access them. They've actually been enhanced to give you a feel for what it was like to walk the boardwalks down by the coast back then in the old days. The ocean breezes, the salt sea air. . . "As did his thoughts, his voice trailed off into silence.

Frida, puzzled by her father's seemingly lost stance, his thoughts lost out over what was now the Atlantic Ocean, glanced up to him. *"Enhanced?"* she probed of him. "Why?"

Keith Hagerton, coming back from it, patted his daughter's head and smiled at her. "Waaaayyyy back," he said, ". . . in the 21st Century, the best visual archives only recorded sight and sound, and even they weren't that immersive, not like today. It was mostly images projected on a wall. What, did you actually think I had firsthand knowledge?" He huffed a laugh. "That was *way* before my time, honey."

"Oh," she uttered, now herself trailing off as both she and her brother lost themselves in the view of the shallow and watery expanse far in the distance.

Keith left the two of them then and joined Kimberly atop the blanket she'd laid upon the grass in the park.

***

"The kids okay?" Kimberly asked Keith.

He nodded. "They're fine. They're just curious about the world, the way it was in the old days when we were still allowed to live out there on the surface."

Kimberly nodded, thoughtfully. "What were they doing before you dragged them up *here?"* she asked, grinning then.

"Visiting Luray Caverns," he told her.

"An old playback?"

He shook his head. "A live feed from the site," he answered.

"So I take it Jeffrey's okay, then," she replied, "with cave exploring?"

"As long as it's not real. I don't know how he'll react tomorrow when we visit one for real."

"I feel like a ghoul," Kimberly Hagerton replied. "I want a Mother/daughter thing with Frida tomorrow in Old Philadelphia, but I know she would rather be with her father exploring Crystal Cave instead of Jeffrey. He's more like me, I have to say, and Frida, she's all you, you and your thirst for visiting the sites out there in the wilderness no one actually goes out to and visits anymore."

"He'll be fine," Keith replied. "It ought to be fun."

"Have you told him where you're taking him?"

Keith shook his head. "Haven't even mentioned it. I'm saving it for a surprise."

"Oh, knowing our Jeffrey, he'll be surprised alright. He'll hate it. He hates going outside."

Keith smirked. "Well, it's a father/son thing," he said. "You want a mother/daughter thing. . ." Keith nodded. "This is my version."

"I think the DNA got those two reversed," Kimberly replied. "Frida's your real son, and Jeffrey's more like the daughter I always wished Frida would be."

"Yeah, well," Keith answered.

"Crystal Cave . . . there's not much to it, if I recall," mused Kimberly.

"No, nothing like the Luray caverns, not even close."

"It's really, actually kind of lame, isn't it?" Kimberly added.

Keith Hagerton shrugged and laughed. "It's nearby, which makes it convenient. And yeah it is sort of lame, which is why Jeff and I are not just going there to visit the old tourist cave. We're going to have some fun."

Kimberly knew her husband, and didn't like the sound of that at all. "How?" she asked. "Where else are you planning to drag my son?"

"There are passages below the main tourist cave that the public never saw because they're a lot harder to get to and involve a lot of crawling around on your belly or on all fours, and trudging probably through ground water. It ought to be interesting. You never know what you'll find down there. We might even find new offshoots that no one's ever seen before. Checking them out ought to be interesting."

"To you, maybe, honey," she replied.

"What do you mean?" he said.

"I've been hearing tales all my life about those supposed places under the main cave, about how people, some of them, go down to explore them and no one ever hears from them ever again." She shook her head. "I don't know, Keith, I have a bad feeling about you doing that."

"It's part of what I'm paid to do, Kim," he said. "I am after all a hired employee of the planet's Recreation Archive Wilderness Recording Society."

"What does that spell again?" she asked of the acronym.

He laughed and shrugged his shoulder.

"Keith, I don't know," she said. "I just . . . have a bad feeling about it."

Keith smiled and took hold of her waist as the two sipped wine and snuggled atop the blanket, the sun shining down from a gorgeous clear blue sky above them beyond the protective bubble.

Keith couldn't wait. . .

CHAPTER TWO

Sunday, October 26, 2415

-1-

Autumn washed the hillsides below. The Blue Mountains of Pennsylvania disappeared into a haze along the southern horizon. Keith and Jeffrey had been in their rented air car, beyond their cocoon city of New Allentown, for over an hour now, and below them swept the emptiness of a realm long ago reclaimed by nature, no more the province of humankind.

"Dad, where are we going?" Jeff suddenly asked of their journey. He'd been silently studying the forests upon the hillsides, and seemed on the verge of falling asleep.

"I told you," Keith answered, "it's a surprise. You'll see."

"Why won't you tell me?" Jeffrey glanced over to his father.

Keith Hagerton smiled. "It would ruin the surprise."

His son frowned, turned and watched the mountains once more.

***

They were on a southwesterly heading, the land below, Berks County, Pennsylvania. At least that was its official name as recorded on the old historical documents of the region. It was thought of as simply wilderness these days, as was most of the inhabitable surface of the Earth. No one had lived out in the open spaces for centuries; all trace of the ancient ground cities and towns from the old days had either been cleared and removed ages ago or had been allowed to crumble away into dust.

New Allentown, fifty kilometers away by now and far to the north, lay deep in the hills of eastern Pennsylvania, one-hundred miles north of the old and abandoned land-based city of Allentown, Pennsylvania, from which the new city got its name. Initial construction had begun in the late 21st Century, back in the days when humankind still gave serious consideration to maybe building a Noah's Arc starship and leaving the solar system and Earth once and for all. They even had a name for it. They were going to call it Exodus II. As if just the notion of such a thing wasn't in itself pathetic; to base the very idea on an incredibly unlikely biblical story from days of old was exceptionally pathetic. Fortunately, that craziness was quickly dispensed with and serious efforts to begin reversing humanity's ecological atrocities had soon after begun, and the species began its migration to artificial life centers, the Island Cities, both above and below the surface.

Towering two kilometers above the northern and diminishing foothills of the Blue Mountains, New Allentown lay completely detached from the world below. Twenty-thousand Earth residents called New Allentown home; the city was but one of a hundred such domiciles inhabiting the old continental boundaries of North America.

The remains of a covered, wooden bridge jutted its debris from the surface of a river below. Evidence of a country road stopped short of it on both shorelines. Keith then spotted a long scar running for miles, southward in the distance. *That would be 222,* he thought; a highway that once traversed the region. It was now only vaguely discernible. He banked the air car to the right.

"I think this is the area," he suddenly said.

Above his head, a series of lights descended from the ceiling to select contact points atop Keith's scalp. It was the Neural-Navigational-Interface System. Keith piloted the vehicle by simply communicating his thoughts to the ship's navigational computer. The ship responded to his every whim, and in his mind he instructed the vehicle to drop toward the tree line. The forests below rushed upward for the windshield.

"Where are we?" Jeffrey asked.

"Kutztown, Pennsylvania. It looks pretty much the way it did four centuries ago when ground vehicles still roamed the countryside. You can still see traces of the old back roads. It's almost hard to find them, though. It's been a while since I was here; I hope I haven't forgotten the way." He spotted a series of hills ahead of their flight. "There." He began searching for what appeared after a while to be weaving gaps in the trees and grasslands. Long eroded and overgrown, they were old two-lane roadbeds, country roads, cutting through the forests and winding through the hills.

"Here's where we start weaving through the trees. The little road to this place was never much even in the 21st Century. Ready? We're going down."

The tree line opened up to the west and a great valley hugged the horizon below a cloud be speckled sky. There was a clearing directly ahead. It seemed man-made, and after centuries of being left alone looked only partially on the way back to being consumed by the trees. Something had been here at one time, and indeed Jeffrey saw the remains of old buildings a few meters up the hillsides. The clearing ahead must have at one time been what they used to call a parking lot for ground vehicles. Traces of old asphalt stood among the underbrush and fronted what remained of the buildings.

Keith angled the air car for it. "Hang on. We're going in."

The air car dropped, like a kite losing its updraft, wafting into the remains of the asphalt parking lot. The antigrav propulsion gently settled the vessel onto it. He shut down the drive; the power levels receded.

Keith activated his gull-wing door; it flopped upward, allowing a cool autumn breeze to waft inward.

"Wow," Jeffrey said. "I'll bet no one's been here for centuries."

"Yes they have, Jeff." Keith looked up to the rise of the hillside to their right. Way up toward the center of it, a log cabin made of cedar wood squatted against the hill's ragged face of rock and grass. The trees shadowed the entire extent of it, filled as they were with their slowly dropping leaves of yellow and red. The cabin looked all alone up there. Keith recalled old photographs of the original entrance façade. The original structure from the 1900s had been torn down and replaced by this solitary and ornamental one ages ago. He grinned to the cabin. It was just as he'd recalled it.

"It looks just like the one Frida and I visited yesterday in Virginia," Jeffrey informed his dad of the tiny structure, against the cliff wall on the ridge above them. "Is that what that is," he asked, then, "another cave entrance? We're going cave exploring?"

"Yes, we are. You're going to love it. . . . You and Friddy weren't really in Luray Caverns yesterday," Keith replied of the Virginia tourist site. He glanced to the log cabin. "It's called *Crystal Cave*. Discovered in 1871. Once one of Pennsylvania's more notable landmarks. It's not very large, not like Luray, nowhere near so spectacular, but it's closer to home, and I thought you might like it. Besides, the caverns in Virginia are constantly swamped by tourists. You were lucky to get real *live time* yesterday down there and on a *Saturday*. That Sensor Sphere ball you and Frida accessed gets a lot of use. Must have caught a lull in the public's interest, especially this time in the year: Autumn."

Keith glanced to the wilderness around him, and smelled the air, aware that just a few centuries ago even that would have required a breathing unit, a life-support belt, to compensate for all the toxins in the air. It was risky enough as it was, just being out here without force field protection. No telling what insect vermin might be lurking in the brush, just waiting to bite and cause all kinds of heartaches not just for him or Jeffrey but for everyone back in New Allentown, if a one-time plague virus, thought long eradicated, were to be reintroduced to the human population because of Keith's carelessness. But he would activate force field protection soon enough, once inside the cave. For now he just wanted to enjoy being outside, and in the open. It did get claustrophobic after a while, being forever cooped up in an island city. And it didn't matter if the thing were above or below ground. The above ground ones, like New Allentown, were in fact the rarity and a privilege to dwell within. Construction on them was a bit more sophisticated. It was far easier to erect such cities below ground. But, for all intent and purposes, the cities could just as well have been constructed in Earth orbit, for all the attachment to the planet they held.

"People don't come here anymore?" Jeff asked.

"Not like they once did. A few old buddies and me, back in our twenties, got permission once to come out here and visit the place for real like this. But I doubt if most people even know of it, anymore."

"Is it even worth exploring?" Jeffrey asked, soberly. "Frida would have mentioned it to me before now, if it were, and gone down it." (On a side note, Jeffrey thought it difficult to ever picture his dad . . . twenty . . . and young.)

Keith noted his son's distant expression, puzzled by it. "What?"

Jeffry grinned, sheepishly. "Nothing."

"There are some nice formations down there," Keith nodded then, "but it's a small cave, not much more than a hole in the ground. I thought it might be fun, do you mind?"

Jeffry shrugged. And then, ". . . Is it safe?"

Keith grinned. "We'll be fine." He walked over to the rear of the air car, foraged in the storage bay and found two antigrav lift/force field belts. "Put that on, Jeff. It's a safety precaution, even for out here. I can feel vermin, gnats, buzzing us even now. We can't risk bringing anything undesirable back with us to the city. And for what we're going to do today down in the cave, we may need these things and their antigrav capacities."

"Why, what are we doing?"

Jeffrey reached down and affixed the belt to his waist. With it activated he could fly off into the air, if he so chose, and soar in the wind like a bird. He could also begin to feel the filtering effect it was having on the air. He kind of was enjoying breathing the unprocessed version of the air out in the wilderness for a change. Oh, well. Keith went rummaging in the storage bay once more, removing equipment. "We'll be in the main chamber for the first hour," he said, then. "It's only about forty meters down. I'd like to try out the lower levels also while we're here, Jeff. They're a little harder to explore; the cave's owners never opened them up to the public."

"How **much** harder?" Jeffrey suddenly asked.

Keith smiled. "I don't know. I've never gone down them before. It wouldn't be as much fun, if I had."

Jeffrey saw his father then slip on a pair of wading/hiding boots. "You're taking *them* too?"

"We may run into a few underground ponds down there, the other reason the lower levels were never opened up."

Jeffrey had a sad look on his face.

Keith grinned. "Come on, sport, you'll love it."

Keith left the air car and started for the embankment, his right hand weighted down by a large, gray utility box. Halfway to the cabin, he suddenly glanced back to see his son as yet by the vehicle. Jeff was staring into its rear compartment.

"What are you doing?" he called to Jeff.

"Are we taking this?"

The Hagerton's very own, personal Home Visual-Sensor Sphere, a tiny crystalline sphere, ten centimeters round, floated unsupported toward the ceiling in the aft compartment. Keith sighed. *How the fuck did I forget that?* he asked himself. He dropped the utility box, and started back for the vessel.

He'd left the thing in the back behind them to record their flight. A million sensory receptors, as tiny as human neurons, faceted its surface. It seemed almost alive; it sensed and recorded the world around it in much the same way as the brain and its network of nerve endings did. The sensory data was then stored on tiny wedge-shaped crystals called ViewWafers. A user situated a headset over the main "sensory processing centers" of his or her cerebral cortex. The effect of the data transmissions on the human brain fooled it into believing it was receiving signals from its own bodily nerve endings (transmitted up the spinal cord). The user at such times imagined the Sensor Sphere was an extension of his perceptual "presence."

Keith had left the headset atop the pilot's dashboard. Gray and skeletal, it was a three-quarter round ring with seven arcing fingers which rose and almost touched. He reached for it, placed it square upon his head, and looked over at the sphere.

The Sensor Sphere started moving, daintily wafting on the breezes, like a soap bubble. Exiting the air car through the passenger side door, it lifted itself six meters, and hovered just beyond the air car. Keith had left a viewwafer loaded in the record/playback deck that accompanied the unit. It was recording every move he and Jeffrey made.

Jeffrey glared up at the sphere; he hated it. He'd had to smile through so many family outings and birthdays with it on and recording his every movement just so the family could later play back the recordings to its amusement and enjoyment. Dads and their electronic toys.

Go away, Jeffrey mouthed, silently, and then looked over at his father. Keith gave the sphere one final mental command; then, reaching into the air car's aft compartment for the unit's carry bag, he pulled the headset from his head and stuffed it away. He then slung the bag over his shoulder.

"I've set it for automatic pursuit. It'll follow us at about six meters behind. That way it won't get in the way."

"Do we really need it?" Jeffrey sighed.

Keith shook his head, depressingly. "You do realize, don't you, Jeff, that a lot of those travel visuals you and Friddy enjoy playing, *I* took over the years as part of my *job?*"

Jeffrey only shrugged.

"It's just not the same, huh, when you're the star?"

Jeff nodded, lowly.

Keith grinned. "I promise I won't record you doing anything embarrassing."

Yeah, Jeffrey had heard that one before. When he was four, his father actually got a visual of him naked on the toilet. He hoped to hell his dad hadn't uploaded *that* visual.

"You get to star with me this time," Keith said, then, "on this excursion visual. People the solar system wide will think, *Aw, what a cute kid. And he loves his dad, you can see it.*"

Jeff had been gazing at the dirt at his feet as his father went on, and after a while looked up. "Are you done, Dad?" he wearily asked.

***

It wasn't long after that Keith was halfway up the hill again, with the Sensor Sphere trailing like a faithful dog. Jeffrey sighed and started up the grade after them. He saw his father pause before the tiny cabin. There was a marble marker stone before it bearing an engraved inscription. Keith appeared to be reading it.

CRYSTAL CAVE
Discovered A.D. 1871,
Formerly in the
County of Berks,
In the commonwealth of Pennsylvania.

The gold plaque had been there since Keith's youth. The cabin, flushed against the hillside, from outward appearances looked quite accommodating in a rustic sort of way. Anyone who would escape the confines and claustrophobia of the cities might be tempted to commandeer it as a get-away refuge. Over a century old, it was in mint condition, the wood showing no wear, or any evidence of the cabin's having ever been used as a dwelling. A façade only, it was strictly ornamental in purpose. A solar-powered force shield, a scarlet cocoon encircling it and only faintly visible in daylight, explained how the cabin remained so pristine. Kevin Danhaily, one of Keith's old Instruc buddies, twenty years ago had blundered into the shield and landed on his ass. Keith grinned. The guys had kidded old Kevin about it for hours afterward. Keith was grateful Kevin had done that, actually. Keith knew better now than to simply cross the road and smack into the thing, in a blind pursuit of the cabin's door.

Below the inscription on the marker was also a tiny input slot just above a lighted bar. Keith searched for his Wilderness Society excursion permit and inserted the crystal within the slot. He drew back then and waited.

"Keith Hagerton. Identity confirmed," came a female voice somewhere before him. *"Resident: New Allentown. Entry approval, dated 10/26/15. Warning. Sensor scan reveals second lifeform in area proximity. Identity input required before shield cocoon can be lowered."*

Jeffrey paused and looked up as he ascended the grade. He fished into his vest pocket and found his own identity crystal; he handed it to his dad. The voice repeated the file review for Jeffrey. Keith removed his son's crystal from the slot, and handed it back.

The red bar below the input slot faded to black just as simultaneously the cocoon shield dropped from the cabin.

"Shield will remain lowered until entry," the voice announced, *"or until such time as new approaches enter sensor area."*

Keith crossed for the cabin. The door to it had only a simple lift-latch upon it. It was a dark metal in color and had been fashioned in the antique style of the 1800s. He raised it and creaked open the door. It was a single-roomed interior and barren, except for two old-style windows on the two opposing walls. It had a wooden floor— mostly for show. The whole thing made a great façade from the outside. The mouth of the cave was on the inward, hillside wall and he saw the beginnings of the old stairway that led down into the caverns.

The stairway evaporated into pitch black darkness below. The darkness kept on going. It looked foreboding.

Jeffrey came up beside his father. "It's dark down there," he said.

Keith grinned. "I know. I'll get us some light. It'll be fine, Jeff. You've already done stuff like this before with your sister."

Jeffrey cringed. "Yeah, but somehow this is different this time. I'm really here."

Keith nodded and left for the cabin exterior, where he'd left the utility box out by the inscription marker. He had to squint his eyes in the sunlight as he went out to retrieve it. He brought it in and placed it down on the floor by the stairway entrance. When Keith opened it, he removed to a vest pocket of his jacket a tiny bag of something that clattered like marbles. They were magnesium-loaded marker beacons that one left on the trail, like a line of illuminated breadcrumbs. There was also a large (much larger than the Sensor Sphere) crystal sphere.

Keith removed it and handed it to his son. "Hold this for a second, while I power up the generator."

The rest of the "tool box" was the portable fusion reactor, the sort of safe, efficient unit one always remembered to take along when camping out beyond the city. It could be programmed to microwave beam its generated power to whatever instrument needed it. Keith pressed the power-commit indicator on the top, and the whole top panel alit with status info. He then looked up at the Sensor Sphere. Reaching down to the unit's carry bag beside his waist, he pulled out the headset and attached a crystal microchip— which he found inside the toolbox— to one of the accessory inputs along its side. He put the headset on again and looked over at the sphere his son held. An indicator on the reactor's data board told him the reactor was on line and so he commanded his son's sphere to levitate out of Jeffrey's hand and rise into the room.

Jeffrey felt it tickle his palm as it slowly lifted away and floated over to the mouth of the cave. He looked over at his father, and could imagine in his father's thoughts the mental command Keith sent to the sphere to penetrate the darkness of the cave. The Light Sphere disappeared almost instantly. Jeffrey looked back at his father, and saw him smile. Keith gave the sphere another command in his thoughts. Jeffrey looked back in time to see a great explosion of light. Slanted shafts of brilliant luminescence were thrown upwards into the tiny cabin.

Crystal Cave filled with light; the sphere blazed below them like a miniature sun.

"Better?" Keith asked.

Jeffrey nodded.

"It'll keep to the ceiling as much as possible, but try not to stare up at it, if you can avoid it."

The limestone walls, angling down into the cave, were charcoal-brown and craggy; the air dampened and cooled off rapidly as they descended the stairs. The temperature hovered then around eleven degrees Celsius at the bottom.

"Aah!" Jeffrey exclaimed as he slapped at his face. Keith had instructed him to for now shut down his force field while up here in the main tourist cave. The danger of contamination from the topside world was not so great down here, he told Jeff. And this way, for the time being without the force field protection, they could experience the real, true on spelunking experience. And that Jeffrey did.

Keith grinned as he saw his son swipe at a droplet of water that hit him square on his nose. "I'm sure that happened as well to you and your sister down there in Luray," he said.

Jeff only looked at his dad, pissed.

Ground water seeped and fell constantly from points upon the ceiling, splashing off stalagmites or whatever else was under the droplets at the time. Jeffrey got splashed three times already, and he and his father had only penetrated the interior fifty meters. Jeff never had to worry over the splashing's before, because they'd only been simulations. But this down-here-for-real-stuff was . . . for him, anyway . . . something he could probably flush down the toilet and not miss afterward.

Being here for real was seriously starting to annoy Jeff. He felt the drop in temperature almost immediately upon entering the cave; he had a weird feeling of no longer being out amid fresh air. There was a thing about being in a cave, underground; it went beyond simply the change in temperature or the draping humidity. It was the ambiance of being *beneath the Earth*. Perhaps it was the old association with death; life dwelled above in the open, upon the surface. Here on the other hand floated the specter of entombment.

An enormous and black limestone block, shaped like a wedge, lay in front of them. It had broken loose from the ceiling and fallen— probably from a long ago earthquake— millions of years ago. The old tour route went around it, hugging the left side wall. The black metal guardrails were still intact, though heavily rusted; standing out from the dark rock were cone-shaped, plaster moldings where the cave's old arc lights used to go.

Jeffrey remembered the light sphere and felt its illumination high above him. The sphere was hovering several meters away and toward the cavern's ceiling. He took a quick glance up to it, and then down again, noting how its light lit up the cave. *Crystal Cave* probably hadn't been illuminated in this way in years, since the power— no doubt— to the place had been cut.

It felt lonely here.

A half hour later they were back by the stairway, leading to the topside cabin. "Jeff?" Keith called. Nearby was an area fronted by an overhang rock canopy, and by this low and white limestone "Flowstone" formation that looked like a batter of white cake mix had been thrown against a protruding boulder and allowed to run and harden. Off to the side of it and below was a slit opening which bent downward into the bowels of the Earth. Keith stared down into it. "That's the way to the lower levels," he said. "So I was told."

Jeffrey looked over to it. He looked back up at his father, and swallowed. "Do you really want to go down there, Dad?"

"Don't you?"

Jeffrey suddenly thought of his sister and his Mom. God, he wished he'd gone with them today. There were times when he actually wished he'd been lucky enough to be born Frida's younger sister. He'd so much rather be with his Mom and his sister right now . . . and a girl. Because if his father was expecting him to man up and enjoy this dark, dank shithole, Jeffrey really didn't feel like he had it in him.

He looked back up to his father.

To be honest, no, Jeffrey did not want to go down there. It was just a feeling he had. But his father did.

He nodded okay, anyway.

CHAPTER THREE

-1-

Kimberly Hagerton, far to the southeast in Historic Old Philadelphia, was in the circle before the Art Museum in preserved Fairmount Park, admiring the mounted figure of George Washington. It was just after nine A.M.; the day was a gorgeous blue and cool. She and Frida were visiting the preserved remains of that grand old land-based city that Sunday morning, as an alternative to following the two Hagerton men out into the wilderness.

A fabulous view of Old Philadelphia awaited Kimberly at the top of the Art Museum's famous steps. She crossed for them, and began her ascent.

***

Her parents' family, the Hinderbeins, hailed from New Philadelphia, a subterranean "cocoon" city about thirty miles to the west in what used to be called West Chester. It was there she met Keith in 2408. He was twenty; she, eighteen and a year out of Instruct. She had landed a position on the Philadelphia Chamber Music Society Ensemble as a flutist. Keith, graduated from the New Allentown Instruc two years before in 2406, had taken a position at the Philadelphia Instruc as an art history instructor. He was something of an artist in his spare time, a student of the old art of landscape painting, and was quite good at it. He joined the city's Fine Arts Society, successfully getting a few of his landscape oils hung and displayed. He and Kimberly met one late-summer night in September of 2408 as Kimberly and the Ensemble performed Johann Sebastian Bach's Brandenburg Concerto Number Two. Keith had gone backstage to compliment her on her performance. They fell in love almost right off.

Settling in New Allentown, where they began to raise their family, Kimberly continued with the New Philadelphia Ensemble, while Keith lent his services to the entertainment division of New Allentown's Interplanetary Information Network. He recorded wilderness imagery in full-sensory surround, replicating the experience (for those not able to leave the city and experience it themselves) of being out in the wilderness. The off-world ports mostly desired them. Ship propulsion technology had opened up the solar system to exploration and inhabitation. To live on Earth was considered passé. But for those who still called the Earth home, the land beyond the island cities was off-limits. The environmental damage to the planet in the past was only now beginning to heal; it was decided that people could never live on the land itself again without harming it. To attempt to do so was discouraged. And permission to tour the wilderness areas was a gift to be savored. Keith's work took him beyond the city's walls repeatedly, and to exotic locales all over the planet. He and his family were permitted to leave the city practically whenever they requested it, which explained why no one had questioned the purpose of his visit to Kutztown that morning.

Kimberly, reaching the top of the Art Museum's steps, turned and faced back to the remains of Old Philadelphia. It was magnificent; the city had been leveled years ago and landscaped as one huge preserve. Its streets and row houses, storefronts, high-rises, and business districts had all been cleared away. Only Independence Hall, the Ben Franklin Parkway, Fairmount Park and City Hall remained. William Penn's statue stood atop it as yet, staring down now upon only oak and maple trees. No longer would taller, more utilitarian buildings dwarf its ornately detailed tower.

High overhead, meanwhile, though not at present active in full force during the daylight hours, several scarlet blue force shields protected the city and its landmarks from the elements and from any would be desecraters.

Kimberly squinted sunward, closed her eyes and breathed in the fresh air. It felt heavenly.

Frida Hagerton, Keith's and Kimberly's only daughter and Jeffrey's older sister, had no desire to test her mettle and follow her mom up the Art Museum's steps. She had asked for permission instead to wander the park on her own for a while. Kimberly had given it to her.

Reaching as far down the Parkway as the Franklin Institute, Frida there encountered a small group of off-world vacationers gathered at the base of its main entrance steps. They were admiring the cityscape before them in the early morning sunlight. Frida did so as well. The air felt cool, ruffling the strands of her long blond hair, a different type of cool, the only word for it had to be *natural* as opposed to what she was used to within the enclosed periphery of New Allentown.

She was a quiet and pensive thirteen year old, about a meter and a half tall, slim, her Swedish origins even more pronounced than on Jeffrey. That at thirteen Frida was already a beautifully developed young lady was apparent even to the boys in her Instruc classes. They'd started taking notice. But Frida, although she didn't discourage them, was more interested in the universe, the stars, the unknown places that she had never yet seen. She got that from her father. Jeffrey, she would smile to herself, acted more like his mom when it came to doing things he had never done before. Frida really wished her dad would have taken **her** today to *Crystal Cave*. She knew how much Jeffrey would hate it. It wasn't fair.

She passed Ben Franklin in the museum's domed rotunda. He was huge. Did he look sullen to her somehow, despite the pleasant expression the sculptor had affixed to Ben's marble face? The statue once greeted hordes of energetic children every day, children eager to break loose from their chaperones and check out the museum's delightful exhibits. Frida had seen holograms and imaging plates of the days when the Franklin Institute was a showcase for science past and present. Now it was merely a preserved relic of a bygone era. Not one child—

(besides her)

(and anyone who called her one was asking for trouble)

—was anywhere near this city that morning. If children her age were the least bit curious about this rotunda these days all they had to do was request their city's library computer pull a viewwafer crystal of Old Philadelphia and access the sub-chapter *Franklin Institute*. The **illusion** that they were actually where she was now could be just as real and just as sensually rewarding.

Frida glanced to the glass showcases along the rotunda's walls. Behind them were printing tools and personals that once belonged to Ben Franklin. She wondered of his time. He lived so long ago. Too long for her to even imagine what life back then was like. But there was one thing about Ben Franklin's time she liked. It reminded her of her own. The continent then was almost as minimally settled as it was now, the landscape as wild and pristine.

Everything else about those ancient times she felt could be tossed.

Kimberly caught up with Frida an hour or so later. An old Omnimax feature, "Mars: Mariner Valley," was the program being shown that day in the museum's old Omniverse Theater. A 350 seat auditorium curved around a huge eyeball-shaped screen, illuminated by an old horizontally-racked 70mm "film" projector. The projector was loaded with film-stock down in the glass-fronted projection room beneath the auditorium and was then hydraulically raised to its berth in the auditorium. The film, fed from a huge spool below, rose up and down again to an equally massive take up reel. Frida and Kimberly observed the thread-up process down in the theater lobby. The projection room was as much a part of the "exhibit" as the Omnimax experience itself was supposed to be, and thus the room was fronted by a huge glass wall, so that its technology could be examined by all before the feature began. Frida thought the entire layout primitive and whispered as much to Kimberly as the two waited with the vacationing off-worlders for the doors to the theater to open.

Named after a space probe, Mariner 9, launched back in the 1900s, Mariner Valley was larger than the United States and ploughed more than six kilometers into the Martian soil. The film was mostly a silent visual homage to the canyon's massive spectacle.

Travel between the eight planets of the solar system, though no longer the difficult and time consuming enterprise it had been back when this Mars feature was made, still wasn't the sort of thing one did for no good reason. The outer worlds contained little for the mere adventure-minded. Jupiter and its moons, for instance, were bathed in lethal radiation from the gaseous giant itself. No practical way to settle or even tour Jupiter or its moons was ever found. And Mars, though far more accessible to human colonization, itself took anywhere from a day to four days to reach, depending upon the travel arrangements. People settled where they did— either on Earth or on one of the artificially adapted off-world ports— and for the most part stayed there.

***

"That was a strange experience, Mom," Frida told her mother of the Omnimax feature, later, after the show as mother and daughter exited the theater. "Watching that thing was kind of boring. It was just an oversized image projection. What was so great about that?"

"In its day," her mother answered, "it was considered the closest thing to being there."

"The Viewwafer playbacks get in your head and make you feel like you're really there," said Frida. She pointed up to the massive curving screen above them as they walked the front pathway out to the exits. "That thing sucked."

Kimberly smiled. "You're used to life in the 25th Century, Friddy. I liked the movie. I thought it was nice. It was like watching a moving version of one of your father's paintings."

"Mariner Valley bothers me, Mom," Frida all at once said. She took a breath. "I've never told you that. I've never even told Dory that. . . ."

(Dory was her best friend in New Allentown.)

"It sounds silly, I know," she continued. "I watch the Mars Viewwafers all the time, because they do things to me."

Kimberly frowned at her. "What things, honey?"

Frida paused. "I've never been there, have I, Mom?"

"Of course you haven't. Frida, what on Earth would possess you to think you had?"

She shrugged. "I feel like I have. It's weird."

Kimberly didn't know how to respond to that one. Once in a while, her daughter would say things like that, describe outer-worldly things as if she were already familiar with them, and Kimberly (at least in the past) would just tell herself her daughter simply had an overactive imagination.

"Mom, why didn't we **all** go to Crystal Cave today?" Frida suddenly asked.

"That was my fault, Friddy," she answered after a pause. "You know how I am about caves. I don't like them the way Keith does. And the first bat I run across . . . I'm out of there." She then explained to Frida about fathers and sons, and how fathers needed to pass on their interests to their sons. It had something to do with male relationships, just as she and Frida could share things that the men could never share. "You're not too disappointed we came **here**, instead, are you?"

Frida grinned weakly, and shook her head. "No, I liked visiting this old city. But, Mom, "Frida began, gathering her nerve to take this next subject to where she wanted to take it. She furrowed her brow. "Male and female . . . They're really becoming outmoded concepts; that's what Jeffrey and I keep being told in our Instruc classes. Did kids really once have to leave home every morning, get up early, to get taught, to have to physically assemble IN PERSON with all the other kids in a specific place? We still do that today, gather in one place, but we never have to leave our bedrooms."

Kimberly chuckled. "*Real Classrooms* was a bit before my time, baby." She nodded. "Yes, that's the way it once was before virtual reality changed all that, made it possible to go anywhere and still never leave home. There are archive 'movies" from the 20th Century that you can access to see how common it was in those days."

"Movies," mused Frida. She glanced again to the Omnimax screen above her. "Like that?"

"Basically."

"Mom, Jeffrey might disappoint Dad if Dad clings to the old ways where sons were sons." Frida shook her head. "It's not like that anymore. I mean, when humanity lost the ability to reproduce without artificial assistance, it kind of took all the fire out of the difference between being born one gender or the other. Dad can't be that provincial, can he?"

"You're really growing up, aren't you?" Kimberly smiled at her command of the English language. She stopped near the exits and gently cupped her fingers in her daughter's chin.

"I guess," Frida shrugged.

"I suppose you're right about that. But boys still try to be like they once were, even if puberty never really bites them in the rear and turns them into 'MEN.' Why, Friddy, what's Jeffrey doing? Has he been doing stuff a little 'not right' for a boy?"

Frida smiled. "You mean like trying on my old clothes from back when I was nine?" she asked. She laughed now. "Yes, he's done that and I like dressing him up as my sister once in a while, but I know a lot of guys my age who like to do that too, more than boys used to— my Instruc teachers say. But . . ."

"What, Friddy?" worried Kimberly. "What's he been doing?"

"Watching stuff in the Viewing Chamber. Stuff. . ."

"Yes?"

"Well, you know, you can POV record anything you want. Just wear the headset and it will record for others to play what it feels like to be you. You know Jeffrey's girlfriend, Ginny, that he talks with all the time over the communication system?"

"Yeah . . . What are they doing, Friddy?"

"I found a few ViewWafers stashed in one of the secret places I know Jeffrey keeps things in his room. There are a couple Visuals Ginny obviously downloaded for him as a gift, stuff of her getting dressed in her prettiest dresses and outfits. . . ."

"Oh . . . well."

". . . *One* of her even taking a *shower.*"

"*Excuse me?*" Kimberly asked, suddenly.

Frida nodded. "I played it. The playback registers he's played it more than a hundred times. I think he likes fantasizing he's Ginny, taking a shower. In some ways, Mom, I think Jeffrey's more your daughter than I am. Should we be worried?"

Kimberly pondered that one as they exited the museum for outside. "It really won't matter one way or the other in the long run, honey," Kimberly decided, ultimately. "If those two hook up someday, Ginny obviously doesn't mind what Jeff likes to do, become her, and . . . if they do want to join like your father and me and have a family one day . . ." She took a breath as she pondered it. ". . . You know how it works, right? And how it used to work? You've studied that much about biology in Instruc as well, am I right?"

Frida nodded. "Men and women don't mate like that, anymore," pondered Frida. "They can't. The DNA has to be extracted and a baby created in a baby sarcophagus."

"They called that artificial insemination a long time ago," Kimberly added, "and if the mother, herself, couldn't grow the fertilized egg inside her, they usually found a donor mom to carry the child to term. Now, it's all done in artificial placenta sacks in a fertility facility somewhere out west. Babies aren't requisitioned to replace elderly citizens that often. People live way longer than they once did."

"I wasn't trying to get Jeffrey in trouble," Frida said. "There's nothing wrong with what he's doing, not really. And it doesn't harm anyone. I just wanted to point out that Dad might not be as . . . pleased with Jeffrey's manhood as he might . . . I don't know."

Kimberly nodded and hugged her daughter. "I wouldn't worry about it."

". . . It's weird to think people once lived spread out this way over *kilometers.* . . ." Frida said then, changing the subject as they began walking the grounds beyond the art museum. "And the fall colors along the walkways are really nice this time of year. . . ."

"Yes, they are," nodded Kimberly, absently.

"But I **still** wish we'd gone with Dad and Jeffrey, Mom," Frida suddenly said.

Kimberly sighed and then smiled as they continued their walk through old Philadelphia.

CHAPTER FOUR

-1-

"It's narrowing again," Keith told Jeffrey of their path through the lower level offshoots beneath Crystal Cave.

Spelunkers had a name for places where it was too low and too narrow to squeeze through. They called it *Tall man's headache, and fat man's misery.*

These were no easy tourist pathways now, and any minute it seemed a certainty they'd reach a dead end, as if the underground river that had long ago cut the limestone down this far had barely begun to complete the job before its waters had receded. The main chambers topside had taken the brunt of the ancient river's force, and thus were the most accessible and cavernous. But down here, anything you wanted to see you had to labor to reach. Jeffrey felt his arm and leg muscles getting a workout, even with his antigrav/life-belt now activated and reducing the pull of gravity around him.

The Light Sphere was now flying at eye level as it illuminated the way forward. The glare from it was giving Keith a headache, and made it difficult for him to see the rock walls surrounding it. With his thoughts, he sent it ahead, hoping that would reduce its white-out effect and allow him to see past it to what existed beyond. It didn't. The path narrowed around him to a half meter in width, and . . .

Shit.

. . . He banged his head on the ceiling as he crouched down on all fours and started crawling. He ordered the Light Sphere to reduce its light level to minimum intensity.

"Hold up, son," he said. Keith held up his palm to blot out the light, squinting to see past the sphere. "This tunnel might be ending as solid rock farther up. I can't tell. I'm ordering the Light Sphere to go as far back into it as it can to verify what's down there. It's getting too narrow to even crawl."

Jeffrey crossed his fingers that the tunnel would soon end, and began eyeing the route back to the surface. He remembered, abruptly, the Home Visual Sensor Sphere; it was only a half meter in front of him. At that distance it would easily pick up his facial expressions. Anyone scanning the playback later would have no difficulty interpreting his feelings about continuing on. He wiped all trace of it from his face. "Okay, Dad," he said, feigning interest.

Keith crawled a few meters farther into the tunnel and squinted to identify what lay beyond the Light Sphere as it continued down. Suddenly, he saw it highlight what looked like a long, vertical slit. The sphere slipped past it and into what seemed a great cavern chamber beyond. The light of the now distant Light Sphere found its way feebly back to the tunnel interior around him.

"Sphere stop," Keith ordered in his mind, and brightened its light level. The illumination in the tunnel abruptly rose.

Keith pulled one of the marker beacons he'd brought along from a pocket of his jacket and ordered it to ignite. It did, and he aimed it first back at Jeffrey and then into the tunnel. "I want to check this out," Keith said. He crept away for the vertical opening, his eyes and ears attuned to what lay ahead. With the antigrav belts for lift support, they could certainly jump down for it, despite the distance, and safely land among the rocks. There were in no real danger of causing injury to their ankles. The gravity influence settings could be reduced all the way to zero, if required.

Keith looked into the diminishing shadows, cast by the stalactites, falling from the ceiling, and heard the sound of droplets impacting upon water. He and Jeff had come upon an underground lake. Ground water, seeping through cracks in the limestone bedrock, fell as liquid limestone solution, plipping its surface, and by the diminishing echoes it sounded like it went back quite a ways.

The water looked quite deep, but there was sufficient shoreline rock for him to descend to.

"Jeff, come see this," he called. "I think we've found something that no one else even knows about."

Jeffrey was about three meters behind. He watched the Sensor Sphere dart away and sail past Keith, stopping a meter beyond the drop off. Jeff crawled the rest of the way to the ledge, slithering in beside his father. He looked out. The lake and the huge cavern looked haunted in the dim light cast by the Light Sphere, and the distant echoing of water droplets far down it, made it even worse.

"Where are we?" Jeff asked.

"It looks like the shoreline of an underground lake," said Keith. "We weren't supposed to find this. Nothing this impressive was supposed to be down here." He studied the edges of the crevice again. "A weak wall," he said, touching it. "Must have broken away in the last couple centuries. Probably a tremor brought it down."

Jeffrey looked at him, and then down into the chamber area below. He saw the rocks littering the floor. He saw also that the break was shear and straight.

Keith glanced to the Light Sphere, and in his mind commanded it to drift farther into the chamber. What little he could see of the area beyond seemed far more open than anywhere he'd yet seen since entering Crystal Cave. The Light Sphere reached about thirty meters out; the lake beneath it seemed to stretch on even farther, until it faded into darkness.

"Brighten," he ordered of the Light Sphere in his mind. "20x current intensity."

The chamber room pulled out of the darkness. Stalactites and stalagmite formations and encrustations against the walls abruptly shown like none either of them had yet seen down here. Full length columns were everywhere, and the scene looked a wonderland of colored rock and jagged surfaces. It was awesome.

"Wow," Jeffrey said. He looked to the mirror-like surface of the lake. Perfect likenesses of the overhead stalactites and the cavern's ceiling reflected upward, the water so pure it seemed not there.

"The tunnel," said Keith, in reflection, "I think the lower levels were thought to end here. No one knew about this lake. Look at it, it's every bit as nice down here as in Luray. It would have made a great addition to the Crystal Cave tour route in the old days, **if** they had found a more convenient way for the tourists to get down here. . . . Jeff?" Keith asked then.

"Yeah, Dad?" Jeffrey wasn't at all sure he liked what was coming.

Keith grinned. Jeff was already showing signs of wanting to leave, and exploring subterranean lakes was probably something Keith ought to do with his hiking buddies from the old days. Maybe, he should even get a ViewWafer crew out here to make a top-notch Travel Visual of it.

"Son, I know that you haven't been too crazy about this whole thing, being here in the flesh, I mean, but we can easily get off this ledge and down there and check out that lake using our mag-belts to ease us down, and we do have an inflatable with provisions for a river trip, back in the air car. Just think. We might be the first to ever explore the lake, learn where it ends up, if anywhere. It might even end above ground. We already have this much of it recorded on viewwafer. The network might take an interest in our find, maybe even make a bid on our recordings. Our little adventure down here could go out on the interplanetary feeds as a Travel Visual, you and me, discovering a whole new cavern. Think of that. You'll be famous, seen throughout the solar system."

"What if it doesn't, Dad?" Jeffrey replied.

Keith frowned. "What if what doesn't what?"

"What if the lake doesn't end above ground? What if it shallows to nothing?"

Jeff knew it was hopeless to sound disparaging. His father would never pass up an opportunity like this at any rate.

Keith removed a hand scanner from his pocket. He aimed it forward and waited for the neural readout to image in his thoughts. "No, I'm getting indications that the lake does narrow in places, but it's nothing we can't handle. And the ceiling doesn't close in on us, either." He nodded. "This river goes north and to the west about ten kilometers." He inputted a time-request. "It's just after twelve, son. We've plenty of time, if you're willing. It'll be a lot more interesting an adventure than what I planned for us for the rest of the afternoon."

"We have to go back for the raft?"

Keith nodded. "We can reduce the antigrav settings all the way to zero, if you like, and make the climb back no sweat at all."

Jeffrey grinned, weakly. "You really want to do this, don't you, Dad?"

Keith nodded. "I guess I'm just a little kid when it comes to stuff like this, son."

Jeffrey frowned and smiled. "You know I love you, Dad, you know that, right?"

Keith knocked him one on his shoulder. "It'll be great, I promise."

Jeffrey nodded.

About an hour or so later, they'd returned to the same spot in the narrow tunnel, and stood again at the ledge drop-off, listening to the sounds of ground water seepage, dropping for the massive underground lake. Keith had sent the Light and Sensor spheres ahead as before to light and record the way, activating the light unit to a high brilliance level as it and the Sensor Sphere hung several meters away from the drop-off ledge. Then reducing his mag-belt to near one-sixth Earth gravity (the same as the gravity level on the Moon) and with a deep breath, he shoved himself off the precipice, to slowly waft down to the rock-strewn floor before the lake. Jeffrey watched him the whole time as Keith then worked his way through the boulders and rocks at the drop-off's bottom. He continued to watch his father as Keith seemed to stop and go into a meditative stance. In actuality, what he was really doing was interfacing with the thought processers in his mag-belt, requesting the unit return his gravity level to Earth normal. Keith then proceeded to approach the lake, crouching down at the water's edge and extending a hand to it. He ran his fingers across the water's surface and nodded. Glancing up to his son, he said, "Let's have the raft, Jeff."

Jeff reached behind his back and worked the backpack containing the inflatable raft past his body in the narrow passage and let it drop to the floor. It did so, quickly, and with a low thud.

Keith went to retrieve it, pausing to look up at his son, who still hung with his feet over the drop-off in the narrow opening in the wall above. "The rest of it?"

Jeff nodded, disappearing into the tunnel and reappearing with a large canvas sack full of their provisions. The sack was secured by a nylon rope. Jeff inched the sack over the ledge and grabbed the rope, praying the weight of the thing didn't pull him down with it. He proceeded to lower the sack slowly down to his father, who grabbed it and moved it off to the side. Keith then looked back up to his son.

"You coming?" he asked.

Jeff glanced down at the mag-belt around his waist to make sure it was snug. (He'd slip out of it, if it wasn't, and he'd reach the bottom a lot sooner than he'd like to.) And with a deep breath, as his father had (as if the two of them were about to take a dive into a lake or some such thing), Jeff pushed off and let the one-sixth gravity reduction from his mag-belt gently waft him down to the rocks and to beside his father. Both crystalline spheres watched his descent, as if they somehow had a sentient presence behind them. It felt to Jeffrey as if they were alive, somehow.

Keith took hold of him as he landed, so that he didn't risk twisting an ankle on the rocks all around. Keith grinned. "That wasn't so bad, wasn't it?" he said to Jeff.

"It was actually fun," Jeff said. "I almost want to do it again."

Keith tousled the lock of hair drooping down Jeff's forehead and grinned. "Let's get moving. See where this lake winds up."

"Are we going to have to drag all this stuff back up to the surface again?" Jeffrey asked, exhausted. Along with the raft, they'd needed to secure food and camping provisions should they be forced to spend the night down here. They'd also had to retrieve the portable fusion reactor (its transmission range went only so far and certainly not ten kilometers down the lake.) All that, hand carried or strapped to their backs, as they slithered through the narrow passage, made the return to the lower level one hell of an ordeal.

I must really be nuts, Keith had thought to himself. *If Kimmy knew I was doing this, AND DOWN HERE, she'd have called me a total idiot. Didn't she say something yesterday about old legends of bad things happening in this area around Crystal Cave? It's superstitious silliness, it has to be. I hope so.*

"Let's just hope," he said aloud, finally, to Jeffrey, "that the lake empties somewhere above ground." He checked his coat pocket to make sure he'd brought along the transponder/homing device. He'd summon the air car to their exit point, if they managed so lucky a feat as to find one.

It was a beautiful day topside, Keith thought, recalling the autumn breeze and sun against his face as he and Jeffrey unloaded the provisions from the air car. The trees, surrounding the entrance to Crystal Cave, had suggested many an inviting place for him and his son to repose beneath and just enjoy the falling leaves. It was a great day to be outside and not be confined to a cocoon city like New Allentown.

So why am I spending all my time down here? He wondered.

Jeffrey spoke again, breaking Keith out of his reverie. "And if it doesn't, Dad," Jeff continued of the lake's ending above ground, "it's back to here again, isn't it?"

"I'm afraid so, son. . . ."

Soon after, their gear and the raft all in the water, Jeff hopped in and Keith pushed the raft forward into the water, climbing in a second later. Grabbing one of the paddles, he stabbed at the mirrored surface. The inflatable floated out and away from shore. Jeffrey watched the bank recede. The ledge (their route back to the surface) lost itself in the gathering darkness. The Light and Sensor spheres kept pace, as the raft became engulfed by the hanging stalactites as it drifted downstream.

The return airbus to New Allentown (off-loading at stops south and east, including New Philadelphia and Gloucester City) had left Historic "Old" Philadelphia around three-thirty. The route north eventually met the beginnings of the Blue Mountains chain and followed the mountains thereafter until they diminished once more to foothills in the vicinity of New Allentown. The city hung jewel-like in the afternoon light, a silvery bubble of metal and crystal. The countryside devoured it. New Allentown seemed strange from this distance, thought Kimberly. From within, it seemed huge and limitless; from out here, tiny and insignificant.

Kimberly glanced to her daughter, beside her in the window seat. Frida likewise contemplated the wilderness surrounding New Allentown. Like Kimberly, she seemed awed by how small, lost, her city seemed. Kimberly smiled and stroked her daughter's hair. "We had fun today, didn't we, baby?" Kimberly asked.

Frida nodded. "It was all right, Mom." She sighed. "Mom?"

"What, honey?"

Frida turned finally from the window and faced her mother. "I'm tired of being on Earth. I wish we could leave."

Kimberly smiled, faintly. "That's quite a statement, Frida. Earth is your home; you were born here."

"There's a whole universe above us. I want to travel the solar system, the outer planets, and if it were possible even visit the stars. I don't want to stay on Earth, get older and only have meeting boys to look forward to. I don't want to settle for only that. I mean New Allentown is beautiful, and so are the mountains, but I'd at least like to visit the Moon, and I know Jeffrey would like to do that too. He told me."

"Jeffrey, **OUR** Jeffrey?" she asked.

"He would."

Kimberly nestled her daughter's head in her shoulder. "Frida, do you have any idea how many off-worlders wish they could get visas to come here, to visit Earth?"

Frida nodded, pensively. "I know, but I envy them being out there."

"They don't; that's why there's such a great demand for those Travel

Visuals your father likes to make."

"And we've gone with him just about everywhere on the planet to make them." She shrugged. "I know viewing them is almost the same as being there, at least they feel the same, but if that's true, while everyone else is trying to capture being on Earth with Dad's sensor visuals, I'm pouring through the ones we get from space."

"Frida, Earth is so beautiful, just ask your Mimi Mariatta. She and your grandpop lived on Mars for several years, before I was born, and they can't imagine ever wanting to return."

Granny Mariatta, Kimberly's mom, in her youth had been stationed on Mars in Mariner Vallley. She was a member of the Outer Planets Discovery Program. It was there she met Ansel Hinderbein, Kimberly's Dad. By the time they had Kimberly, Ansel and Mariatta had moved back to Earth, and to their ancestral home, Shengele, Sweden, a quaint mountain village. In the northern Norland territory, Shengele lay some forty kilometers west of Kiruna, in the shadow of Mount Kebnekaise. The town had been preserved exactly as it had looked back in the 18th Century, with the same wooden houses and huts of the days when people still got around on foot or on horse and ox driven wagons. Kimberly was born there.

"Keith and I can't afford to take trips off the Earth right now, honey," Kimberly said. "We just can't."

Frida nodded and silently watched the wilderness once more.

New Allentown, large now in the window ports of the airbus, the city's flight deck came into view. The airbus slipped past the entry gateways, and was abruptly down and upon the deck. A half hour later, Kimberly and her daughter were in the hallways beyond the transport facility and in search of the nearest elevator for their level and their home.

CHAPTER FIVE

Five p.m. came around, and Keith looked into the new sector of tunnel the raft was entering. So far the subterranean lake had shown no sign of ending or exiting above ground. Even a rearward current would suggest that up ahead the waters were descending from a higher elevation. The lake remained deep and placid. There'd been a few times on the way north where it hadn't been, where it had shallowed to almost a trickle. They'd even had to get out and walk, pulling the raft and its provisions along through the shallows and seeing the way sometimes constrict quite claustrophobically, their heads at times bending low just to avoid a harsh rap against the diminishing ceiling. But in other locales the lake flourished once more, and at times it looked as if the reason it had narrowed at all was because Keith had taken a wrong turn, when the lake divided into offshoots and Keith had to decide which of them was the one the lake called its "true course."

He pulled a hand scanner out of his pocket and aimed it at the water. Images (scanner data) visualized in his thoughts. He nodded. "We're coming to the end of the tunnel, Jeff," he said, breaking the silence. The two had been relaxing for some time since the raft last showed signs of bottoming out among the shallows. "She'll end about another half kilometer west of here, the lake with it."

Jeffrey looked down the surface of the lake and to the corridor it cut through the rock. The route arced rightward farther up the way, and there seemed signs that the caverns might be widening again beyond the lake's banks. Keith was still gleaning imagery information from the pocket scanner. Jeffrey waited for him to continue.

Keith nodded. "It's looking good, son. The rock is hollowing out above us. We may find a route back to the surface, yet."

"How far down are we, Dad?"

"Eighty meters."

Stalagmite encrustations fell like splattered, multi-colored paint down the walls to either side; the cavern was only ten meters wide in this sector. It had been a far better spectacle down here than Crystal Cave, itself, so far back now to the southeast. They'd gotten some great images to replay for Kimberly and Frida when they got back to New Allentown.

The path ahead curved around a large boulder. Keith glanced at it, all five meters of it, jutting out of the water, and noted the canopied hole in the roof where it must have fallen from a long time ago. *Jeez*, he thought of the splash and reverberation throughout the cavern that boulder must have made when it let go from the ceiling. He paddled the raft clear of it.

His expression changed all at once, and he froze. Jeffrey looked over at him in puzzlement. Keith seemed possessed.

The residual momentum of the raft was taking it right for the boulder. Jeffrey looked first at his father, and then at it. He stabbed out at it with his paddle as they drew near; the raft bumped up against it harmlessly.

"Dad?"

Keith pulled the portable scanner from his pocket and extended it in front of him again. "The alert code on the scanner just went off," he said. "There's something out there."

Jeffrey probed the darkness beyond the rightward bank of the lake. **"What?"**

The cavern went back a ways in that sector, creating a shoreline. Beyond it, within the darkness only now beginning to become touched by the Light Sphere's light, Jeffrey detected a rustic-colored wonderland of limestone pinnacles and bridges. It was a haunting sight.

"Dad, *what's out there*?"

Keith frowned. "I don't know. I can't get a readout on the composition."

"Is it alive?"

He shrugged. "It's putting out energy, like a power source." Keith nodded. "Something is definitely down there." He frowned and shook his head. ". . . about a half-kilometer away and to the northeast."

Jeffrey suddenly felt the flesh on his arms goose-pimple. "A secret renegade colony?" he asked.

Renegades. Keith looked over at him, pensively, and considered it. They weren't all bad, these rebellious humans who refused to live in the cities. At first at least some of them actually left to commune with nature, because they so loved the outdoors and the wilderness that they couldn't conceive of never being permitted to venture out amid it ever again. But that was generations ago, and their descendants had lived on out here never knowing the life of the cities or the civilized existence that they accorded humanity. There was no telling, thus, whether these descendants would evolve into peace-loving natives, or bloodthirsty hunters and barbarians.

"It's way too small for a renegade encampment," Keith answered of the data readouts. "It's small, very small, maybe twelve inches tops, but the scanner says . . . it's **organic!** I'm sensing only an object, no internal structure to it at all, just energy. . . . How can it be **alive?**" He pondered it and shook his head. *What the fuck had he gotten his son and himself into? What the hell was that thing?*

"Renegades, Jeff, would never get past the force shield cocoon back at the entrance cabin. That's why it's there, why it's identity code-keyed, to prevent that sort of thing. Unless there's another way into the caves no one knows about. But those power emanations, spectrum readouts . . . they're not from known power sources or human metals."

"And it's *alive?*" Jeffrey swallowed hard and drew breath to again speak.

43

"Dad, are you trying to scare me? We're going back, right, the way we came? We're leaving now, pretend like none of this ever happened?"

Keith grinned. He wasn't feeling real great at the moment himself. The flesh on his neck began to crawl up his scalp as he looked out at the rock formations. The scanner couldn't identify the anomaly's distant molecular pattern against any it had ever been programmed to recognize, and that included all the various elements that had been logged as present in the core rocks discovered within the outer planets in the solar system, or even in the circling comets beyond.

Keith looked down to the scanner in his hand and inspected it. What was worse, he wondered: stumbling onto a renegade encampment, or onto something completely unknown?

Whatever's out there could already know we're here, he abruptly feared.

"Please say we're turning around," his son repeated, voicing the course of action that even Keith now thought might be a good one.

Keith took a breath, and then looked over at the boulder. Its top was slanted but mostly level. They could easily climb to the top of it and find lodging. He made up his mind.

"Come on, Jeff."

"Where?"

He paddled the raft flush against the boulder and reached for the mooring line. "Get up there," he said, indicating the boulder's crest.

"Why? We're staying?" Jeff asked, incredulously.

Keith persisted, helping his son onto the rock. Securing the Sensor Sphere carry bag, he hoisted himself up after Jeff, tossing Jeff the mooring line. "Hang onto that," he said. He looked over at the Sensor Sphere. "We should see what that is. I'm going to check it out. Maybe the humidity down here has affected the scanner, and this is just a glitch. That thing **can't** be organic." He decided. "I'll send the spheres to check out the shore area. If something **is** out there, we'll have a half kilometer start before it decides to come after us."

Jeffrey swallowed. "Dad, why don't we just go?" he tried to reason almost pleadingly.

Keith smiled. "It'll be okay. Don't be scared. These mag-belts have cocoon shields. If something threatens us, we'll be safe within them. Nothing can get past them, not pack wolves, black bears, not even water moccasins."

Oh, great, his father was talking about snakes now.

Keith reached into the Sensor Sphere carry bag and found a *playback only* headset which he proceeded to hand to his son. Jeffrey put it on. With its seven arching ribs secure atop his head, it looked exactly like Keith's command headset. The only difference between them was that Jeffrey's was a passive unit. It received transmissions only; it could not transmit commands.

Keith tucked his legs under him atop the boulder as he heard the plip plop of droplets all around him. He reached into the inner pocket of his jacket and fished out a handful of marker beacons. He took a deep breath.

Jeffrey tucked his own legs under him, as Keith created a crude circle of light around them both with the markers. He then instructed the beacons to light, and their faces were suddenly illuminated, long upward shadows making ghouls out of the two of them.

"Ready?" asked Keith.

"Are you sure you want to do this?" Jeff answered.

Keith nodded. "We'll be fine. We're not leaving the boulder. We're fine." He activated the monitor mode on the Sensor Sphere-record unit, and data transmissions from the sphere were relayed from it to both their headsets.

Jeffrey's consciousness clouded, he became confused. He felt one second on the boulder with his father, his attention fixed on the Sensor sphere. The next second, thoughts not his were in his head; he seemed not atop the boulder at all, but out over the water. He saw the raft directly below him and the water around it. He saw the Light Sphere floating in the air just a few meters away. He could "see" in all directions at once, a complete three-sixty vista. He saw the Light Sphere out over the water nearby, but he could not "see" the Sensor Sphere.

That was because he was *inside it.* He **was** the Sensor Sphere.

Jeff centered his attention on his and his father's forms atop the boulder. Both of their bodies seemed lifeless. He concentrated hard, imagining his eyelids and demanding them to open. When they did he got a double exposure image of himself beside his dad: one up close facing his father, and the other from a distance just beyond the boulder.

"Your eyes are open, Jeff!" his father informed him. Keith's voice seemed to originate simultaneously from up close and from far away. "Stop fighting it. Get oriented."

Jeff closed them once more, and once again in his mind's eye he was swept back over the water. "It makes me dizzy," he answered.

"Quit opening your eyes and it won't."

Jeff nodded. "Okay . . . I'm okay now."

"All right," Keith answered. Very slowly, then, at Keith's command, they felt themselves waft away from the boulder. The Light Sphere's intense beam in this state registered as only warmth and brilliance. It didn't hurt to stare at it, Keith felt no pain doing so, which was fortunate because there was no "looking away." Keith concentrated on ignoring its presence. He felt a momentary disorientation as he tried to ignore the sight of his body back atop the boulder. He felt himself shunting back and forth between the two perspectives. Keith was as bad as his son, and he was **used** to it. He let go awareness of his body.

He ordered the Light Sphere to dim. The farthest reaches of the cavern receded back into shadows. Steering the Sensor Sphere now, he felt himself float northward upriver and toward the distant shoreline.

Beyond the shoreline came an eerie gleam of purple light. Keith didn't have access to his pocket scanner in this state; he couldn't request further analysis of the strange light's origin. He commanded the sphere to continue on for the shore.

The cavern was only six meters wide in this sector, but the ceiling was awesome; large drapery stalactites hung above them like bath towels on a clothesline. The Light Sphere rose and slipped past them, its dim glow making them eerie-looking and ominous. Jeffrey felt nervous just seeing them. Suddenly everything in the cave seemed as if it were hiding a dark and threatening secret.

Keith directed the Sensor Sphere over to the shoreline. The ceiling was low and studded with stalactites. The cavern went back for meters. He dimmed the Light Sphere even more, and had the two spheres head off for the source of the purple glow. The rock formations passed to the rear ominously and ever so slowly, the twilight dimness almost nauseating, but he did not dare do anything about raising the level, for the glow was that dim, and he'd miss it otherwise.

Scanning the cave's shadows, alert for the slightest unnatural sound the Sensor Sphere might detect, his breathing was heavy; he could feel it. It bothered him. He took a long breath. The sound of it, so near, reminded him that his body was back (and safe) atop the now distant boulder. He took some small comfort in that.

He was safe. It was his conscious *essence* that was venturing places that maybe was a bad idea.

He stopped the sphere, suddenly, and took in the three—sixty degree view.

"Dad?" Jeff called.

This was the hard part. How to tell someone monitoring the vista with you in which direction to turn or where to fixate one's thoughts within the three-hundred-sixty degree vista. The purple glow was originating from an area far back along the rear wall and off about thirty meters to the right, facing away from the lake. Keith inched the sphere a single meter forward in its direction.

"Holy Fuck," whispered Keith, forgetting his son was near and could hear him swear.

Jeff gasped.

"Do you see it?" Keith asked Jeff.

"Oh, God, Dad, **YES.** *What IS that?"* He tried to keep the fear out of his words, but it leaked through, anyway.

Lost in the shadows of a grotto, a ghostly specter revealed itself amid the darkness. It glowed in a purple light. The color emanated from it. A cocoon shield also of dim purple light encircled the thing, some three meters in width. Keith tensed. Jeffrey looked over and felt a shiver go up his body.

Keith directed his thoughts on the Light Sphere; he ordered it illuminate full intensity. When it did—

"*What **IS** that, Dad?*" Jeff asked again.

He heard his father under his breath, utter, "***Damn!***"

The object, whatever it was, was little more than a ball of pure energy, said energy being self-contained in a crystal mass of some sort. It was no more than maybe a foot round and **hung** in the air several inches and with no visible means of support above a stalagmite formation two meters in height. The stalagmite appeared to be a natural formation, the result of years of limestone solution, dripping from the ceiling to slowly fashion it into the monolithic rock mass it now was. Its top tapered to a rounded point, as if a finger pointed up to the energy ball; it lent further proof that eons of limestone drippings was in fact how the stalagmite had ended up there. One almost got the impression the energy ball *chose* to repose above it as it did, deliberately.

It was sentient, that was certain, there was an ambiance about it that left the two sure that there was intelligence, an organic intelligence behind that thing's presence. Keith stood poised to emergency-recall the two spheres back to the boulder. Whoever or whatever left that thing down here probably had programmed the plasma ball to not take kindly to intruders. Time to pack up and get moving out of here, leave it, whatever the hell it was, to its own affairs. He was almost glad now he'd not done this in person. He expected any minute now it would begin coming after the two crystals and then go after him and Jeff as well. But nothing changed. He then scanned with his mind's eye the three-sixty vista of the cavern it reposed within. He saw only rock.

Jeff forced his eyes open to remind himself he wasn't really "there." He saw in double exposure the dim circle of beacon lights surrounding himself and his dad. It made him dizzy again. He very seriously considered removing the headset.

"Whatever that is," Keith said, "no renegade colony left it behind. And it's not standing guard in front of anything either."

Jeffrey closed his eyes again. "Are we capable of making something like that?" he asked.

Keith grunted a laugh. The air surrounding the plasma ball's cocoon shield felt tingly, electrified. It registered upon the "feel" sensors of the Sensor Sphere. Keith and Jeff both felt it. "No," Keith replied to his son. "Human beings aren't even close to fashioning whatever that is. That's a plasma ball of pure energy." Keith furrowed his brow. "I'm having trouble, Jeff, recalling the spheres. They're not answering my commands. We may have to leave them behind."

Keith opened his eyes; Jeff had his open as well and fixed on his Dad.

He was nodding, totally in agreement with his father's decision.

Jeff felt his mind abruptly redirected back to the grotto where the plasma ball resided. Something was suddenly happening. "DAD!"

The ball of plasma was suddenly very large in the image in his mind. It had left its berth above the stalagmite and was approaching fast. It was so near the two distant spheres he could feel the static charges emanating from the thing affecting the neural circuitry of the Sensor Sphere. It kept on coming and was about to "seemingly" overtake the two Hagerton males.

Jeff tensed and tore off the headset in time to see something completely terrifying happen to his father and to Jeff's headset. His father's reflexes hadn't been as swift as his own. Both Keith —and Jeff's headset— disappeared, the headset tickling Jeff's fingers as it disintegrated. Suddenly, it was gone from his hand, and his dad was just plain gone, departed without a moment's warning.

The circle of light beacons he alone now resided within cast but a feeble glow upon the boulder top. Their light barely illuminated the edges of the boulder, and only subtly bathed the ceiling. Jeffrey heard the lake around him (the water droplets plipping into the water), but it was lost to him, lost in pitch black darkness. He was terrified to move, afraid he'd slip and fall into the water, afraid to make any move, certain at any moment the anomaly would come for him next. He couldn't think; his mind wouldn't work. His awareness of being back and present on the boulder in full measure was only now returning.

"Dad?" Somewhere in the back of his logical mind, he knew it was stupid to call out such a thing, summon his dad, even meekly, as he did. But he had to disbelieve the truth, call it a lie. *Come on, Dad, stop not being here!* was what his "logical" mind wanted to exclaim.

It didn't help

CHAPTER SIX

His father was dead, Jeffrey imagined. That thing had reached through the Sensor Sphere and was somehow able to annihilate his dad, and only missed doing the same to himself because he'd been quick enough to remove the playback headset in time.

No, maybe it used the Sensor Sphere as a homing device, perhaps for matter transport purposes.

Maybe.

It would be something to hope that, anyway.

***

Jeffrey couldn't say exactly how long he sat there too frightened to move, and too overwhelmed with shock to do more than assume a near fetal position atop the boulder.

He felt nothing, thought nothing, or so it seemed to him, breathed and just attempted to survive the ordeal he was in now. Eventually, he found a solution, a small one, but one which brought him back to an awareness of time and the universe. He made himself list what the positive attributes about the situation were (the situation itself, he thought, sucked). He thanked good fortune for one for the lighted ring of lights encircling him. Jeff would have now been hopelessly in the dark without them, no real hope of ever successfully moving from this spot and finding his way back to the surface.

His father had been wearing the command-headset when he'd disappeared. Jeffrey in panic had torn off his "playback only" headset, and had seen it disappear. It gave him chills to think that— had he left it on— he might have vanished too. And maybe that wouldn't have been as bad a thing as it felt like it should have been, because was his present predicament any better? His Dad was mysteriously gone.

Slowly, he reached up to his nose and eyes, swiped at them, sniffed once (he'd been crying), and then reached down timidly for one of the beacons. He peered over the boulder's edge to the blackness beyond, and saw a faint impression of the lake. He saw the raft down there as well.

"Dad!" he suddenly called into the darkness. "Dad!"

Suffice to say that after about a minute of vainly hoping his father would answer, he gave up. Jeffrey didn't completely buy that his father was dead; although it was just as likely, even more logical, that he was. He just didn't want to believe that. If that plasma ball was designed to be as defensive against intruders and as aggressive as all that, why not come up the lake itself and do the job in person?

This felt like something other, and also like he was beginning to repeat himself, his mind circling around the same issues and the same optimistically plausible "points", as he wavered over what his next move should be. He wondered if he should venture down there and attempt to confront the thing, if it really were intelligent and "organic" and inquire just why in the hell did it have to do what it did. Why couldn't it choose a more civil way to say hello, or *"Get out!"* He wondered if— on the chance that his dad was still not dead, he could negotiate with the thing, or would that end up doing more damage than good? If he could get back to the surface and call for assistance, maybe he could get the proper authorities down here and let them figure out how to deal with an entity/anomaly like that one.

He pondered the notion of paddling back upstream with only the feeble beacon lights for illumination. With the mag-belt set at near zero gravity pull, reaching the surface should be possible, eventually, and calling New Allentown from the air car would be the solution.

Unless his father was already dead.

In which case did doing anything matter, really?

Shit.

He felt the chill of these underground depths and wanted to curse it. It was even chillier and more damp this far down than up near the surface.

He genuinely could not see a solution to his quandary. Which course of action to take? Go in search of his dad's fate, or leave?

He gathered up the beacons into his palm. His fist glowed red, the white light of the beacons filtering through his hand's flesh and blood vessels, no doubt. The light levels, with them all in a bunch like that, still sucked, but was more now he realized like the candlelight intensities the first cave explorers centuries ago had had to endure when they first explored Crystal Cave back in 1871.

He had been sitting the whole time on the mooring rope to the raft, making sure the raft wouldn't drift off. He took the marker beacons and stuck most of them in his pocket. Retaining one, he then grabbed the rope with his other hand, and carefully descended the boulder. He pulled on the rope, securing the raft flush up against the boulder, and then dropped down into it.

It bobbed only slightly, and immediately began to push off on its own (by the nudge his descent into it had given it) and enter the waterway. It started down the lake in the direction of the distant shoreline where the anomaly reposed. Jeffrey hadn't been sure which direction he wanted to paddle in. Though the raft on its own seemed to make the decision for him, he told it that he still retained final say on the direction, and would change it if he chose to. He didn't.

Jeffrey took a breath and slowly laid the beacon lights out on the floor of the raft, before the fusion reactor "utility box." Once doing that, he reached over for one of the paddles. Suddenly, he sensed activity out the corner of his eye, and he heard himself gasp.

The as yet unseen (with his eyes anyway) plasma ball was now evidently making quite a spectacle of itself up the way. Its purple light was strobing against the shoreline and the opposing wall beyond the shore itself, the strobing pattern reminiscent of archive material he scanned of welders and the arc light bursts they caused as their welding arcs stabbed at the metal surfaces they were attaching. The effect was an eerie series of purples flashes, very brilliant explosions, popping off over and over. That thing was getting ready to emerge into view, he was sure of it, and come for him. He concluded now was a very good time to turn around in his seat in the raft and begin paddling back the other way.

Two shapes suddenly emerged from beyond the distant shoreline, just as he was about to do that. Jeffrey couldn't turn away; he wanted so badly to just do that and leave. But he didn't; he was curious to know just what they were.

The Light and Sensor spheres wafted into view down upon that distant shoreline and stopped short of the lake itself. Once again as before, only this time he was certain of it, the two units acted as if that had a sentient presence behind them, and no doubt that was in fact probably right. They appeared to be waiting for him, lighting the way and "recording" his possible progress. "Oh, shit," he whispered. "Is that thing using the Sensor Sphere as a remote set of eyes?"

"Dad?" he called then, hoping maybe his father had somehow been able to commandeer the two units and were controlling them. "Dad?" he said again, hoping if so, his father would make some sort of gesture with the two units that would indicate it was he behind their antics. There was no such indication, nothing. The spheres simply hovered there, waiting by the shore.

"Where's my father?" he shouted, convinced it wasn't his father controlling them at all. "Who are you, and what have you done to him?"

That didn't help, either.

Jeffrey took a breath and looked down to the fusion reactor utility box. He flipped up the lid and read the status indicators. He got an idea, and reached down for the legend marked "Light Sphere." He pressed it . . . and looked up.

This time goosebumps rode up his arms. The light sphere should have powered down; there was no change. It no longer fed off the power emanations of the fusion reactor. That thing down there obviously was controlling it.

"Nuts to both of you!" he said aloud. Jeffrey again reached for a paddle and slowly eased it into the water. He was leaving. He took a pull and turned the raft around.

"Jeffrey, don't go, please," came a female voice, either all around him in the

cave, or in his mind, either way it felt as if the voice were right there beside him. "Your father is not dead. He awaits you . . . within me. Come to me. I'll not further frighten you by making any further aggressive actions."

"Who are you?" he demanded.

"My name is Athena," the voice answered.

"How do you know my name? From my father's thoughts?"

"Your sister has spoken of you often. I've seen you in her thoughts. She and I have talked many times, although she does not remember the occasions after."

That stunned him. "My sister! What are you talking about?"

"I have been waiting for your arrival for some time, your family's. You are the last. My time is almost nigh. I tried to plant the desire for Frida herself to accompany your Dad. She wanted it to be, but he preferred you, his son. No matter. All will work out in the end. Come, Jeffrey. Within me, I will make your fondest wishes and desires come true."

"No," he simply answered.

"Jeffrey," suddenly came his father's voice. "It's all right. Come son. The way back to the surface, that way, is a path you should not pursue. You will see. Things will be so much better from here on. Athena will now go in search of Frida and your mom, to complete her mission. She's leaving it to you, son, to come of your own free will. Don't disappoint her. She means you no harm. Don't abandon me like this, son. You know you can't."

"Are you really my father?" he asked. "You talk like you're still *her.*"

"I'm in your thoughts, Jeffrey, it's me; you know it to be true. Son, please, it will make sense to you soon why this must be so."

The raft, unbeknownst to Jeffrey all the while, had been idly wafting downstream toward the shore on its own. Obviously, the current was moving in that direction at present. If he did nothing more, he would end up down there soon anyway. He turned around again in his seat and began to again lower his paddle into the water and pull the raft forward. *She would fulfill his fondest wishes,* had said this Athena. What did she mean by that? Could she know about his secret infatuation with being like his best friend, Ginny? Oh, God, if this Athena had already mind melded with his dad, Dad probably already knew what Athena was implying by that. How could he face his dad knowing that his father knew he secretly wished he been born a girl, like his sister?

But he had to admit one thing. At present, concern over a silly thing like that was the least of his concerns.

Idly, he continued pulling on the paddle, inching the raft ever closer to the waiting spheres down the way. It became easier to maneuver the raft, the more strokes he made.

Above him, as if a warning of ominous events on the horizon, the hanging "drapery" formations were coming up upon his raft. He would pass under them in moments. They were scary presences, especially in this light, looking as if at any moment they might gain living sentience and detach themselves like giant bats to descend upon him and feast on his flesh. The whole area felt like the lair of an alien world, in a place where winged night creatures and creepy crawlers dwelled. All he needed now was to see an actual bat dart across the cavern ceiling, and he'd probably lose it. He'd heard his mother utter the same aversion. She hated bats. He'd inherited her phobia. Too bad that was all he'd inherited; her femininity would have been a pleasant acquisition as well. He wouldn't have minded being her daughter.

Why are you fixating on that again? he asked himself. *"Quit it!"*

***

Past the draperies finally, he looked back for the boulder and could barely see it. It had faded eerily into the twilight. He faced the shoreline ahead, and paddled for it, probing its shadowy reaches for the way back to where this "Athena" entity reposed.

Getting out as the raft glided onto shore, he pulled it all the way out of the water. The spheres were right in front of him. He finished what he was doing and then walked up to them. "Well?" he asked.

Slowly they began to penetrate the caverns beyond the shoreline, the Light Sphere's light bringing the passages ahead out of the shadows. The ceiling was low and studded with toothy stalactites. The caverns went back for meters.

Within minutes he saw the grotto, the stalagmite sentinel and the purple orb that called itself Athena aglow above it. Jeffrey had a feeling that lake behind him now was very close to an exit point to outside. He pondered the thought of just activating his mag-belt, telling the two spheres and Athena to go to hell, and "flying" the mag-unit up the remainder of the lake and leaving here. But then he thought of his father, and the possibility that he might still be his dad and of need of Jeff's help, and hated himself for thinking only of his own well-being.

***

Jeffrey studied the plasma ball before him. It didn't seem real somehow. He almost wished there was another more logical explanation for its presence other than that it was alive. It reminded him of one of those old static-filled globes whose fiery filaments changed their erratic dancing patterns and all of them angled straight for a hand that touched the crystal's surface. He wondered if something like that would happen now.

"Well, I'm here," he told it. "Now what?"

The two meter height of the stalagmite formation was way too high for Jeff to reach up and touch the plasma ball. It promptly left its station above the formation and wafted down to before him, whereupon it abruptly rose in intensity and elongated to the shape of a humanoid figure; her female form slowly took shape upon it and long golden blond hair cascaded down from an incredibly angelic young woman's face. She smiled to Jeffrey as she stood there, her billowing white ethereal gown blowing as if in a swift breeze, the trailing bits of its hem trailing off into wisps of ethereal energy that seemed to detach and disappear.

Jeffrey stood motionless, totally amazed and impressed. The Light and Sensor spheres were right behind him, standing sentinel, as if his escorts.

"This is but a fragment of my total 'Me,'" she informed him. "I am not here in full."

She spoke but it was as if in his thoughts that he appeared to hear her.

"What are you exactly?" he said to her.

"What you see before you is an externalized fragment of my total self, which lies elsewhere. You would call this my Avatar. I have limited powers while inhabiting it as I do now, but still many you would find impressive. I greet you, young one. How are you?"

"Where's my Dad?"

"Fret not of him. You will be reunited with him soon. *All* your inquiries will be answered, Jeffrey. You want to be Frida's sister? I can do that, make your wish come true."

"It won't be real, not for real," he said. "It'll just be an illusion. Like you?"

She grinned a beauteous grin. "I am called an Eleution, and I am not an illusion."

"Is this your real form?"

"I have no form to speak of, young one. We are creatures of pure energy now, although once eons ago we were much like you. Your body comes from energy as well," she said. "Transmuted into physical mass. It is simply a collection of molecules. They can be rearranged to whatever pattern you desire. Your male sex is nothing of consequence. It can be altered with a simple command."

Athena waved her wispy hand before her and a trail of energy strands curled and drifted off, suddenly engulfing him. Jeffrey first felt his clothes transform. He looked down at himself; he still seemed himself, but he wasn't dressed in his original denim jeans, corduroy shirt and leather jacket for spelunking in dark, damp caves. He was attired instead in an off-white turtleneck, tan hiking shorts, brown leggings and tan hiking boots.

"Hey!" he protested.

But then a million tiny needles began to infect his physical "presence." He felt his entire body undergo a metamorphose, as if his body were undergoing a total molecular reorganization. He felt his body eventually resettle, his consciousness adjusting to all the new sensations that were suddenly flooding through his "body."

He looked adorable. But it was all wrong . . . felt that way as well, and to his thinking he hadn't requested any of it. Was this what it felt like to be a young girl? He'd donned outfits such as this in the past with Frida, when she and he were playing dress up in her bedroom in New Allentown, but this was the first time it all felt "right" on him, like it were meant for him. He felt weird all over.

"I didn't say **do it!**" he said. "You've turned me into a girl!"

He *was* one . . . just like that. Appearance wise, the only real difference, besides the cute outfit, was in the softness of his long brown hair, which had been quite the way down past his ears and longish before. The only other major change he could sense about himself "down there" wasn't something at this point he wished to expose himself to verify.

"Change me back!" he ordered. Even his voice was the same. "It doesn't feel all that different anyway."

"You're only nine, Jeffrey. At your age, there isn't much that CAN change. There isn't that dramatic a difference between your two genders, anyway, especially now at this stage in your species' evolution. "

"Change me back!"

"Join with your father within me. He awaits you. Then we'll see if that is what you really desire. In my reality, you can become what you most wish. You will see. The choice of gender will be yours."

"I can't go back home like this. No one will believe it's me!"

He heard Athena laugh; she was obviously enjoying this very much.

"You are an adorable child, young one. Your sister really does enjoy you. You are fortunate."

"Why do you know my sister? What is she to you?"

"She is more to me than you can ever imagine," Athena replied. "The day is waning, young one. We have work to be done. Tarry no longer."

"You'll change me back?"

"If you really wish it."

"Do not fear me. I take this form, a true representation of my benevolent nature. I am no threat to you."

"What do you need me to do?"

She extended her hand. "Take my hand."

He swallowed hard and extended his own, gently making contact Athena's ethereal energy. Jeffrey felt a weird tingling all over. His body appeared to be acquiring a static charge, and felt his very physical presence began to break down . . . **again.** He was dissolving. It sort of reminded him of an old archive program from centuries ago where the leads used a similar method to "beam down" from their space vessel to the planets they wished to explore.

I'm coming, Dad, he spoke in his mind.

***

A minute later, his physical presence completely dissolved and he was no more. And a minute after that the two sentinel crystal spheres that had escorted him to this point joined him . . . in wherever and whatever fate awaited him in this domain that called itself Athena. . . .

CHAPTER SEVEN

-1-

Jeff saw only a murky twilight around him. He "awoke" —because that was how it felt— crouched like a cat curled up upon a cold hard floor. He wanted to say a hard, *metallic* floor, or even one of concrete, but no, it was more like the texture of hard bone or fossilized stone. It was dark all around him, very damp and warm. As lairs go it was a creepy place, like being a microbiologist reduced in size to traverse the interior of a living organism, to see it from the inside out. He felt very weird and very strange. And as he propped himself up on one arm, his palm resting and supporting his head and chin, he felt a great amount of hair all around his face, more so than he'd ever allowed there to be, and it felt soft and fluffy. He looked down at himself; he still wore the turtleneck top, shorts, tights and hiking boots. But now he felt even more like a little girl than even before, and this time reached into the tight tan shorts and felt panties— like his sister's— and nothing under them that was supposed to be there. Not that it had ever been all that emphatic a male endowment before. Course on the other hand he never really gave the thing much thought anyway, except when he needed to pee. It was hard to say he even felt the thing's absence. How could something be missed when you gave it no mind to start?

"Dad?" he called out into the misty darkness all around him. *Christ, his tonal inflections even sounded more girl-like than previously.* "He's never going to believe it's me now. Thanks a lot, Athena!"

He rose on his spindly-feeling legs and was incredibly impressed by how "real" all this felt. None of it could be real, not as he knew reality. Where was this anyway? Athena's domain? Is that how she described it? Her lair, a construct, an imagined place only? He glanced to the "realm" before him and cringed. *This is awful, Athena,* he whispered under his breath. *Is it really how you imagine a fun place to be?*

"Dad, I'm here," he called. "It's your son. Honestly, it's me. Don't be fooled. Where are you?"

He almost felt like cute little Alice Liddle in *Alice in Wonderland;* imagined he sounded a lot like her as well. And here, wherever this truly was, felt to be as morbidly depressing as some of the locales she visited in Lewis Carrol's stories.

***

The wall behind him was ebony black, lost in shadows; he could see a reflection of himself in it in the tights and shorts. "I wonder what's on the other side of that," he said. "Oh, fuck, I'm even talking to myself like Alice. All I need is the blue dress, an apron with a big bow tied in the back, and some cute knee socks. I'm already a girl. All I need is a pair of maryjanes to complete the outfit. *Oh no! Stop!*"

Seconds later, his outfit totally changed to an Alice in Wonderland one.

***

He felt something wrapped around his neck, and quickly faced the back wall to catch his reflection.

Was that a black choke collar with a red heart on the front?

"Aah, are you kidding me?!! I look like my sister! This stuff only happens to people in *their dreams*. Is this what this place is, a dream state? **This** is what your holding pen looks like, Athena, for people you entrap? *Wonderland?* **Put me back!"**

But it wasn't happening, and now dressed like a modern day Alice, in a cute blue dress that barely covered his panties, a checkered petticoat with black threads hanging down and white knee socks ending —yep— in a pair of cute, patent leather maryjanes with a strap around the top. Oh, shit. If Frida could see him now, she'd probably shout something like, *Hey, no fair! If you want to be my sister, fine, but I'm the blond one. I'm Alice. You can be Little Bo Peep. . . .*

Curiouser and Curiouser.

***

Jeffrey daintily extended his little girl hand to the wall behind him and felt it. It felt almost like living tissue. He suspected, if there was a way out, it might be through this wall where he "came to" when he first awoke here. He had to make a note of it, mark the place somehow. What was it about Alice and her story? She had reached into a pocket on her apron and found a thimble to hand the Dodo bird. No thimble, and no pockets as well, not in that tiny apron he was in with all the hearts, spades, clovers and diamonds embossed on the fringe. He'd just have to try and remember where this was. He turned and surveyed the scene before him.

The air smelled fresh, if it even was real air and not just imagined air for imaginary lungs. The interior of wherever this place was felt as damp and cold as the caves, themselves, and as mysterious. It was unlike any ship interior he'd ever been in before. He felt his skin crawl.

"Dad?" he called again, fearful of what else might hear him as well. He studied the twilight before him. The interior walls were supported by buttresses and vertical columns, dividing the interior into various compartments. The scene looked dismal, like a cave's; an indigo glow radiated from everywhere. It seemed to originate from the walls, themselves, as if a form of bioluminescence. There was no other light. It

58

was eerie.

A white sheen washed the columns before him all at once. He turned. A fiery circle of light appeared on the wall behind him and subsequently grew brighter and larger each second. Jeffrey tensed. He felt a shiver go up his spine. All at once the light became a fiery crystal, and Jeffrey recognized the shape of the Light Sphere, as most of it now slipped through the membrane and into the room. Its light flooded the interior. He almost wanted to smile at it in relief, until he reminded himself that it was now being guided on its way by Athena and under her control.

The Sensor Sphere entered behind it, subsequently, and took a position a little above and in front of him as if there for one job only— to observe and record. He'd always hated the sight of that thing, watching and recording his every move for all the world to see. Now he wondered exactly for whom was it "watching."

"Go away," he said to it.

He reached back and felt the wall again where the two units had just emerged. If they could come through it, why not he exit out of here the same way? He pressed his hand against it a little more to test that notion. But no it would not give. It was (for him) just a wall. An impenetrable wall.

Resigned to be stuck in this horrid place, Jeffrey turned again to scan the interior of this . . . whatever and wherever this place was. With the light from the Light Sphere now available to him as extra illumination, he was able to "shed more light on the subject."

Dumb, Jeff, he told himself of making jokes at this juncture. He glanced down at himself in the Alice get up. *And a lame one, you . . . **girl**. . . ."*

The domain he reposed within now looked even more dismal than before. It was brownish-orange, the color of the caves, and contained no walls or corridors in the familiar sense. It looked more like the neural fiber network of the human brain with ribbon lengths of something that resembled webbing or angel hair (fiber optic tissue?), angling every which way amid pinnacles and buttresses and disappearing against walls that, should one squint hard to discern them as such, one would eventually realize they were the equivalent of rooms and corridors aboard human-made spaceships. God! Is that where he was? The interior of a spaceship? Athena's plasma ball avatar was indeed like a space vessel, because it could facilitate passage, evidently, for whomever she allowed to ride with her as she journeyed through the cosmos. It started to make sense what Athena's avatar crystal was and what it was doing down there in the subterranean bowels beneath Crystal Cave. It was a capture device, like a Venus flytrap— snare anyone who came too close and then deliver them to wherever it was programed to take them.

The Athena crystal was a transport device and he and his Dad were its new acquisitions. And Athena had every intention of rounding up the rest of the family, especially Frida.

Oh, fuck.

This was no ordinary transport. The place was *alive*, he just knew it. The entire interior was like a thinking brain. He saw wisps of light, whites and reds and blues, streak through fiber optic-like tissue as if they were neural brain data being shunted from one lobe of the brain to another. There were blotches of red running against the walls in some places, and Jeffrey really felt as if he'd entered a living organism, itself.

"DAD?" he called, more agitated now. A part of him hoped his father was nowhere among all this. This place seemed more the lair of a malevolent monster that enjoyed feasting on whatever souls fell into its trap.

***

The Light and Sensor spheres followed him as he slipped past the columns and around stalagmite-type mounds upon the floor. The place looked a cross between the human brain and the caves, themselves, as if Athena had a thing about dark, dreary lairs.

He stepped daintily, having no choice, not so much used as he was to getting around in maryjanes and a dress so short he wondered how girls could stand going out in public in such flimsy outfits. Still, it felt as cute on him as he looked in it.

Before him how lay what looked like a small arena room; it reminded him of the ruins of ancient Greek amphitheaters he'd scanned in historical archive visuals. The room ahead seemed also almost deliberately thought out, self-enclosed and circular. Like an amphitheater, it had concentric rows of what resembled aisle seating that descended to a circular pit. A large crystal sat in the pit area at the bottom. It glowed a dull orange, and Jeffrey heard it hum, ever so faintly. It felt alive somehow, and he was afraid to venture nearer to it.

"It's not real, none of it; it's all in my head! Why did you even fashion all of this, Athena? Is it really necessary?"

The back retaining wall to the room to this one rose only three-quarter way to a ceiling dew-dropped with tiny stalactite encrustations. Tiny stalagmite mounds, like sculptured figurines that could resemble anything the imagination wished them to, inhabited natural-looking shelf nooks, as if they were exhibits along a museum wall. Aglow in indigo, the nooks receded into the shadows to the remainder of wherever this place was.

The Light Sphere stayed with him, illuminating the way, as if lighting the scene to assure a good Sensor Sphere record. Because there it too was as well, the Sensor Sphere, gliding forward across the ceiling, taking what seemed a permanent position, then, directly above the crystal mass, and no doubt archiving every move he made.

Jeffrey bit his lower lip. This was Athena's idea of a spaceship interior? He expected weird, alien lairs filled with alien devices and artifacts, and long winding hallways, like in the cruise vessels that sailed between the Earth and planet Mars. He certainly wasn't expecting to see this. This was just plain depraved.

Athena. She called herself an Eleution. From where, though? What world in what solar system? How many light years away in space from his own? He tried to imagine Athena hailing from another planet and solar system, a place far far away place out in space.

How many centuries now had the human race wished it could travel among the stars in a period of time brief enough to actually make it worth the effort?

Hyper drive, Trans- dimensional space travel, was a novelty concept that even at his young age he'd heard of, although in truth he got most of his knowledge of such things from the old Sci-Fi entertainment visuals in the archive libraries of the city. As a means of propulsion through space, Hyper drive travel was supposed to be possible in theory. The same concepts of distorted space were used to describe black holes, those areas in the universe where collapsed giant stars had concentrated so much matter into so small an area that the universe could no longer contain them three-dimensionally, and thus warped space around them, literally creating a hyper dimensional realm that no longer made sense in three dimensions. Such were black holes, which had been known as fact for five centuries, now. Traveling in hyper dimensions, however, in the hope of shortcutting the journey to other stars, was outright fantasy. No one had ever figured out how to do it. It made for good entertainment, and was fun to dream about. Years ago, however, serious research on the subject fell prey to ridicule, was considered pointless and just plain dumb. The stars, it was eventually decided, were simply too far away for voyages to them to ever be attempted, not using known and proven methods of space exploration in use since the mid-1900s, but which unfortunately meant that travel between worlds was limited to only the eight worlds (and Pluto) of Jeffrey's own solar system. And that was kind of depressing.

Not one of those worlds were good for much at all; certainly they couldn't accommodate human visitors from Earth. Atmospherically, and ecologically speaking, they were nothing like Earth at all.

Could Athena, a lifeform of pure energy, and as such not bound by the rules of physical matter . . . could she really do what was thought impossible? Had she come here from another world? What sort of people had these Eleutions once been, and how many eons did it take, before they eventually evolved themselves right out of the restraints imposed by lesser matter-based lifeforms, and allowed them to come and go through the cosmos with no concern over how far away in space distances really were? It was pretty obvious to Jeff that this "illusion" of a space vessel was occupied at present by only him. He hadn't yet even located his father. And Athena? This was all her ruse. She was carrying him and his dad, as a mother kangaroo carried her young in a pouch. Athena, as such, could become her own "spaceship" for the benefit of more inferior "Earthplane"-bound entities like Jeffrey's own. And that could make her quite enviable to the human race if it were to find some way to subdue her and use her for its own narcissistic ambitions where the universe was concerned.

How long had Athena's "avatar" been down here in this cave, waiting for hapless innocents like himself and his dad to wander by? The way into the subterranean depths below Crystal Cave that his father and he had found this day showed every indication of having only been newly opened up. There HAD to be other ways to get to here. Jeffrey could not believe he and his Dad were Athena's first captives.

"Come on, Dad!" he shouted now in his little girl voice, with growing impatience, *"will you quit not being here?! This is getting old!"*

He felt his heartbeat racing again, and he paused a second to take a deep breath and attempt to breathe normal. It was then that he noticed a strange cavity, a nook or anteroom, down the way just off the amphitheater. He wondered of it. It reminded him of a storage room, off the main pit area. It lay on the other side of the amphitheater from him, and resembled a stage directly in front of the angled, rising tiers. Limestone formations drooped from the ceiling within it or rose from the floor.

No, that wasn't right at all. Those cave formations were **real.** He was seeing what appeared to be a way back out into the cave, and could see all the way back to the subterranean lake where he'd left the raft to come in search of Athena's orb. But how could that be? It was pitch black out there in the cave without the Light Sphere to light the way. Was that really an exit, a way out of Athena's pretend place?

He hurried down for it, saw movement above him. The Sensor Sphere left its station, and like an inquisitive cat dropped to investigate his actions.

"Leave me alone you pain in the ass!" he told the Sensor Sphere globe. "This place *isn't real and neither are you!* I don't know why Athena even bothered to pattern you into her dream world for."

Realizing then that this version of the Sensor Sphere was itself like someone's remote "eyes", he knew Athena herself was watching him, interested no doubt in the path Jeffrey took to coming to grips with his new reality. Jeff paused, faced the Sphere squarely and grinned. He pinched two opposing ends of the dress's hem (it had a white trim encircling it) with his fingers and did a curtsy, like a proper little Victorian English girl. "Like my dress?" he asked, grinning sarcastically to the Sphere, certain Athena was watching and aware. "You're sick. How long do I have to stay stuck wearing this stupid thing? I feel like I'm dressed for a Halloween party. Isn't it enough that you've turned me into a little girl? Why do I have to wear **this?**"

The sphere just stood there observing him. After a time passed with no hint of his ever getting a response from it or Athena, he turned and again faced the anteroom "stage." He faced back to the Sensor Sphere, intent on entering the anteroom. "Is that real?" he asked Athena. "If I go in there will I be back outside and in the cave . . . for real?"

He would have liked for her to verify that she was indeed watching his every move by filling the room with the sound of her voice. But no such thing subsequently transpired. The silence all around him was the silence of a tomb.

"Fine," he nodded. "I'll find out myself, but I bet I already know the answer. You're messing with me. It can't be that easy: to walk in there and leave this all, I mean."

Jeff then entered the anteroom and soon found he was correct. The scene was little more than like a holodeck chamber, a room outfitted to create authentic 3D image simulations. Indeed, for all intent and purposes it seemed as if he were back out among the formations, in the subterranean cavern itself. Only no, he wasn't. That became clear the moment he tried touching one of the stalagmites, his hand went right through it. And of course there was no sign of Athena's plasma ball. There wouldn't be. He wasn't out there in the grotto of the cave. His life essence had "melded" with Athena's. He was inside her. Facing down, he could see the tapered top of the stalagmite above which Athena's globe reposed.

This whole place was pattered to resemble someone's concept *of a ship's Bridge.* This "anteroom" was the forward viewport. He gazed back to the arena levels, the tiers, angling away and upward, and imagined this "holodeck" to in fact be that very thing. He pictured an alien crew seated upon the tiers, watching the images displayed before them in this pretend holodeck "pit." All this effort just for ambiance? No, Jeff began to suspect that maybe Athena chose this "imagery" for other reasons, perhaps she did so because it was her go-to "manifestation," as if to suggest that maybe in fact she provided it regularly for other species to occupy and while away their time as they crossed the cosmos inside her. It would be as if an entertaining distraction, a way to while away the time until their destination was reached.

Wow, what thoughts went through his head. But he'd bet anything he was correct.

It was at that moment that it happened. The tapered top of the stalagmite "moved" as if "Athena" had begun to lift her essence upward and away from the stalagmite beneath her orb. Jeff felt himself within the holodeck pit waft upward and away from the grotto and back toward where the lake reposed. "Oh, shit," he thought. "We're actually doing it. We're taking off. She's snared Dad and me and now we're leaving here and going to where she stores her captives."

What followed next was like the traveling images he saw whenever he and Frida sent a remote Sensor Sphere globe anywhere he wished to visit on old Earth, like yesterday when he and Frida visited Luray Caverns in Virginia. It was as if he were now airborne and riding a magic carpet.

The scene threaded past the hanging columns and sped off for the lake. Then it followed it north in the direction opposite the route Jeff and his dad had come. There was a slight incline now and the depth of the lake began to recede until finally it became a mere trickle. Eventually there was a slit opening ahead and sure enough seconds later the light levels exploded, the scene opened to the world above.

Jeffrey had to shield his eyes a second until his pupils adjusted.

The view hovered briefly now above a small stream that seemed to purposely flow alongside what at one point a long time ago may have been a back country road. Traces of it occasionally revealed itself among the overgrowth. Soon after that the image took flight upward and cleared the trees and took off for the clouds.

"Jeffrey?" came a voice suddenly behind him. He turned and saw his father, standing in the entry to the anteroom. He was looking right at his son.

"**Dad!**" said Jeffrey. With his appearance in the dress, maryjanes and knee socks, he looked like a little girl, jubilant to again be reunited with her father.

And that was the way he looked, like an Alice from Wonderland lookalike. He met up with Keith Hagerton and threw his arms around his dad and wrapped them tight. He hugged his father.

Keith Hagerton glanced down at his "son," Jeff's girlish arms in the short sleeved dress, with the white and blue shoulder puff outs, wrapped tight against Keith. He hugged him back. "Jeff?" he asked, lowly, noting his son's appearance. "Is there something you want to tell me?"

Jeffrey looked up at him. "What?" he uttered in his little girl voice. "No, I was worried for you, Dad. You're all right. I thought Athena killed you back there when you vanished from the boulder."

Keith nodded. "And you didn't abandon me and run away. I'm proud of you . . . son. You ARE still my son, aren't you?" Keith found the situation somewhat amusing in a weird sort of way.

Jeffrey grinned, sheepishly. "I can't make this girl costume go away," he replied. "It's as if I'm stuck this way."

"It's not just the get up, Jeff. You're a real little girl."

Jeff frowned and slowly nodded in agreement.

"And you're okay with that?" Keith queried.

Jeffrey shrugged. "I guess I have to be. I think Athena did this to me on purpose. She knew I secretly like looking this way—"

"You do?"

"Dad, this is embarrassing. If I could make it go away right now and make myself male again, I would." He shrugged again. "It's not happening."

64

"Probably because deep down you're enjoying it too much," Keith said. "Wow, this is quite a reveal, Jeff. I didn't know you felt this way. I thought you were okay being my son."

"Dad . . . !" Jeff pleaded.

"And what's with the Alice in Wonderland get up, anyway?"

Jeffrey shrugged again. "It sort of just happened."

Keith grunted an acknowledgment. He glanced to the area before him and the airborne scene it displayed.

"We've left the caves," he observed. "We're topside."

Jeff nodded. "We've taken off. Athena's orb is a spaceship."

"Huh," pondered Keith, nodding his agreement as he thought about it.

Jeffrey turned around in his father's arms and glanced down to the image of their flight as well. "Where is she taking us?" he asked his dad.

The air surrounding the Crystal Cave parking lot was colder now, much colder than it had been at One that afternoon when Jeff had last seen the surface. Maiden Creek ran northward to the west, a ribbon of gray in the advancing twilight. The Blue Mountains rolled off across the westward expanse.

A flock of geese honked by far above, mere silhouettes in the dark, flying northward in a ragged V-formation. An autumn breeze blew across the expanse. Jeff actually could feel it. He looked up now beside his Dad and realized they were no longer at present in an illusion of an alien spaceship. Only the "scene" remained around them, like one would while accessing images from a Sensor Sphere. The rest of the "ship" had disappeared. It was as if they were now riding a large force field soap bubble.

Athena's orb "bubble" hovered then about a hundred meters above the hillside into which Crystal Cave descended. The two Hagerton's spotted their parked air car nestled in the tall grass that only obliquely suggested it once were a parking lot. It was mostly eroded away now and grown over. Athena's orb remained motionless directly above the air car, as if studying it intently. Jeffrey looked up at his father.

Keith seemed to stare as if in a trance, as if he were interfacing directly with Athena's essence, listening to her.

"Dad?" asked Jeff. He glanced to the air car. "Is she letting us go?"

"No, son, she is not. She's . . . cleaning up."

Jeff puzzled over that one from his dad, when all of sudden he saw a strobe flash, and a blue beam of light spear away from Athena's orb, and strike the air car. The vehicle began to glow. A second later the air car was gone, and the beam retracted. *"She destroyed it!"* he exclaimed. "Why did she do that?"

"No, not destroyed," Keith replied, still seemingly preoccupied with his direct musings with Athena. "Stored as molecular pattern data."

"Why? Dad, what is it? What is she doing?"

"Son," he only answered. "Attend."

The land suddenly dropped away, the scene leaving the surrounding hills to enter the cloudbanks. Jeffrey saw the moon swimming in a pale blue sky. He felt nausea sweep over him. Athena's orb climb made him dizzy. She climbed then even faster and higher, the ground growing smaller as it receded. The Earth began to lose its flatness. It contoured into that of a sphere, of the planet it was when seen from high orbit. Slowly, the Earth slipped into the blackness of outer space. Athena climbed through the thin layer of Earth's atmosphere, which now ringed the planet in a blue-green band. The atmosphere thinned and the stars pierced the growing blackness. Jeff felt a gnawing unease eating at his stomach. He wasn't used to the sight of such a thing. He was kilometers above the only home he had ever known. All his life he'd lived down there beneath the clouds of Earth.

And just as suddenly the view began to descend again, Athena arced back down toward the Earth, but not before Jeffrey could clearly see (for real, for he'd never really been out here above Earth like this before) the Eastern contour of the North American continent. He and Frida just yesterday had asked their Dad about the New Jersey coastline and its once famous Atlantic Ocean beaches. As he wandered his gaze up the eastern coastline, he clearly saw what remained of New Jersey. The entire Lower Peninsula portion was submerged to varying degrees, totally under water and gone. Florida for the most part, he gleaned, glancing down to the U.S.'s south had lost most of its jutting lower half as well. Gone thus went Miami and its famous beachfront property.

Earth's contour began to flatten again. Within seconds it became obvious they were re-entering the Earth's atmosphere, en route for the northeast United States.

Jeff felt Keith's hand rest upon his shoulder. "Dad?" he questioned.

Keith's continence had seemed to change as if he was no longer simply himself, but— like a puppet— remotely being controlled by another. "Athena's orb," said Keith, "was left here on Earth a long time ago. I have not been told why, only that humans were meant to one day find it. Athena craves companionship. She is used to being in psychic bond with those who need a lift across the galaxy and can't because they still exist as corporeal entities. She's been in our home solar system now for many years. She misses the opportunity to serve and be sent out into the stars. Immortality, Jeff, can get pretty boring when you live forever and long for something fulfilling, distracting to do."

"Dad," Jeff queried. "What is she doing to you? Athena, stop it. Give me back my father. Stop being so mean."

Keith grinned, weakly. "She answers, son: 'that you sounded just like a real nine year old Earth girl just then.' She thinks femininity suits you. It seems more in line with your basic nature. . .

"We were chosen for a reason, Jeff, you and I, and Kimmy and Frida, I don't yet know why. You see, Jeffrey, Athena, being an advanced, non-corporeal entity, has the potential to travel far into the universe via hyperspace. Living entities such as ourselves would not survive the stresses of transdimensional crossings. Athena's 'guests' joined with her, became one with her for a time, willfully allowing their physical mass to be stored as energy, their *patterns* remembered for when the voyage was done and they could again exist separate from her and in the flesh, as physical beings. But while melded with Athena, for a time they had to surrender their physical beings. Athena fashioned the illusion of suitable accommodations for her passengers, like that spaceship interior we saw earlier. You and I, as such; our patterns, I mean, are in storage for now. . . ." He pointed at the Earth. ". . . You are being sent home. You are being returned to New Allentown."

Jeff pondered that a second and finally uttered, "And you? Dad, what about you? She's not letting you go as well?"

Keith Hagerton had a blank, almost possessed look upon his face. He didn't answer.

Within moments, the view passed through the wispy cloud layer a few kilometers above the Earth's surface, and eastern Pennsylvania spread out below it.

"No one in New Allentown will know we've come, Jeff," Keith said. "Athena's orb at most will be mistaken for a shooting star."

"Dad," Jeffrey persisted, apprehensively, "why is Athena using you to tell me all this?"

Keith only grinned and glanced out to the night beyond the orb cocoon field. "Son, look," he said.

A jewel of light, brilliantly alit to the north of their journey, then emerged from the ground mists, settling across the Blue Mountains of Pennsylvania. New Allentown. It grew rapidly larger.

"Do not be afraid, son. You are going to be reassembled and transported back to the city. It won't hurt. It will be as if you simply 'woke up' from a brief nap."

"But what about you, Dad?" Jeff only replied.

At his feet, suddenly, Jeffrey saw his dad's Sensor Sphere "carry bag" solidify into presence.

"You are asked to take the Record Deck with you to replay the visuals we made today. Show them to your mother. It will help her believe you. I love you, son. And if you wish from here on to be my daughter that is all right. I want for you whatever 'you' want. I will see you and your mom and sister, very shortly."

New Allentown grew large now in the view ahead. The view was zeroing in right for it, and soon the tiny orb slipped effortlessly right through the city's deflector shield barriers and outer walls. And just like that they were inside the Hagerton family's apartment in the city. The image slowed and settled then beside the long couch in their living room. Jeff glanced up to his dad.

"Take care, son," he said to Jeff.

***

It took several moments for Jeffrey's mind to recover, to realize he was no longer with his dad inside Athena's orb bubble and within Athena's energy "realm." The darkened interior of his family's living room faintly revealed itself against the silence of the advancing night. He saw what remained of the day in the terrace window on the westward wall. And he saw himself. . . .

He was still female, although at least the Alice in Wonderland get up was gone and he was back now in the shorts, tights and hiking boots. Athena wouldn't even give him back his boy clothes.

As for Athena herself and her orb, they were gone and so was his father.

The Hagerton apartment was located along the city's outer perimeter and thus allowed the family a real terrace view (not one generated from a hologram display panel) of the terrain beyond. Jeffrey walked over to it and attempted to locate Athena's orb in the night sky, hoping he could somehow spot it as it streaked away and into the night. He couldn't. He went into the kitchen and tried the hologram window over top the sink. He called up a southern exposure request, verbally, and stared upon the image it displayed. He saw a shooting star fall into the hills south of the city, and the brilliant constellations showcased within the heavens above the tree line.

"Shut off," he requested of the display.

"Your vocal inflections match those of Jeffrey Hagerton," informed the apartment's master computer interface, *"but a slight deflection in tonal delivery suggests you might not be. Please confirm your user identity."*

Jeffrey looked down at himself and had to grin at that, at the thought of the unit's confusion. His voice wasn't all that different, slightly softer, more feminine now perhaps, but not really, not at his young age. He told it, and the system accepted his response and complied.

Jeff re-entered the living room and walked over to one of the chairs which flanked the center sofa. He sat down and gazed out at the mountains, searching the heavens yet again for a sign of the orb.

"Why did Athena do that to you, Dad?" he asked, lowly. "Why did she get rid of **me**? *And leave me this way, a girl,* he wondered. She could just as easily have reassembled him the way he was before— a boy.

68

He spotted the Sensor Sphere carry bag atop the sofa. Like him, it too had been reassembled as physical matter. Jeff remembered what his Dad had said about the viewwafer recording of their adventures in the caves that day. He gazed first at the bag and then out the window to the stars. "I'm to show this to Mom," he uttered. That was why Athena had sent him back.

He waited for her and his sister to return.

CHAPTER EIGHT

-1-

Kimberly didn't understand it. She hadn't heard from Keith *all day.* Usually, he made <u>some</u> attempt to call her. No matter where he was, communication was possible, even when below the surface exploring subterranean caves, not like the old days centuries ago when phone service depended on how near you were to a local "reception tower." *A cell, I think they used to call them,* mused Kimberly. *No Service.* There once was a time when such annoyances were the rule, not the exception and had to be tolerated. She reached down to the pocket of her slacks and pulled from it her phone. She fingered it absently.

(Take it wherever you go, the folks at Global Communications, based in Tokyo, Japan, were always advising of the gold pendant she pulled from her slacks. *For that all important occasion when contacting the <u>right</u> person is only an arm's reach away.)*

I could always call him, she supposed. She imagined he and Jeffrey were too absorbed in their adventures to think of it.

"Time, please?"

"5:34 p.m.," came the phone's reply in her thoughts all at once.

You're becoming an old worry wart, she told herself. *They'll be here. It isn't that late, yet.*

She gazed off to the mountains. The foothills surrounding New Allentown rolled off in darkness for the horizons. The view was wondrous— a full three-sixty degree vista.

She and Frida, shortly after getting back, had left the apartment and gone to the City Top Terrace, the city's highest lookout point. They'd gone to watch the sun set behind the foothills. They'd had a late-day meal after at one of the authentic Italian food shops on the veranda level just below the terrace. Nothing beat a "hand cooked" meal. The synthetic concoctions prepared by the nutrition services and made available to each apartment in a dumbwaiter distribution set-up, were adequate enough, but the ambiance of an old-time restaurant serving real food couldn't be topped.

***

The entire top floor of the city was a wooded park, with trees and ponds and various small animals and birds. It was not at all unusual to encounter the occasional rabbit or squirrel as one walked amid the birches and evergreens. The ceiling and exterior wall were transparent crystal. Like a promenade deck, they gave the citizens of New Allentown a panoramic view of the sky and countryside beyond.

Virtually every dome city on Earth had a park much as this one, even the subterranean cities. Theirs poked the surface allowing real sunlight to filter down into the submerged mega structures. The concept had been based on "Central Park" in old land-based New York City, as a way to preserve and bring a piece of the wilderness to a domain locked in on all sides by concrete and steel. The real Central Park and New York City of course no longer existed as did all trace of above ground cities as it once was so many centuries before. And Manhattan Island, scrubbed eventually of all residual traces of the old city, was allowed to return to its pristine state. With the decades the soil gradually began to show signs of nurturing life. By the 2200's, the entire region looked as it might have back in the early 1600s before the first Dutch settlers had begun to develop it.

The sunset tonight had been gorgeous. Evening settled a crimson red among the foothills to the west. The forests beyond the city were graying to obscurity. It was a peaceful sight.

"Keith, where the hell are you?" she asked of the fading day.

"No sign of them, yet, Mom?" Frida asked as she met up with her.

Kimberly shook her head. "No. I called Transport. There's been no sign of them."

"I'm starting to get worried, Mom. This isn't like Dad."

"Keith's a big boy," she answered. "If he had a problem, he'd call . . . if he could." Kimberly smiled and took hold of her daughter's waist. "I'm sure it's nothing, Friddy. Shall we go wait for them back at the apartment?"

Frida shrugged. "I guess so."

***

They exited the park, following a footpath that briefly led into the greenery behind them, and eventually intersected a descending promenade walkway. Like a gossamer wing, the walkway gracefully angled downward for the restaurants below.

The stars slowly flourished into view above the mountains as the day faded into evening.

HAGERTON
APT. 1024, SECTOR 9
QUADRANT 2

Jeffrey heard voices outside in the corridor beyond the apartment. Kimberly and Frida were chatting, amiably. He heard them stop before it, and imagined one of them inputting the entry code into the keypad. The panel slid open; a light came on in the foyer; his mother entered the living room.

Kimberly innocently activated the room lights. She saw her son seated in a chair; she jolted.

"Jeffrey?" She wasn't sure he was. "Jeffrey?" she asked again, approaching him.

Before her in the room was this adorable nine year girl, long brunette hair who in a female sort of way resembled facially her son. And it wasn't even that the girl was attired in a tan turtleneck sweater, tan shorts, tights and hiking boots. Everything about the creature before her read GIRL.

"Jeffrey?" she asked again.

He seemed in a daze. He looked at her, silently.

Frida, who had been en route for her bedroom but had still been within range, heard her mother call to him, and headed back down the hallway.

"They're back?" Frida re-entered the living room, looked first at the girl seated in the chair and then at her mom. "Mom?" she whispered, fearfully, approaching her mother and whispering in her ear. "Who is that?"

Jeffrey seemed to briefly regain a semblance of awareness and glanced to her; he smiled. "Hi, sis," he said.

Frida's mouth opened wide. "Jeffrey?" She glanced back to Kimberly. "Mom? What's going on?" And again staring open-mouth at her brother. "Jeffrey?"

"Go check the den, or my room," Kimberly told Frida, abruptly, touching Frida's arm as if to dissuade her from pressing Jeffrey further. "See if your father is in there,"

"Mom," Frida whispered, "that **can't** be Jeffrey." She glanced to the young girl on the lounge chair once more. She shook his head. *No way,* she thought.

"Frida!" he mother whispered back. *"Go!"*

Frida studied her, and then nodded, walking the hallway down to her parents' room.

Kimberly glanced to her son, went down on one knee and touched his cheek. "Honey?" she asked.

He looked at her. "He's not here, Mom," Jeffrey said,

"Your father?"

He nodded.

"Where is he?"

He shrugged. The living room around him and his mother all looked as if he were observing them from a distance, as if from the wrong end of an old twentieth century telescope. He remembered the viewwafer he had removed from the carry bag and which rested on his lap. He could sense that his mother was still looking at him (one could only wonder why), and that her face was a study in concern, worry and total confusion. He had to tell her about the viewwafer. Dad had said to show it to her and Frida. It would explain everything. How could he ever do so with any real believability? But Jeffrey didn't know how to do that, tell her to view it. His body felt detached from him. He couldn't feel his arms, or the hand which now took hold of the data crystal in his lap.

Kimberly glanced down to the viewwafer, and sensed his desire to give it to her. She took it, and then looked up to him, again.

"The stories are true, Mom," he was finally able to say.

"Stories?" she asked.

"About Crystal Cave. They're true. People go missing. They were supposed to be just stories. Why did they have to be real?"

"Frida!" Kimberly called, abruptly, pondering the viewwafer and what was on it.

Her daughter returned to the living room, approaching her mother, carefully. Kimberly faced her.

"Daddy's not in his bedroom, Mom," Frida said, "or the den!" She shook her head. "Mom, what's happened to Jeffrey? Why does he look like that? Where's Dad?"

"Come and help me take your brother to his room. I think he's in shock. That's right, he's your brother, get over that and help me. I'm going to put him to bed. I don't know, Friddy. I don't want to let it get me scared. I think your brother wants us to play this in the viewing chamber."

"What is that?" Frida asked of the crystal. "Is that what they recorded today on the trip?"

"It might be," said Kimberly. "Maybe. I don't know."

"Mom, if that really is Jeffrey and here's HERE, why isn't Dad?" She looked at her brother again.

Kimberly fought back the impulse to get overly upset by it all, but her body was ringing with a nervous shimmer all over and it made her feel so very hot and clammy. She wanted to keep her calm about her for her kids' sake. But what in the name of God had happened to her son, and where was Keith? What did Jeffrey mean about Crystal Cave's "missing people" stories being true?

"Frida, come on," she answered. "Help me with your brother."

The doorbell chimed. Kimberly jolted and glanced over at it. "Who the hell is that?"

"Shall I get it, Mom?"

"NO! You take care of Jeffrey. *I'll* get it."

She turned and approached the foyer. "Yes?" she called into the communications device attached to the door chime. "This is the Hagertons."

"Excuse me, Ms. Hagerton," came a polite male voice. "I'm with the transportation department. My name is Gregory Phillips."

Kimberly touched the door opener. As the panel slid open, a casually dressed young man of about two meters in height, with dirty blond hair and blue eyes, stood behind it. He must have been in his mid-twenties, and was wearing the blue and yellow outfit of a <u>Transport Personnel</u> employee.

"I'm sorry to disturb you, Ms. Hagerton," he said. "Your husband rented a recreational vehicle this morning, and took it out into the wilderness a few kilometers south of New Allentown."

"Yes?" Kimberly nodded, impatiently.

He nodded back. "Your husband listed his return time as five p.m. It's long past that. My department is becoming concerned. He listed his destination as the old tourist attraction, Crystal Cave, in the old Kutztown district. He hadn't planned any other stops, not according to his flight log. We don't want to worry you, but we're going to have to begin a search for your husband and son soon if we don't get some indication that they and their craft are all right. We've even lost the transponder signal from it that allows us to home in on it. We have no way of knowing what's become of them or the craft." He shook his head. "I hope I'm not prematurely alarming you. I don't mean to create worry. But under the circumstances we have an unusual situation."

No shit.

Kimberly felt that wave of anxiety trace through her body again, as she stood there trying to remain calm. She glanced quickly to the bedroom to make sure that Frida had safely maneuvered Jeffrey out of view. She turned back to the young man and tried to look appropriately concerned, but not overly, as if she might already know something was wrong.

"Could there simply be a problem with the transponder?" she asked forcing a smile.

"You mean a malfunction?"

She nodded. "If I know Keith, he's late; he loves it out there beyond the city. He's probably on his way home right now. I hope so. I don't want to start worrying, or fearing the worst."

The young man smiled, politely. "I can go along with that. We're standing by on communications, hoping your husband calls in soon. We'll keep you posted. Thank you, Mrs. Hagerton. I'm sure you're right about the situation. But if you yourself should hear from your husband, please let us know. And, as I have said, we will have to begin exploratory measures very soon, if the situation doesn't resolve itself."

Kimberly nodded. "I understand, Mr. Phillips. And thank you. I appreciate your delivering this in person."

"No problem at all, ma'am," he answered. He nodded, then, and drew back from the doorway. Kimberly pressed the door wafer again, and the panel silently closed.

She reached down for her pendant phone and held it in front of her. "Keith? This is Kimberly. Keith, honey, where are you? Are you all right?"

The pendant remained silent. She put it away.

"Mom?" Frida neared her, hesitantly. She had a frightened look on her face; she'd been listening just out of sight in Jeffrey's bedroom doorway.

Kimberly nodded, her eyes betraying her wish not to appear upset by it all. Frida saw the frightened, worried look in her eyes. She saw her mom's eyes misting. She went up to her mom and hugged her, resting her face against Kimberly's breasts.

Kimberly cupped her hand against her daughter's head. "I know, baby," she said. "Something's terribly wrong. Keith's in trouble. And Jeffrey . . ." she shook her head.

"He fell asleep," Frida said.

Kimberly paused. "Did he talk to you first? Did he say anything . . . ?"

Frida nodded. "He said he's my sister now."

Kimberly was in no mood for even more strange news. She simply studied her daughter's eyes. Frida was dead serious. Kimberly detached from her and hurried off to Jeffrey's room.

Frida waited for her return by the terrace window; she gazed out into the night.

***

When Kimberly returned a few minutes later, she had a totally exhausted look on her face. She nodded to her daughter. She remembered the tiny viewwafer she'd hidden from Gregory Phillips within her slacks. Kimberly knew what she had to do.

CHAPTER NINE

The viewing chamber was a five-meter, spherical room just off the den, and lit in a subdued blue glow from indirect light. Kimberly and Frida entered it from a side panel and silently padded onto the cushioned floor. Sensor Sphere "ViewWafer" recordings did not have to be viewed in such locales, but for the best, undisturbed experience, they were the like the one time Home Theaters of centuries past. You entered them to concentrate on the playback archive; it was understood that while you were within the View Chamber you sought to not be disturbed by outside distractions. It was advisable most anywhere when using Sensor Sphere ViewWafers that one wear both the playback headsets AND a visor, which was little more than a pair of sunglasses. The glasses didn't so much screen out all exterior distraction, should one accidentally open one's eyes while accessing the ViewWafer data, as they reduced the headache inducing effect of a mental "double exposure." As it was impossible most often to keep one's eyes closed the whole while playing a ViewWafer recording (as it might induce one to fall asleep), the visors were effective in allowing one to "enjoy a ViewWafer" with others, to see them alongside of you and still avoid the headaches of a double image from your own eyes and the info from the ViewWafer data crystals.) View Chambers came equipped with only padded walls and floor, there were no chairs; one simply reposed upon the floor. Kimberly and Frida did so. Kimberly placed a portable playback unit before her and Frida (similar to the one Frida and Jeffrey had used to visit "Luray Caverns" in Virginia the day before), and loaded the viewwafer into it. She then handed Frida a headset and visor and placed hers upon her head. She played with the headset a little, until suddenly a thought impression flooded into her consciousness:

HEADSET PLACEMENT CORRECT

It then vanished. She called, "Image start," and watched the home-video-like-account of Keith and Jeffrey's sojourn into the southern regions of the Blue Mountains— and their journey for Crystal Cave— get under way. In the beginning, the archive's contents from earlier that day seemed innocent, and not a little mundane as the account showed in real time the largely uneventful flight of the air car amid the rolling hills and their autumn colors. Kimberly grew impatient with the recording.

"Rapid forward," she continually requested, hastening the recording on to its more eventful and later segments.

Frida, meanwhile, found it hard to separate the two sensations running parallel within her being: a dread of what the recording might reveal, and the beauty of her father's and brother's journey, of which she herself had so much wished she could have participated. The experience of seeing it here recreated in the View Chamber was so very authentic that it was difficult to imagine how much more she might have received from actually having gone along, and in a way that worried her, for whatever caused her brother to return home not himself, literally, and with no explanation of how he managed his return all on his own without his father or their vehicle, could very well be recorded farther down this account of his experiences.

"Dad?" Kimberly heard Jeffrey call to his father in the playback as the two sat in an inflatable raft. The view from the Sensor Sphere was from above it as the claustrophobic walls of the subterranean lake authentically closed in around her. It made her queasy. She did *hate* caves, after all.

"The alert code on the scanner just went off," Keith announced. "There's something out there." Keith seemed lost in thought suddenly, and Kimberly realized he was accessing the data from his pocket scanner.

"What?" Jeffrey asked.

Kimberly and Frida felt their arm hairs bristle.

Keith frowned. "I don't know. I can't get a readout on the composition."

"Is it alive?"

Keith shrugged. "It's putting out energy, like a power source." He nodded. "Something is definitely down there." He frowned and shook his head. ". . . About a half-kilometer away and to the north east."

"A secret renegade colony?" Jeffrey asked.

Kimberly heard her husband explain why it couldn't be those dreadful lowlife types who refused to live in the cities. But when she heard him reveal ". . . It's small, very small, twelve inches tops . . . the scanner says it's *organic!* . . . How can it be *alive?*" and then her little boy in fear reply, "Dad, are you trying to scare me?" she was ready to run from the View Chamber. She listened to what her husband proposed to do. He wanted to send the two spheres the rest of the way down the tunnel, while he and Jeffrey, from atop a boulder, monitored whatever was discovered beyond the shoreline of the subterranean lake.

"Keith, why didn't you just *leave?*" Kim asked aloud, her arms quaking.

"Mom?" she heard a voice call beside her. She pulled the visor off and saw in double exposure the image of her daughter awash in the dim blue light of the chamber interior. Kimberly called, "Image halt. . ." The double exposure ended.

"I'm all right, kitten." She smiled. "You know me and caves. They bother me."

"Whatever is down there, Mom, can't hurt **us**," Frida answered. She shook her head to emphasize the statement.

Kimberly smiled yet again and then nodded. She saw Frida pull her visor back over her eyes, and she did the same. She called, "Resume playback," and she watched as Keith and Jeffrey assumed Lotus-like positions atop the boulder. The two females then began to "experience" the very same revelatory events Keith and Jeffrey had. Kimberly saw her husband's and son's bodies slowly grow small with distance as the Sensor Sphere departed for the distant shoreline that led up to the grotto where Athena's orb had so long reposed. Kimmy edged over on the cushions and took hold of her daughter's waist. Frida responded in kind, grabbing her mother's tiny waist just as tightly.

Large drapery formations, as if giant and winged cave creatures, passed overhead. Frida wanted to shut out the sensory transmissions. The things looked very much as if they could drop to her at any second. She was glad when the scene left them behind.

The shoreline grew nearer. A rustic-colored wonderland of limestone pinnacles and archways went back from the shore and to the grotto. Far in the distance and lost amid the shadows, a tiny orb hovered in the air, above a two meter tall solitary stalagmite, seemingly with no support, and glowed with an unearthly purple light.

Frida felt a shiver go up her body. "Mom," she whispered. "What is that?"

Her mother only squeezed her daughter's waist, tighter.

The output level of the Light Sphere rose amid the limestone formations, melting the shadows from the scene ahead. And then—

Both of them grabbed each other and screamed. The orb all at once was right there, right in front of them, or so it seemed. The image went black then. Frida screamed a second time, because at that very moment a hand touched her shoulder, her *left* shoulder. Kimberly was to her right. Frida bolted to her feet.

Kimberly looked over at the sound. She and Frida both simultaneously grabbed at their visors and ripped them from their heads.

Jeffrey.

"God!" Frida exclaimed, grabbing her chest.

"Jeffrey!" Kimberly called to her son —or new daughter— gasping for breath. Kimberly's heart felt way up her throat. Jeff was dewy-eyed; he'd been asleep for an hour or so, but it had not worn well with him. He still seemed entirely unwell and troubled. He had changed from the girly outfit Athena had lent him and was now back in one of his standard fall-winter pullovers, a pair of denim shorts (near as short and identical to a pair his sister wore as well) and bare feet. The get up did nothing to assuage the truth— he was all girl and it showed. He had cute toes and feet like his sister. His long brunette hair ran halfway down his back, and immeasurably furthered the sight of him as such.

"That was Athena, just then, Mom," he said so lowly he sounded almost like a little child again.

"Jeffrey, that was who?" his mother asked.

Jeffrey smiled weakly and nodded. "Athena. You met Athena. She's an Eleution."

That answer of course meant nothing to her. Jeffrey did not elaborate. Instead, he walked to her other side and nestled down against her. He was wearing a headset (and had obviously entered some few moments earlier and had monitored what his mother and sister saw, right up until the moment the scene went black). He had a visor in his hand, atop his thigh, and there he temporarily left it. He stared forward to the blue-tinted wall before him. He waited for his mom to sit down and resume the playback.

"I think it goes black for a few minutes, Mom," he uttered, absently. He seemed a little more in control of himself, now. But his eyes remained vacant. "I *think* it recorded what it did after it came back for me. . . Uh. . ." He paused then, embarrassed to even bring up the next topic. "Can you and Friddy give me some pointers after on how to be and act more like a girl, seeing as I am one now? I don't think Athena is going to change be back."

He's still in shock, she thought. *But starting to come down from it, thank God. Oh my god,* she thought, then. *Someone* **did** *this to him. I've got TWO daughters now.*

"Jeffrey, honey," she said aloud, eventually. "What were you saying before? What was that thing?"

"She's an Eleution," he repeated. "That's her natural form, pure energy. She's been down in the cave waiting for people like Dad and me for ages, taking them. Dad and I decided to use the Sensor Sphere to scout what was down there first to make sure it was safe for us. We were monitoring the images atop the boulder, when Dad suddenly disappeared. I got scared, and pulled off my headset. Dad didn't. Athena took him."

Frida looked over at her new sister, as she/he sat there beside the two of them so quiet, docile. Frida looked over at her mother, fearfully. Kimberly nodded to Frida to sit down and refit her visor. Jeffrey took that as his cue to refit his own over his eyes. Kimberly exhaled, silently and fastened hers against her eyes as well. Sitting down then between her two "girls," she pulled them toward her. "Resume," she called to the playback unit. "Rapid forward!"

Kimberly and Frida sat there in the darkness, waiting for the replay to again fill their senses, and dreading it at the same time. They saw finally how and when Athena confronted Jeffrey about his female yearnings, and how easily she could fix that for him. The two females, mother and daughter, glanced over across from their new "daughter/sister" at each other, enduring the double exposure of actual sight and the images from the recording. They both shook their heads in disbelief.

Jeffrey leaned over to his sister across his mother's lap, and whispered to her, "Frida, what do those feel like?" he asked her of her young, newly budding breasts. "Is that going to happen to me?"

"Mom?" pleaded Frida, glancing up to her mother

Despite all she was seeing, Kimberly had to laugh at that. She glanced to her "son." "We'll cross that bridge, Jeffrey, when we come to it," she said to him. She concentrated once again on the recordings in her mind.

"My name is Athena," Athena informed Jeffrey (still male at the time) on the playback at that point in the recording when he resolved to return upstream and head back up to Crystal Cave.

"Jeffrey?" said Frida to the real him opposite their mom. "I know that name, I've heard it before. Where have I heard of it? That's so weird."

Jeffrey glanced over at her, and laughed to himself. "Not weird at all, sis," he replied. "Keep watching."

"How do you know my name?" asked Jeffrey on the playback. "From my father's thoughts?"

"Your sister has spoken of you often. I've seen you in her thoughts. She and I have talked many times, although she does not remember the occasions after."

"Image STOP!" declared Frida. It paused. She tore off the visor and headset and stared at him as he smiled and removed his own. *"What does she mean by that? When have she and I talked?"*

"She's been waiting for you," he calmly answered. "It was you she called to the cave, not me. But Dad wanted me."

"What does that mean? Why does she want ME?" Frida replied in a fearful whisper.

"I'm not really sure." He then re-fixed the visor and headset upon him, and waited for someone to call "Image resume."

". . . I will make your fondest wishes and desires come true," Athena promised Jeffrey.

***

And later at the scenes in Athena's grotto, Kimberly and Frida watched Jeffrey approached Athena's floating orb above the stalagmite, reach up to touch it, and watched it descend and reshape itself into that of a beautiful blond woman; she was as like an ethereal specter in a ghost story. Frida gasped once again, even as Athena waved her hand and physically morphed Jeffrey into a nine year old girl. She stood straight up and again yelled "STOP!" ripping the headset and visor off her head. She slowly inched backward until she felt the back cushioned wall of the View Chamber against her back.

Kimberly removed her visor/headset combo as well, and requested the light levels to raise. "Honey, what is it?" She got up and went over to her. "What's the matter? It's all right, you don't have to be scared."

"She's not, Mom," Jeffrey interjected, before her and still seated on the cushioned floor where the three had reposed. Kimberly turned to his way too placid expression and calm demeanor. He was too docile; it worried her. "What do you mean?" she asked him.

Jeffrey smiled. "She's seen Athena before. Can't you tell?"

Kimberly looked back at her (other) daughter. Frida timidly nodded. "I've dreamed her. For years. Since I first started being able to remember my dreams. Oh, my God, mother. That's her. That's the woman in my dreams! She's taken me everywhere— all the planets, Mars, the Venus, the Moon, all over the galaxy, even to her home world. I thought it was me. I thought I was secretly attracted to my own gender and she was my ideal." She shrugged.

Kimberly nodded. She knew what Frida meant. She smiled.

"Mother. Athena . . . ." Frida nodded. "That's her. I remember now. Oh my God, all those dreams were real?" She looked to Jeffrey then. "And she made you a girl," she said. "Because she knew I *liked* having you for a younger brother, we got along so well, and I love you to death, but I wished— uh, I . . . *she knew it!*"

Jeffrey eyes lost their docile stare; he looked at her. "You mean I have you to thank for this?" he said of his predicament.

Frida got defensive. "Oh, you can't put that all on me, little brother. You loved when I dressed you up and we pretended you were . . . my. . . ."

"Say it!" he insisted. "Your little sister."

She nodded. "You even said it once. You wished you were my little sister. We could have had so much more fun together, had you been, you said."

Jeff nodded. "And you agreed. I think Athena did it as much to please you as because she knew I wouldn't really hate it. But now what am I going to do? Is she going to leave me this way? You should see what she did to me a few minutes later."

"Oh no, honey," dreaded Kimberly. "What now?"

Jeff encouraged the two to resume their places on the cushioned floor and re-don their visor/headsets.

Soon after, this appeared on the archive:

Jeffrey dressed in a little girl's Alice in Wonderland outfit.

"Aww, how cute!" called Kimberly. She couldn't help throwing her arm around Jeff and hugging the crap out of him. "Oh, honey you're adorable!" she said.

"Mom!" moaned Jeff.

"I wish you had kept that outfit," mused Kimberly. "I'd love to see you in it for real."

"Why do *you* get to be Alice?" insisted Frida, frowning. "You're a brunette."

Jeff had to laugh at that one. *I knew it,* he thought. He shrugged, meekly. "I felt half naked in that thing. How do you guys stand it? Don't you get cold?"

"Welcome to girlhood," said Frida. "You make a cute Alice, brother."

"Thanks."

***

When the recording finally ended about an hour later, Kimberly and Frida were exhausted. Mother and daughter removed their visors and looked over at Jeffrey. He seemed a lot better now, now that the tale had been told. He quietly removed his headset and visor and tossed them both to the floor beside the playback unit.

Kimberly was monumentally floored. The powers this Athena possessed. The things she could so easily do to Jeffrey, a full on molecular transition from boy to girl. That was impossible. Sexual and gender reassignment "surgery" and cosmetic theatrics had been performed by humans for centuries, and got better with every advancing century, but a full on chromosomal metamorphose? Humans weren't even close to that.

She eyed her son, squarely. "It isn't over is it?" she asked.

Jeff shook his head.

"Is all that going to happen to us, too?" asked Frida. "She sent you back to prepare us for our being taken as well?"

"She's been waiting *for you,* Frid, for ages." He nodded, pensively.

"Oh, Mom!" moaned Frida, rising off the cushion, retreating to where Kimberly sat alongside Jeffrey and grabbing and hugging Kimberly for dear life.

Kimberly thought about the last part of the recording, and how the Sensor Sphere in Athena's lair would only have been a phantom one, an illusion, at that point, like everything else in the pretend "Bridge," and any data at that point laid down on the data crystal in Keith's record unit would have had to be placed there deliberately by Athena herself. Which meant Athena meant for her and Frida to see ALL of what had transpired. And the sight of Keith at the end, sending their son off and back for New Allentown. It was as if he wasn't even Keith anymore. He seemed as if a man possessed, or only a pretend manifestation of himself, merely mouthing Athena's words, in her behalf. The pure thought of it gave her chills.

"Come on, kids," she began, then, as she got to her feet, dragging Frida with her. She started for the exit.

"And go where, Mom?" asked Jeffy. "Where is there to go? When Athena comes for us, she's going to get us. It's inevitable. Dad said, he'll see us soon. And me? I can't be seen like this. I am recorded in the city population rolls as a boy. The authorities are going to want an explanation for ME. What do we tell them . . . about any of this?"

Kimberly exhaled in fatigue. "I don't know, Jeff. I swear to God, I just don't know. We have to take this one step at a time. And *don't ask me what that means!*"

There was a sudden whine from somewhere above them. The three looked up, startled, as a shimmer enveloped the chamber, and suddenly an image evolved upon its walls. *"What the hell?"* Kimberly asked.

She couldn't remember if she had ordered the playback to shut down, or if she had just left it to do so on its own. The recording must have recycled itself, or skipped back a few paces, because suddenly the three of them were surrounded again by the interior of the arena "Bridge" of Athena's spaceship interior.

"Jeffrey, **what's this?** What's wrong with that recording? Yank it out of its slot. I don't want to play it back again."

Kimberly glanced around her to the sensory image replay. The walls of Athena's pretend "Bridge set" were bioluminescent indigo. The scene had them down before the center crystal in the pit area before the main holodeck "anteroom/view screen." In the cavity view screen beyond it came the sight of their living room and the scene had them going right through it and outside beyond the city. There came a swift upward climb, and soon the Earth hung large and wondrous. Athena's orb looked apparently to have gone into orbit; the Earth hung amid the starlight, a dark sphere of blue and gray in the advancing light of evening. On its western terminator descended a blood red sun, slipping below the Earth's rim. It was a view that in real time would put the sun's setting somewhere over California by this hour. Kimberly noted the darkened east coast. New Allentown was but one of a handful of brilliant alit dots upon it. The thought of existing as such so many kilometers above her in orbit gave Kimberly chills. She couldn't stand it.

"Image **off!**" she yelled to the playback unit. She looked down at her son. He saw it too, the arena room in Athena's "lair." But he no longer wore the playback headset *upon his head.* Kimberly felt a quiver run up her arms. She pulled her own headset off and dropped it to the floor; it was at that moment that the truth hit her. *This was no illusion!* Goose-pimples rode up her arms.

"Mom . . ." Jeffrey began in resignation. He was expecting something like this since the moment he and his dad parted company. He pointed to the floor beneath them. The cushioned floor upholstery was gone, so was his headset and the playback deck, all gone. "We're back," he said.

Frida let out a gasp. She leapt to her feet, tore her headset off, and ran for the rear wall. "We're really **here!**" she exclaimed. She felt down the length of it, by the exit archway. It was neither rock, nor metal. She felt a throbbing pulse under the surface of whatever material it pretended to be, and she pulled her hand away. She noted again its faint bioluminescent gleam. "We're in something *alive!*" she gasped. "Mom?"

Jeffrey went over to her to calm her. "Frida, stop. It's not real, any of it. It's all illusion. We're been reduced to pattern data inside Athena's mind. This is all like a dream."

"You mean, we're really here! She's already taken us?"

Frida ran to Kim and grabbed her mother's side. Kimberly called to Jeffrey and cradled both her "daughters" in her arms against her. "It's okay, baby," she said to Frida. "We're not dead. We still exist. Jeffrey, why?" she faced him. "Why like this?"

He never got to answer. Like a special effect in an old Sci-Fi movie, he and his sister faded into nothing and were gone. Kimberly was there, suddenly, all alone in Athena's pretend alien Bridge set. She felt the walls about her; she felt the living "presence" they radiated. For a "dream" it all felt so real, so frightfully real. As she'd thought before, seeing it recreated on the Sensor Sphere playback, the arena room was a horrible looking thing, like something belonging in a ghost ship. She lunged at the pit crystal and began to pound on it. "I want my **babies!**" she yelled in hysteria. **"Athena, you BITCH, give me back my babies! . . . Keith,"** she called then. **"Where are you?"**

She glanced to the rest of the room. Keith was nowhere. She faced the pit crystal again. She knew it somehow represented Athena herself. She could feel it. **"You bitch, give me back my family!"**

She felt herself falling, and collapsed against the crystal. Her eyes were swollen with tears, but she looked up anyway to the forward imaging cavity. The Earth's surface moved ever so subtly, suggesting the orb's flight above it.

Kimberly remained there for what felt like forever. . . .

CHAPTER TEN

Kimberly felt a sudden brilliance upon her neck. She turned and almost shrieked. The Light Sphere hovered only a meter away, having soundlessly entered from where it had reposed. Its light bathed the arena room. She rose to full height and stared at it. The incandescent warmth was like the sun's from her terrace view window back in the apartment.

What do you want? she asked it in her mind.

The Light Sphere simply hung, bathing her in its light. Kimberly knew it had to have been sent by Athena. This was her lair. Everything that happened here in this place did so with Athena's knowledge and consent.

She stared in fascination at the room. She had seen her son enter it in the playback, but it felt very different to know that this time it was no sensory playback. She was actually here. She saw the imaging "anteroom" with its hologram display, acting as a "view screen" for whomever it was Athena allowed passage within her as she plied the galactic depths. She made her way over toward it.

A sea of stars surrounded her the moment she entered. It was like being out in space for real, without even a spacesuit, just naked, fully prone, out there alone with the Earth miles beneath her and the stars overhead, hinting at a universe whose reaches and length defied imagining. She wondered how far back this holodeck chamber went and if the Earth was merely a projection upon the back wall. She walked for it, her toes soon stubbing against it. She reached to touch the Earth's sphere. She felt only the back wall. The planet, itself, appeared to be on the other side of it, though the wall was clearly not transparent. It was a clever illusion.

She faced back to the chamber's entry point.

Keith Hagerton stood in the center of it. He smiled at her. "Hello, angel," he said.

"Keith," she replied. There seemed within her no desire at this point for any emotional reaction. It was her husband, and she was glad to see him, that he was all right. But was it *really* him, and not another cruel trick of Athena's?

"It's me, Kimmy." He took a step toward her. "It really is."

"How can I be sure?"

He palmed his chest with both hands, and then extended them, splaying his fingers. "It's me."

"Touching yourself, Keith, is not proof. Nothing here can be trusted to be what it appears. You might only be a simulation."

"Kim, honey. Why would Athena need to do that? Trust me. I'm NOT a simulation. It's me."

"Was it you when you sent Jeffrey back with all that info about Athena's mission?"

"I wasn't myself," he only responded.

She nodded. "No, you weren't. Why would this Athena do that to you?"

Keith shrugged. "It's her domain to do with as she pleases. She calls the shots."

She nodded to that too. "But not at present? It's all you?"

"Are YOU all you?" he replied.

She grinned. "Good point. How would I really know?"

"I guess we just have to take each other's word for it, then," he said, drawing near.

"Yes, I guess we do." She approached him. He reached a hand for her. She extended her own to take it. Her fingers closed around his own.

"Okay?" Keith queried.

She took a breath. "Jeffrey showed us what happened."

He nodded. "Do you like having two daughters, now?"

"Is he that way, permanently?"

"From the way I read Athena's bend of mind . . ." He nodded. "She claims she's doing it because that is what he truly wants . . . deep inside."

"This is a world of illusion, this place," she said, glancing all around her. "Shouldn't we have the option of profiling as whomever and whatever we want?"

"I think, Kimmy," he answered, "the only way to describe this realm of Athena's is to say she wants as best she can to *keep it real.*

"But in this state we're neither male nor female, we're nothing. Conscious awareness only."

"Best not to wrack your brain over that too much, Kimmy and just roll with it."

"*Roll with it?*" she smiled and nodded. "You're full of centuries' old clichés tonight, aren't you?"

"Kimmy. . . . Don't be that way."

"Didn't you have ANY say in all of this?" she asked then. "You couldn't insist Athena let us be, abduct some other family?"

"It would have been a waste," he said. "She's been awaiting her time with Frida for some time now."

"She even told that to you as well?"

Keith shrugged. "I just know it, somehow."

"Where are our children, Keith?"

"They're fine, Kimmy."

"Where are they?"

Keith faced back toward the crystal. It began to hum, its light output rose along with the sound. To either side of it, images of his now two daughters materialized. They were representations only, as one could still see the arena steps behind them right through their bodies. They didn't appear conscious, but more like . . . inert figures, like wax museum likenesses.

She turned to him in anger. "I want my *children,* Keith, not ransom photos!"

"The point, I think, Kimberly, that you're supposed to get, is that they're no less real like that, or no less <u>here</u>, then when you can actually touch them. They've been here all along." He looked to the walls of the Bridge, to the life energy that flowed amid them. "Technically, we're all in the same place. We're HERE."

Kimberly only regarded him, crossly. "Tell Athena, then," she answered, "that that's not good enough!"

Keith shrugged. "I'll pass it along."

He looked down at the crystal mass. With a flourish of light, Frida and Jeffrey suddenly solidified into solid beings. They both got a confused, frightened look on their faces as they realized they were conscious once more. They looked at each other, and then at their parents.

"Daddy?" Frida called, shyly. "Is it really you?"

Keith smiled. "It's daddy, Friddy.'

Jeffrey looked first at him, and then at his mom. He ran to Kim and cradled her waist.

Frida looked down at her body, to assure herself that she was whole, and slowly neared her father. "What happened to me?" she asked.

"Don't you remember?" He took her into his arms.

"I had a dream. Jeffrey and I were together, and you were there too, but it was all so . . . I don't know. It felt so real, but it couldn't have been."

"Mom?" Jeffrey whispered to his mother, as he peered up at her.

She hugged his head against her chest. "Yes, baby, it's Mommy."

"I thought we were <u>dead</u> . . ." He faced his sister and father. "All of us, except you."

I thought that too, she answered to herself as she dropped her chin against Jeffrey's hair.

"Where were we, Dad?" Frida asked, softly.

"I can't answer that, baby," he said, "because I'm not sure if we're even anywhere in the real sense now. I don't know where we were. We just weren't 'aware.' Does that help?"

Frida shrugged. "Is that what death is like?"

Keith grinned. "I hope not, because if that's all we have to look forward to after we die, no conscious reality at all, then what's the point of any of this?"

"Keith," cautioned Kimberly. "You're going to give her nightmares. You don't know. Just leave it at that."

Keith smiled and nodded. He grinned to his daughter. "I don't know."

"Why was mommy not with us?" asked Jeffrey to Keith.

Mommy? pondered Keith of his "son's' word usage. *He never calls her that;*

he calls her Mom. I'm losing my "son."

"I wondered about that also," said Kimberly. "Why can't I connect with this 'Athena' like the rest of you do?"

"It's your emotions, hon," answered Keith, grateful to be answering her, not Jeffrey, not needing to "deal" with the gender changes that were happening to his 'boy.' "Your emotions, your maternal concern for your family's wellbeing is very powerful. It's too much for Athena. She prefers to not deal with it all for now."

"Well, then I guess you'll have to be my proxy," she said. "Tell her I don't appreciate—"

Keith's face went blank.

Kimberly frowned. "Keith?"

"The viewwafer? . . ." he answered aloud but not to Kimberly.

Athena, Kimberly thought. He's talking to her. Had to be.

"I don't understand," Keith continued. "Why is that a problem?"

Kimberly's concern level rose as Keith's defensiveness to this "someone" rose as well. "Keith?" she queried.

"We didn't know!" Frida all at once insisted. "No, don't you dare blame my mom for leaving it behind!"

Kimberly glanced to her oldest daughter.

Frida, her eyes vacant, looked as if she were defending herself to someone. "You took us *too fast!* We forgot it! I don't care if you are disappointed in me. And don't give me, that *I thought you and I were friends, crap,* Athena. We're sorry okay? You forgot too!"

What is happening to my family? Kimberly thought. Her arms began to tremble. All at once a thought touched her mind. It startled her. It ignited like a light bulb flash in her head. A question was asked of her, and in an instant she knew it to be the same question her family had already been interrogated about. Her answer in her thoughts amounted to little more than her own apology.

Kimberly hadn't been told anything about bringing the viewwafer along, she told the voice. She looked at Keith. "She wants the viewwafer you made in Crystal Cave! She's asking where it is? I left it in the playback unit back in the apartment."

Keith shrugged. "You can hear her now?"

She nodded to him, distantly. "Apparently."

Keith nodded in return. "Athena wants us to go back for it. She doesn't want a thing like that lying around for someone else to find it."

"Why doesn't she just go back and get it?"

"She is. That's what she needs us for."

"So, I guess we're going back, then," she responded.

And as if on cue the view in the view screen cavity began to accelerate forward and down, targeting its Earthbound destination for the north east of the United States. Kimberly glanced back to Keith. She smiled an icy one. "Is she always so forgetful?" she said.

There was a pause, then. Her facial expression appeared to go blank for a second. And then, from Kimberly. "All right, I'm sorry, you're right. We all make mistakes. Somehow I thought a being like you would be beyond all that."

Keith laughed silently. He heard Athena's answer. Something on the line of *nobody's perfect*. And then a whole litany of information flowed into his head, and he could tell that Kimberly received the same report:

Once this "clean up" business with the errant viewwafer back in New Allentown was attended to, Athena's orb was en route with her "charges" i.e. her captives, to a remote underground holding location on the Moon. It was a joint operation this "saving humanity from its own suicidal inclinations." The Eleutions were in with a race in their same solar system who called themselves the Barthonians. They were cute little creatures, indigo skinned, like the interior motif in this pretend "space vessel Bridge" around them. They had slender and oval-shaped little heads, and wispy white hair. They looked almost like little elves, and for the most part they other bothered at all to assume physical shaped when it suited them. They existed in a state of mind-energy most of the time, not quite as advanced as the Eleutions, but way further along on the evolutionary ladder than humans could ever even hope to achieve for hundreds of years yet. They would materialize as physical entities to accommodate the lifeforms they studied and aided in their tour of the galaxy. It was, after all, their intent to help intelligent life to prosper and develop wherever it flourished in the universe. It so happened that the planet Earth was one of those places where their interests and desire to assist had been in progress now for well over two-thousand years.

Kimberly looked over at Keith, ultimately. She had a weary expression on her face. "Tell it enough, Keith! She's giving me a headache. So, what happens to the children while you and I are down there in the apartment?"

"They'll stay here with Athena. They're not needed," he replied. "Athena intends to let them get some sleep, or whatever passes for it in this state. They've had a rough day."

"Sleep where?" She looked around the arena room. This 'Barthonian' space vessel motif was not exactly the Holiday Inn Plaza back in New Allentown up near the City Top Terrace. Instead, it looked more a place where Kimmy's and Keith's cave dwelling ancestors might have reposed in their bearskins as they huddled around a stone fire.

To her question, Keith only smiled.

CHAPTER ELEVEN

Keith showed his family the remainder of Athena's spaceship interior, moving through the spider web alleyways and past various size crystal masses, the whole of the ghoulish spaceship lair likening itself to an All Hallows Eve fun house. Toward the very center of the thirty-meter-wide-spaceship and in what felt to be its deepest part, he showed them this large and iridescent "pond" of glowing crystal.

"They're brain lobes," Keith said of all the crystal masses they'd seen. "According to Athena this one doubles as the vessel's engine and main power plant."

"Dad?" Keith heard his daughter call.

"Yes, baby . . . Sorry, Jeff." It was his *other* daughter.

Jeffrey shrugged. "Why go through all this trouble? It's not real. It's all just . . . pretend."

"Well, son, Athena's Barthonian crew for whatever reason . . . want it this way. It probably helps them pass the time."

"Their real spaceships look like this inside, then, right, you suppose; the ones that can only make short flights in their own solar system?"

"Sounds about right, son," Keith answered.

"Dad?"

"Yeah, son?"

Jeffrey thought about his Dad's confusion over who had called him. "I sound like Frida? I sound like a girl? I can't help it. And I can't change back; I've tried."

"Could be a lot a reasons for that, Jeff," Keith said. "Don't give up hope."

"I won't."

Allowing his two kids to get a little farther up the corridor from him and Kimberly, Keith then reached over and whispered in Kimmy's ear, "He talks like a girl and even has the vocal inflections down," he said to her. "If I didn't know better, I'd swear we traded our son in for a daughter. What have you and Frida been teaching him?

"Not a thing, no time," Kimberly replied. She shrugged. "He's transitioning all on his own."

"Do you think maybe Athena's helping it along somehow?"

Kimberly frowned at that. "If she really knows our Frida like she says she does, I'd say she might be. For Frida. And to help Jeff become our daughter."

"What if he doesn't want to?"

Kimberly considered his question as she watched Jeffrey and Frida walk hand in hand up the sepulcher corridor, both dressed in wintry pullovers and shorts, their bare feet daintily padding across the decks. One would have no trouble believing they were sisters.

"I know my child pretty well, Keith, I don't think it's just Frida's wish and Athena's desire to placate Frida." She nodded. "I'm not sensing she'd do that to our child if she didn't know he didn't mind, even liked it. I've seen Frida and Jeff together. She's always thought of him as her little sister. And I think so has he."

"Am I going to have to start thinking of him as my little girl from now on?" asked Keith.

"When you're ready . . . to abandon those old fashioned notions about fathers and their sons."

"Easy for you," he replied. "You're gaining a daughter. I'm losing a son."

"You can really be an old fossil at times, can't you?" she observed.

****

They came eventually to a sealed archway. That it was sealed— and not simply a solid bulkhead in the shape of a portal arch— was apparent by its metallic luster. Something else about it was wrong: It had a door-actuator button on its side. Kimberly eyed it in confusion. The device was unmistakable; she'd seen hundreds like it all through New Allentown. It lay affixed at the standard height of an average human. That made no apparent sense. The Barthonians were no more than a meter tall at most, and it seemed bizarre to place a door actuator an extra half meter higher than the tallest of them. Keith realized why it was as it was, smiled and touched it. The panel didn't slide upwards, sideways, or in any direction. It simply evaporated, and beyond it—

Frida and Jeffrey gasped in amazement. It was Frida's bedroom from New Allentown, reproduced exactly. Her real room back in the city contained two hologram panels (manufactured by HoloView Windows, Inc.), dressed to look like actual windows. In New Allentown, Frida could program her two to show any scenic view she desired, not simply views from beyond the city walls, but even murals fashioned by her own imagination and inputted into the unit's imaging computers.

These two, however, were filled with views from beyond the vessel in its orbit about Earth.

Kimberly turned to Keith, abruptly. "What is this, Keith?"

"Athena's trying to make us feel more at home," he replied. He laughed. "We're home."

"Mom?" Frida called to her, softly. "Is Athena really sending us off to bed or into nowhere like before? Why can't we go with you and Dad back to our real apartment?"

"Don't you know why, Frid?" whispered Jeff. "She'll lose her leverage if we all leave."

Frida eyed her new little sister. "When did you get so intuitive?" she snided.

"Frida, don't be mean," he begged. He shrugged. "It just makes sense." He faced his father, then. "Do we have to, Dad?"

All at once upon the two kids, their daytime wear vanished and were replaced with white nightshirts, both with kittens on the front. This was a new one for Jeffrey. He'd never wore a girl's sleepshirt before. It felt . . . wrong."

Keith shook his head at what was obviously Athena's reply to Jeffy's last inquiry. "Afraid so, Jeffy." he said.

***

(As noted, earlier, Frida's "floatation bed" was an oval-shaped cylinder of smoky gray plastic. Queen size, the bed's upper surface lay open like a manger; the bed itself reposed on an angle. It had no visible means of support from the floor. It didn't need one. It hovered, perpetually, owing to its antigrav levitation system, built into its bottom. Its interior maintained a zero G environment. A person simply climbed into the thing, and "floated" off to sleep. A blanket was optional.)

***

"Aw, Mom," moaned Jeffy at the sight of the sleepshirt on him, "why do I have to wear this? **Athena!**" he called. "Please. Can't I wear my own boy stuff?"

There was no answer, not verbally (whatever that meant) or in their minds (again, not that there would be a real difference). Athena had no intention of having her decisions brought up before a committee for a vote.

"Guess not . . . *sis*," grinned Frida.

He glared at her. "Oh, you just love it, don't you?" he snapped.

Frida took Jeffrey's hand and pulled him over to the bed.

"With *you* . . . in your bed?" He faced back to his parents. "I don't even get to sleep in my own room?"

"We're sisters now," Frida replied. "Sisters do this all the time."

"It'll be all right, honey," soothed Kimberly. "Tomorrow you can sleep in your own room."

Frida glanced to the large, oval window along the long wall. "I can almost imagine it **is** my room. Only . . ." She was about to verbally command the widow to change its scenic view to one of her own choosing, when a thought occurred to her. She *thought* the command instead in her mind. The Earth image dissolved into one of tropical, multi-colored angel fish, swimming in a green-lit aquarium. It was her favorite "night light" holoview scene.

She looked at her folks and grinned.

Keith glanced to her. "How did you do that?"

"I thought it," she replied. "I asked it in my mind."

"Will you two be all right?" Kimberly asked her kids.

Frida looked at Jeffrey, who shrugged and nodded. She faced her mom again. "Yes."

"Do either of you need to use . . ." (One never knew in this realm.) "—the bathroom."

Frida giggled; so did Jeff. "I don't think that's even possible, Mom," said Frida. "In fact, if it is, even the thought of pretending to need to do it here seems a little stupid."

"Okay, then," said Kimberly. "Get in bed, both of you."

They nodded and climbed into the thing's interior, bobbing around in it as if they were astronauts on a deep space EVA (extravehicular activity) mission.

"You going to be all right, champ?" Keith asked his son, approaching the bed's side.

Jeff grimaced. "No. I feel like a girl," he said. He glanced down at his slender, wispy legs peeking out of the hem of the sleepshirt. "God, Dad, my body feels so different. I even smell different . . ." He glanced to his sister. "Like the way she always smells. I smell like a girl."

He heard Frida break out in a giggle over that. "Gee, I wonder why, brother?"

He glanced over at her. "Shut up, Frida," he said. "You're used to it."

She grabbed by his waist and pulled him up against her. "Yeah, and I can do this with you now, hug you to death, all I want, because you're my sister. God, you feel so squishy soft, like me. This is great. I have a little sister to play with and hug."

"I'm happy for you," he answered. He faced his father again. "Dad?"

Keith grunted a laugh. "You had a hell of a day, today," agreed Keith. He touched his "son's" long brunette hair. "You'll be fine."

"I'll keep him safe, Daddy," said Frida, still clutching Jeff tight against her.

"I'm sure you will," he smiled.

He wanted out of her grasp, and she released him. "Dad?" she began, with reservation, looking up then to her father.

"Yeah, kitten?"

"You and Mom ARE coming back, right?"

Keith smiled, encouragingly, but a part of him wanted to lose it. "You know I am," he answered. "Athena's not really that awful an entity. She just has a mission she's duty bound to carry out. But I think it's all meant to be for humanity's benefit. You know, baby, there were times in the past when it didn't even look like our species would even survive. At one point, the human race even drafted up plans to build a giant spacecraft, way bigger than that one that launched a few years ago for deep space."

"The *Stellar Quest?*" she said.

"Yeah," he nodded. "That one. They even had a name they were going to give it: *Exodus II.*"

"You mean, like the old Noah's Arc story?" cut in Jeffrey, fascinated.

"That's right, son."

"It was going to carry the whole of our civilization at that time away from Earth, never to return."

"It's going to take years for the Stellar Quest to get to Eighty-two Eridani," Jeffrey said. "Wouldn't it have taken the *Exodus II* years as well to reach its destination?"

Keith nodded. "Same laws of physics apply, son, yes, it would have."

"What happened to it," whispered Frida, "to the ship?"

Keith nodded, reassuringly. "They never built it. The public hated it. They called it *Mike's Globally Despised Solution,* for the fool who first thought it up. The situation got better. Maybe that's why Athena is doing this. Maybe we need help again. Maybe."

He turned to leave his two kids.

"Dad?" called Jeff.

"What, Jeff?"

"Tell Athena, if you can, not to be mad at me."

"For what, son?"

"For forgetting to remember the viewwafer. It was put in my charge, and I left it."

Keith tossed a strand of his long hair off his forehead. "Athena knows she screwed up also, son. Don't beat yourself about that. See you in a bit, okay?"

"Goodnight, Dad." He kissed his father, then.

(Jeffrey was right, Keith noted, his son did indeed feel and smell like a girl. He didn't know if he'd ever get used to that.)

"Daddy?" Frida called.

(**Kids, right?**)

"Yeah, kitten?" He smoothed a strand of blond hair off her cheek.

I got two girls, now, he thought.

Frida's expression was serious. "Is this what heaven is supposed to be like?"

"I don't know, honey. I don't know how it's possible to feel alive, to feel anything, here, where we are."

"You know what this feels like?" she returned.

"What?"

She smiled. "Like being free to fly like an eagle anywhere, go wherever you want to go and not worry about gravity anymore. It's almost like one of your travel visuals."

He kissed her cheek. "Goodnight, kitten."

***

Keith and Kimberly exited Frida's bedroom, and discovered that the Barthonian spaceship interior was nowhere to be found. Instead, the door led to the hallway outside that passed the bathroom at the end of the hall, Jeff's room and the master bedroom. It was all flawlessly recreated. It was incredible. One would almost think it was real.

They reached the living room, then and stared out their terrace view to the scene of Earth from high orbit.

"Okay, Athena," said Keith aloud. "Let's go retrieve that viewwafer you're so worried about it."

The image of Earth in the terrace window began a rapid approach. It was way too apparent that Athena's orb was slipping into the atmosphere with no worry over friction build up, no heat-shield worries for Athena. She darted through the night voids effortlessly, like an eagle soaring on the wind. Almost in no time, the Pennsylvania countryside began to become visible as such in the scene below and very gradually they noticed the lights of New Allentown high up in the northern reaches of the night-blue expanse of old Earth.

The orb would reach its destination in no time at all.

"I guess Athena needed time to pattern our 'apartment'," said Kimberly, "before she was ready for us to see it."

"That sounds about right," Keith supposed.

"Are you sure the kids will be all right?"

"She loves those kids. I can tell. And I think she has a thing for females. I think she sees males as being afflicted in the womb with a disease that prevents them from achieving their full potential."

"Did she say that to you?" queried Kimberly, incredulously.

He shook his head. "No, but I got that vibe from her, if that makes any sense."

"You think that's why she transformed our son into a girl?"

"I think it was one of her reasons. In her mind, maybe, she fixed Jeffy, put him back the way he should have been. The way *all we guys should have been.*"

***

The image in the forward terrace view approached New Allentown straight on. It pushed through the deflector shield barriers and force fields surrounding and protecting the city and zeroed in for the residential levels, themselves. It found a particular "terrace window" and headed onward for it. And then it went through it as if the window were not even there. And suddenly — nothing. Keith looked around him to the living room. There was no evidence of a double exposure, the orb's recreation or the actual living room. Nothing. Just the room all around them.

95

"What happened?" asked Kimberly. "Are we still in our fake version or are we home?"

It was then that they felt an energy field behind them, causing static electricity charges to do crazy things to the hair on their heads and arms. Keith and Kimberly looked back, and there behind them was Athena.

No, not her orb. Her. The ethereal vision of a gorgeous blond woman, of normal height (about two meters), the human she'd be in the prime of her life, and perfectly shaped. She was staring at them.

"I'm counting on you to not betray me," she cautioned them.

"You speak," snided Kimberly.

"When it's appropriate. How are you, Kimberly? You may not believe this but I'm a mother as well. I have many I care for. I would never bring harm to your children. And yes, I've given your 'son' a great gift. I made him what biology on your world took from him."

"Athena," defended Keith. "We males exist for a purpose, you know," he said.

"They are other less deleterious ways to propagate your species," she replied, "than allowing the need to reduce some of you to what is in effect a stripped down version of a human being— just to be a gene pool courier and allow the even distribution of available DNA. Even at your primitive point in your evolution, you have embraced one of them. Entrusting the business of DNA distribution and propagation to your artificial devices. Your usefulness, Keith, no offence, in your present diminished and 'Male' form is mostly not necessary anymore."

"We men are useful in other ways," he countered. "We have the extra stamina to build things, our civilization and technology, for instance. The island cities now. There are some tasks that men can just handle better, some men, that is. It takes a certain kind of individual, for instance, to physically do what is necessary to build a skyscraper, or a bridge. We've served our purpose in many productive ways."

"Have you ever heard the phrase, Keith," she answered, *"Nature always finds a way?"*

"Am I really so much worse off, Athena, as I am?"

"Not you, perhaps, but many of your gender do despicable things, awful things, things your species has to learn to shed if you hope to move on to a higher level of being."

"I'm not sure how I'd feel about being given the opportunity to try it as the opposite gender," he said. "Is it really fair to impose such a thing on my son?"

"Nothing is really preventing him from seeing himself in my realm as he was. There is only one explanation for why he remains your daughter. He likes it. Even if he's reluctant to admit it fully even to himself. I will help him find he's made a good choice. When he's ready he'll realize and accept why he's not reverting back."

"I see," Keith only replied.

"Please complete your task now. My energy presence may set off some alarm sensors in your city. We should move with all haste. And I will leave momentarily so that these sensors continue to be ignorant of my presence."

"We're here anyway," said Keith. "Can we bring anything else with us?"

"I have made a full scan of your apartment," she said. "Any items of sentimental value to you will be included in the image matrix I have fashioned for you within my realm. No, you may not. Please do not leave any clue behind that you planned your exit from this city. Leave everything here as it is."

Keith sighed. "All right," he answered her.

"Please proceed."

Athena became an orb again, and with a flourish *pifffit* herself right out of the terrace window, becoming lost quickly in the starry night beyond.

"Okay," said Keith. "You said it's in the playback deck, right?"

"Yes. Do we both need to go get it?"

"No, I'll go. Wait here."

Kimberly set herself upon the long sofa, facing the southern mountains of eastern Pennsylvania, just watching the stars twinkling in the night above them. A few minutes passed and Keith suddenly returned with a puzzled look on his face.

"Did you get it?" she asked him, rising.

"It's not there. Are you sure you left it in the playback deck?"

"Yes," she insisted. "It's got to be there."

"I can't find it anywhere," he told her.

"That can't be," she said. She darted past him and headed for the den. She saw the side entrance to the viewing chamber open and went inside. The room looked exactly as she had last seen it. The playback unit remained there in the center of the cushioned floor where she and the kids had left it. Keith was right. The ViewWafer crystal was not in the playback deck. It was gone.

"Keith, it should be here. Where is it?"

"It beats me, hon," he answered. "Athena wouldn't say it was here if she didn't think it was still supposed to be," he considered, then. "That leaves only one other possibility."

"What?"

"Someone's been in here ahead of us."

"Who would do that?" she asked, lowly. "There's no sign of entry, and how could anyone enter our house without the entry code?"

"Did anyone come around tonight asking about us?" Keith asked. He exited the chamber and went for the Phone-Imagizer Unit in the den, sat down and donned a neuralscan-headset. He asked the phone unit in his mind to replay any incoming calls that might have been recorded in the last few hours.

The imaging disk on the tabletop fluttered with grayish-blue light, which floated just above its surface. And then the image of a young, blond-haired, Transport Division male come onto the screen.

"Hello, Mrs. Hagerton? This is Gregory Phillips of the Transport Department calling you again," came the replay hologram of the young man, just as Kimberly remembered who he was and that he had earlier stopped by. "Ma'am, I've been trying to reach you now for several hours. The department is seriously concerned about your husband's and son's absence. We sent a team out to their last known location for a report, and we're awaiting their communication. I'd like you to contact my office as soon as you return and play this. It's important. I'm sorry to bring you so bleak a report, and again I don't want to upset you over what we at the department fear is developing into a serious mystery. Please get in touch with me at your earliest convenience. Thank you."

The image faded away. Keith pondered the message for several seconds in silence. He looked at Kimberly, then. "He was here?"

"Only for a few minutes," she answered, lowly, "before Frida and I put Jeffrey to bed and played your recording."

"He didn't see Jeffrey, did he?"

"No, but what if he had? Jeffy's a girl now. He wouldn't have recognized him. Only thought probably that Frida had had one of her friends over. But that's all irrelevant. Phillips never saw Jeffrey. I made sure. . . . You think he came back, don't you? He got in here somehow?"

Keith sat back in his chair and only contemplated it. He had no idea at the moment what he should do.

Kimberly gasped, lowly. "Keith!" she called in a whisper.

He looked up. Not four meters from both of them stood the ethereal presence of Athena, her form billowing as if blown by an unseen wind. She was staring at the two of them. She had heard everything they had said about Gregory Phillips.

She was not happy.

PART TWO:
THE PHILLIPS,
INTERWORLD,
AND
THE STELLAR QUEST

CHAPTER TWELVE

Earlier that evening.

Gregory Phillips made numerous attempts during the late afternoon/early evening to contact Kimberly Hagerton. He hadn't been successful.

Eight o'clock that evening, Greg was seated behind his office desk, a desktop full of printed matter and data readout tablets— clerical business— splayed out before him. He'd have to attend to it, eventually, his junior-grade, transportation department duties, and certainly as many of the files from his desk that he eliminated would only in the end make way for even more. So what the hell? Why let its piling up cause him guilt? He leaned back in his chair and distantly watched the pattern of the static field above the phone-imagizing disk atop the desk flutter silently in a solemn gray. Mrs. Hagerton just wasn't going to answer, he realized, and already the situation was causing him much distress. Responsibility for the whereabouts of the air car and the two Hagerton men was partially his. That meant he'd be on call and on duty for almost the entire time it took to resolve the situation, however many days the lousy thing would take to **get** resolved.

He had two missing males lost somewhere south of the city, in all those kilometers of wild and rugged terrain. And then there was always the possibility some renegade group intercepted the ship while it was down and vulnerable, and apprehended (even killed) its two inhabitants. He shook his head. He really did not want to have to deal with that possibility, or be the one to have to ultimately report such a thing to the surviving members of the family.

Which brought him to the second mystery. The two Hagerton women. Where were they? They **might** have gone out, Kimberly Hagerton and her daughter, Frida, he supposed. But wouldn't they instead be just a little worried? And why hadn't Mrs. Hagerton called to say she'd tried to contact her husband and son herself and had not been able to reach them. Why wasn't she some somewhere where the department could contact her? Greg would be hanging on communications and worried sick, if it were someone dear to him.

His father, maybe? Randolph Phillips? Nah. Greg would worry over his mom, maybe, God bless her, but Greg's dad, that egotistical son of a bitch? Probably not.

Randolph Phillips was the chairman of the American division of *InterWorld*, the society for the exploration of the outer planets and beyond. Before his venture into politics, he'd been an aerospace engineer, and once received the Global Peace Prize award for his design of the Stellar Quest, the starship that left the solar system in 2410 for Eighty-two Eridani. Randolph Phillips was a man of high rank in the world government of Earth. No question about it. And Greg? He was the son of a woman the councilman once briefly joined with, believing it would be something permanent. They had petitioned the population control board for permission to make a baby. Greg kept his father's name (he had every right to it). Illegitimacy was almost unheard of today. It was very rare when a man and woman could actually copulate. What they did instead was a combination of mind melding their consciousness during intimacy, coupled with additional assist programs of male and female sex partners recorded centuries ago on early versions of archive data crystals. Seeing as the male rarely could even successfully obtain an erection, let alone achieve climax and seminal release, such "virtual reality" assistance brought back the passion mother nature had taken from humanity centuries ago, when mother nature decided humanity's stewardship of the planet needed tweaking and males and females virtually lost the ability to achieve "coitus" without outside assistance via the DNA coupling centers and baby-making facilities. Mother Nature's strategy worked. The human population was listed in only the millions now. The days of posting population figures in the billions was long gone.

As for Randolph's and Leidia's time together. It was destined to be brief. He pretty much left Leidia to raise young Greg on her own. But though Greg had no reason to really call the guy his "Dad," Randolph's last name proved advantageous, it was a great foot in the door to announce he was Randolph Phillips's offspring. As for the last time he'd seen his father, Greg couldn't recall the last time the councilman even bothered to inquire about him.

Keith Hagerton and his son were long overdue, and Gregory's department was as concerned about the two men now and their fate, as it was about the missing and rented air car.

"Terminate," he called out, finally, to the phone unit. The air above the hologram disk cleared; it became a lifeless circle of aluminum once more.

He then placed a neuralscan-headset atop his head, and requested the unit contact Melanie Richards, a good friend (perhaps maybe a bit more than that) in the passenger records department of the transportation division. He had bypassed the vocal unit, the communications system reading his neural pattern request, and before long a tiny, three-dimensional visualization of a young, twenty-three year old female (dressed only in a white slouch-shirt, which ended just below her hips) evolved above the tiny aluminum disk.

Melanie looked up at him and smiled. "Greg!" she called, "hi. What are you still doing at the office?"

"Melanie, I—"

Her image afloat above the phone disk shrunk, pulled back, to reveal a wider view. She was in her den/workroom. A stool came into view, as she sat down atop it.

God, Greg murmured under his breath. Her dark brown hair hung long and loose against her neck and beyond; he could see her nipples pinpricking the material of the shirt. Her smooth legs draped the stool, demurely. Christ, he could even see her satin panties, just beyond the hem of the shirt. (They were pink.) As a tiny hologram representation atop the imaging disk, Melanie resembled a little girl's toy dress-up doll. Greg wished he could pluck it from the disk and fondle it in his fingers.

All his hand would do, however, if he tried, was simply pass through her image. His own sending camera at the same time would record his actions, transmit them, and give Melanie a suggestion of where his thoughts were. Not that she would necessarily be offended by it. She would probably laugh, probably offer him the real thing the first chance he could get away from his duties. She might anyway before the transmissions ended.

Melanie grinned, demurely. Greg's image of him atop *her* unit in her apartment stared directly at her. She looked down at herself. "They say, Greg, phones were once voice only. You could answer them, naked, and not get self-conscious about it."

"You're doing nutty things to my head, Mel," Greg only answered.

"I'd have put something else on, but when your ID came over the system, I thought . . . for you . . . you've seen me in this before."

"You wanted to torture me, right? Make me pine for something that went out of our species centuries ago?"

"What I was hoping to do," she clarified, "was give you a sample of what you're missing, hanging out at the office so late in the day."

"Thanks."

"Our species isn't dead and gone, yet, Greg. We can still fuck . . . around. We've invented some pretty decent technological work a rounds to compensate for our impotence."

"Until the power goes out and then it's *oops, sorry, nothing's happening down there.* By now I should be sporting one hell of a . . . Doesn't that ever bother you, virtual reality fucking, cutting in toward the end some ancient bloke's hard on and climax?"

She shrugged. "It feels like the real thing. Can you tell the difference? I mean, the female's orgasm in the playback in place of the one that I just can't seem to muster? It's just a matter of cutting in the right couple from the past at the right moment."

"It's a little sick, though, isn't it?"

"You want to try it just us alone, like a couple of in love girls?"

"No," he replied. "Let's just say it's cruel; we guys, most of us, don't get aroused anymore. Mother nature pretty much rescinded our license to—"

"To what, Mike? Quit acting like my delicate feminine ears will be offended. There's nothing 'proper' about me, and I'm proud of it. And you love me for it, so knock it off. What you mean is you miss the old days when guys could and would fuck anything that moved. Right?"

Greg grinned, red-faced. "Yeah."

"So . . . what's up? How much longer do you think you're going to be? I could use the company."

"Mel, I need you to check on someone for me."

". . . Okay," she answered, pondering that. "I'd be happy to. On the up and up, right?"

"Well, it could get kind of interesting," he replied.

"So, it's something fun?" she replied. "Possibly naughty?"

"Well, not exactly ethical and . . ."

"Entirely legal?" She was staring at him, with a mischievous twinkle in her eyes. "Whose privacy ARE we intruding on? Hang on." She leaned forward, placing her neuralscan-headset atop her head and cueing up the system. The view atop Greg's imaging plate once more restricted to only her top half. "Just let me log into the Transport computer banks," she said.

"Technically, this *is* legitimate business, Mel," he offered.

"So, can I log in? If I'm going to be working the next few minutes, you don't mind if I get credit for it, do you?"

"It's what I would do," he simply answered. "You'll know if and when we've entered a gray area."

"A shame there aren't more bad boys like you out there anymore. You're your father's son, Greg Phillips."

"Please don't bring him into the conversation, Mel?"

O-k-a-y, she mouthed, silently, as she powered up her headset. *I hit a wound with that one,* she thought. "So, Greg, who are we investigating so surreptitiously?"

"We have some missing persons out beyond the city, in the wilderness."

"Oh . . ." She frowned. "At *this* hour?"

He nodded, wearily. "Afraid so. A Keith Hagerton and his nine year old son, Jeffrey."

"Oh my God. What happened?"

Greg shrugged. "I don't know. It was supposed to be just a Sunday outing."

"An 'outing?' It wasn't an *Intercity* that went down?"

***

(By that one, Melanie meant a regular airborne shuttle run out of New Allentown and bound for other cities.)

***

"No," he answered, "Keith Hagerton is with one of the networks. According to his file, he records Travel Visuals. He makes visiting the wilderness areas his occupation."

"What are the details?"

"Sending them now," he said, visualizing the info in his mind and transmitting it directly from his neuralscan unit to hers.

Melanie received the data as thought impressions in her head. "Lord," she lamented. "Oh, lord, that child must be scared to death by now. And outside the city, out in the wilds? Oh, fuck."

"Yeah," agreed Greg. He thought about the apartment number. Melanie's likeness temporarily left the hologram disk, replaced by the placard he'd seen earlier in front the Hagerton apartment.

HAGERTON
APT. 1024, SECTOR 9
QUADRANT 2

"'Apartment ten-twenty—

"I'm receiving it, Greg, stop," she said. "It's in your thoughts and coming up on the imaging plate. "I've got it. Let me go to work, now."

Clear, he mentally requested. The imaging plate emptied of the text, and Melanie Richard's likeness returned upon it.

She thought scanned the family name into the network, mentally summoning current data on the family's whereabouts. She looked up at him again. "Keith and Jeffrey Hagerton." She nodded. "They left this morning for . . . Crystal Cave? The old tourist caverns?"

He nodded.

"What were they doing there? No one goes there anymore."

"Keith Hagerton does."

"Return time should have been five o'clock. Three hours ago. The air car's transponder signal is off-line. . . . No updates, no additional information."

"What about the rest of the family?" Greg asked.

She scanned. "Mother and daughter spent the day in Old Philadelphia. No recorded sightings at any lifts or specialized entry sectors, not since they left the City Top Terrace around Six. According to the summary, mother and daughter should be home."

"<u>Should</u> be," he agreed.

"Do you want me to try their residence code?"

"You'll just get the message recorder. Melanie, what are the chances of my getting authorization to do a bio-scan of their premises?"

She smirked. "Greg, that's a bit extreme, don't you think?"

"It'll tell me if they're home or not."

"Yeah, and unless you and I can show just cause before a review board,

104

they'll fire our asses, and probably punish us. This is that gray area you hinted at, isn't it?"

Greg got a little red-faced again. "It'll tell me if they're home or not. They've been made aware that father and son are missing, no transponder signal. 'I' would be worried. They don't seem to be. I want to know why."

"You don't ask for much, do you?" she replied. She exhaled in fatigue. "Wow. . . . Maybe mother and daughter are visiting neighbors, or heavily immersed in some viewwafer."

"That's what the bio-scan will tell me."

"Greg, if I found out someone ran one of those on my premises to check up on me, I'd went them prosecuted."

"Melanie, something's not right. I've been to the Hagerton apartment once already tonight. Kimberly Hagerton couldn't wait for me to leave. She kept insisting her husband's tardiness was typical for him, and that she wasn't worried. Why hasn't she been after me for updates, for information? She's not even making herself available for *us* to contact *her*. Hell, I wouldn't blame her if he demanded we let her go out with a search detail to look for them herself. "

"What have we done," she inquired, "about finding them?"

He nodded. "I sent a team out to Kutztown. I'm waiting for the on-site report."

"Then short of going to Kutztown yourself to look for them, you've done all you can for the time being. Relax, Greg. Don't piss off the higher ups over this. You got your people out." She smiled, then. "Stop over. We can monitor the search updates together, on and off."

Greg grinned. "Nice as that sounds, Mel," he said, "I still have to notify the Wilderness Society, apprise them of the situation. Missing persons beyond city limits is their department. They live for that sort of a thing."

"And you have to be in your office to do that? I've got everything you need right here, Greg. Quit acting like a devoted member of the organization, working overtime at the office. Work it with me, here, at my place."

"I have something better in mind, Melanie, and it's why I need your help."

"Oh, why don't I like the sound of that?" she fretted.

"What if you and I," he said, "go visit the Hagerton apartment, and if they're not home, we go in and see what's up?"

Melanie eyed him, incredulously. "How are you going to get entry authorization? You planning to break the door down?"

"No, I—"

"And how would you justify the need for the request if you did? Especially if it turns out the Hagerton women are only out visiting?"

"I'd have a friend help me get it," he nodded toward her, "a friend with good connections, and a way with secret access codes."

"Greg!"

"You won't regret it," he said, appealing to the one thing she had a weakness for: the promise of a night of passionate lovemaking. She liked him, and everyone at Transport knew it. He liked her, although they both knew, unfortunately, Greg liked *himself* a whole lot more.

She straightened her sitting stance into a more rigid one, as she pondered all the consequences and benefits of going along with his scheme. And then she darted her eyes back toward his tiny image in her hologram receiver. "I'd better not regret it," she warned him, "because if we do this, after tonight, we're both going to have to get lost way far from here." She shook her head. "This is not going to go down well. I'm going to need a lot more from you than tantric sex, Greg Phillips. You better be planning on joining with me as my mate for the long haul."

"Melanie, hon," he said. "We'll be fine. And it'll be the best fun we've ever had in our lives. I really want to do this."

"You better be one hell of great partner without reliance of those playback archives, all you for the next year, Greg Phillips, because it's going to be you and me for that long, if not longer."

"Don't be such a pessimist, Mel," he said. "It might not be that bad."

"No, people know who your dad is. They might want to back off a little on the heat, considering the possible repercussions."

"I don't need my father and his reputation to fight my battles, Mel," he defended.

"You still have it, it's there, whether you want to acknowledge it or not. . . ."

Greg smiled. "You're going to do it, aren't you?" he brightened.

She took a breath. "It beats looking forward to only washing my hair tonight."

"Okay!" Greg only replied.

"Hey, Greg?" she replied.

"Yes, Mel?"

"You're a dick, you know that?"

"So you've told me many times. . . ."

They both had a laugh over that one. . . .

CHAPTER THIRTEEN

-1-

InterWorld, the human race's collective effort to further its knowledge of the universe, was headquartered in Mariner Valley on distant planet Mars. Randolph Phillips, Greg's father, was chairman of the American division in the United States, the main Earth headquarters constructed in the mountains outside of Sydney, Australia.

The councilman was on a VIP suborbital shuttle with his staff, en route for the eastern seaboard of North America. It was the return leg of a trip to Sydney. Randolph had declined the complementary "viewwafer" recording of the London Symphony Orchestra's Tchaikovsky symphony "Pathetique" (Number Six in B Minor), which they'd performed back in 2344. As he looked down the compartment, however, to the "luxury class" seating (cushioned swivel chairs informally arranged as if in an elegant parlor room), he noted that several of his staff had *not*, and upon their heads and faces were the headsets and visors that accorded them the requisite privacy they would need to fully appreciate the experience of attending the English concert.

He looked out instead one of the tiny oval port windows and to the flat horizon of open land, the plains of the mid-west United States, east of the Rocky Mountains. It was Eight o'clock p.m. Eastern Standard Time in Capital City, the nation's new Island City capital and his destination; Randolph was tired. The trip to Sydney had been exhausting. The sun made a slow dive into the westward plains behind him.

InterWorld, here on Earth had connected with the entire interplanetary membership throughout the solar system via Sensor Sphere link-up (taking into account the five minute time lag between Earth and Mars). The main, Martian facility in the high country near the great "Grand Canyon" gorge that was Mariner Valley had just finished reviewing the latest telemetry from the *Stellar Quest* starship, the first vessel to ever leave the solar system for a voyage to another star. In its final communique four years earlier before the eight person crew retired to their long sleep in cryogenic hibernation, (twenty-three years would pass on Earth, although on-board it would only seem like ten), the crew had sent home both public and private messages and offered the standard tripe about being in fine form, fit and in good spirits. Then, one by one, they had entered their hibernaculums and gone to sleep.

The ship was now four light years into its voyage and traveling at ninety percent the speed of light. It was not certain what effect such speeds would have on human tissue and mental acuity; could the warping effect of enduring both a volume decrease and a mass increase as predicted by the great Albert Einstein centuries ago leave the *Stellar Quest*'s crew somehow chromosomally damaged, especially after being bodily subjected to such a stressful rate of travel for twenty-three long years? Only time would tell. And perhaps it was a good thing that the crew was not awake and aware of it. Maybe it was indeed harmless and no great matter at all. Only one way to know.

It was hoped the mission would rekindle humanity's thirst for adventure, something that seemed lost these days anymore.

Stellar Quest would reach Eighty-two Eridani in A.D. 2433. Twenty years later her first signals from the new system would finally reach Earth. Any desire for a reply would spend another twenty years again crossing the distance back to Eight-two Eradani. For this reason, more than any other, the mission had cost *InterWorld*, the most in selling its merits to the human race. No one really got excited over travel much anymore. As *InterWorld*, feared might happen, the human race had already lost interest in the voyage. The time involved was just too great for most people, and Randolph himself wondered if he'd even be alive when news of the crew's arrival reached Earth. For all the good it did, the crew of the *Stellar Quest* might just as well have ceased to exist.

***

Randolph Phillips had added his words of encouragement to the myriad others that comprised the return communique *InterWorld*, sent, knowing full well of course that the signal would never catch up to the ship until it reached Eighty-two Eridani. Moving at ninety percent light speed and already four light years out, the starship would force an Earth-sent transmission— dispatched from the solar system this very night and traveling at one-hundred percent light speed— to gain a whole light year on the retreating starship every ten years. After forty years (were the voyage to take that long, which it wouldn't), a signal sent out this day would finally overtake her. No messages, thus, from the Earth to the *Stellar Quest* (no serious ones) were transmitted. What <u>was</u> being sent was done so for the sake of the crew, for the 2430s when the starship reached its destination.

Capital City, the new site of Washington D.C. in the hills of Leesburg, Virginia, and some thirty kilometers north east of the old capital, rose finally into view for Randolph's and his staff. He entered his suite's living room around the same hour that Keith Hagerton realized someone back in New Allentown had entered his apartment and stolen the viewwafer. The city, towering above the countryside on its concrete supports, lay just north of the ruins of Dulles International Airport. Although Washington

D.C. itself had decayed into oblivion centuries ago, the Mall complex and government buildings, the old Congress, White House and presidential monuments had been preserved in their original condition as museum pieces for the ages and were visible in the distance just barely by the new Island City that replaced it. Like the old Smithsonian Institute nearby to them, the old city's remains were now a major tourist spot. Because life in the island cities could become claustrophobic after a while (all that open land just beyond their sealed perimeters), such planet-based tourist sites as old Washington D.C., the caverns of Virginia, Niagara Falls, the Grand Canyon, etc. were maintained, thus to aid the race in its need to leave the city confines occasionally and to "breathe," spiritually. As a New Jersey delegate to the American branch of the World Council, Randolph Phillips even joined his fellow delegates every July Fourth in the old Congress to conduct that day's business in the very halls where their ancestors had once done so daily. It was one of the few days of the year he actually felt good about his duties, and the principles upon which they had been founded.

***

Randolph lived alone in what he believed was a suite too big for only one man. He was fifty-two, and had been divorced from Rhea for five years now. Greg was his son from his old affair with Leidia whom he'd met in his twenties and during the days when Randolph was still a student at the Fort Lee Instruc facility in Fort Lee, New Jersey (an island city, replacing its old land-based counterpart in the northern territory of New Jersey, the only remaining part still above the water line). He had been born there. He hardly remembered Leidia. She had been a fellow student at the Fort Lee Instruc, someone he had sharpened his lovemaking expertise on in the days when he was still in what he liked to call his experimental phase. As far as he knew, Greg, who was now in his twenties and on his own, only saw his mom whenever he had reason to leave his apprentice job in New Allentown and travel north to visit her. In the few times Randolph, himself, had actually seen his son, Greg had never really spoke much of his mother, or for that matter showed much enthusiasm for his father as well. Although Randolph had never actually denied any knowledge of or responsibility for his offspring, there was never time for more than a marginal participation in Greg's upbringing, such occasions as a birthday once in a while, or a gift during the "Winter" holiday. Perhaps that was why Greg insisted on making his own way in the world. There had never been much room in Randolph's life for a real family, even when he was married to Rhea, and perhaps that explained why they never had any children of their own, or why after ten years of marriage his wife had finally ended it. Randolph was just too bent on reaching the top of the political ladder, and realizing his space exploration goals. His colleagues and rivals always knew him as a man not to be underestimated. He knew where he wished to go, and who or what

109

he had to conquer to get there.

-3-

Greg would have been flattered to know that his father was thinking of him that hour of the night. He and Randolph when they did meet were civil enough around each other, but it had never been a relationship that Greg would have called loving. He had spent his childhood in Fort Lee with his mom. She was a good woman, but didn't understand Greg's thirst for more than a meager life and career in Fort Lee, any more than she ever understood his father's love for the stars and his need to leave his home roots and explore the ends of the Earth.

Greg shared his father's love for travel and his obsession with the stars. What he had discovered this night at the Hagertons would probably be the answer to his father's dreams.

Melanie Richards had come through, accompanied Greg to the Hagerton apartment. Although she had earlier feigned approval of his outrageous antics, she now secretly hoped he'd be disappointed. She had had time to come down from the euphoria of ending up as two young lovers on the run from the authorities, moving across the wild expanses beyond the Island Cities, eluding capture. She prayed instead that the female Hagertons, Kimberly and Frida, were home as they should have been under circumstances such as these.

The apartment had been empty, no answer to their entry request. Melanie had wanted to leave it at that, to end whatever mystery Greg had hoped to create from the whole ordeal. But Greg had wanted to enter and look around, and begged Melanie to key in her "appropriated" entry code.

"I don't believe you!" she had whispered, wishing not to be overheard, and forgetting like so many others always did that the walls were completely soundproofed for privacy, and that no one was likely to hear them. "Greg, they're not home. Let's just go."

"I thought you wanted to have some fun?" he only replied.

"We're about to commit an offence that will ruin the two of us. Are you sure you want to do this?"

"This is a departmental matter," he had defended and excused of his actions. "We're on official business."

"Bullshit. You're just massaging your ego. I hate this!"

"Melanie, I'll make it up to you. Nothing will happen to us. I can fix it."

She remembered who his father was, and had only nodded to herself that Randolph Phillips could probably extricate his son from near anything. Somehow, that made Greg a little less of the kind of male she would ever want to get serious with.

"I'd better not end up incarcerated over this," she warned.

He had assumed that impish grin that she had found so enticing before, as he approached her. Resting his arms against her shoulders and placing his hands on the wall behind her, he pressed her back into it as he kissed her on the lips. "You won't," he said.

Melanie smirked and pulled out from a vest pocket in her blouse a tiny transparent wafer. She turned sideways, seeking the entry input slot before the Hagerton door. Greg removed an arm from against her to allow her passage. She inserted the micro wafer and watched as the door quietly withdrew into the leftward wall. She looked over at Greg. He slipped past her and entered the entry foyer to the Hagerton home.

Nothing in the least bit felt wrong or peculiar within. The Hagertons appeared not to be home, and Melanie could not help once more feel as if this were an unjust intrusion, and she said so, repeatedly.

"It still *feels* wrong," Greg insisted after they had spent several minutes simply scanning the living room over from its entrance foyer.

"Can we go now?"

Greg paused and exhaled in contemplation. He shook his head. "I want to check out some of the bedrooms. We ought to be thorough."

"We shouldn't even be *in here!*"

He looked at her again and only nodded. He departed for the foyer, and Melanie in frustration exhaled and flopped down on the sofa. She noticed and then stared in interest out the terrace window. You could tell: The view was a real one, and not a hologram image. Her own place was too far within the city to possess an actual view of the mountains. She heard Greg milling about in one of the adjoining bedrooms, and she tried to let the scene out the terrace take her mind from the indignity of it.

***

Thinking maybe Mrs. Hagerton and her daughter might have fallen asleep watching an entertainment visual in their viewing chamber, Greg entered it carefully, ready to apologize should his sudden intrusion amid the recording scare the piss out of them.

It was almost a relief to him to find the chamber empty; the thought of having to explain what he was doing in their apartment suddenly made him feel ill. He was about to leave when he noticed the playback unit on the floor. A neuralscan-headset and visor lay beside it; he grew curious. The Hagertons hadn't put their toys away, and perhaps a viewwafer was still in the playback bay. He checked it out, and sure enough there was one within it. Even more puzzling was the glowing "Power" button on the playback deck, indicating that the unit was still on. He'd forgotten to turn things off like that himself on occasion, and he always hated it because it wasn't good for the equipment. But this made him wonder:

Where were they?

"Greg, what are you doing?" Melanie suddenly said from the entrance.

Greg jolted.

"They're not home." He placed the headset and visor on his head then, and sat on the floor. He pointed toward the storage nook, recessed into the wall beside the entrance.

Melanie looked over to it. "What?"

"See if they're any more sets in the cabinet, and then sit down. I want to see what's on this viewwafer."

"Oh, for Christ's sake, Greg!"

"Come on. It's probably a home visual. Ought to be good for a few laughs. It won't take long; what harm will it do? Sit down." He grinned then that way that made him look so cute.

She smiled back and reluctantly opened the cabinet, searching for a headset and visor. Finding a set, she put them on and joined him on the cushion. "If it gets personal, you **will** shut it off, won't you?"

"Yeah."

***

Twenty minutes of skipping through the contents of the recording's first couple hours told Greg that something wasn't right. What he was viewing should not have been present in the Hagerton home, not yet, not while Keith and Jeffrey Hagerton were still supposedly away from the city and this recording with them.

He shut it down and extracted the wafer from the unit, removing his visor from his eyes to study it.

"What's wrong?" Melanie asked, in the silence as the image faded from her consciousness. She pulled off the visor glasses. "Why did you shut it off? I liked it. I've never actually seen any visuals from Crystal Cave. It's nicer than I thought it was."

"I am actually shaking," he said, studying his hands and then looking up to her. "God!"

"Greg, what? It's just a home visual of one of their trips to Crystal Cave. You said Keith Hagerton likes to go there."

"You don't get it, do you?" he said. "Look at the date!"

He showed her the engraving etched into the crystal's edge, no doubt by Keith Hagerton himself before he left the city.

Crystal Cave Trip
Jeffrey and me. 10/26/2415

"Today's date"! Greg said. "Why is this *here*?"

"He sent them a copy?" she suggested of Keith Hagerton, his wife and daughter.

Greg shook his head. "This is the original, look at it." He removed the headset and dropped it to the floor as he got up. "Come on, Melanie, we're leaving, and I'm taking this with me."

"No, you're not!" she returned of the viewwafer as she went to grab it. He'd already turned for the exit. "Greg, *put it back*. You'll get us both arrested for breaking and entering . . . *and theft*."

He faced back and shook his head. "One of our air cars is missing, Mellie. This wafer may explain why, and our department will want any information that helps explain what happened. I'm going to watch this thing all the way."

"Put it back where you found it, Greg! You can make an anonymous call that you have information, leave it, and then hang up. But you can't mention in any report that we were ever here. The Hagertons will sue the department for every last token it possesses. Make the report you would have made before coming here, and let the department and the city handle the rest of it. That's the way it's supposed to be done."

"I'll make my report," he assured her, "in my own time. But first I have to play this. Don't you realize what this is? This is an anomaly. It'll be okay. I told you. I can handle it."

"You mean, your father can."

Melanie, he knew, was well aware that Greg Phillips held little fondness for his father, yet prided himself on his ability to make use of the clout his old man's position in the government granted Greg.

"I know what I'm doing," he answered, annoyed at her, as he pocketed the crystal. He subsequently withdrew from the den, and then the apartment.

***

He was all alone now in his apartment, in his bedroom and atop the bed. His back propped up against the headboard of his centuries old, antique waterbed, he sat straight up and just allowed the images from his neuralscan headset to feed him the images being sent to it from his portable playback unit beside him atop the mattress. The unit completed its replay of the Crystal Cave excursion, and silence descended upon Greg. His bedroom suggested itself darkly beyond the dark-lensed visor glasses. He removed them and looked down his body to his waist and to the playback unit. He picked it up and held it in front of him. It and the bedroom had been there all along; he simply hadn't noticed as he'd lain on the bed mesmerized by the signals being transmitted into his brain. He was numb, without comment or even thought. He only contemplated the room before him.

The call alert from the phone system signaled him, suddenly. Greg took a breath at its insistence, and slowly rose, pulling the neuralscan headset off his head and dropping it on the pillow.

The phone imaging disk was on the nightstand; Greg looked over at it

113

as the unit continued to beep for him. Then, he sat down next to it on the bed, and uttered, "Go."

An image slowly solidified into presence above the disk. It was the image of a colleague in the transport department, a Reily Stoddard, attached to the investigative unit in charge of recovering misplaced transport vehicles.

"Mr. Phillips?"

Greg knew of Reily Stoddard, and he was sure Stoddard had heard of him. As neither, though, was on a first name basis with the other, Greg returned his greeting with one of equal formality. "This is Phillips," he said. "What have you got?"

Reily Stoddard was standing before a large white vehicle (a search team runabout). Several of Stoddard's team members milled about in the area behind him and to his side. They appeared to be stowing their gear back in the craft. It was a wide angle view, and Greg recognized the hillside beside them. They were in the Old Crystal Cave parking lot. Greg recognized the location of the call, immediately, having just been there, sort of, via the viewwafer playback.

"Mr. Phillips," Stoddard said, "we've done a thorough check of the cave. It's remarkably intact— the stairways and entrances— for so long being abandoned. If the Hagertons were here, they're long gone. We ran an ID scan on the field cocoon. . . ." Stoddard looked down at a transparent imaging plate. ". . . Around ten this morning it did admit one Keith Michael and Jeffrey Allen Hagerton. But there is no log-out time. The system would have recorded the second field drop to let them exit. There isn't one. It's possible they're still down there somewhere, but I can't imagine where. The cave isn't all that big, and there are only a few small openings along the ground level that look as if they might go down a few meters farther into the rock. . . ." He read down a new "page" on the imaging plate. ". . . The specs on this place say that the lower level off-shoots aren't very open or extensive. I doubt they're down there, but if you want us to check it out, I'll send down a team."

Greg thought about an answer to that for a moment. Then, he shook his head. "No. I believe they took with them spelunking gear: lift packs, light globes and assorted power units? You have the equipment, correct, to detect output transmissions from such units?"

Reily Stoddard nodded pensively. "True. We don't read any emissions at all— not even organic life signs. You're right, they're not down there. It's almost as if you *knew that,* Phillips."

Greg's arm hairs bristled at the affront, but he kept his wits about himself. "The air car isn't there; it just made sense the two Hagerton men weren't, either."

The team leader nodded; Greg's reasoning made sense, as well. "Do you want us to remain in the area a while longer, expand the search to the neighboring hills?"

Again, Greg paused in his answer, and held back an urge to smile at the irony of that. "No, wait for the daylight. Come on back in."

"Okay, Phillips. We'll be in in a while."

"Right. Good job, Reily. Thanks."

"End," Greg then faintly called. Reily Stoddard and his search vessel faded from the phone-imaging disk. Greg shook his head again.

Search the area, he thought. *What a waste of time that would be? The Hagerton males were nowhere upon the Earth.*

His search teams were looking in the wrong place; the air car was as good as permanently gone.

CHAPTER FOURTEEN

-1-

It was approaching ten in the evening when Greg Phillips petitioned his department for the use of an air car. There had been a moment's pause amid the maintenance staff at his request, so late in the night, at the seriousness of it.

"I need it," he had simply answered.

"Your flight plan?" Doug Manning of Craft Storage and Maintenance had inquired with amused innocence. The man was intimidating, Greg knew. As head man over the entire fleet of vehicles the department owned, he had to be. And he was a formidable man at that: over two meters in height and one-hundred and thirteen kilograms heavy.

He could be one mean motherfucker, Greg had heard. Greg didn't care. "Just give me authorization, so I can take the fucking thing," Greg said. "If anybody asks, tell them I had to talk to my old man."

Manning knew Greg's father was in Capital City these days. He gave Greg a simple look of amusement.

Greg looked back with a, *"don't say it!"* warning on his face.

Fifteen minutes later, he was in an air car and beyond the city limits, on his way west for old Leesburg, Virginia. He hardly glanced out the air car's windows to the rolling countryside beneath him, or took notice of how radiant were the stars in the absolute darkness beyond the city. The silence all around him was deep and like a numbing cold in sub-freezing weather. It was not a little disconcerting. He tried to ignore it.

Melanie had not gone with Greg back to his apartment. She had not been in a mood to do much of anything with him by that hour. She was pissed at how callously he violated other people's rights of privacy. He didn't care, especially now, after viewing the rest of the Hagerton's home visual. He could still feel his hands shaking as he contemplated the images of Keith and Jeffrey Hagerton entering the Crystal Cave caverns and slowly penetrating the hidden and till now never-before-seen sectors of the cave. And then there was that bit with the alien, Athena. She called herself an Eleution, and what she had so easily done to poor nine year old Jeffrey— strip his manhood from him and turn him into a little girl, and so effortlessly, as if that sort of thing were possible and done every day— was enough to make one . . . very uncomfortable.

Strange, very strange.

Greg glanced again to the Hagerton's viewwafer that he'd appropriated from their premises and wondered what he should actually do about the aforementioned document. It was valuable beyond belief, that went without question, but would it be believed by anyone or even accepted?

He wondered what his father would want to do with it, beyond curse the fact that the Hagertons had in all probability been taken from their home and were all by now halfway to the other side of the galaxy. But it would be good to show this to his father. He and the *InterWorld* Society would want this information, and unless Greg was prepared to destroy the recording right this minute, he had better see to it that the proper people had control of it. Oddities such as this always became public knowledge sooner or later. The World Government would ultimately be informed of it, and when it did, it might be more willing to accept its contents as authentic, if the recording by then hadn't already been splashed across every news service this side of Pluto. There was the impact of such a revelation on society to consider— proof once and for all that humanity was not alone in the universe, the very proof the *Stellar Quest* had been sent out into the universe to uncover and investigate.

What of the Hagertons? He pondered again. The last recorded image on the viewwafer was of Keith Hagerton and his "son" (his daughter now, apparently) as ethereal energy preserved inside Athena's essence as they rode her "energy bubble" up into the stratosphere and then back again for a landing inside the Hagerton's apartment. Jeffrey then being off-loaded and made physical again to wait for his mother and sister to get back from their visit to Old Philadelphia and relate the tale of what he and his dad had experienced. What an incredible sight the whole of it was. Athena could convert matter to energy and back again or rearrange it to whatever pattern she chose as if it were all child's play. And such ease at getting around in the physical universe. No need of clunky metallic tin cans (space vessels) that struggled just to overpower gravity and actually get going somewhere.

So, young Jeffrey Hagerton had gone back to the city with the viewwafer, and now all three remaining Hagertons were "missing." Greg felt shudders all down his arms simply at the thought of all of it. What did this Athena want with them, where was her race from in the cosmos, and why was she waiting down there beneath the Earth surface to begin with? How many innocent souls had she already snared in her Venus fly trap?

"Dad's going to love this," he thought, grinning a nervous grin, his whole body aquiver. "Now I know why Kimberly Hagerton was so elusive with me before. She didn't want me to hang around too long and find out she now had a new daughter, her husband was being held hostage by an alien super consciousness. Wow. And now probably all of them are. We've had an inner-city kidnapping, and by perpetrators who probably see us as like vermin at their feet."

And then there was the matter of what Athena could do. Not only could she herself travel the galaxy in mindless abandon, as the urge compelled her, she could also be used as a taxi service, ferrying lessor races like Earth's own to wherever in the universe they might wish to go. If only some way could be employed to persuade her into "cooperating."

A transponder signal identified itself, suddenly, upon one of his forward imaging screens. Capital City was nearing. He'd have to call soon to announce his approach. He thought of his father again and only felt the anticipation of it cause his skin to goose bump. He shook his head.

Randolph Phillips was surprised that anyone would be calling on him so late in the day. It wouldn't have been any of his colleagues on the assembly, or even one of his many social and female acquaintances on such last minute notice. He was therefore totally taken aback when he opened the door, and found his son in the entrance corridor in a casual pair of blue trousers and a rumpled tan sweater.

"Greg?" he simply acknowledged.

"Dad. May I come in?"

"Yes, of course. This is quite a surprise, son."

"I know. I should have called first." Greg sounded distant, almost cold. Despite the news he had for his dad, he still didn't like him all that much.

"No, son, it's all right. It's great to see you."

"You too, Dad. "How's the *Stellar Quest* doing?"

Randolph Phillips nodded, amiably. "She's doing fine, so far as we know. The specs on the crew's sleep were all in the green, ship status diagnostics are reporting everything's working as it should. At least they were as of two years ago." The man grinned. "No way to know what the status is as of today."

"Why?" puzzled Greg.

"The telemetry we just received tonight was sent out by the ship's automatics two years ago, son," he told Greg. "Two years ago the *Stellar Quest* was only two light years from Earth. It took those signals two years to reach us. Tonight's telemetry updates we won't get for another four years."

Greg smirked. "And I thought it was irritating to receive a communique from Mars. What's their time lag, something like fifteen minutes?"

"It varies" he answered, "but that's about right. The lag for the *Stellar Quest* will only get worse the more time passes, son," he returned. "Each day, they put another fourteen billion miles between us and them. And of course by the time they reach Eighty-two Eridani, the vessel will be twenty light years away . . . as the crow flies."

"But they're due to get there around 2433?"

He nodded. "They're only moving at nine-tenths light speed. So instead of it taking twenty years, it'll take a few years longer."

"And how much is time slowed for them inside the ship at that speed?"

"They're asleep, son," he said. "It'll seem to them as if no time at all will pass when they're revived. They're in suspended animation. How would you like to skip over the next twenty-three years?"

Greg smiled. It was off-subject but he contemplated it anyway. "There are days. . ." he admitted. "But if they were awake, what's the compression rate?"

Randolph laughed. "Two point two-nine-four . . . and a few more numbers after that. For every year they experience aboard ship, two years and roughly four months pass back here. Meaning, their ship's clocks will record that only ten years have come and gone when they awaken, but in reality, twenty-three." Randolph went reflective after that. "Greg, I can't believe you came all this way in the middle of the night just for a lesson in relativity theory."

"No, I didn't," Greg simply answered. He wandered over to the terrace view patio. In reality, his dad's suite of rooms was too far inward Capital City for it to be a real patio balcony overlooking the old land-based capital city to the east. It was a hologram/holodeck simulation. Open the patio doors and withdraw to its "exterior" and you'd swear it was totally authentic, that you really were outside the city and breathing in real countryside air. Someone as important in the world politics as Randolph Phillips could demand such posh amenities. No doubt about it, Greg's dad enjoyed his lot in life, the hand life had dealt him. Greg took note particularly of the twin blinking lights atop the distant Washington Monument. The long white marble column was clearly visible even at the distance the designers of the holoview simulation had selected and it was a beautiful monument to behold at night, the monument bathed in a golden wash of illumination, marking the ancient site of Washington D.C.

"I stumbled onto something, Dad," Greg said, ultimately as he stepped "outside" and took in the "night air." Randolph Phillips followed him out onto the patio and to the thing's wrought iron railing. Not turning to face his dad now beside him, he was aware nonetheless of his dad's presence.

"You stumbled onto what, son?" asked his dad.

Greg pulled the viewwafer from his pants pocket, and handed it to him. "You're not going to believe what's on this thing. It's mind boggling. I may need a favor of you after, because of the way I obtained this, should anyone try to bring breaking and entering charges against me."

"What's on this thing?" Randolph asked, eyeing the viewwafer every which way.

"It's a home visual I stole from a family's household, tonight."

"Do they know about it?"

"No, and I doubt they'll be coming back for it. I doubt they even meant to leave it behind, they probably didn't even know they *would* be leaving it behind. When you find out why, it'll make your hair stand on end. This thing will scare the shit out of you, Dad, I guarantee it. I've uncovered a kidnapping like none I've ever heard of before, but I had to break into a home to get this, Dad. I smooth-talked a friend of mine into getting me the right entry code. Like father, like son."

Greg smiled. Randolph Phillips glanced at him at that one.

"The family is missing, and my department is concerned over that, because there's no rational explanation that they know of. Watch this with me? You won't regret it. In fact, you'll probably call me bringing this to you the first useful thing you've ever known me to do."

His father contemplated Greg for several seconds, and then turned his gaze upon the recording. "You brought something with you to wash this down with, I hope," Randolph answered. He started to smile, then, and finally Greg did the same.

***

Greg spared his father the pain of watching the entire recording, and for that his father was grateful. The two passed on the thought of viewing the viewwafer in Randolph's posh Viewing Chamber. Here on the patio in the lounge chairs with the nighttime view of Washington D.C. off in the distance would do fine. The two got comfortable within them, set Randolph's portable playback unit on the little cocktail table between them and donned headsets and visors. Greg called "Image Start."

The replay at first glance seemed like so many other dismal home recordings Randolph had had the misfortune to sit through. It wasn't the images themselves that made them dismal, but the fact that like most home recordings it was all unedited, raw footage. Tedious to endure? That didn't describe most such experiences by half.

Greg began with a brief description of the two males, and their eventual destination. And after a quick overview of their activities in the cave— for no other reason than to prove to his father that Keith and Jeffrey Hagerton had in fact gone there— he cut to the final portion . . .

The illumination from Keith's Hagerton's Light Sphere rose and suddenly the Sensor Sphere could see all the way to be back of the chamber room. Something aglow with an unearthly light caught Randolph's eye.

"What in the hell is that?" he asked his son of Athena's orb, hanging motionless above the upward jutting stalagmite. The apparition, whatever it was, crackled and snapped like heat lightning.

"Just wait," Greg said.

Athena eventually reshaped her ethereal presence into that of a beautiful woman for young Jeffrey Hagerton's benefit, right before of course she changed him into one himself.

"Whoa," said Randolph at the sight of it.

It amused Greg to glance to his Dad —through Greg's visor sunglasses— and faintly note the intensity of his father's incredulous stare. Randolph Phillips was mesmerized. It was as plain as that. He looked over at Greg, pulling up over the bridge of his nose his own visor glasses. "Is this for real?"

"Assuming it is," Greg answered, still seeing Athena and her ethereal form in his mind, "what do you make of her?"

His father shook his head. "I don't know."

"Her name is Athena," Greg smiled. "Watch the rest. You won't believe it."

Randolph Phillips was enthralled. Truth was he was astounded. When Athena— with Keith and Jeffrey enveloped in a near invisible force field bubble— left the subterranean depths finally to seek out their rented air car in the Crystal Cave parking lot, and appeared to destroy it, the replay of the event was so authentic that Randolph actually felt his adrenalin begin to pump into his blood stream. Her subsequent climb into the clouds and into a low Earth orbit was both silent and without visible strain. It was as if he were in a soap bubble and riding an incredible updraft. Randolph really believed he was leaving the Earth, and only when he thought of his son or his Holodeck patio beyond his visor, had he noticed the truth flooding into his eyes. He had shut them and let the experience wash over him, he totally "felt" the climb into orbit.

The recording ended right where Jeffrey was about to disembark from Athena's lair and re-enter his apartment. Randolph Phillips's patio abruptly reinstated its presence around him. He looked over at Greg. His son was without question enthralled by all he'd seen; he lay as yet quite content in a reclining position on his patio lounge chair beside his dad.

"I would have loved to have done that last part myself, gone into orbit like that," he told his father, "just to experience for real what it felt like. So . . . Dad. What do you think?"

His dad nodded, absently. "I don't know what to think," he admitted. "What do you expect me to do with this, Greg?" he asked.

"That's up to you," Greg replied, rising to a sitting position and twisting himself to face his dad. "I thought you'd get a kick out of seeing it. It sort of answers an important question, though, doesn't it? I mean, you did go through a lot of trouble to build a space ship, launch it into space, and hope like hell it reached where it was going, all to possibly answer a really big question, one of the biggies."

"Which is?"

Greg smirked. "*ARE WE ALONE IN THE UNIVERSE?* I'd say that was a 'NO.'"

Randolph glanced back to the viewwafer in the playback deck. He suddenly felt very ill, not physically ill, the terrible kind of ill, the kind that gets a person deep in his very soul.

He hated it.

CHAPTER FIFTEEN

-1-

A very unhappy Athena, meanwhile, was in Keith and Kimberly's apartment deciding what to do about the missing viewwafer. Keith's supposition that quite possibly this young Transport Department upstart, Gregory Phillips, might have absconded with it, didn't sit too well with her as well. He couldn't help feel a little amused by her piqued expression; he shrugged and frowned a little too whimsically.

Athena, her ethereal, ghostly apparition approaching them, simply pointed to them and then to herself. What she meant was, *"Return! Now!*

They both gave the living room a final glance. Kimberly felt a dizzying rush of energy overcome her as she was consumed in Athena's essence. And then . . . It was as if nothing had happened at all. All she saw before her was evidence of Athena's orb bubble acting as a barrier, her living room as yet but an arm's length away. Kimberly reached out for the bubble. It rippled like the surface of a pond when disturbed.

"We're sorry about this," offered Keith. "It complicates things I know, but perhaps nothing will come of it. Please don't be mad at us."

There was no answer from Athena. Instead the two felt the bubble rush forward for the terrace window and break through it. Soon Athena and her tiny blue orb were outside in the cold Pennsylvania air and rapidly ascending New Allentown, its three pillared struts, holding it up as if a pedestal supporting and showcasing a fine and delicate piece of art under glass and in a museum. She cleared the top of the structure and headed straight for the night above.

Keith and Kimberly saw the Earth's flat expanse begin to contour, become the planet it was, and the stars of the Milky Way galaxy glowed in the night above it with a piercing clarity rarely seen upon the Earth itself.

Eventually, Athena and her orb settled into orbit around the planet and for the sake of Keith and Kimberly, she recreated for them the living room they had just a few minutes before departed. The two remained fixated upon the scene in the terrace view: Earth's surface was engulfed in evening darkness, a smattering of brilliant "island city" lights scattered across the face of the North American continent.

"At this time of the night," Keith spoke lowly and after a while, "once upon a time that entire surface was alit with ground clutter illumination. Light pollution it used to be called. The Earth looks almost pristine again like it did before humans learned how to build stuff."

Kimberly nodded. "Greg Philips took the viewwafer, didn't he?" Kimberly said of the archive, and bringing the topic back to what was really

122

on both their minds. "He came back while we were out and he took it."

"Yes, and I'm pretty sure Athena believes that as well," said Keith. "I think she's a little miffed about it."

"What do you think she'll do?"

Keith shrugged, and then glanced again to the Earth. "I don't know. "Why was it so damn important to that kid to search our apartment?" Keith asked suddenly of Greg. "What was he looking for?"

"Greg Phillips is an arrogant little bastard," Athena suddenly said. *"He's not getting away with this, rest assured of that."*

"What are you going to do to him, Athena?" Keith replied aware that he and Kimberly and their children in this realm really possessed no privacy in their conversations.

The view in the terrace window subtly began to change, the Earth flattened once more as the living room seemed to fall back into the planet's atmosphere. Keith looked over at Kimberly; he slid his arm around her waist. "This can't be good," he said to her.

"What's she doing?" uttered Kimberly.

"We're heading down. *You're actually doing it, aren't you, Athena?*" he addressed aloud. "You're going after the little prick, aren't you?"

"Yes," she only replied. "And you two are going to help me do that."

"When?"

"Does now sound soon enough?" she answered in feigned innocence.

"Athena," spoke up Kimberly, softly. "Can I see my kids again, look in on them? Just to see them again?"

"I've made you a fully accurate reproduction of your apartment," she answered Kim. "You know the way. See them all you want."

Kimberly smiled at Keith, kissed him on the cheek and faced back to the hallway leading to the bedrooms. "Thank you, Athena." And to Keith: "I won't be long."

He nodded. And as she departed for her kids, Keith retreated for the long sofa facing the terrace view. "Could you bring the lights down a little in the room, please, Athena?" he asked, lowly. "Usually, I'd ask the voice recognition system, but seeing as it's —"

The lights promptly dimmed to a more nighttime setting, a wash of blue issuing from the overhead lighting.

"Many thanks," he said. He took a seat then on the couch and waited, watching the contour of eastern North America grow larger in the view before him.

She's really going back for it, Kimberly thought to herself of Athena and the viewwafer. Kimberly was glad in a way. It meant that she would be allowed a few more hours of transition time before being taken from her home world, probably forever. But, on the other hand, she almost hoped Athena never did recover the wafer. It reminded her of a *Note in a bottle* cast adrift at sea in old Twentieth Century "novels" she had scanned. The viewwafer would show evidence to her race that she hadn't simply vanished into nothing; would finally solve for them the riddle of why so many before her and her family had gone missing after visiting that Kutztown cave. Maybe even her parents would learn of the wafer's existence one day, and view it, if fate were to be so kind. But only if Athena failed in her desire to retrieve it.

She shook her head at the conflicting desires within herself, and centered her attention on the hallway to her children's bedrooms.

Jeffrey and Frida, looking very much like sisters together, were asleep against one another in the solemn green glow of the aquarium program in the large HoloView portal along the forward wall. The littler, circular window port to the side still showed the vibrant stars above a night vista of old Earth. God, what a sight it was, coupled with the serenity of angel fish, swimming at peace in the holoview scene. Athena had maintained (as per Frida's wish) the aquarium scene, despite the fact that Frida no longer remained in a "conscious" or aware state in this illusionary recreation of her bedroom. Were Kimberly's kids really *asleep?* For surely as disembodied entities, such a concept as being asleep did not precipitate the need to lie down and rest one's body, when certainly one no longer *had a body,* possessed such an unnecessary appendage— unless (on some level of super conscious awareness) Frida and Jeffrey still needed the illusion of physical forms, reposing in a bedroom, in a semblance of conventional sleep.

Illusion or no, Athena was providing Kimberly with a "localized" depiction of her children's continued presence as sentient energy forms, and since it seemed as real as reality itself, she went over to her children, and touched them— smoothed her older daughter's hair off her cheek, kissed her "younger daughter" (that would be Jeffy) on his/her left one. She quietly exited the room, then, and returned to her husband and their "living room."

"Are they all right?" Keith asked.

Kimberly nodded. "They're fine. You'd think we were all back home, our real home." She frowned as she thought about it. "There's no real way for us in this state to even tell if we are home or aren't. Are we even alive, Keith? Do we even still exist? Or are we just mental programs, memories, stored in Athena's 'essence?' I'm not even sure I know what I'm talking about. This . . ." she trailed off.

He took her into this arms. "What, Kimmy?" he asked.

"The kids are sleeping! But are they really? Do the dead sleep?"

"They're not dead, baby," he whispered. "None of us. We're aware. We still exist."

"Keith, this whole thing can make a person insane." She grabbed her arms, as if suddenly chilly. "I'm not sure how I can remain okay with all this. I mean, when is a person really dead? When our brain stops working, stops processing thoughts and sensory data? Is that all life is? Just awareness of being alive?"

Keith smiled. "You answered your own question. We're aware."

"Hmmm," she murmured. "I always thought that when people slept, their souls sailed on the wind, astral projected, happy for a few hours to escape the confines of a human body. By that definition, none of us should need *sleep* when we're pure energy like this."

He rubbed his hands gently up and down her shoulders. "If the illusion of sleeping works for us while we're in that state, and serves as one way to pass the time, the hell with trying to rationalize *what is* and *what isn't*. You'll give yourself a migraine over it."

"How is that even possible?" she asked. "A migraine. Here? We're not real."

She rested her forehead against his, closing her eyes. She pulled back, eventually, opened them again, and asked him: "So, when will Athena allow *you and me* to take a break? Has she made any progress with Phillips, yet?"

He nodded. "In fact she's made a lot," he said. "She's got a good bead on him."

"Where is he?"

"Capital City/Leesburg, Virginia."

"He left New Allentown for real, didn't just use virtual reality?"

Keith shrugged. "Apparently, he has as much clout as I have when it comes to going on excursions beyond the city."

"What's in Capital City?" she asked.

"His father. Greg's gone to have a chat with his old man— about us I would assume. This thing just keeps getting more interesting."

Kimberly smiled at that. "Are you absolutely sure, Keith, that Greg took the wafer?"

Keith nodded. "Athena's already obtained everything from New Allentown she needed to prove it."

"Even this high up in orbit?"

He nodded again and this time smiled. "Yes. A young woman named Melanie Richards helped our intrepid boy down there get everything he wanted to know about what we all did today. Apparently, if need be, anyone in the city can be tracked by surveillance scans that largely are intended for other purposes. Which reminds me, how was the sunset tonight from the City Top Terrace?" he suddenly asked.

Kimberly eyed him, incredulously. "Nice." She smiled then. "It would have been even nicer, had you watched it with me. They know Frida and I went to the veranda and had a genuine Italian meal?"

"Even what you two ordered off the menu. How was the linguini by the way? You used your ID to register payment for the meal, didn't you?"

She nodded. She huffed, irritably, then under her breath. "Doesn't anyone respect people's privacy anymore? What does Athena want to do about this Melanie person?" she asked then."

"Nothing. Greg's the one Athena's got issues with."

She nodded, lowly. "So we're headed for Capital City to have a talk with him?"

"*No*," answered Athena herself finally.

"Hey, Athena," smiled Kimberly. "You must be really mad about now."

"I'm handling the situation, Kimberly. Keith, there is something I need you to do for me right now."

"Here? While we're still in orbit?" asked Keith.

"Yes," she replied.

"What?"

"I need you to make a long distance phone call."

Randolph Phillips thought his life had totally turned upside down. Here was the very proof of other intelligent life in the universe he'd been searching for and there seemed realistically little he could do with the knowledge.

Greg had gone to the den to make himself and his dad a drink. Randolph remained on the pretend patio deck and in his lounge chair, pondering the playback deck beside him on the cocktail table and the viewwafer it contained. Its sensory data would have to be analyzed diligently. There was a wealth of information within even it, to keep *InterWorld* busy for the next twelve months. With all those ancient accounts— about alien sightings and their somnambulant craft doing what human science had never found a way to explain in the physical universe— filling up space in the archive banks of Earth's libraries, and all of them so easily dismissed as garbage, this chronicle his son had deposited with him was almost an unwelcome irritation. For now the truth would have to be accepted. Life existed on other worlds. And not just intelligent life, but god-like intelligent life, super advanced life that had evolved beyond the need and dependency on physical bodies. The tradition of debunking such absurdities as UFOs and alien visitations among serious thinkers and people of science was one even he had shared. Despite how much he wanted to believe beings such as Athena exited, beings who could fulfill humanity's dream of leaving the home solar system and exploring its universe, proving she was real was going to be a hard sell. And the funniest thing about it all was, what did he really have with this recording? What could be proven? The Hagertons would probably never be heard from again, and any outlandish suppositions linking them to this recording would be met with as much negativism as had all the ancient accounts of humans being taken aboard alien vessels and later returning to tell their tales. God, it was all so annoying. Greg had given him nothing in the final analysis, though the boy meant well. He had in fact taken from Randolph his long standing belief that voyages between stars by any means was largely fantasy. Greg had just shot that theory to hell. But of what use would this new revelation be?

If he hadn't already been sitting down, he'd want to.

"Dad?"

Randolph turned to see his son re-enter the patio deck. Greg had a curious look in his eyes.

"What, Greg?"

"My pendant phone signaled while I was in the den." Greg looked dismayed. "I don't know how, but Keith Hagerton tracked me to Capital City and hacked my pendant account. He called me. He knows I stole the viewwafer. I need to give it back. *Athena*, he said, is 'a little miffed' with me."

"Oh wow, Greg, that's a little worrisome," said his father. "Why does that sound to me like you managed to piss off a . . . an omnipotent being. It's like pissing off one of the gods atop Mount Olympus. You don't look so good, son."

"You don't think I know what I've done?" He thought of little Jeffrey Hagerton. Making Greg a female would be the least awful thing she might do to Greg. What she did to that poor little boy, she did in kindness, in her mind. She knew Jeffrey Hagerton secretly wished he'd been born a girl. But him? With a single thought, there might be a scorched rug stain on the floor where Greg had been standing just a second earlier. Greg wasn't sure he wanted that drink anymore. He almost wished that patio balcony was real; he wanted to rush over to the rail and throw up. "Dad, I need a minute," he told his father, and hurried off to his father's nearest restroom facility.

It was at that moment, as Greg sped out of the patio, that Randolph's pendant beeped. He touched it, allowing its neural circuits to communicate directly with his brain. "Phillips, what is it?" he said in his mind and out loud. There was no answer for several seconds but he sensed someone was there. "Who is this?" he pursued. "How did you get this code? It's my private number."

"Congressman, how are you? I take it Greg's a little worried he pissed off Athena?"

"WHO IS THIS?"

"I gave Greg Athena's message, but it looks as if he's too 'upset' at the moment to finish repeating it. Athena wants to arrange a meeting."

"You're Keith Hagerton from New Allentown?"

"Congressman, stop wasting our time. Yes, it's Keith Hagerton from New Allentown. Athena has requested the pleasure of your company and she wants me to pass on a request, actually a demand."

"How did you get this number?" insisted Randolph.

"Do you really want to try Athena's patience with nonsense?" he asked. "It's not you, not yet, that she's angry with. But you can get there very quickly."

"Are you threatening me?" Randolph could hear the man chuckling at that, almost as if Keith Hagerton were purposely mocking him, deliberately taunting him.

"You have worse things to worry about than anything I can do. You viewed my viewwafer, no need to deny it. I already know you did."

"What is it you want, Hagerton?" Randolph spat.

"Return the archive Greg took and forget you ever saw it."

"And why should I do that?"

"Congressman, do you really want to piss off a being like Athena that way?"

"Okay. Should I expect <u>you</u> or will she be coming to retrieve it herself."

"Yeah, that's really amusing, Phillips," spat Keith. "No. She'll/we'll meet you in the old city in an hour."

"The old city? D.C.?"

"That's the one. At the top of the Washington Monument. Take the stairs, top floor, the Observation Deck. Some really nice views of the old city from up there. Athena's not expecting you to wait for her at the tip, outside, although that is a sight I'd get a kick out of seeing: you with the Washington Monument's pyramidion tip poking you in the butt."

"You want me to climb all those steps to the top of the Washington Monument?"

"Well, if you can't handle it, I suppose there's always the elevator."

"It's shut down after dark. Not available."

"The stairs it is, then," replied Keith.

"The Mall's closed. So is the city. We can't get in."

"The great Randolph Phillips? A man who pretty much gets what he wants? You'll be there. Don't force Athena to come to you in your suite of rooms. She might not be so willing to let you off so easy."

"You want me to come alone?"

"God, no," said Keith. "Take that miserable excuse of a son along. He's the one Athena's really got an issue with. As soon as he's done getting his stomach to settle back down that is."

"What makes you think my son is upset?"

"Because I see you," Keith Hagerton flatly replied.

A spectral manifestation of a young man in his thirties suddenly appeared beyond the balcony railing, his ethereal essence fluttering as if in an unseen breeze. He simply gazed almost hauntingly at Randolph. Greg's dad couldn't move; his heart felt like it was suddenly beating a mile a minute. The man's visage reminded him of all those ancient stories about ghostly presences appearing in the dark of night, uttering not a word, only staring as if to deliberately intimidate the living.

"Sorry, Dad," Randolph heard his son speak from the living room as Greg approached the patio. "I made it just in time to not make a mess in that really nice shitbox of yours, and. . . *Oh, shit! Dad! Oh my god!"*

Greg's pendant phone beeped in his mind. A weird crackling accompanied the voice that filled his brain. "Feeling better, Greg?" came what sounded like only an approximation of Keith Hagerton's voice.

Greg stood mesmerized by the sight of Athena's manifestation. Her fiery presence totally lit up the darkened patio.

"Athena is asking me if you like this little show of her abilities. I've never looked better, right?" Keith Hagerton continued to the two of them as his spectral visage continued to silently stare them down. "We're serious about this, gentlemen. We'll see you two in one hour. Washington Monument. Observation Deck. We'll be waiting."

Just as quickly as Keith's presence had entered, he departed again, fading as if a candle slowly dimming until it was totally gone. The silence that suddenly pervaded the patio was worse than that of being in the bowels of the Earth beneath Crystal Cave. The two only looked at each other.

"Dad, I'm sorry," Greg told his father. "I've got you messed up in something very . . ."

"That's all right, Greg," an obviously very rattled Randolph answered.

"Dad?" queried a totally confused Greg.

"He wasn't really here," Randolph declared.

"How do you know?" Greg asked.

"If he were truly here, a manifestation like that would have set off intruder alert sensors in the whole damn city. Do you hear any blaring?"

Greg focused his hearing to pick up the subtlest suggestion of distant claxon alarms. He heard none. "That was all just . . . what was it, then?" he asked his dad.

Randolph nodded. "What those paranormal types call an *astral projection.*" He nodded and pulled out his pendant phone. "Security," he spoke into it.

"Capital City security. Main surveillance center. Go ahead."

"This is Congressman Randolph Phillips in Sector 8, Level 3, and Executive Suite 504."

"Yes, Congressman, how are you tonight?"

"Fine, for the most part. Are you reporting any disturbances in the city?"

The officer down in the main surveillance center did a quick check of his equipment. "All readings are normal. Is everything all right, Mr. Phillips?"

"Yes, just checking. Thank you. Goodnight."

"Good evening to you as well, Congressman."

Randolph glanced to his son once more. He shook his head. "That was impressive. Wherever that entity of yours is she wasn't about to risk coming here. She sent us an image of one of her captives as proof of what she was capable of."

"She projected that image of Keith Hagerton just to—" began Greg.

"Yeah," nodded Randolph, ". . . to impress us, and scare the crap out of us. Speaking of which, how are you feeling now?" He grinned at the thought of his son's situation a few moments before.

Greg nodded. "I've been better." He nodded some more. "I'll live."

"Keith Hagerton sounded strange to me. Like it wasn't really him. Did you pick it up on that too?"

Greg considered it. "You mean like his voice wasn't quite real?"

Randolph nodded. "Almost as if it were synthetic. We were picking it up in our neural synapses. That's the way these pendants work, assuring us total privacy. But I'm not sure that was really your Keith Hagerton we were talking with. He may be this Athena's prisoner. We'll find out eventually, I'm sure. In the meantime, they're waiting for us at the top of the Washington Monument."

"We're really going out there . . . at this hour of the night?"

"You said it yourself," Randolph answered. "Pissing off a god-like entity like that one?" He shook his head. "Bad move." Randolph smiled then. "This Athena of yours is one impressive lady. I haven't felt a rush like this since the *Stellar Quest* left the solar system. Guess I ought to thank you."

Greg was too off-put to know how to respond to that. "Glad to help . . . I think," he only returned.

CHAPTER SIXTEEN

-1-

In an hour, thought Keith of the rendezvous with the Phillips's. He sat before his desk in his apartment's study, the surface of which (like his real one back on Earth) could be made to become a full surface imaging panel. On it at the moment he had painted an image of their descent back for the Earth. The angle was low just a few hundred meters above and west of New Allentown. Kimberly was many levels down in this pretend version of the island city, in the transport department's main flight deck. Rows of air transport of various size and use were on racks and shelves before her. Like the rest of the city, in this version, all of New Allentown was a deserted city. Only Keith, Kimberly and their kids inhabited the place. Athena had the schematics to the whole city and could "pattern" any part for wherever within it the Hagerton clan wished to visit. But it was eerie, alone like this, walking through an entire seemingly abandoned city. It just felt empty.

***

Before her lay a departure ramp and a "pretend" force field barrier keeping out the outside world of upper Berks County in Pennsylvania (pretend wise of course; none of it was real.) But it sure felt like it was. Before one of the massive deck's egress portals sat a sleek, silvery gray air car, its gull wings raised for her inspection, at rest upon the flooring that led out to the world beyond. It was an interesting design, in the shape of an old style expensive sports car, a Lamborghini, she believed Athena likened it to.

***

Like herself in this realm of Athena's essence, it was an image recreation. She and Keith had had Athena create both a phantom image of the air car (from its stored memories of the air car's molecular pattern) and the flight deck Athena intended to return it to. It was hard to believe that it was the very same vehicle that had started all this, the very one Keith and Jeffrey had used early yesterday morning to leave the real New Allentown and visit Crystal Cave. Keith wanted to return the rented real one he and his son had used that day to its proper berth in the real New Allentown. Would it actually be the REAL air car they'd used, and not an energy to matter rematerialization, a copy in effect? Who cared? They'd get it back. The Hagertons could not be blamed for absconding with a valuable piece of city property. At Keith's request, Kimberly had gone down to the Hanger deck (although in her case all she had to do was picture herself there and in seconds she was) to thoroughly check out the air car's interior to make sure everything had been stowed within it, properly. Keith wanted to make sure that when he sent the air car back to New Allentown, the transport department had no complaints about its condition.

Onto his desk now in his study he called up the layout of the New Allentown flight deck, the real one with all the vehicles perched in their proper berths. He found and verified the location where his and Jeffrey's belonged. He had asked Athena why she was assigning all this to him, why she didn't just attend to it herself like she'd done everything else. She had only responded, "Keith, honey, you and Kimberly need something to do for the next hour. Enjoy the distraction."

He had harrumphed an "Uh huh," and got to work.

When Kimberly eventually returned, rematerialized back in the apartment and informed him that her inspection was complete, he would deposit the craft in its very own berth within the flight deck garage. The city's computer file on the craft's maintenance specs had been as accurate as to even give him the correct berth.

"They're never going to believe it," Kimberly had said of the task Athena had assigned them.

"It'll shock the shit out of them," Keith had said, grinning, weakly.

It was approaching one-thirty in the new morning. Keith felt the effects of the long day that had just an hour ago passed. He leaned back in his desk chair, and arched his back. His behind felt sore from sitting so long, which was impossible, he didn't really possess a real behind to get sore. He had to do try some ancient meditation technique, from Tibet perhaps, to train his brain to quit expecting things to cause aches in this realm as they did in the real world. It was a silly bad habit he thought he was developing. He even if he allowed it could feel the urgent need to run to a bathroom and attend to some primitive bodily functions and "needs."

Old habits, he thought. *Got to work on that.*

He rose and stretched, leaving his study for the living room terrace view. New Allentown's lights and navigations beacons (the real New Allentown just below and on the surface) twinkled, solemnly, in the advancing night. He closed his eyes and made the pretend living room go away. When he opened them again he was in Athena's orb bubble and seemingly suspended only a thousand feet or so above the Blue Mountains and their foothills. He imagined that only a thin piece of glass held him so high above them, and kept him from falling to his death. It made him dizzy; he told himself to stop looking directly down.

He gazed to the stars in the night all around him. The effect was nothing less than awesome. He was like an enthusiast riding a hand glider over the Pennsylvania countryside. He smelled the scents of autumn, and felt the breeze of so high an elevation. And he was elated to be offered such an immersive experience of the world beyond Athena's orb. The chill he felt upon his arms kept him alert for the activities Athena still had planned for them for the remainder of the night.

"Keith?" He felt Kimberly's hand suddenly upon his shoulder. She was right in front of him before the terrace view window in their living room. "Where were you just then?" she asked.

The stars north of the city haloed her thirty-year old slender form.

"Kimberly?" he said.

"Keith, you looked a million miles away. Where were you?"

"You saw me here the whole time?"

"Yes, weren't you?"

"I guess that just proves we're not really anywhere at all. Check this out, Kimmy," he said. "Close your eyes and picture yourself in Athena's orb, where we're really are."

"*Oh my god,*" she exclaimed. "Jesus, Keith, is this safe? I feel like I'm about to step off the rim of the city and into air." She fixated her attention upon the rim of the real New Allentown before them both. "That's the real thing down there, right?" she queried.

He nodded. "We're right above the city. There's where we were yesterday and you and Frida last night." He pointed. "The City Top Terrace."

Under its glass-enclosed bubble were revealed colored fountains, amid a myriad variety of trees and shrubbery and flora. "The terrace looks so small from this angle," she said, looking up to the mountainous region the city reposed within.

"It's just like seeing it in a hologram exhibit," Keith returned.

"But at least in one of them," she replied, "you know where the floor should be. This bubble of Athena's looks like it could pop any second. Is Athena's orb in danger of being seen?" Kim asked, turning to look back upon the remainder of the city.

"Not likely, at this hour of the night. And you forget how tiny Athena's orb really is. Is the air car okay?"

"It's fine. You and Jeffy weren't that messy with it."

Keith grinned. "Athena?"

The view abruptly fell forward and swept toward the lower levels of the city, finding its way for one of the real New Allentown's flight deck portals into the city. There was a real, authentic force beam barrier before this one they now approached, keeping out the topside world of the Earth that humanity had forsaken for the planet's sake. It also however assured that no disease carrying microbes entered the city.

By this point the vertigo inducing effect of the rapid sweep for the city was having a very dizzying effect on Kimberly's and Keith's well-being, but it was better. Athena's orb slipped right through the force shield as if were nothing at all, and wandered around in search of the berth Athena, Kimberly and now Keith knew was the borrowed air car's place of repose. When she (Athena) located it, being as small and virtually inconspicuous as the orb really was, it climbed the shelves and settled inside the berth and hovered there for several seconds. The flight deck was of course occupied even at this late hour of the night, but by only a few personnel and it never would have occurred to the half dozing inhabitants at that hour to even be on the lookout for such an oddity entering their city.

Before Keith and Kimberly came an impression of the air car in the deserted pretend flight deck of Athena's. The air car as yet at rest on the flight deck departure ramp melted into nothing.

"Transport and molecular reassembly commencing," Athena replied.

She (her orb that is) removed herself from the berth and at once a real version of the air car that Athena had seemingly "destroyed" yesterday in the Crystal Cave parking lot solidified into presence in its berth, now officially returned to the city, and ending in everyone's minds that this was a matter that had until then had yet to be resolved.

Now it was, and as surreptitiously as when she had entered the city, Athena just as stealthily departed it again, removing her orb presence right out the same egress panel she had entered. Soon, Kim and Keith felt the sweeping sensation once more as they were lifted far up into the air, New Allentown (the real one) falling away and losing itself against the autumn tinted landscapes of hills and mountains all around it.

***

"I'd love to be there when they find it," Kim said of the air car, the thought making her smile.

Keith smiled as well, lowly shaking his head. "Care for a quick hop over to historic Washington D.C.?"

She smiled again, nodding.

"The hour up yet, Athena?"

"Commencing D.C. excursion NOW," she answered.

"Like this?" Kimberly asked of Athena's field bubble. "I feel like I'm on a magic carpet."

"That's as good a simile as any," he returned.

Slowly, the terrain beneath their flight turned and Athena's orb descended for the west. In seconds it was skirting the hills and valleys of upper Pennsylvania on its way to Virginia.

Kim watched the terrain roller coaster past them.

"Like it?" asked Keith.

"Yes."

"I had a feeling you might."

"You're liking this too much, Keith," she said. "We're captives, remember?"

134

"I know."

Athena's orb continued into the night.

"I don't know, Dad," contemplated Greg as he and his father seated themselves in the air car Greg had requisitioned from New Allentown. "When I told your flight people here in your city you and I were only going for a spin around the old capital, just to check it out, I had to remind them you were my father. They looked at me, strangely— two guys, at this hour of the night."

"You're not my type, Greg," his father said.

Greg looked over at him. "Don't worry. I gave up a night with Melanie Richards for this."

"Is she cute?"

Greg smiled and nodded. "She's great. Although I'd say about now I'm probably the last person she wants to see." His father looked over at him. Greg shook his head. "It's a long story."

"Oh."

"You really woke up Commodore Roger Stakely for this?" Greg asked.

His father laughed and then nodded. "The old guy probably wishes I drop dead, disturbing his sleep like that, simpy to alert D.C. security we'd be buzzing around the Mall Complex historical buildings, but I got us permission, just the same. (The commodore, retired, was head of District Columbia historical management and was curator of the old Smithsonian Institute Society.) "He said I was really pushing our acquaintanceship."

"I'm sure you handled it like a true diplomat," Greg grinned. "You bullshitted him, no doubt."

"Whatever gets the job done."

Greg grinned. He saw movement then ahead of him in the viewport. The egress panels of the flight deck yawned opened before them. The beautifully star-filled night shimmered solemnly above the rolling hills, and off in the distance the Potomac River glinted tranquilly in the moonlight. Its presence weaved south-eastward toward the old city, and would make an effective navigational fix for Greg to follow.

"You're cleared gentlemen," came a technician's voice over communications. "Please signal over channel A 7, Mall Complex Security, when you pass over the area so they can drop the cocoon. Enjoy."

"Thank you," Greg responded. He pressed the Neural/LaserScan actuator on the dashboard before him. "Leaving now, I mean . . . commencing departure." A network of beams descended from the ceiling and onto his head. He took a breath, and with a silent nod, ordered the air car to leave the flight deck and to enter the night. Soon the jewel-like Capital City, suspended upon its four pedestal struts and residing upon a shallow hill within a kilometer of the banks of the Potomac, fell behind, receding into the wilderness of upper Virginia. To the south west Randolph noted the beginnings of the Blue Ridge Mountains down by the ancient town of Front Royal, and their solemn march southward amid the gray of the night. For humans in an age when life could be spent forever within sealed megastructures (the island cities), such open vistas as this seen in the dead of night was as alien as the desolate landscapes of the Moon must have been to the early lunar settlers back in the 2100s, or perhaps, contemplated Randolph, this is how the terrain must have looked and felt to the first English pioneers such as Sir Walter Raleigh back in the 1500s. The Earth had been given back to its rightful owner; Nature. Humans no longer considered the planet their birthright. If the Earth were to survive, humanity would have to reduce its existence upon it to even lessor extents than presently, as detached as that now was. Out here alone with the stars, as the wilderness consumed the horizons, Randolph knew that humanity could never claim the Earth again, must never attempt so, must instead move on. He looked up at the Milky Way, streaking across the sky, and wondered where amid it humans could eventually settle if they were even given the opportunity. It bothered him that he and his son were simply submitting to this Keith Hagerton character's conditions for a meeting. He would have preferred making some arrangements to assure that Hagerton and his family — and that incredible orb entity, Athena, would be prevented from departing the planet. Athena, as advanced as she was, in all probability could solve all the issues humanity currently had designing vehicles that could transcend the boundaries of space and time. She obviously crossed space with a nonchalant ease that unsettled him. She had to be detained, studied, her wraith notwithstanding, it was too important. The thought that her knowledge might be lost and this modern-day Swiss Family Hagerton (Robinson, whatever) was just going to sit back, do nothing and allow it, turned his stomach.

Historic Washington D.C. — or what remained of it— glinted on the horizon, a brilliantly lit area of ancient monuments, parks and federal department buildings. Above it in the shape of half spheres, scarlet blue cocoons of energy glowed faintly like veils above the Mall Complex, Arlington Cemetery, and other neighboring parks and institutions.

Chris MacIntire, late-duty guard in the Mall Complex Security Division (located in a small marble building camouflaged to look like yet another monument and situated on the grounds of what at one time was the Nation's Pentagon complex) had just returned from answering some special, on-site check request from one of the monitoring consoles. There'd been a potential problem in the Air and Space Museum in the

Smithsonian complex. A surveillance sentinel had reported that one of the chains, holding up the Kitty Hawk airplane, had looked as if it might be coming loose.

It hadn't been. He intended to recheck the "trouble-shooting" programs when he returned. Such a report was absurd, considering the care to which the artifacts in the museum complex were given.

The Pentagon itself, now totally gone, some argued should have been made a monument itself, an homage to a time when "global security" was pursued with a paranoiac vengeance. The world had not known the likes of its kind for almost three-hundred years. It amused Chris that his duties were housed in a place where such military politics were practiced in the past. He often times paused on the exterior grounds and tried to imagine the days when men and women traversed the Pentagon's halls, defending humanity against its own immaturity.

Nothing noteworthy had occurred, he learned upon his return to the facility. All the displays read normal, not an *Attention Alert* upon any of them. He stretched his muscles and drifted over to the huge 3-D display hologram of the Washington D.C. Park before him on an illuminated table. It recreated in miniature the entire Mall area (surrounded by a miniature simulation of the trees and hills that perimetered the old D.C. area for ten square kilometers). It reminded him of the tiny Mall complex model that was showcased in the Smithsonian reception lobby and which dated from the Twentieth Century. The only difference between that one and this one was that that one was showcased under glass and contained actual models that had been meticulously crafted and patterned after their real counterparts outside along the Mall. This one on the other hand could be changed to isolate (for detailed surveillance and inspection) a specific building or sector anywhere within the ten kilometer range of the surveillance cameras, and it didn't require a glass bubble shield to protect the models. Should Chris reach down to touch one of the tiny building holograms, his hand would only go right through it and reveal it to be only an image field recreation.

It always struck him as funny to see the tiny Potomac River within it— just off the Lincoln Memorial and running north until it seemingly fell off the image display surface— slowly churning and slithering as if a thing alive. He was tempted often to touch the "river" relief, and always fully expected to get his hand wet, because the image looked so real. But all he did was touch the base of the imaging surface beneath the holographic display.

He was alone. Joe Slater, his co-worker, was off checking the north quadrant, beyond the main force shields. Chris MacIntire had the entire facility to himself.

Nothing of any consequence ever really threatened the Mall. Rarely did the surveillance network spot anyone nosing around the outer cocoon area. Renegades inhabited a few of the more intact buildings about the old city's perimeter. They were rumored to be like the rugged "mountain men" of the nineteenth century, citizens of the planet who needed to go off on their own in the wild and live on the land. They were kept in check. So long as none of them attempted to re-establish land-based societies and lifestyles that would threaten the ecology of the open wilderness, they were left to live out their lives in their self-imposed solitude and isolation.

In those times, when renegades did come too closely to the restricted areas, it required little more of Chris than to watch them fail to breach the shields. Only once this year did he actually have to run off someone who had tried to dig his way underneath them. The shield extended beneath the soil, totally enveloping the area. Chris had simply taken a runabout out to the area and told the old fellow to get moving.

The blinking red pyramidion beacons of the Washington Monument began to glow filmy to his eyes as the silence began to work on his attentiveness. He felt himself wanting to whisk the whole scene away with an abrupt sweep of his eyelids. He rubbed them, just as he saw what he thought was a tiny speck of silver entering the far North West sector of the image. It was following the Potomac. He went over to the peripheral sensors and verified the target for what it was.

-4-

Greg had brought the air car in low over the river, following its leisurely wind southward for the entire flight, and now pulled the craft over toward its shoreline above the span of the old Arlington Memorial Bridge. In the moonlight he and his father saw the rectangular length of the Lincoln Memorial. It looked as stately as it must have when the ancient city used to surround it. Just ahead, beyond the still intact Reflection Pool, was the one-hundred, fifty meter column of the Washington Monument dedicated to the nation's first and most honored leader. It rose in its flood of orange light, a stabbing finger of white marble towering above the Mall complex. Greg scanned the perimeter area beneath its base and pondered a place to touchdown.

"I'm sure security must be aware of our presence," said Greg.

"We're supposed to call in," Randolph reminded.

But it wasn't necessary. Below them, suddenly, the force shield cocoons faded into nothing, leaving the area open for their perusal. Greg looked over at his father. "Now, how do we land without getting them pissed off at us?"

"Make a broad sweep of the Mall," his father answered. "Then, head back to the Potomac. Let them think we're heading home, leave the area in fact, and then put down in the water. Do you think you can maneuver in the currents and beach the ship over by the Arlington Bridge, hide the ship under it? We can wade onto the bank, then walk across to the Monument."

Greg smiled and shook his head. "We'll still have to find a way to breach the shield once we get on shore."

"I know."

"And we can just walk across the Park without tripping any alarms?"

"They won't be expecting anyone to. No one usually gets past the shields."

"Well, okay, if you don't mind us getting our feet wet," said Greg, " and then walking a kilometer or two, not to mention at least a half hour drifting down river. We'll lose time."

"So, they wait for us," Randolph said.

"What about breaking into the monument, though?" Greg asked.

"I have that covered too," answered his dad.

Greg noted his answer, quietly, and then pulled the air car right up and over the top of the monument, making a wide sweep of the D.C. area. He looked down to the overgrown regions beyond the Mall Complex. Even in daylight it was hard to find evidence of the old city. The Wilderness Society debated constantly whether it made more sense to leave the crumbling townhouses and business high rises to their decay or to just pull them down and clear the land for the elements to reclaim it. For now, however, the debate went on.

***

Fifteen kilometers North West of the city and amid the placid rippling of the Potomac's length, Greg activated the communication network. "Mall Complex Security," he uttered, lowly, into it. "This is Greg Phillips and his father, Randolph, of *InterWorld*, we're leaving the area now. Thanks a lot, guys."

Chris MacIntire, glancing over to the relief display from his central console, indifferently confirmed the communication, wished them both a goodnight, and touch-activated a few wafers on his console.

Randolph, out his side view window, saw the distant landmarks of D.C. again consumed in the scarlet-blue cocoon shields. He looked over to Greg, and nodded.

Greg nodded in return, and brought the air car down to within a meter of the river's surface. He found himself subsequently becoming hypnotized by the river's shimmering surface as it passed beneath the ship. With his thoughts, he nudged the ship ever so gently forward as he killed the thrust all together. The ship floated down onto the river surface with hardly even a splash. Very faintly the hull began to bob amid the current. Greg permitted the ship to follow the flow southward for the time being. He'd make adjustments on the course later using the attitude stylizers.

He saw Washington's Monument faintly aglow against the horizon in the distance. He wasn't looking forward to climbing it.

"Well," he told his dad, "now we wait."

Randolph nodded, vaguely, as the air car continued down river.

Security Chief MacIntire was over by the image display. He'd watched the tiny air car sail off in a general North West heading, about ten centimeters above the surface of the hologram relief. It almost resembled an insect, circling the imagery showcased within the display field. He was tempted to swat at it, but thought better of indulging in such nonsense. It reached the table's edge, and abruptly vanished. Watching, Chris then examined the waters of the Potomac at its northernmost point. A tiny speck at the table's edge subsequently fringed into presence, and then resolved more clearly into the shape of the tiny craft. It drifted upon the water's currents now, southward. He studied its progress for several seconds and then grinned. He walked over to the center console and darted his gaze leftward to the "phone imagizer" unit over by the far wall. He punched out a code and waited. The air above the imaging disk stirred, became ethereal. A bedroom scene resolved into focus. A man, only now stirring from sleep within it, rose and faced his own and smaller unit by his nightstand. Chris saw the night light beside it come on, and the features of the man become even clearer. The man rubbed his eyes and noted the identity of the figure within his own imaging unit.

"Commodore . . ." said Chris.

CHAPTER SEVENTEEN

-1-

Greg worked diligently now. The air car was a flying vessel after all, and maneuvering through the Potomac's currents, although possible, was actually a bit nerve racking. It wasn't as if the ship had a rudder. He very carefully tweaked the attitude "antigrav" beam stylizers, nudging the vessel so that it remained along the leftward shoreline, where its progress could be masked— should anyone be monitoring— among the over brush that protruded out into the river.

Greg took a long breath and exhaled; he looked over at his dad. Randolph was starting to nod off with the advance of the morning. Greg shook his head; he envied him.

I could be asleep myself by this time, he thought. He could have also by now been involved in some very pleasurable antics with Melanie. If only he had left well enough alone in the Hagerton home, once he and Melanie had established that the Hagertons were not there.

He looked ahead again; the air car was once more drifting toward the river's middle. *Go ahead,* he decided, easing back and placing his hands behind his head. He took in the view, instead, enjoying the utter silence and peace of the night. The trees along the riverbanks were dropping their autumn-tinted leaves into the banks before them; the whole area lay alive with the season. He wished he could open a window and feel the night with his senses. But he'd get enough of that as soon as they reached the shore. God, this was a different sort of quiet all together from the deliberately soundproofed interiors of the city. Even a session in the viewing chamber, with an environment visual running, couldn't produce quite the same attitudes within him. He shook his head.

In the distance, then, he saw the Arlington Bridge, and off to the shoreline, the illuminated outline of the Lincoln Memorial as it slowly grew in size. He nudged the stylizers once again, aiming the vessel for a landing before the bridge's span.

This is it, he thought. Very faintly, he noticed the scarlet blue outline of the force shield perimetering the length of shoreline in the vicinity of the bridge. He looked over at his father.

"Dad?"

Randolph Phillips jumped at the sound. Looking up, he saw the phantom shape of the old bridge pylons looming only a few meters ahead of the air car.

"I hope you brought your wading boots, Greg said.

His father nodded, shaking the cobwebs out of his brain.

The stylizers weren't enough for Greg; he brought the main antigrav unit back on line, and gave it the slightest energy burst. The momentum overwhelmed the insistence of the current, and the air car quietly drifted over to the bank. It made contact with a gentle bump.

"Well," Greg told his father then, "we'd better get a tether line out of the back and attach it to a tree, or this thing will drift off with the current. Have you figured out yet how we're going to breach that security shield?"

"I told you, Greg, don't worry about it," he said, departing his chair and entering the tiny compartment behind him. He came out with a tether line and some other hiking gear as Greg locked down the instrument panel, and shut the power down. He didn't want someone (a renegade?) finding the air car and attempting to borrow it while he was away. When he was finished, he removed himself from his pilot's chair and joined his dad in the rear.

"Here," said Randolph, handing him a belt, "strap this around your waist."

"A maintenance belt?" returned Greg, looking down at it.

"You really don't *want* to trudge eight-hundred and ninety-eight steps up to the top of that monument, do you, son? Wouldn't you rather float up those flights, like a hot air balloon?"

Greg nodded. "Yes, but why an *Orbit-Class* model?" he asked of the lift-belt.

As opposed to the lift-only model that Keith and Jeff Hagerton had used in the caverns, an "Orbit-Class" model also doubled as an environment suit. It provided its own internal air and life-support with skin-outlining force field contouring.

Greg studied it and then grinned up at his father. "I get it, Dad," he said. "When we're done with the Hagertons, we'll be so high off the ground anyway, in the observation deck of the tower, we might as well keep going, all the way up into orbit. We can always find work with one of the maintenance crews up there. I'm sure they can always use a few more hands."

"You're getting tired, son," his father said. "Rule number one, concerning the cracking of jokes? If it takes a second breath to get to the end of one, it's too long and probably not worth telling. So, if you have any more like that you plan to make tonight, don't. We've work to do."

Greg managed a grin.

"They're modified," his father said of the belts as he strapped his on. "Just watch what they'll do."

A purple body-contouring shimmer enveloped Randolph's form as he activated his belt. He turned then and pulled open the left side door to the air car.

Greg felt the cool night air enter the craft's interior, and heard the quiet lapping of breaking waves against the hull of the ship. He activated his belt then, and suddenly lost all of it, as the field cocoon enclosed around him. The only sounds he heard now were from his father's belt communicator, when he spoke to Greg.

"You could walk all the way to the river's bottom, if you wanted, and it wouldn't kill you," said Randolph. "You're on internal air and the field acts like a wet-suit."

"Is that necessary?" Greg spoke into his own communicator.

"Until we breach the shield cocoon, yes. For a lot of reasons, including you might catch something out here that no way will you be allowed to bring back with you to the cities."

"What good," asked Greg, "is having done all that environmental work to restore the planet to a pristine state, the air especially? It's breathable again. And yet. . . ."

"The air is fine, the planet's in great shape," his father agreed. "It's **us**. We've spent the last four centuries in sealed cities. Being out here in the wild like this is risky. No telling what can happen. Poison Ivy plants for instance. They grow everywhere out here. We never were immune to their toxins, a lot of us. You brush against a single leaf of those little bastards, get that oil on your skin, you'll get a rash that after all the centuries we've spent indoors might put you in anaphylactic shock. And God forbid if we get stung by a bee out here. No son, it sucks, I know. We worked so hard to reverse what our species did to the planet, and at the same time lost our immunity to a lot of the things that exist in the wild out here. It's a risk to even be out here."

"And that's why we're wearing them?" clarified Greg.

Randolph considered that and then creased his brown. ". . . That's . . . *one* reason."

As Greg paused to ponder why his dad was being so cagey, Randolph departed for the vessel's exterior; there was the sound of water splashing as his feet clomped around in the shallow waters of the Potomac near the bank. Greg noted immediately how the life-belt's field cocoon molded around his father's body and parted the water around Randolph's ankles so that he never even got wet. Randolph threw one end of the tether line to Greg. "Find something in there to latch that to," he said, as he waded to shore and selected an appropriate tree to fasten the other end to.

Greg looked around in the air car cabin and chose his flight seat, which looked sufficiently secured to the floor. Then, he closed the hatch behind him (as well as he could with the rope sticking through), and followed his father to the shore. He noted yet again how the force shield cocoon around him manifested that it was on and present as he nudged his foot idly in the shallow water and felt the water lap up against his ankles and yet not penetrate his clothing. It acted like an outer skin. He liked it.

When they were satisfied the ship was moored, they ascended the bank. The rear of the Lincoln Memorial loomed beyond amid the spotlights. The sky above it showed the effects of both the moonlight to the south west and the ground lighting of the city. There were practically no stars visible; the glare from the park lighting washed them away. The crickets chirped out a concert all around them. It was a hell of a night, an experience that more than made up for whatever inconveniences they would soon endure to accommodate Keith Hagerton.

Greg saw the force shield cocoon rise to ninety meters above him before it arced inward to include the entire Mall. The monument, soaring another seventy-five, blistered a second cocoon around it, piercing the top of the main shield and continuing locally to the full height of the landmark before arcing down to the main city shield on its other side. As they came up before the main shield there by the river front, Greg looked over at his father.

"So what now?" asked Greg, hearing the slight energy hum emanating from the force field barrier. "You know a magic word or something that will create a hole in that shield large enough for us to slip through?

Randolph smiled, and simply walked into the shield. A local fluttering surrounded his body, a disruption in the force field. Like the ripples caused by a pebble's being thrown into a lake, the disturbance slowly cleared and the area of his father's entry became stable once more. Randolph looked back at his son. He motioned to Greg to follow. Greg drew his body up against the shield and watched it come into contact with the one generated by his life belt. The two melded into one another, like two drops of olive oil in a bowl of water being forced up against one another. And as this melding occurred, suddenly the way forward was as simple as advancing two steps more right into and past the field. He slipped easily through. The city shield should have stung him a mild jolt for trying to breach it, and then repelled him back, the same way a thick wall of stone might have denied access to an intruder in an earlier time.

"You can turn it off for now, if you want," Randolph said of the life-support belt when Greg was completely through the shield. He approached his son. "We'll get through the one around the Monument the same way."

"How?" Greg asked. "How did we do that, just now?"

Randolph smiled. "It involves something called frequency beam compatibility. It's the same principal that allows the Monument's personal shield to coexist with and overlap the main shield."

"So that's what that courier delivered to the apartment before we left—these belts."

"Yes, one of the benefits of being affiliated with the space program."

"It can't be *this* easy to get in," mused Greg. "I've never heard of this happening before."

"Well, not just any old *orbit-class* belt will fool the shield like that. You have to retool the belt so that its shield frequency matches the frequency of the wall you wish to breach."

"And you were able to get access to something that unique this quick?" asked an incredulous Greg.

"Can we just assume, son," a very weary Randolph requested, "that the answer is yes, and leave it at that?" He smiled over at his son.

"Okay, answer this then. It's important."

His father sighed. "Yes?"

"How did you know it was exactly eight-hundred and ninety-*eight* steps to the top of that thing?" Greg asked of the monument.

His father laughed. Greg had his father's gift for wit. "You don't think I asked?" he replied, straight-faced. "I asked." He faced forward then to the Monument far off across the Reflecting Pool. "Ready?"

Greg searched the sky. "I don't see the orb anywhere."

Randolph nodded. "They know what we're up to," he stated with confidence. "They're nearby, I'm sure of it."

***

He started forward then, taking a foot path around the right face of the Lincoln Memorial and heading for the Pool.

"Dad?" Greg called.

Randolph turned and stared at him, quizzically.

"These things are also lift-belts. Why don't we just hop over the pool instead of getting our feet wet, wading through it?"

(The Reflecting Pool.)

Randolph laughed. "Sure, and we can yell at the top of our lungs the whole way. We'll be lucky if the surveillance cameras don't pick us up, taking a stroll through the pond like this, as it is. Just activate your force field again."

He smiled at his son, a fatherly smile, now. Greg nodded, and then sighed. He followed his dad across the grounds.

-2-

Surrounding the rise of the green laws of the hill— atop which the Washington Monument stood- were the fifty American flags representing each state in the nation. And before it, the old park benches and roadways encircled it, the asphalt highways dating from the days when ground transport vehicles belched their petro-chemicals into the air as they motored around the Mall area and around the city as a whole in what today would be considered an example of utter madness. And just before the start of the lawns to the Monument, came the distended field cocoon that surrounded the Washington Monument all the way to its pyramidion. Greg and Randolph, their force beam belts still active from their trek across the Reflecting Pool, entered the shield as if it were only a wall of mist created by some vertical-spraying, lawn-irrigation system.

145

Once beyond it, they stared at the rise of the marble obelisk before them. It seemed a spear aimed for the universe of stars beyond it.

"Now all we have to do is reach the top," nodded Randolph.

"We have to get **in** first," answered Greg. "How can you be sure we will?"

"It's easy," said his father. "We open the door and **go** in."

"You mean, it's not *locked*?"

His father shook his head, no, and looked back to the contours of the two cocoon shields. "Why should it? Who's going to get past all that?" he asked of the two force fields.

"Us?"

Randolph grinned. "Trust me, it's all uphill from here."

Greg stopped suddenly in his ascent of the hill, he glanced back to his father. "Look who's cracking stupid jokes now?"

Randolph laughed. "You're right, son," he replied, "but it's way past my bedtime. What do you want?"

There was something so very *Alice in Wonderland-ish* about their conversation, Greg thought, which reminded him again of that sad look on poor little Jeffrey Hagerton's face in the archive when he turned and saw a reflection of himself in the shiny ebony outer wall of that alien space vessel interior. The kid did make a cute looking little girl though. It was a cute outfit. It was a cute outfit. As for now? Greg could never recall having ever enjoyed so laid-back a time with his dad. It felt good.

***

They completed the distance to the Monument, and true to Randolph's prediction, the door was unlocked. They simply opened the double-doored entrance and went in. The elevator sat immediately ahead, dimly visible in the light from the illuminated exit sign above the door. They were carrying one each a marker beacon like the ones Keith Hagerton had used to light the way in the caverns. Greg saw his dad bring out his and command it to light; Greg did the same with his own. It made things inside the downstairs entrance a little easier to see.

In a recessed nook to the right began the upward wind of the stairs, all eight-hundred and ninety-eight steps of them, straight up. Randolph reached down for his life/lift belt and secured the tiny forehead sensor, which he fastened around his skull like a headband. "See you up there," he said to Greg, and like a shot, lifted off the ground level and began to ascend the staircases.

Greg only looked at him as his father ascended. He reminded Greg of a character in an old children's story.

Peter Pan?

Peter Pan never wanted to grow-up, he told himself. Pan wanted to stay a little boy, flying off to adventures, forever. Did that describe his father, who never seemed to find time for Greg's mom, or Greg, himself? Randolph Phillips had been too busy pursuing adventures, pushing back the boundaries of humanity's ignorance concerning the universe, to give any thought to growing up.

You're no prize, yourself, asshole, a voice inside Greg informed him. *Look at you, out here <u>with</u> him! Stable family man you'd make, chasing alien anomalies.*

He took a breath, let it out slowly, and then sent a power-up command to his lift unit's neural-sensor. He lifted off the ground and glanced up to the darkness above him. It was a long way to the top.

***

Randolph paused at a stone engraving, donated from the state of Iowa, embossed upon a wall. He peered up the shaft (it seemed to climb upward forever), and wondered how he would have had the strength and energy to walk the staircases all the way to the top.

Greg came up beside him, touching down upon the landing of the next flight of steps. "Did people really do this on foot?" he asked.

"They forbade the practice," Randolph answered, "in the late 1900s, forcing people to only take the elevator; they were afraid someone might have a heart attack. And there wasn't a quick way out of the monument if a person keeled over halfway up the column. The elevator only made two stops: one at the bottom and one at the top."

"Comforting," said Greg. "I'll wager anything Hagerton was hoping we were too stupid to think of bringing lift belts, and would try walking all the way to the top." He looked up yet again to the shadowed darkness far above the range of his hand-held lantern. "I might have made it, probably. I don't know about you; you're an old man. . ."

Before Randolph had a chance to respond to that, Greg shot a wry glance at him and then shot straight up the shaft. He suddenly recalled an old entertainment visual he'd watched years ago when he was a kid. He reminded himself of some super hero type in a red cape and blue tights, but he couldn't recall the name.

Randolph shook his head, humorously, and directed his lift-belt upward. He soon caught up with his son. An endless flight of steps remained yet above.

CHAPTER EIGHTEEN

-1-

As exhilarating as the "airborne" ascent of the staircase-stairwell might have been, it was necessary near the top to go back to physically climbing the last few winding and roughhewn stone landings that led to the observation "bunker". The observation deck itself at the very top of the monument was neither spacious nor stylish, in fact it was downright drab, gray-colored stone, quite narrow, looking very much like a World War Two forward command bunker. The last few flights of steps themselves attested to how it was not the location itself that was the tourist draw:
It was the view.

The centuries old views out the eight windows— which were reputed to make the trek to the top worth the effort— hung ahead of the two men as they trudged upward on foot the last few winding steps that led to the topmost level of the monument— beneath the pyramidion tip itself. Father and son leaned toward the bunker-like observation lookouts on the eastward side and to the remains of the once great city below them. They faced and congratulated one another for making it to the top.

The night lights below brought the city into view. Remote, but impressive, the view looked exactly as it had in a viewwafer of the Washington Monument Greg had once played, recorded a few years back by the Wilderness Society. Being here in the flesh this time didn't feel all that different. The security cocoon shields glowed and shimmered below like colored bubbles around it all.

"Imagine Earth in the 1800s when these stones were laid, Greg," said Randolph. "People didn't fly in those days; they walked, cities were ground level and kept expanding, taking over the green land. You needed a hot air balloon to see the city from this high up."

Greg tried to imagine a society that knew only this as the one great view of the city. He couldn't.

"They used to line up at the bottom just to see their city from up this high," his father added, absently. "You could wait for hours some days, just for the opportunity, and then had to edge yourself in past a hoard of other tourists up here with you simply to get a turn at the windows." He glanced to the narrow 360 degree "deck" that encircled the elevator, for there was little room at all for much else up this high. Cramped described the place perfectly.

Greg rounded the overlook perimeter, reveling in the knowledge that he had the windows all to himself.

"So where are they?" Greg said of the Hagertons.

"I don't know," Randolph returned.

Greg nodded. The night beyond was hushed, dream-like; open and unspoiled. It was perfect.

Then it happened. It seemed at first as if an electrified sheen enveloped the entire length of the observation deck. A radiant orange light seared across the stone walls as if static had suddenly got loose and spread like a virus.

"What in the fuck was that?" asked Greg.

"I don't know," Randolph answered. He palmed and felt up his chest and hips as if he were doing a crude physical diagnostic on himself. He faced his son. "A scan maybe?" he thought. "To make sure we were here?"

"I hope that's all that was," breathed Greg, taken aback by it. "Dad, she's here." Greg pointed to one of the two "bunkers" on the east-facing side. Emerging from the glass as if it weren't even there and rising to one of the scenic "East Side" photos above the window came Athena's orb, sparking and crackling and very much looking as if it were a static ball or heat lightning somehow invading the observation deck.

It remained there above the window port, its presence dimming now and its snapping, sputtering sounds abating. It lit up the room so well the two of them no longer needed the use of their hand-held marble beacons.

Greg looked to his father; Randolph did the same. "Shall I say hello?!" queried an anxious Greg in near a whisper. It was clear he was very much put aback by it.

"Greg!" whispered his father. "Ease it down at little. We were expecting something like this, so relax."

Greg nodded. He faced the orb once more, bravely approaching it, yet not wanting to get too close. He was well aware that doing so might cause him *and his dad* to end up inside the thing, yet another of Athena's collected captives.

"We are here," he spoke with a forced calm.

But there was nothing in response from the orb. It merely hung there as if only waiting.

Greg looked back to his father again and shrugged, dumbly. He honestly had no idea how to proceed.

"Just as you asked," he said facing back to the orb. "We've come."

A blue spark all at once set the inward wall ablaze. The two Phillips men tensed. It ignited, became vertical, and from out of it Keith Hagerton emerged. He stood there in the shadows before the two men, and simply observed them.

"Gentlemen," he said, amiably, "pretty night, isn't it? A good night for touring the landmarks."

"Are you really here this time?" came an icy retort from the congressman.

"Greg. You don't mind if I call you that? I feel we're well acquainted by this point, considering how much time you've spent fixating on me and my family." He turned to Randolph, then. "Congressman." He extended his hand, again good-naturedly. "It's an honor, sir. Thank you for coming."

Randolph Phillips shook his hand, suspiciously. It felt real enough, he thought.

"Yes, in the flesh, congressman," Keith Hagerton calmly replied.

Randolph glanced back to Athena's orb. "She keeps sending **you**," he observed, dryly. "Won't she speak for herself? Or is it that she can't."

Keith closed his eyes as he answered, "I've been fully briefed; and it's fun to feel a real body again, if only for a little while. So, shall we get down to it?"

Greg crowded near and in a hushed voice asked, "Are you and your family okay? Look, I'm sorry about busting into your apartment that way. I was taking my job a little too seriously, I'm afraid. We're ready to help you, my father and me, to break free from that thing. Just say the word. Can you speak freely, or is this Athena holding your family accountable for whatever you say?"

Keith reviewed Greg's words, assessing their sincerity. Surprisingly, he felt, the younger Phillips really seemed concerned for his and his family's well-being.

"We're fine," Keith said, "but I doubt Athena would allow us to leave, if we tried to. And as you say we are being monitored."

"Hagerton, you understand the seriousness of the situation, I trust," spoke Randolph. "You must allow us to help you any way you can. Tell this Athena, this Eleution, as she calls herself, we need a private place to talk; this is no good. We want to help you break free of that 'thing's' bondage. I can have hostage negotiators out here on a moment's notice, but you have to give us room to work."

"I didn't call you here for my freedom," Keith answered, "or my family's. You have something Athena wants. I've been sent to get it."

"I see," Randolph flatly replied.

"I would just as soon you keep the stupid recording," said Keith. "No one's ever going to accept it as authentic, anyway."

"You know it's difficult to give aid when the recipient can't see it's being offered. Or is it— he won't . . . ? What do you have to gain from your captivity?"

"Well, if you must know, simply a look at the unknown, a chance to go somewhere I've never been before."

"And how does your family feel about it all?"

"They're making the best of the situation. Athena will get wants she wants, whether we cooperate or not."

"Aren't you even a little bothered by what she did to your son? As a father of a boy myself I'd be pretty miffed about it."

Keith pondered that. "Jeffrey seems okay with it. Who am I to tell him he can't be whatever he wants to be? What kind of life is that? Going through life knowing you're something other than what Mother Nature made you, and you're powerless to do anything really authentic to correct it?" Keith nodded, "He seems happy. He's happy; I'm happy."

"You are what you are," coldly answered Randolph, "the person you're born as. There's a reason for it. . But not in your world, I take it. Don't like the hand the universe dealt you? Change it. What gives any human, Mr. Hagerton, the right to seriously try to make an end run around Mother Nature?' You were given a son."

"We'll learn how to do the same thing ourselves, someday. It's just knowledge. Have you brought the wafer or not, Congressman?"

Randolph pulled the tiny crystal out from his pocket and trained his beacon marble upon it. "Satisfied?"

Keith went over to him. He learned toward it and read the tiny ID legend he, himself, had had engraved on the wafer's front. It was his data disk, chronicling yesterday's Crystal Cave excursion.

Phillips stuffed it back in his pocket. One would never believe, he thought, this innocent fool could be worth so much trouble, or capable of producing it. He looked so ordinary. "Before I turn it over to you," Randolph said, finally, "you have to do something for me."

Keith nodded. "Naturally. What?"

"We want to talk with the rest of your family, make sure they are still your family, still exist as themselves, and not been forced to surrender their identities."

"Sure thing, just approach Athena and ask permission to enter her 'lair.'"

Randolph grinned. "And become her prisoner as well?"

"If she wanted you to be you'd be already, Phillips," said Keith, acidly.

"Out here," pointed Randolph. "I need to speak with them out here, where I know they won't be possibly only illusions created by her to deceive me. Tell her to release her captives, so I can talk with them."

"And that's the last she'll see of any of us, correct? A man like you, even with only an hour to get a rescue operation up and mobile, has it probably organized and ready to go into action the moment she releases all of us. Besides, my kids are asleep. I'd rather not wake them."

"You call what they're in, sleeping? What's happening inside that orb of yours is my idea of what hell itself might be like, if there really was such a place."

"Or even heaven, right?" grinned Keith. "Either one there's no leaving after?"

"Those are the terms, Hagerton. I want to meet with your family members, out here!"

"You can't. Athena won't permit that and you know it."

"Let me speak with her, directly," he ordered. Randolph glanced again to the floating orb by the window, who seemed intent to say or do nothing, except observe.

Keith appeared to be thinking. He looked at Randolph again. He shook his head. "I'm sorry. That's not going to happen either. Athena wants the wafer back, that's the end of it."

"Tell her, it can't be. This is way more complicated than that," Randolph answered.

"Of course it is! Which is why my family and I are probably in safer hands, held captive by her, than we'll ever be in yours. Let's not play games with each other, all right? You want her, or more precisely her knowledge. I can see why. She knows stuff about reality, about the universe, that we can't imagine. Did you ever think maybe we can't imagine it because we're not ready? She knows your thoughts, councilman. You're Randolph Phillips, head of the American branch of *InterWorld*. You're on the world council. And as a former aerospace designer/engineer, space exploration is one of your passions. There's nothing you'd like more than to find a way to subdue her, get her to spill everything she knows, leapfrog humanity's knowledge of all things beyond its wildest dreams. Not going to happen, congressman. You have no idea what you're dealing with."

"I usually get what I want, Hagerton."

"I know," said Keith. "Like the controversy in '09, before the *Stellar Quest* left Earth. How many members of *InterWorld* did your committee bribe to get that project approved? I've tried to do specials on the number of scandals that very conveniently came out back then. Several careers went bust. They were the members who wouldn't back down, weren't they? I scanned several of the debates for rebroadcast in New Allentown and Philadelphia. The arguments against a hopeless one-way flight into the galaxy got really heated at times. Like a lot of us, your opponents thought the *Stellar Quest*'s voyage was a waste of time. You might just as easily have sent a probe, they said. That way, if something went wrong, and the probe never reached its destination, it wouldn't be so bad. You're not really going to learn a whole lot form Eighty-two Eridani doing it this way, anyhow. Not only may that crew never come back, there is also no guarantee once they get there that any of their transmissions will ever reach us."

"Those are brave people, I'll have you know, who went on that voyage, Hagerton. They wanted to go. Like you, they were called by the unknown. It's not for you or anyone else to say what they'll be able to achieve once they arrive."

"All I know is the Network told me to back off an in-depth report on your committee, and I suspect the pressure came from very high up."

Randolph grinned. "You're lucky; your outfit is strictly local. If you were one of the global affiliates or worse— an interplanetary, I might have got wind of your presence. You would not have wanted to become a pain in my butt."

"You really are smug, aren't you?" said Keith.

Randolph's grin faded. "Were at a standoff here, Hagerton. You know we can't give back the recording, or allow this Eleution to take you from here and to wherever she's going. She has to cooperate with us first, give us an idea of the people she represents."

"You're kidding?" answered Keith, dryly. "You're lucky she's patient with you at all. That's like a teenager arguing with his old man. Quit embarrassing us all, Phillips, all of humanity, I mean. We're fortunate the Eleutions are benevolent enough to not just consider us a nuisance and end us once and for all."

"And YOU are a citizen of the Terran Federation! You can't just leave! And *I've been very patient with you!*"

"So have I— *with you*! Keith said. "You won't get your way this time, councilman. If you won't give me what I came for . . ." He shrugged. "No one can say I didn't try. We're going to have to do it the hard way." Keith glanced back to the Athena's orb. He nodded. "I'm sorry, gentlemen."

"So are we," said Randolph all at once. He pulled a stun gun from his parka, and aimed it at him. Keith faced back. He'd seen one before, the thing resembled an old-style remote control device from the early 2000s. Randolph Phillips let the light from Athena's orb clearly identify what he held.

Keith smiled. "Do you really think she can by swayed by threats to me?"

"You'll end up on a dissection table, for all we know," said Randolph.

"I'll take my chances," Keith said, "like I did leaving Athena's protection and coming out here. When your political machinery on Earth gets its hands on Athena, if that's even possible, my family and I will probably, conveniently disappear. Debriefing, I think they used to call it."

"You've been watching too many visuals from the Twentieth Century. We don't behave that way, anymore. I don't want to kill you, Hagerton, but if it takes that to get this Athena to release the rest of your family, well . . ."

"Fuck off, Phillips, put that thing away! You remind me of one of those old macho-jock-types whom people once admired four centuries ago."

Randolph fired; an amber-red bolt of energy erupted from the unit's front and tore into Keith's form.

"*Keith*!

Keith jolted. Kimberly Hagerton's desperate cry reverberated through the observation deck. Randolph and Greg Phillips suddenly looked up to the walls at the sound, and then back toward Keith.

A blue spark behind Keith set the rear wall of the monument afire. From out of it a very frenzied Kimberly emerged and hurried to her husband. She took hold of him.

Keith looked down at himself, and then up at her.

Randolph looked puzzled; Keith was fine. The stun beam hadn't even fazed him. Keith smiled, and took Kimberly into his arms.

"Are you all right?" she whispered. "I wasn't sure how far Athena would take this."

"I'm fine, darling," he returned. He looked up to the Phillips again.

Randolph and Greg stared at them both. Keith shook his head and grinned at Randolph. "Feel better now?"

Randolph Phillips saw red. He flipped the beam setting to "lethal," took a step forward, point-blank against Keith, and took aim.

"Dad!" yelled Greg, grabbing his father's arm, "you'll only damage the wall! He's a hologram; he's not really here!" He faced Keith. "*Right?*" Greg was close enough to reach out with his hand. But instead of it passing through Keith and Kimberly's bodies, they strangely felt as real and as whole as he was.

"No, not a hologram," answered Keith. "I like you, Greg," said Keith. "You may be a little stuck on yourself, a little too disrespectful of others even, but you're not really as rotten as you try to be— not yet anyway. There's still hope for you. It's a shame you can't come with us. You'd enjoy it. Athena has hinted that this odyssey we're about to embark on ought to be some great adventure."

"Why didn't my father's shot injure you?" he only replied. "You're as real as I am."

"Yes, we are," Keith said of himself and Kim. "Think about that." He faced Athena's orb then. "Athena?"

The orb disappeared. The "scene" of their presence in the Washington Monument's observation deck "moved," whisked out from under them. They were outside suddenly in the cold night air, all four of them, meters beyond the sloping pyramidion tip of the Washington Monument. Greg looked quickly around him, Randolph as well. Greg's pulse rate suddenly quickened. One hundred, fifty meters below, the old city— its buildings, parks and rivers— hugged the four horizons beneath a canopy of black sky. Greg couldn't help think that in the next microsecond the forces of gravity would awaken and send all of them plummeting to the ground and to their deaths.

Keith glanced down to the ground far below. "Impressive view, is it not?" he said.

Greg told himself to relax, it couldn't be real; he'd dead already if it were. The old city beneath him from this view looked awesome, compared to the view from inside the monument. The monument (speaking of it), all sixteen and half meters of its pyramidion, was right there before them, resembling a pharaoh's tomb from old Egypt. Its red navigation lights were like small suns from this proximity and when they blinked they red-tinted the entire scene around Greg. Just two meters above the pyramid tip, Greg noted the bubble-like bend of the cocoon shield wrapping around the structure, spreading out, and careening down to its distant base. He saw the lawns and hill atop which the monument had been erected. It seemed so very far down.

"Figured it out yet?" asked Keith. "The world you're seeing out there is real. We're not. You're already a part of Athena's lair. You were the moment you reached the top of the monument."

"That orange light that went through the place," recalled Greg. "That was *us* transitioning?"

Keith grinned. "Yes. You entered her field bubble and never even suspected you were leaving the corporeal world behind. Getting an idea now what you're up against with these *Eleutions*? My advice. Stop embarrassing the human race in front of them. We've centuries behind us of doing that. It's got to end."

"You're a pretty smug son of a bitch yourself, Hagerton!" spat Randolph. "So we're captives, ourselves, now?"

"You're Athena's guests for the moment. Welcome to her lair. How does it feel, Greg? To actually be here now, and not just watching an archive re-imagining of the thing?"

Greg said nothing; he merely felt himself up and down, surreptitiously. He felt no different. He then gazed at Kimberly. "And you're children aren't stressed out by all this?" he asked her.

"They're fine, Mr. Phillips. They're *home*, in *bed* and *sleeping*." She smiled.

Greg nodded. "I'd feel better if you meant they were in their *real home* in the city."

"It feels real enough to them. What is reality, Mr. Phillips?"

Greg looked at his father and gestured with his hand. Randolph grinned and then nodded.

"It sounds to me," said Randolph, "like you both have lost your minds, just don't realize it. I wonder if you're even fit to retain custody of your children."

Keith grinned. "You're welcome to secure a court order against us, but I doubt the courts will grant you custody in time. And I can't imagine Athena taking the court order seriously." And then to Greg. "I'm sorry, son," Keith said, "Athena took the wafer back the moment you entered her lair; she wants the copy your father made as well." He nodded then and glanced to Randolph. "She knows your thoughts, Randy old boy. It's easy to do in here. We have no secrets, not really, in this domain, from her at any rate. She's telling me it's in your apartment back in Capital City, she can see where you hid it, clear as a bell. Well, that's where it is for now. It won't be there by the time you get back. . . . Okay, gentlemen, it's been fun. It really has. They're going to wonder, back in Capital City, where you guys are. Athena will grant you one last kindness, speed you on your way."

Like being in an open air elevator that made a quick descent, the scene below rushed for them stopping many feet from impact with the ground. The view then wafted past the fifty American flags encircling the Washington Monument and headed off for the Reflecting Pool, then climbing briefly to clear the Lincoln Memorial and aiming for the Potomac and the shoreline area just before the Arlington Bridge.

The view came to rest then in the grassy bank just above the descent to the air car, no more than two meters from the city's force shield presence, rising seemingly out of the ground, a true round sphere in fact, just that the remainder of it went underground. It was quite clear to both Randolph and Greg that they were inside Athena's orb bubble. They could see the faint outline of its spherical presence just inches from where they stood. Greg reached out to touch it.

"This is where you get off," said Keith. "I've always liked that old phrase," he grinned. *"Just WHERE do you get off, anyway?!* Right here. When they ask where you guys have been, say you've been taking a moonlight cruise. Have a safe trip back."

Kimberly waved, bidding the two men goodnight. Athena's orb suddenly lifted upward, leaving the two Phillips men standing there on the bank before the river. Before long her orb lost itself in the starry night above and was gone.

Greg collected his wits about him and looked first at the Lincoln Memorial, and then to the distant column of the Washington Monument. He heard the river behind him, lapping against the shoreline below. His father was already down by the ship, preparing to untie the mooring line. He seemed preoccupied, or something else. Greg didn't want to risk angering his father by inquiring. He turned then and descended the bank to help his dad.

The eastern coastline of the United States took shape beneath Keith and Kimberly. Off toward Europe the new day's sun begun to rise and burn upon the planet's rim. The stars, that had been masked by the lights of the city, came out now in all their power all around them. The sight was haunting, and Keith and Kimberly pondered them. Then, Kim sighed and looked over at Keith. "That was fun," she said of what had just happened. "Do we call it a night, now?"

"Absolutely," Keith answered. "Did we do all right, Athena?" he asked aloud.

"I enjoyed that as well," she replied. "I haven't had this much fun in several centuries since I was assigned the Earth project. You two have earned a few hours repose."

"Our living room, then, if you please?" he requested.

In an ethereal shimmer the orb bubble morphed into their living room. The two found themselves down by the center sofa, before the terrace view, the room soft-lit in night lighting of blue. Instead of the rolling foothills of Pennsylvania, which belonged there outside their living room on Earth, all of North America instead splayed out before them in the terrace view in darkness and night.

"Do you know where we're going?" asked Kim.

"No," said Keith. "She's saving that one for a surprise."

CHAPTER NINETEEN

-1-

Greg and his father were mostly silent as they prepared the air car for its return trek upriver. Greg was seated at the helm and vaguely touch-activated the laserscan network actuator, the points of laser light descending to his skull and locking onto his brain's conscious command center. He silently requested the ship to power up, and the dashboard brightened into illumination. He touched a few wafers and felt the ship's antigrav propulsion come on line. He commanded the attitude sytlizers to hold the ship at station, where it was in the water. When the readout confirmed that the request had been carried out, Greg looked back to his father who was waiting by the entry hatch.

"Okay, Dad," he said, lowly.

Randolph slipped into the night beyond, and Greg heard him enter the water as he waded onto shore. A few moments later he reappeared in the entrance with the tether line, which he proceeded to unfasten from around Greg's flight seat floor mount. When he finished, he looked down at his force shield belt, powered it down, and then removed it. He looked over at his son, and then down at Greg's unit still around Greg's waist and activated. Greg powered it down and subsequently handed it to Randolph. Greg then looked down at the helm displays, as his father retreated to the rear compartment. Greg ordered the stylizers to turn the ship. He powered up the main drive, and nudged the ship forward against the current. Slowly, the ship began to leave its place beside the Arlington Bridge pylons and head upriver. At his angle in the forward window, already the main attractions of the Mall were behind him, and only the lonely course of the river northward greeted him ahead.

Randolph returned from the rear storage compartment, and took his seat beside Greg.

"Dad?" Greg began.

"It's been an interesting night, hasn't it?" Randolph said. "So that's what being disembodied feels like. We reached the observation deck and didn't notice the change." He shook his head at the subtlety of it all. "An interesting night," he repeated.

"I'm sorry it didn't turn out more the way you wanted it to."

His father suddenly smiled. "Everything went about as I expected it would."

"It did?"

"We may not have Hagerton's home visual anymore, but we're hardly going to look like fools when we try to convince *InterWorld* of what we saw."

Greg looked over at him.

"You didn't really think it would be that easy to penetrate the Mall without security knowing we were in there, did you? As a matter of fact, this Athena probably put on a hell of a show when she whisked all of us outside the monument tip."

"You have visuals? How did you arrange that?"

Randolph smiled. "I didn't get where I am, son, without having some reliable connections. Yes sir, we're all right."

"Athena's orb is only about this big around," Greg returned describing with his hands a sphere the size of a basketball. "You couldn't have got that much of an impressive reveal of anything."

"It's enough to convince the council that *something* occurred up there. You don't see a manifestation like that, a controlled, intelligently powered ball of heat lightning doing what that thing could do."

"I still can't believe we were trapped inside that thing the whole time," Greg pondered.

"Yeah, well, as I said, *it was an interesting night*. It's just a shame Hagerton had enough sense to anticipate my making a copy of that wafer. I didn't think he could ever get to it, not the way he did, anyway."

"Dad?"

"What Greg?"

"You mean, Athena? You don't seem to be giving her any credit for the brilliant strategies at all. Why do you keep ascribing it all to Keith Hagerton?"

"Her, I can't defeat. I actually admire her, what her species has achieved . . . omnipotence, immortality. . . . Hagerton's just an ordinary asshole human being; a nobody. Worse, he's a prime example of all the fight that's gone out of the human race. No wonder his kid would rather be a girl. Who wouldn't, anymore? Men have more or less been marginalized by Mother Nature herself. Hagerton. Got to throw the blame at somebody for all our failures, somebody who can be hurt. Why not him?" He faced his boy. "You okay?"

Greg nodded, pondering all that. "You wouldn't have really killed him, would you?"

Randolph took a breath. Greg had his mother's compassion, not his pop's ruthlessness. A good boy, but not one who'd probably ever get very far in the political arena. "Wound him a little, maybe," he said. "Just enough to get this Athena person to give me what I want. For all of what she is, she has a female heart. Kind of like where our species is headed if we don't put the skids on it."

"And that's a bad thing?"

Randolph scratched his chin. "I'd say it is. I get it, few agree with me anymore. Guess I'm sort of a throwback. Women, though, all compassion, not suited at all for war."

"Is that what this is, a war?"

"With human beings, Greg, yes. Everything's a war, everything's a contest. It's been that way for ages. It's never going to change."

"I hope you're wrong, Dad."

Randolph looked over at him. "Oh? Why?"

"As a species, before Mother Nature sent us scurrying underground and off the planet, all we ever did was make war. Like we can't conceive of it being any other way."

"Like I said, *it's never going to change.*"

"So what you're saying is, as a species we're *fucked.*"

His dad faced him, with an inquiring look on his face.

"If what it takes to get where this Eleution species has reached means embracing a more female outlook on life. . ." Greg nodded. ". . . and we humans just won't let go of . . . testosterone . . . "He nodded again. "We're fucked."

"Probably, in the end, I suppose, but in the meantime . . . think of the adventures that await us in the future."

Greg glanced to the sky. "You mean up there?"

"If we ever learn how to actually get anywhere besides the eight worlds of our own solar system, yes. There's a whole universe of worlds to explore and . . . well, I know conquest isn't exactly in humanity's playbook right now. We're in a low spot at present as a species, pretty much regrouping, waiting for things to open up again, like the way they were back at the turn of the millennium. They will, things always do turn around eventually."

"What about the *Stellar Quest?*"

"What about it?"

"You helped get that project going. Was it worth it?"

"The universe and its immutable laws," he spat. "Can't get past Albert Einstein's general theory of relativity. Can't travel faster than light itself. Fuck that. We're going out there anyway. Giving up is usually a prelude to losing all desire to keep on living. And our species is doing a pretty good job of being that way right now."

"And what about Mitch Katill and his crew? Will they actually make it to Eighty-two Eridani?"

Randolph sighed. "I don't know, son. We can only hope we ironed out all the problems outfitting a ship with enough fuel to last the trip."

"You really want the human race out there bad, don't you?"

Randolph nodded. "Yes. We have to. Look at us— living in sealed cities, so not used to our own outdoors now that it's potentially lethal to us, from things even as pathetic as mosquito bites. You call this living? We can't even reproduce on our own, like in the old days. The universe is trying to obsolete us. We can't let it. We're already at war . . . with it. So . . . about your copy of the viewwafer, Greg, is it safe?

Greg turned to him. "How did you know I made a copy of my own?"

Randolph Phillips grinned. "Where is it?"

"My apartment, in New Allentown. I was surprised that Athena didn't catch it in my thoughts. I tried not to think it, but you know how hard that is."

His father knocked him one on the shoulder. "Good for you. It hasn't been a bad night after all. What do you say we crank up this crate and go home?

Greg looked out at the Potomac. "We're not far enough upriver yet."

Randolph grinned. "Don't worry about it."

Randolph looked down at the displays. He touched a wafer upon it, and a duplicate band of laser points dropped from the ceiling and onto his skull. A mental confirmation informed him he was on-line; he ordered up a relief of the region and the quickest route back to Capital City. He then ordered the ship into flight mode. There was the slightest jolt, and the ship rose into the air, as if it had hit a sudden updraft. The liftoff was that smooth. A second later the Potomac River receded beneath them and into the shadows behind them. Far off to the west they saw the navigation lights of Capital City. The ship was on course and heading home.

Amanda Stakely, wife of Commodore Roger Stakely (District of Columbia historical manager and curator of the old Smithsonian Institute Society) rose from her side of the bed as she noted her husband absent from his own. She put on her night robe, and departed the bedroom in search of him.

"Roger, are you all right?"

The commodore was in the kitchen, helping himself to a brandy, and as he sat at the table, the dim light from above the food dispenser beamed the only illumination into the room. He was in his old, blue robe, which fit poorly upon him that hour. The man looked as if he would have preferred anything to being up at this ungodly hour. His graying hair was sticking out in a dozen directions and his equally graying whiskers made him look like the sort of "outcast"(renegade) he'd routinely chased from his beloved park in his years as Smithsonian curator.

Amanda only shook her head, sadly. "Can't sleep?"

"It's nothing, dear," he answered, hoarsely. "I just had something on my mind that seems to be keeping me up. So I thought some brandy would help me get rid of it."

She smiled. She always knew when he was making up some story to cover what he was really doing. "The Mall?" she asked.

He nodded, awkwardly, and then shrugged. "I'm expecting word on something allegedly important. With Randolph Phillips, you never know, though."

"Do you want me to wait up with you?"

He shook his head. "I'll be right in, I promise. I'm not going to wait forever for this nonsense."

"What is it?"

"I wish I could tell you, Mandy. If it weren't so late, and both of us half dead at this hour, we could both probably appreciate the laugh. I don't know. You go on."

She smiled and kissed him on the forehead. "Goodnight."

He kissed her back.

Phillips, he thought with irritation, as Amanda departed into the hallway for their bedroom. He thought of all the dealings he had had with the man in the past, and of all the stories he'd heard about that character. The man could be downright scary. Downright persistent was what he was, he told himself. He shook his head.

The phone signaled in the den, and he got up for it.

"Go," he ordered it. Onto its surface evolved an image of the Security Complex in the old city, and before a console came the face of the man who had awakened him a few hours earlier.

"It's MacIntire again, sir," the man acknowledged.

The commodore nodded. "Yes, chief."

"They're out and away now, sir, the Phillips. I just finished tracking their craft out over the Potomac. They didn't even wait this time to get beyond range of the peripheral sensors."

"Did you make a visual of what Phillips wanted? Anything unusual?"

Chris MacIntire looked at the likeness of the commodore on his imagizer. Commodore Stakely noted it and the display of the security chief on his own unit.

"Chief?"

"Would you like a copy of it transmitted now, sir, or would you rather wait till morning to come to the center and view the replay?"

"You *have* something?"

"A small something. Honest to God I can't figure out what the heck that thing was. Is it worth all the fuss your political friend is making about it? I don't know."

"What did you see?"

Chris MacIntire described Athena's orb for him. "The only weird part for me is what it did after it left the Monument. It went down by the river, where your congressman moored his craft, and briefly landed atop the bank."

"And? Come on, man, what's the problem?"

Christ MacIntire looked as if he were rattled some. "It took on the shape of a very large soap bubble, of a size large enough to carry a person, and that's when our two interlopers suddenly materialized on the bank.

One minute nothing, the next, there they were. I can't get over that. It literally deposited them there, like it transported them there from inside the monument or something."

"Huh," pondered the commodore. "Then what happened?"

"It became a tiny blue thing again and just shot upward. Straight up."

"Where's it now?"

"Dang if I know, Commodore. It's just gone, that's all I know."

"Did you call the local traffic net?"

MacIntire grinned and then nodded. "Yes. And I felt a fool for it. They had no idea what I was talking about. They said the sky above me was all clear; they did call back a few minutes later to tell me about the councilman's ship. I told them to never mind about that one."

The news perked the commodore up a bit; he rubbed his chin. "Hmm, and Phillips and his son, did they seem all right?"

"They seemed fine. They acted like materializing out of thin air was something they did every day. Descended the bank for their craft and left."

"No point, then, in worrying anymore about this tonight, I suppose. It's gone, huh?"

"Like a bat out of hell. Straight up into the sky. Didn't take long to lose it, the resolution of the sensors is only so good."

"All right, chief. I'll come around to see that visual in the morning. I'll probably be getting a visit from Phillips, which means he'll either be joining me or wanting a copy for his own files. Either way, you better prepare him one."

"Yes, sir."

"Very good, chief. Thank you."

"Have a good night, sir."

The commodore looked at him. "I was, until Phillips decided to involve me in his nonsense. Have a good one yourself, chief."

***

Chief MacIntire departed his center command console and returned to the display relief hologram of the Mall area. The scene was again quiet, no unusual activity among the various, lighted monuments, and nothing along the outer perimeters. He moved over to the relief's memory unit, blanked out the current display and cued up a Playback/Time-Code entry.

The display field lit up once more with a replay of the orb, hovering like a Sensor or Light Sphere in the air, then entered the observation deck of the Washington Monument. Emerging from it again sometime after it wafted downward to the bank and deposited the two Phillips on the bank.

Chris MacIntire froze the playback there, getting his closest shot of the orb.

He shook his head.

Randolph Phillips's *InterWorld* staff was waiting for him and Greg in Capital City's Transport hub, and greeted them as their air car touched down upon the flight deck. Prior to his leaving the city, Randolph had had his staff access the Earth's archive computers and gather all the most recent intelligence (or lack thereof, if you preferred) that had been logged concerning strange encounters with unknown anomalies. They had prepared a summary, detailing prior reports of sightings and weird phenomena in the Berks County region of Pennsylvania over the last few centuries.

Dreary eyed, Greg had paced his father's study, trying desperately to keep from nodding off.

"All right, Marion," Randolph Phillips had eventually begun, "I appointed you team leader of this inquiry. Have you learned anything?"

"Sir, this is a really strange field of inquiry you set for me and my team, and at this hour."

The rest of her team, seated, grinned weakly and nodded.

"Is that your way of saying you found nothing at all?" he retorted, staring reproachfully at the two men.

"No, that's not it at all. Yes, we did; we learned a lot. It's just that this whole area of inquiry is just so . . . *weird*."

Randolph touched his forehead and shook his head. "Noted. What do you got for me?"

"Sir, are you interested in hopefully tracking or locating where this object of yours possibly is going?"

He studied her, curiosly. "Halfway to the other side of the galaxy, I would believe. No?"

"There's a possibility, a faint one, that it's . . . that it's headed for the Moon."

"For the Moon," he repeated. "Our Moon?"

"Earth's." She smiled, weakly, and nodded.

Dexter Sellick and Brian Howser, the other two members of the team, awkwardly shuffled in the sofa's leather upholstery as they handled info tablets and filed through pages of transcript that ran across them. It was obvious they were tired.

"Councilman," Marion answered. She handed him a data tablet with a list of names. "There have been almost fifty different sightings of an object like the one you and your son described, reported over the last four-hundred years in the Berks County, Pennsylvania area, that also coincided with people mysteriously going missing after last being seen in that particular area. The Unaccounted-For list soars well into the hundreds. They've never been heard from again. Sir, have you ever heard of a young boy named Michael DeAngelo and his girlfriend, Melinda Shepherd?"

The councilman tried in vain to stifle a yawn. He looked up. "What's that now?"

"Michael DeAngelo. . ." she began to re-say.

"Vaguely. I know that name from somewhere, but at this hour, my brain's insisting on taking a sabbatical."

"Exodus II?"

"Anyone in aerospace engineer, my field, knows of that." He turned to his son. "Even my son, here, has heard of the *Exodus I.I* In a way it gave me the inspiration to shove the *Stellar Quest* down the Terran Council's throat. But the *Exodus II* was just a proposal; it never made it past the first stages of even being taken seriously. . . . Michael DeAngelo? Wasn't he the high school student from South Jersey before it sank under the sea who wrote a paper about that as part of his entry essay to MIT?"

"Yes sir. And a Charles Mistalavich came across it years later and took it the Terran Council. The rest . . . well, you know. It never came to anything. We're all still here in the solar system. We never left."

"And what about this Michael DeAngelo?"

"He and his girlfriend— Mindy, she went by— she, her mother and father, Michael and Michael's mother . . . Gone."

"Gone?"

"Without a trace. And not a moment too soon. DeAngelo's dad, before he disappeared too, rigged the propane tanks to the house to . . . cause an explosion."

Randolph only looked at her.

"Levelled the house," she said. "This all happened on the day the two kids were due to graduate from high school; they skipped the closing ceremonies. The last traces of info about any of them was a record of their checking into an Inn in Chadds Ford, Pa. And then nothing. They never checked out. The management discovered them gone, no trace of their vehicles or them. There were rumors the two could... open wormholes—"

"*Wormholes?*" repeated Randolph. "I trust you mean the kind those little slimy critters create when they slither through the ground?"

Marion swallowed. "No sir. The fabric of space kind." She pointed upward, drawing a pretend circle in the air with her finger. "Several students claimed to have seen them make them . . . in the air right in front of them. Not big ones. Just large enough to maybe put your arm through."

"Marion, come on," he begged.

"And something also about astral projection," she continued. "There was a weird event that happened at their Senior Prom," she finished. "Some students used the phrase *Poltergeist*-like."

"If they could do all that, Dad," said Greg, "no wonder Athena swiped them."

"Marion," Randolph pleaded. "It's too early for this."

"I have more, sir."

He waved her on.

"The FBI never got to question the kids. But it was pretty difficult to just disappear back then and leave no trace. Surveillance had reached new heights in privacy invasion. It was almost impossible not to find yourself under constant surveillance by any means, and with a population as big as it was in those days, people saw stuff and reported what they saw. The FBI was pretty sure the kids left their parents at the Inn for a few hours and on their own went to the Crystal Cave area. They were later seen returning to the Inn. An eye witness swore he saw the entire group soon after climb into their two vehicles and head up Route 100. After that . . . nothing. They were just . . . gone."

"And this all happened when?"

"2014," she read.

"How do you know, Marion," Randolph soberly asked, "that any of that involved what my son and I are involved with here?"

"The FBI," she said, "uncovered evidence the two kids were planning to do some cave exploring when they should have been getting ready to go to the ceremony to get their diplomas. But there's no record of their having ever gone to Crystal Cave." She nodded. "They must have known another way in."

Greg turned to his dad. "Keith Hagerton kept insisting there was another way out besides the way he and Jeff entered. And it looked as if Athena used it on *her* way out."

"All very interesting," said Randolph, requesting from the apartment's master computer the hour. "But how does any of that figure in this stuff about the Moon?"

"I doesn't," Brian Howser said. "Not really."

"Of course it doesn't," said Randolph.

Marion swallowed, ill at ease. "This next part . . . is a little out there."

Randolph laughed. "I can't wait."

She retrieved her tablet from the councilman and accessed a new file. A middle-aged, heavy-set man, balding, with graying hair fringing his temples, appeared upon its surface. He looked rugged, outdoorsy. The bio beneath his photo read:

WILLARD SOMEDALE
InterWorld Personnel #13567:A7
Clearance Code 9G
SubClass: Subterranean Excavation.
Deceased: November 27, 2304

"After he retired, councilman, for years he lived like a hermit in the trenches of Mariner Valley. He claimed when he was ten and still living on Earth that he saw and was abducted by aliens in a flying saucer. I don't have his full story because he only told so much, and what he did was usually over drinks with his co-workers at the Martian facility."

"So, this is second-hand testimony from them?"

"Yes."

"Okay."

"Willard was told by these . . . little alien creatures . . . purple-skinned . . ." she palmed her hand waist-level in front of her, ". . . about this tall . . ."

"The Barthonians?" queried Greg to his dad.

"Excuse me?" came Marion.

"Just continue," said Randolph.

"These . . . little aliens told Willard of how they left behind a specimen-capture network on Earth and on planet Mars. Humans, who stumbled onto the network, were delivered to a holding facility on the Moon. When a sufficient number were taken, someone from their home planet would haul all the captives . . . uh, back." She glanced upward. "To the home world."

From Randolph. "Is that all?"

"Willard said he was told, after he grew up and became a man, he was to go live on Mars, work and locate the Martian snare network because a miscalculation had resulted in the site's becoming buried during a cave-in that occurred sometime before. It was supposedly caused by a seismic quake, very local, and inconsequential. They wanted Willard to unearth their artifact."

"Their *artifact?*"

"Actually, he described it as a glowing orb."

That one perked Randolph up a bit. "*Where* were these *aliens* that they couldn't retrieve it, themselves?"

She shrugged. "It doesn't say."

Randolph sighed. "Marion, that's quite a report."

"I know, sir. It's *weird*. . . . but it does tie into a little of what you and your son say you witnessed, and then there's this snare network here on Earth and on Mars. All in our backyard."

Randolph smiled, weakly. "And Somedale?"

"Sir?"

"Did he ever find that Martian 'orb'?"

Marion herself couldn't help chuckling lightly at this next paragraph. "It won't make a conclusive claim to that, councilman. There's an artifact in a museum in Mariner Valley attributed to Willard, which he claims he donated to the museum and that he allegedly found in the rubble of an excavation site, but no has ever come forward to ever corroborate his assertions. The report concludes with a vague acknowledgement of his death in 2304."

"Uh, Dad?" called Greg to his father in an aside. "I think I saw what she's talking about, that one time you took me on that trip to Mars." He nodded. "I've seen that artifact, and the legend about the guy who claimed to have found it." He nodded again. "Yeah, I remember that."

Randolph nodded in vague acknowledgement, and then turned again to Marion. "Does it report where, Marion, on our Moon that this whole snare network was based?" asked Randolph. "It's rather large."

"It does actually. The northern highlands. The mountains near the Mare Imbrium valley."

"Which ones?"

Marion nodded over to Dexter on the sofa. He promptly rose and handed Randolph his info tablet.

"Back in 2210, Mr. Phillips," Dexter began. "When the original Cassini moon base facility went up in the crater, there was a weird report of this unexplained electrical phenomena . . ."

"Let me guess: orb-like?"

"Yes sir. November 20th of that year. It was seen tracking in for the Northern Alps, and then disappeared. June 27th, 2210, a young girl, Cassandra Hemmel, a member of one of the first families to arrive at Cassini with the original construction crew, stirred up new fervor about visitations from beyond our solar system for a time after she insisted she'd seen a large fireball pulling up out of the same mountains, disappearing into deep space. She was ten years old. The object wasn't picked up on local sensor arrays. Everyone patted the little girl on the head and humored her."

Randolph Phillips went over to his genuine oak desk, sat down, and buried his chin in his head. He took a breath and considered all of it, pensively. He looked up, then. "If I read you three right, are you proposing we launch a *rescue*?"

"It's a mystery, councilman," said Dexter, "and as Marion said, it's in our own backyard."

Randolph buried his head in his hand, and shook it. "Right, thank you. I'd like all the bases in the vicinity of that lunar range alerted. Tell them to watch the skies, employ good old-fashioned visual sighting techniques, and forget their fancy tracking equipment. Don't say anything about little purple aliens, or orbs, not yet; I'll do that. It'll sound more genuine coming from me, not much, but a little. If what we're investigating gets out prematurely—"

"You'll be laughed right off the council floor," finished Greg.

"Thank you, Greg," he told him.

The three staff members as a group, rose and bid their goodnights.

***

After they left, Greg watched his dad grab his forehead and head for the den. Whatever he was pouring, Greg imagined, it would probably be a double.

"Wow," said Greg.

"Talk about grasping for straws."

"I think about now you probably wish I'd never stole that viewwafer. You'd have got a decent night's sleep."

Randolph took his brandy shot and saluted Greg on that one. He gulped it down. "What can I get you?

"Nothing for me, pop," he answered. "I'm barely standing as it is. I got to crash."

His father grunted a yes. "Time?" he called.

It was almost five.

"The whole damn night's gone," Randolph said.

"You'll want me to fly back to New Allentown, tomorrow, won't you?" Greg inquired.

"For?"

"My copy of the viewwafer. Yours is not here, right, as Keith promised?"

"Yeah, it's gone; I checked. I don't know how they do that, enter the city and leave again, and the sensors don't go nuts? But yeah, it's gone."

"So, are you coming with me to New Allentown?" Greg asked.

His father made himself another drink. "Can we talk about that one in the morning? We can work out the details, then. Get some sleep, son. Tomorrow ought to be quite a day."

Greg nodded. "Goodnight, Dad," he answered.

PART THREE: MOON.

CHAPTER TWENTY

The <u>Stellar</u> <u>Quest</u>.
Mission Status and Location:
"On Course and Four Light Years out."
CREW STATUS: IN HIBERNATION.

October 24, 2415, three days prior
Earth time, one and a half, ship time.

Mitch Katill, *Stellar Quest*'s commander, his eyes as yet closed, took a long breath and let it out slowly. He began to have thoughts, small ones at first, inconsequential stuff, of no real importance, he only knew he was Mitch Katill and that he had always wanted to be a pilot, even if in his time those who were as employed as such were in a mostly passé occupation as humanity for the most part no longer needed to really go anywhere physically, not when doing so could be accomplished so consummately with virtual reality. Access a Sensor Sphere crystal afloat in any of the solar system ports humans these days called home and it didn't matter where your physical body reposed; it only mattered that your "mind" through the sensory array within the Sensor Sphere crystal could give one the reality of being wherever the crystal unit itself currently was situated.

There was only one place left where no Sensor Sphere crystals reposed and could be "rented" for use, and that was beyond the orbit of Pluto and the great as yet unexplored and empty nothing that existed beyond the Earth's home solar system. Mitch always wondered what it might be like to try leaving the home system and venturing out there. Too bad that for the most part that "sci-fi fantasy" notion was only a pointless dream. There was no practical reason to do it, most stellar destinations were too far away.

His mind was losing the fog of sleep now, and he was beginning to recall. He remembered that last day in December of 2410, a month or so out beyond Pluto and the ship left in the high-tech control of the "artificial intelligence" systems on board, that in all probability could probably fly a space vessel way better than any human ever could. He remembered his crew. Doug Bahner, second in command, Monica Cressler, Stellar Quest's communications officer (of any real importance in the first days of the flight when direct communication with *InterWorld* and the solar system was still possible and practical). But as to Monica, that flirty small-framed brunette with the short bob and perky demeanor, she could do so much more than make phone calls back to Earth. She was on board to listen to the music of the stars themselves, their EM signatures. There was his chief engineer, Dexter Ziegler, Angelique Bonnachelli, food and agriculture specialist. He smiled. Angelique, vivacious, blond, tall Angelique. A beauty if there ever was one and as decent a person as they came.

To name a few. All good people. It seemed as if the days following departure from space dock went by very quickly, there was so much to do monitoring the EM drive as it powered the ship upward to ninety percent light speed. The month that passed once they attained their cruising speed, itself felt like a blur, mostly because there wasn't much to really do anymore after leaving Pluto and the solar system. They were in the interstellar voids between solar systems and moving at the speeds they were, all the star patterns out the window ports were gone, their starlight Doppler shifted toward infrared and ultraviolet. And he remembered now, each of his crew bidding their goodbyes for the long sleep (ten years to them, twenty-three in actuality) as they entered their hibernation chambers. And then he all alone for an hour or so, walking the silent ship and wondering if he, they, or even the Stellar Quest would still exist when the time for them all to be revived . . . arrived. Making port of call within a whole other star system, the thought of it, something no human before them had ever attempted to do.

On that last day, a month out and beyond Pluto, he had sat before Monica's communications station on the Bridge, and had calculated that a signal sent back to Earth that day needed at least six, seven hours to thread its way Earthward, and that was ONLY if the antennae calibration had a reliable and positive "lock" on Earth. If not, the farther into the voyage the ship went, the narrower and more precise the calibration had to be to assure the signal hit the Earth (and the Solar System) and not missed both entirely.

Mitch felt really fine, now, content. His thoughts were organizing themselves more coherently than just even a few minutes earlier. He was ready to "wake up," open his eyes; he glanced around to his surroundings, aware that just a short time ago he had awakened, with no idea at all who he was, where he was, and how long he'd been asleep.

He knew the first two for certain (who he was, where he was ;) but that last one. If he were awake it meant the Stellar Quest had hit the outer boundaries of Eighty-Two Eridani's solar system and it was now the year 2433.

He rose finally from his hibernation chamber and looked the "sleep center" over, saw clearly the proximity to Engineering the location was. It was definitely all returning to him. But there was one question that puzzled him. The others. They remained in their chambers and were still fast asleep. The main computer had not yet bothered to even begin the process of bringing them around.

"Computer," he called out. "Are you on-line? Initiate verbal communication mode."

"System on-line," came the response.

"What year is it?" he asked.

"2215," it answered, "Earth time, October 24, 2415."

"Five years?" he clarified. "Only five years have passed?"

"Affirmative. On board chronometers now read elapsed mission time as 19093.2868 hours."

"Which would be what," he asked, "using December 25, 2410 as our voyage begin date?"

"795.553617 days," it replied.

"Just over two years," he calculated. "Two years, two months? That would make it for us about February, 2413."

"Affirmative."

Two years, he thought, *the Time Dilation effect slowing down the very pace of time itself.* He felt fine, like he wasn't any worse for it. The motioning dampening systems on board, and the artificial gravity plating really helped mitigate the effects of such an incredible rate of travel as the Stellar Quest with its EM drive was making through the galaxy. And yet for all its haste, the Stellar Quest was a snail, moving through the voids at a snail's pace.

"Computer," he called then. "Why was I awaken? Is anything wrong?"

"Emergency protocol 001," it returned. "Senior officer aboard to be informed of any and all anomalies potentially capable of jeopardizing or endangering the mission."

"What anomalies?"

"Extravehicular EM spectrum event, source location indeterminate. Type and composition unknown."

"Shit," Mitch thought. "The fuck is wrong?"

He got his head on straight right quick and double-timed it straight for the bridge.

-2-

Several hours later now, the entire crew now revived, it being his decision to do so, Monica Cressler was on station in the bridge doing radio frequency scans, attempting yet again to filter out the Sun's EM emissions noise as it blasted its frequencies of cosmic radiation into the universe behind the *Stellar Quest*. Mitch noticed how her placid, almost bored expression took on a sudden interest, and he had to leave his tinkering's with the log entries to go over and see what she was receiving.

"Yep, here it comes again," she said, "that weird blip over the EM band at a frequency I've never heard of before. God, what a configuration." She took a long breath and shook her head. "The ship woke us up to explain what this is? The fuck does the *Stellar Quest* think we are? I've never seen anything like this. It acts like a radio burst, almost as if our sun were a pulsar and every so often let out a discharge, but Mitch it ain't regular, and it's not a natural radio wave frequency at all, or anything that I've ever seen. In fact, it reads like little more than a weird type of static that the high-gain antennae is just sensitive enough to even detect. I'll be fucked if I know what it is."

"So it's a radio burst coming from our home system? That can't be," mused Mitch. "No signal can travel that fast. We're four years out. It would have to be have been sent—"

"Four years ago! No kidding!" she replied. "Four years ago we were one year out beyond the solar system. The math's all wrong. We can send telemetry and even messages back to Earth, but anything they send us will never catch up to us in time. It's all going to hit us when we slow down and enter 82 Eridani. It's been that way for years now, while we were asleep. Mitch, I don't know what the hell this thing is, but the son of a bitch acts like it just left Earth today. "

"That can't happen," he flatly replied.

She grinned. "Which is why the ship woke you up. It's as confused trying to explain this one as we are. Want to know the worse part? It gets better."

"Am I going to regret saying *go ahead?*"

"Absolutely.

"Let's have it, then, Communications Officer."

"Uh huh," she said of his formal reference of her position among the crew. "An hour ago I got a similar EM burst but from the **opposite direction**, from **Eighty-two Eridani!**"

"You mean like they're talking to each other?"

"Uh huh," she nodded.

"That's not possible either."

"No shit it ain't," she agreed.

"Who?"

"Hah!" she said. "Like I know?"

"Mitch? Remember in the old days of household plumbing, you know the archives from when people lived in 'houses' on the Earth's surface? Water faucets?"

"A faucet? You mean a water dispenser?"

She nodded. "They used to use such things as the end nozzle to a long network of piping. They called it plumbing. And sometimes the seals weren't always tight, and your faucet developed a leak. It used to drive people up the wall at night, *drip drip drip.*" She grinned at that. "Anyway, if you stuck your finger over the spout, sooner or later the pressure would build up and would burst from your finger in an explosive rush. That's what this reminds me of."

Doug Bahner came over from navigation at her plumbing "metaphor". "Monica, what's that got to do with this?" he asked. "What exactly does that mean?"

The two men eyed her curiously, awaiting her answer.

"It's as if somehow we're interfering, we're getting in the way, of someone's two-way conversation, and occasionally there's a pressure build up, that manifests itself as a massive energy blast against the hull. But again, what kind of energy, or EM frequency, and whose? I don't know. The computer will only log it as static, but crazy static, because just before I receive it, it seems to Doppler, as if it's being reduced to a frequency we can perceive as it smacks right up against the ship. Which means whatever the hell this signal is, it doesn't originate in normal space, it can't, not to travel that fast. I don't know what it is, but it must have an almost super-intelligent origin. But Mitch, from <u>both</u> directions, not just from the star system in front of us, but back where we came?"

"Is there any test you can run?" asked Mitch.

"It doesn't last long enough, and it's too random. I wouldn't know how to begin. It's like trying to record a lightning strike. You never know when the next one is going to flash."

"Then, I take it, you can't even isolate where back in the solar system this one just came from. The sun, itself?"

"I doubt it, but at this distance, we're so far out already that to us the eight planets—"

"And Pluto," said Doug Bahner.

She smirked. "*And Pluto*. They're all in a straight line, with the sun's output overshadowing just about everything else. I'm going to have to intercept a few more to seriously convince myself I'm reading a real anomaly, and not just a maladjustment in the machinery."

"Have you done a full diagnostic yet?" Mitch asked.

"An hour ago, but that doesn't mean I didn't miss something, something messing up on a sporadic basis. I may request your permission to leave the sensor array active 24/7."

"Do it. The ship woke us up over this. Might as well be thorough."

"It woke YOU up. But damnit, <u>I'm</u> the one whose hair is going gray over all this."

Doug Bahner laughed. "You might also want to notify *InterWorld*, Monica," he said, "let them know what you recorded leaving the solar system, so that they can begin an investigation on their end."

Doug and Mitch both were standing above her station. Monica remained seated before it. She looked at him, incredulously. "Yeah, good idea, Doug. Four years from now when they receive it, they'll get right on it. Doug, go wander the ship, playing first officer, or something. You're not helping."

"She's right," said Mitch to his first officer. "They can't help us back home, not in time anyway, if this thing gets any worse and endangers the ship. You think it will, Monica?" he asked his communications officer.

Monica Cressler stuck an earpiece in her ear and touched a few wafers on her console. "The *Stellar Quest* must think so. It woke you up after all."

In the forward viewscreen, in the Doppler shift compensated rendering of the view ahead, Eighty-two Eridani loomed a tiny beacon of cold white light, astride the wispy panoramic backdrop of the Milky Way. The waveband algorithm compensator was on. They could see the starlight again before them in the night, even if it was only a waveband correction. Not what really was visible to anyone else of the crew passing the many window ports along the back side of the ship.

It made for a nice image to see real stars and not that damn starbow.

At least they had that.

CHAPTER TWENTY-ONE

-1-

Aboard the Stellar Quest

Monica Cressler spent the next twenty-four hours (her time, not Earth-time) fine-tuning her instruments to try once again to intercept a "transmission burst" as it flew past in either direction— for Earth, the home solar system or Eighty-Two Eridani. Success so far had not come.

It was now autumn of 2415 back home in the American continent. Monica could just imagine the peaks of the Blue Ridge Mountains in her home town of Charlottesville, Virginia, decked out in the bright colors of the fall season. She couldn't help feeling a little sad. Four autumns like it had come and gone, and yet she'd only been gone two months, at least that's how it felt. She wondered if she would ever see the likes of an east coast autumn ever again in her lifetime.

Mitch pondered much the same around Six p.m. that evening, ship time, as he walked the long corridor from the galley, up to the Bridge. He'd just joined the civilian members of the *Stellar Quest* crew to an impromptu meal that Angelique Bonnachelli had concocted out of stores in the freezers for just such an emergency as their prematurely exiting hibernation. Not a few of them were still coming off the effects of being asleep for five years. The meal was a vegetable-synthesized concoction that was supposed to resemble a sirloin cut steak. The mash potatoes she included with them were from real potatoes, also in cold storage, albeit hydroponics grown in the weeks before the entire ship was shut down for the long nap. Mitch, nevertheless, considered it a somewhat halfway decent meal.

Doug and Monica were topside that hour, Doug doing his thing as second in command, satisfying himself that all aspects of the ship's course were in synch. Monica continued to run triangulation scans of the nearby stars to assure her that the "rearward" telemetry signals were in fact aimed precisely back for the home solar system. She also periodically monitored the computers as they automatically ran a surveillance check of those high-band frequencies that had forced the crew to awaken and come out of hibernation the day before. Getting to the bottom of the mystery was becoming an obsession with her, especially because since this morning she'd detected no anomalies at all, after learning the *Stellar Quest* had logged four of them on its own before awakening the crew.

Although Mitch had more or less outlined his recommendations concerning her probe of this matter, last evening the crew had assembled for another one of their impromptu "meetings." It was decided there that it made sense to hold off returning to hibernation until this matter resolved itself one way or another, and as for sending a report to *InterWorld*, that too was placed on the backburner. They would wait until Monica actually had something definite to report. By the time *InterWorld* received such a report from the *Stellar Quest*, humanity back home should have long before discovered the anomalies on its own. If not, it would probably make little difference by that point either way.

"No real point in bothering them with this," Harry Michaelson, planetary systems expert, offered up at the meeting. "This is really our problem; we're all alone out here."

"Thank you, Harry," said Doug Bahner, "for stating the obvious. Now we can move on. Thank you."

Michaelson gave him a return glance, but no point would be gained from exploring that one any further.

All gathered around the conference room table had silently nodded to Harry's assertions and reflected on the implications of it all. Mitch recommended, nonetheless, that the following morning Monica concentrate her scans rearward (back for Earth) because at least in that direction the crew knew what it was dealing with in so far as the presence of an intelligent species was concerned.

***

All of that would soon become moot, however, for Mitch as he strolled idly now through the long corridor for the Bridge. He could see the hatchway to the Bridge just another ten meters ahead of him in the blue-tinted corridor. Suddenly, he heard the following issue from Monica as she called Doug Bahner over to her station:

"Oh, my God, Doug, look! Look what the computer just processed for me!"

Mitch ran the rest of the way, entering the Bridge. "What?" he said. Doug was already by communications, and across Monica's display screens fuzzy pictures of Earth (shots of autumn-tinted hillsides and such) fluttered in and out of focus upon her displays.

"Mitch, you won't believe this!" she said, turning to him. "Look!"

He glanced across her board to the images. It was fall foliage shots from some mountainous hillside region. It could have been anywhere on the Earth, but it was definitely Earth. However, a second shot resolved a series of fast-scanned images from the surface of the *Moon*. Various views of a lunar mountain range (its peaks and ridges) faded in and out upon the screens, within what seemed a series of superimposed symbols (commentary?), running across them.

"Are those images what I think they are?"

"Got to be," she declared. "That's the Moon. No mistaking that desolate landscape, and that was definitely Earth a moment ago. The north east America by the look of it. The question is, *who is transmitting this off the home world?* And Mitch . . . they're live! From right now. Right this second."

"That's not possible," insisted Mitch Katill. "They can't be. Nothing from Earth can reach here that fast."

"Mitch, believe it or don't. But they're current, today. And for god's sake, Mitch, I haven't had time to run them back yet in normal speed, but look at them. What kind of writing **is** that?" Squiggly, wavy symbols, inverted v's, and other geometric shapes wafted across the images as if commentary.

"What frequency band did these come in on?" he asked.

She shook her head. "I was tuned **way** off the high band scale. Let me work, okay. There may be more coming in. I'll have a summary for you as soon as I can."

Mitch turned to Doug. He nodded. "Doug, assemble the crew. A half hour too soon?" he inquired of Monica.

"Fine," she said, absently, her eyes glued to her monitors.

Mitch turned to his first officer. "Conference room, 1800 hours. Everyone. You have the Bridge, Doug. . . ." If you need me I'll be in my ready room.

Doug nodded, and leaned down over Monica's shoulder. Her eyes remained glued to her monitors.

The Conference room was a white with red trim facility about eight meters round, back on level two of the *Stellar Quest*'s three main levels.

Mitch Katill looked over at his communications officer. "All right, Monica, tell us about your strange signals."

She nodded and cued up a series of visuals. Onto the imaging disk in the table's center came a representation of the geometric symbols that she had seen superimposed beneath the visuals. "They're meaningless," she said. "Without an alien culture's version of a Rosetta Stone as a guide, we have no way to make any sense of the symbols, what they mean, anything."

Rita Knowler, civilian, Linguistics expert, spoke up: "Unfortunately, without references, you're right. But I want a copy of the original sequences, anyway. I'd like to study them for groupings and such. There's a recognizable pattern in anything created by an intelligent mind. I don't promise anything, but I'd like to look them over."

"I make you a copy," Monica promised her.

"Monica?" Mitch interjected. "Is that it?"

"No. The whole transmission lasted about 150 milliseconds, just a signal burst. We're talking way sophisticated stuff. Between my tinkering's and the computer's persistence, we managed to hit the right deciphering code that dropped the carrier frequency and allowed us to download the information it contained. It just happened. I couldn't guarantee it would ever happen again. I just got lucky. I just hope their intended recipient in 82 Eridani doesn't get too pissed off to find we swiped their email. We didn't just read it; we downloaded it." She shook her head at the thought of what type entity was wondering about now how and by whom their reply email got hijacked. "Oh boy," she said.

"You insist," Harry Michaelson interjected, "they were sent this very day . . . from back home. Isn't that an incredible postulation?"

She shrugged. "You have a better explanation? I have plenty of *theories*. I'm sure you do too. *Tachyons*, elemental particles of matter that behave just the opposite from other subatomic particles: they can't travel *slower* than the speed of light. Maybe there's a way to lay signals on them piggy back-like, like the old AM and FM carrier wave frequencies from the old days when radio was first pioneered. You want to hear my other theories?"

"If that's all you got," said Mitch.

"Yeah, well," she said. "The computer is freaking out over this whole thing as it is. The transmissions are definitely back and forth, between our solar system and *theirs*. Listen to this commentary, accompanying the visuals."

A low droning voice that almost sounded synthetic, not human at any rate, seemed to narrate. Accompanying the vocals, were pages of test, wedge-shaped symbols, flashing one after the other. The aforementioned fall foliage shots from Earth were shown, which included those of anonymous "Island Cities," suspended above various countryside vistas. Faces of ordinary humans filled the hologram imaging disk, and then: "Mug" shots, as if the individuals captured within them were part of some "List." No one around the table recognized any of them, but it nevertheless gave them all chills to see such ordinary faces as part of an alien race's communique. Wedge-shaped symbols seemingly identified each individual, and an accompanying narration from the dispassionate voice droned on in a language that Rita was no closer to deciphering after a half hour of attempting to do so than she'd been when Monica had first called her to the Bridge to hear it.

An image of the northern highlands of the Moon, then, were shown next, with further summaries. The images blurred then into murky obscurity, and subsequently faded.

Monica looked up at Mitch. "I think one of the reasons I can't identify the original bandwidths of the carrier frequencies is because, whether they're Tachyon type or no, they almost *have* to be Transdimensional, or what the fiction storytellers once liked to label *Subspace Radio*. It was first coined in an old 20th Century space opera series, I believe." She grinned and nodded. "How prophetic and insightful of them. It refers, I imagine, to the notion that the carrier frequencies were actually crossing the galaxy in dimensions of space that for want of a better description could be called *folded space,* dimensions of time and space where time and distance and everything we know as real doesn't apply. *SubSpace Radio, Transdimensional Radio,* whatever. The facts speak for themselves, guys. Some highly intelligent species directly in front of us is trying to have conversations with someone back in our solar system, and *we're interfering with the signal.*"

Serina Cruthers (zoology expert, landing party team) looked over at her, confusedly. "*Why?*"

"Excuse me?" Monica replied.

"Space is so big, so vast, there's so much of it. How can our little ship be in the way?"

Monica sighed and shook her head. "Specialists," she said of Serina. "All knowledgeable and experts in their own field of study; dumber than a box of rocks in every other field."

Serina glared at her. The two of them played verbal volleyball often; it helped pass the time. Probably because both females had had a special thing going on with Commander Douglas (Doug) Bahner in the weeks before the crew entered hibernation. Doug had also helped pass the time for both of them.

Still, they considered themselves on other occasions to be the best of friends. "Mon?" she called to Monica. She gave her the finger and then saluted with it. "Is this broadening myself enough for you?"

"Yes, it actually suits you," she shot back.

"All right, you two, quit it," ordered Mitch. "Do that later when we're passed all this and can re-enter hibernation." He looked over at Zoologist Cruthers. "Serina, it's like this: In space, distances are so far, you can't imagine the pinpoint accuracy a radio beam must have if it hopes to land dead on the solar system it's heading for. In fact, *InterWorld* had better hope that whatever they've sent out behind us, right this moment trying to race and catch up with us, had better be precisely aimed for the solar system ahead. If not, they'll miss it, and we'll never even know they sent anything at all. Now of course normal radio frequencies start to spread, conically, outward . . ." He fashioned his thumbs and forefingers into a near circle and then slowly widened the gap between them, as he pulled his hands away. "In that way," he continued, "signals laving Earth over normal laser carrier beam end up widening to cover a lot of ground, however concentrated they were when they started out at their source. It makes it easier to be a little off, but it also means that the signal erodes itself, spreads itself too thin. Sent too far into the galaxy and such a signal would eventually become garbled nonsense, hardly recognizable from background static." He turned to Monica, then. "This one is very precisely aimed, but whomever did the aiming didn't anticipate we'd be traveling the same route."

"Guys," offered up Monica, "here's my theory in a nutshell. The *Stellar Quest* is getting in the way of the transmission, and we're like a clog four and a half light years into someone's communication pipeline."

Charles Houser (Environmental specialist, expert on atmospheres) chuckled and added. "And someone at either end might decide to send a drain cleaner down the pipe to break us up and flush us out?"

Laughter peppered the conference table; it was only beginning to get started and relieved much of the tension in the air. But then the general alarm claxon shrilled into life.

Mitch jumped up from his chair. "Stations, everybody, now!" he ordered.

All nine of them suddenly bolted for the room.

A high frequency energy beam swept down the length of the ship. It passed through the halls, like when a cloud passing over the sun casts a moving shadow of itself on the ground below. Mitch, as he and his bridge crew tore through the hatchways leading up to to Level One and the Bridge, saw an orange haze waft past him, along the halls, floor and ceiling, only to disappear into the corridors and compartments aft.

The danger— or whatever it had been— had passed by the time the three reached he Bridge. Doug and Monica hurried to their stations and ran a quick diagnostic of all systems.

"Well?" Mitch said after a minute or so.

They both shrugged. Monica looked up at him. "We're fine. Whatever that was, passed harmlessly through the ship."

"Instrumentation checks out, Mitch," Doug assured him.

Mitch nodded.

Monica requested of the master computer a summary of the event that had just transpired. The system signaled that it was working, and when it finished it flashed its findings over her displays. Mitch was still with Doug over by the ship-wide status board, and when he saw her attractive and young, brunette continence assume a look of incredulous shock, he motioned to Doug and hurried over to her station. "What?" he demanded.

"I don't believe this!" she said.

"Monica," he said. "What was it? Which direction was that from? Earth?"

She shook her head. "No, from Eighty-two Eridani."

"You know yet what that was?"

"The computer only lists that sweep as an unknown type of energy. *Patterned* energy! Its analysis is that . . . Jesus, Mitch! According to the computer we've just been <u>probed</u> by Eighty-two Eridani, sixteen light years away! Who could manage a beam like that?"

"**Probed?**" asked Mitch.

"Probed!" she replied.

"By whom?"

She glanced to him. "Whoever they are, when they decide to get around to it, I suppose they'll tell us who they are, themselves."

"Christ, Mitch," Doug Bahner began, "if Monica's right, and we are blocking their normal pipeline, then they just sent out a probe to learn who and what we were. That means they know we're coming. We can only hope they're okay with that."

Mitch grunted a laugh. "Are you thinking, we'll know about it, soon?"

Doug nodded, pensively. "Yeah, that's a fair supposition. Mitch?"

"What?"

"We still have time to turn around, if you want, or move out of the way."

Doug picked the wrong moment to crack a joke at times, like now. Mitch turned to the spectrum-adjusted forward view screen (and its depiction of the Eridanus constellation, still light years ahead of them); he wondered just what the *Stellar Quest* had in store for it out there.

"Doug, not now," he simply asked his second in command.

CHAPTER TWENTY-TWO

-1-

Jeffrey felt his sister nudging him; he didn't like it. He'd had a full day Sunday, and roaming the wilderness with his father usually exhausted him. He wanted to continue sleeping. The bedroom was dark; it still had to be night out. True, there was no way he could know it was night from within his room, it did not face an exterior city wall and therefore contained no conventional windows. But if morning had come, his image display windows would be filled with views of the new day, and he'd feel the raised light levels they'd be flooding into the room. It still felt like night.

"Come on, Frida!" he begged as he twirled his body over in the zero gravity. "I'm tired from all the walking Dad made me do yesterday."

"Jeffrey!" she called again, nudging his shoulder. She felt charged with energy and awe. She'd awakened and remembered, seeing the starlight streaming in like vibrant jewels against black velvet. It had confused her at first, because she couldn't remember programming the scene into her image-display window. But then she had turned to the other one with the angel fish.

"Forward view, please," she said to it. It was the same command she gave it most every morning.

The angel fish faded away. The cratered contour of the Moon hung large and near all at once in the window. It was then she verified it. However much like her room this place resembled it, she was no longer in New Allentown or on Earth. So many times she had wished her mom and dad would take the family on a trip to the Moon, and so many times she had been told the excursion was too impracticable and costly, or that maybe someday the family *might* consider it, whatever that meant. And here it now was.

"Jeffrey," she called again, "we're in orbit around the Moon! You should see it!"

Jeffrey opened his eyes and glanced out at the bedroom. *Oh jeez!* he thought. He was in his *sister's room!*

Stuffed toys banked a bureau before him; more were neatly dispersed about the floor— a panda teddy, a Persian cat, koala bear, old dolls Frida had outgrown in recent years. Shit, and on top of all that she was annoying him when all he wanted to do was sleep. He wanted to get up and go back to his own room.

"What, Frida?" he asked, squinting as he turned over again and faced her. Her long blond hair hung loosely across her left shoulder as she floated in the antigrav sleep chamber and faced him; he could read the excitement in her wide, blue eyes over some crazy thing or another.

"Hey, little brother," she said when he finally looked awake enough.

"Uh huh. Hi, what time is it?"

She shrugged and smiled. "I don't know."

He yawned, glanced around her room again, and then down at the white sleepshirt he was wearing with the kitten on the front; it stopped at mid-thigh, his legs doing a great job of making him look even more girly for it, if that was even possible. Beneath the sleepshirt he *felt*— and through the fabric of the sleepshirt— he *saw* a pair of blue panties encircling his waist. "Aw crap, damnit," he exclaimed. "Frida, why do you keep making me do this?" he asked.

"Do what, brother?" she queried.

"Dress up as your little sister in matching sleepshirts and girl's underwear! I'm a **boy**! How did I even get here? Did you come into my room, like when I was younger, pick me up and carry me while I was asleep into your room, and then later force me to dress in your stuff?"

"No," she insisted, smiling at the memory of that. "No, brother, I didn't. Jeffrey—"

"No?" he questioned, interrupting her. "You say you didn't? *Look at me?*" He felt the long locks of his brunette hair draping his shoulders and back. "I'm going back to my room and taking all this crap off. I'm a boy goddamnit!" he swore.

"No, you're not," she informed him.

"I'm nine!" he insisted. "If you don't quit pretending I'm your little sister, I'm going to tell Mom to make you quit it!"

"Jeffrey. . . ." But Frida was way too amused by the way he was totally misreading the situation to really say much more. "Jeffrey . . . where do you think you are?"

"*Your* ROOM." he replied. "But not for long. I'm going to mine. But first if you must know I have to pee. I thought I'd throw that out there."

"No you don't," she said.

Jeffrey looked at her confused. "What do you mean, *I don't?* Yes, I do. I know when I have to pee."

"Jeffrey, you don't have to pee. Not here, it won't be real, nothing is."

"I'm going back to my room when I'm done," he declared. "See ya, big sister."

He grabbed hold of the sleep chamber's edge and pulled his body up level with it, throwing his legs over the side of it then, and felt the room's gravity take hold of him. He stepped down off the bed and padded off for the hallway.

Frida stepped down after him, absolutely amazed and amused that her brother was not yet up to speed on his current whereabouts and personal situation. The plush blue carpet of her room felt warm and cozy against her bare feet, and more importantly it felt real. She had to hand it to

Athena. If one didn't know better one would swear it was the real thing.

Now by the door to her bedroom, Frida paused to watch her brother depart. Looking as adorable a nine year old girl as one could, he padded down the hall for the bathroom facility at the end of it, one foot in front of the other, so girl-like, glancing to the closed door of his parents, and wondering . . . *what day was it?* He didn't seem to know the answer to that one. *What time was it?* That one either. *Or why everything felt so . . . weird?*

He reached the bathroom and quietly closed the door.

Frida stood in shock at the entrance to her bedroom, glancing to the distant and now closed bathroom door. Somehow, she just knew what was coming next.

"*EEEEEEEEEEE*!!!" came the totally terrified scream of a little girl in that high-pitched vocal range that only little girls could manage. It sounded like something straight out of a horror entertainment archive.

Frida started for the distant bathroom to help her new little sister out. She heard a rustle from her parent's bedroom and the sound of her mother's barefooted footsteps padding across the carpeted floor of her and Keith's room for the door.

Kimberly Hagerton, looking very haggard and dewy-eyed appeared in the opening door, glancing to her daughter, stopped now beside it in the hall.

"Frida, what in the hell?" she whispered so not as to wake Keith. "Was that Jeffy?"

Frida tried not to completely lose it; she nodded or tried to. "Yeah," she eventually said. "He said he had to pee. I think he just found something out again."

The door to the distant bathroom slowly opened and cute little "female" Jeffrey Hagerton, looking all so cute in his little sleepshirt, long brunette hair down to his waist and thin, adorable little legs, stood there in the door with what had to be the saddest expression Kimberly had ever seen him make.

"Umm . . . Oh." he announced, finally. "I just remembered. . . . Hi, Mom," he said to her.

"What's wrong, honey?" Kimberly innocently asked, trying hard not to start giggling like a teenage girl.

"It's not funny, Mom," he replied. "I tried to use the bathroom like I always do, but . . ."

"Yes?"

"Everything is different down there. What do I do?"

Frida started snorting again as she went up to him. "First, little sister, you sit down. You've done that before, and don't say boys don't. You have to when you have to go the other way, as well."

"Frida," chided her mother. "Do you have so be so crude?" she asked.

She grinned, weakly, at Kimberly. And facing her brother again. "I know you know how to do it, sitting down, brother. So just sit down and . . . pee. But after don't forget to—"

"Frida!" persisted Kimberly.

"Forget to what?" Jeffrey replied, concerned it was something really dreadful.

"Mom . . . ?" encouraged Frida of her mother, grinning and turning to her and implying by her tone, *if I can't tell him, one of us has to.*

Kimberly approached her son, and whispered in his ear. "You have to wipe after you're done, sweetie. It's not like when you were a boy."

Jeffrey looked down at himself, and picturing in his mind what that would be like. "Oh, fuck," he replied.

"Jeffrey!" Kimberly chided.

"I never had to care about a thing like **that** before," he said in his defense.

"Well, you do now, little brother," Frida said, giving him a bear hug and mashing his face against her own as she kissed him on the cheek. "Don't want to walk around all day feeling wet down there."

"Eeew," he said. "And I'm glad you think this is so funny."

"It's hilarious," she replied. "None of it is real, not here inside Athena's lair, Jeffrey. Last night maybe while you were still in the real world, and a real girl in our apartment. Didn't you have to pee then?"

"No, this new body didn't need to, and then I forgot all about it."

"And now here it's not real," said Frida.

"Then why does it *feel* so real?" he asked.

"Because you're used to having to do it," Frida whispered in his ear.

"And *you* can just make '*needing to*' go away?" he said of the urge.

She thought about it. "I don't know. I hope so. You try it, and tell me if it works."

Jeffrey concentrated hard, and then: "Be back in a second. I can't even make that go away, let alone make myself a boy again."

He closed the door to the bathroom, and mother and daughter had a private laugh about the whole ordeal as they gave Jeffy some privacy; the two females headed for the living room.

***

Kimberly stared in awe at the spectacular view of the Moonscape in the terrace view. "Ugh, there it is," she said. "The Moon. And it's so . . . so *bleah.*"

A lunar mountain range, hardly more than mounds of stark, sun-bleached sand dunes above the level plains, swept across the Moon's surface. They were not like Earth's mountains at all. In fact the whole scene reminded one of a long forgotten and dust bunny infested attic crawlspace, somewhere you might never in a million years ever consider visiting for any longer than necessary. A long time ago, a twentieth century Apollo astronaut referred to the Moon's surface as "Magnificent desolation." Magnificent? Only because nothing like it on Earth (thankfully) existed in quite such a stark, glaring, bleached out a way as the surface of the Moon did and it was the first time human beings had taken a bold step off their parent world to land elsewhere in the universe. But *magnificent?* It really did resemble a crawlspace, somewhere that needed to exist but in no way a pretty, desirable place to visit. If one did deign to come here, it wasn't for the view; it was for its value as real estate.

"What time is it, honey?" Frida asked her daughter.

Frida shrugged. "I didn't ask," she said of the info address system her real home possessed.

"It is eight in the morning back in New Allentown, the real one, Kimberly," came Athena's voice in both Kim's and Frida's minds.

"Thank you, Athena."

"Your planet's Moon is not so bad," Athena commented about it. "As planetary moon's go. I've seen way worse. . . . Is Jeffrey all right?" she asked.

Kimberly smiled. "He's just having a hard time making adjustments."

"I'm not the mastermind behind his transition, Kimberly," Athena insisted. "If he really wanted to go back to being as he was, he would have done so by now. When he finally stops fighting all the time the reality that nothing stays the same forever, that change is inevitable whether you're willing to accept it or not, he'll see who and what is behind his transition."

"Give him time, Athena," Kimberly said. "Is everything all right?"

"Everything is fine," she answered. "I usually do not spend this much time with and delivering my latest 'acquisitions,' but you four are special, and always will be. So I'm giving all of you time to get adjusted, and hopefully soon Jeffrey will accept things for what they are as well."

"I'm fine," he insisted and suddenly said, from the back hallway as he entered the living room. "This is all ME, making me this way, Athena? I *like this?*"

"It's *your* personal new adventure," she replied. "And I'm happy to make it possible for you. So I hope you are enjoying it."

Jeffrey grunted a laugh. "At least none of my friends back in the city can see me like this. Where we're going no one else knows me as I was?"

"No. They will see you only as you wish to be seen and known."

Jeffrey glanced down at his adorable little legs. "I'm going to have to get used to peeing sitting down now, aren't I?" he said to all the females present in the room.

Kimberly and Frida smiled.

"How's Dad?" Frida asked her mom.

Kimberly grinned to her daughter, weakly. "All right. He's exhausted. Athena really put him to work last night."

"Oh, he was enjoying himself," answered Athena. "I could tell."

"What happened last night?" Frida pursued. "Did you and Dad get the viewwafer back from the guy you thought stole it last night?"

Kimberly rounded up her two "daughters" and sat them down on opposite sides of her on the sofa. "Yes, we did." she answered. . . .

"You visited Washington D.C. and the Washington Monument . . . for real?" asked Jeffrey.

Kimberly nodded. "Your father, Athena and I had to return to the surface and track down that young man who stopped over last night." She turned serious, then. "The wrong people know what we've found. I think they want Athena."

"Yes, that is my perception, as well," Athena added to the conversation. "As if. . . ."

Kimberly laughed at that. She turned to her kids. "You got to love her," she said. "She's not stuffy."

"Thank you, Kimmy," she returned. "I like you too."

"Why, Mom?" pursued Frida. "Why do they want her?"

"Honey," she answered. "To some people, finding a super advanced being like Athena is like the pot of gold at the end of the rainbow. She has answers to questions that human beings have sought answers to for time on end."

"Was Athena in danger?"

"No. Worry not over that," Athena added. "It was actually quite fun what happened."

Kimberly smiled and nodded. "But it's dangerous for us to ever go back home, now. If we're caught, they might arrest us, put us away."

"They'll put us in jail?" That was from Jeffrey.

"Worse, honey— where we can never tell anyone what we've seen, what we know about the truth."

"What's that?" the two kids asked in unison.

"That we're not alone in the universe. That they're really is intelligent life out there in the night. That is an unknown that frightens governments, kids, because they have no defenses against things they can't even explain. And since these other races have never landed and revealed themselves publicly to the whole world at the same time, no one government has ever had to deal with them as a genuine reality. The official stance then is that they don't exist. People will come to accept anything as true, even if it isn't, if the lie is pushed on them hard enough. That way they'll never have to deal with the actual truth."

"Mom, would they **really** get rid of us?"

"Maybe."

"*Kill us?*"

"Honey, I don't know."

Frida looked at her brother, and then pondered the possibility for a while. Finally, she glanced up to the ceiling. "Athena? Mom and Dad visited *D.C. Park* last night, and you didn't *wake us?* Why not?" And then facing her mother. "I've always wanted to go there."

Kimberly stared to smile. So did Jeffrey. "Oh, Frida," Kimberly answered. She grabbed her kids and hugged them against her.

Keith Hagerton awoke about an hour later, and he was surprised to notice the Moon so large and near in his bedroom window. He honestly had thought that Athena would take them much farther out than just to Earth's Moon. He thought about the events of the night before, and found it hard to believe that here in his heated floatation bed, he could ever have been involved in anything so incredibly bizarre. He only wanted to remain here in this illusion of serenity. Suddenly, he noticed a little girl with long shoulder-length brown hair, sitting cross-legged, backlit, upon the floor before the Moonscape in blue-denim jeans, sneaks, and an off tan cable-knit pullover, long enough to have been worn as a sweater-dress, minus the jeans.

"Jeffrey?"

"Hi, Dad?" his son answered.

Keith yawned, and looked over to the time display on his side of the bed. "What are you doing, Jeff?"

"I'm gazing at the Moon."

Keith pondered that a second; he could see as much.

"I was waiting for you to wake up, Dad."

"Where's your mom and sister?"

"The City Top Terrace. They had Athena make them one. They wanted to see the stars and the galaxy all above them from up there."

Keith grinned. He nodded. "Have you had breakfast, yet?" Keith asked.

He saw Jeffrey smile. "No, but I learned how to pee like a girl. Fun."

Keith laughed to himself. "Oh. Okay."

"Come on over here, champ," Keith requested as he contemplated his son's quiet stance.

Jeffrey did. He climbed into the bed chamber and floated over to his dad; Keith put his arm around his son's shoulder and stroked his hair like he often did Frida. Not so much with Jeff. Suddenly, it felt right to do it to him as well. They both stared then to the Moon and saw a lunar city on the horizon. The Moon's surface was in night, and the city gleamed brightly amid the shadowy-gray soil, its navigation lights twinkling like starlight. From this altitude the lunar city seemed so quiet, placid, no evidence of commercial traffic adrift above its length.

"Do they know we're up here?" Jeffrey asked of the people in the city below.

"I doubt it."

"Where *are* we going, Dad?"

Keith shrugged. "To the Moon, it would seem."

"Mom says Athena sent you back to Earth to get back the viewwafer."

Keith nodded. "Yes, she did. We actually got back *two* of them, the original and a copy of it. Athena now believes we might only have wasted our time."

"Why?"

"Because if there were one copy, chances are there were many. Anyone seeing what was on the wafer would be smart to start cranking out duplicates left and right."

"Why, Dad?"

"Because, son, it's the proof the race has been seeking for centuries that Earth has been visited in the past by other species from other worlds. It's the first real evidence. If I had thought to send my network a copy of it, for instance . . ." he shook his head, "they would have eaten it up. As it was, I didn't, and luck being the way it always is, the wafer was found by the very people who would see to it that no one else ever found out about it."

Jeff nodded. "Mom told us. Do governments really bury proof?"

Keith smiled. "That's been the persistent rumor since the millennium began, son. Even when classified documents, that suggested the government did, were uncovered and made public, somehow the truth still never came out. They used to call it *Disinformation*."

"What's that?"

"It's when you pretend to reveal something, but instead you deliberately distort the facts. That way you mislead and delude people, and the truth is still never reported."

"Are people afraid of the truth?"

Keith nodded. "People, even governments, are afraid of losing control of their lives. It's why people all down the centuries have always hated change and loved keeping things just as they always were. People hate surprises. They fear the unknown. You can't predict or control how something never before encountered will turn out. To some people that is something so scary they'd rather not deal with it. And as long as these aliens never make a public appearance no one has to treat them as a serious threat."

"But they exist," said Jeff.

Keith shrugged. "Up till now nothing came along to prove that, son." He glanced out to the Moon again, and to the Northern Alps, which were only now orbiting into view upon the horizon.

"Mom said we can never go home again," said Jeff. "The government

191

people will take us away. Would they really kill us?"

Keith smirked. "They'll have to catch us first, son. I think Athena is too smart for them."

Jeffrey smiled; he reached over and kissed Keith on the cheek.

"What was that for?"

"Last night when you sent me back to Earth I got so scared, I thought I'd never see you again. I thought something awful had happened to you, that you weren't my father anymore. I love you, Dad. I hope I didn't let you down last night." He grabbed his father's neck, then, and hugged him.

Keith cuddled his son tighter to himself and kissed him back. Everything about Jeffrey said he was Keith's son, it was only his appearance that suggested otherwise. Appearances. . . .

"Let's join your mom and sister topside, see from up there where this place is, Athena is taking us"

"We can go anywhere in New Allentown we want, can't we?"

"Yeah, I suppose we can," smiled Keith. "Just like in dreams. . ."

CHAPTER TWENTY-THREE

-1-

Kimberly and Frida were nestled in the grass and among the evergreen trees of the City Top Terrace, their gazes angled upward to the starlight showcased in the overhead glass dome. If this had been the real terrace in New Allentown, the facility would be populated by maintenance personnel and early morning visitors, there to catch the sun rise over the eastern foothills. But as this was only a dream recreation, that extra bit of human ambiance had evidently been omitted from the simulation.

"Mom," Frida called out to Kim, ultimately.

Kimberly rolled over on her side and eyed her. "Yeah, kitten? This is nice, isn't it? The stars, the Moon. Almost like our real one, come nightfall."

Frida nodded. "But it's so *quiet*! No crickets or birds chirping. And other people. Athena forgot to add them."

"None of those things would be real, Friddy. And if one of our New Allentown acquaintances did come over and said hello, it would freak me out. I'd have to run back to our apartment."

"I talk to people I know in my dreams, all the time . . . and some I don't know."

"But you don't know you're dreaming when you do. You think you're awake. We on the other hand know none of this real."

Kimberly and her daughter were no longer in their matching white sleepshirts. Now dressed in a red snow bunny outfit, Kimberly's long blond hair fanned down the back of it, standing out from it, strikingly. She wished the outfit upon herself, as Jeffrey had earlier when he'd wanted out of his own girly sleepshirt and into something a little more like he was used to. Kimberly hadn't risked waking Keith in the apartment, by returning to it to fetch the outfit from the bedroom dresser and slip into it. She and Frida simply lay there in the Terrace Park in their bare feet and wished the nightshirts away. Frida now wore red shorts with matching suspender straps over a striped shirt, wooly leggings and dark brown ankle boots. She *appeared to be dressed in* was the appropriate phrase here. The outfit felt on her, but she knew it was no more real than *her body* or the greenery surrounding her in the terrace. Athena's leisurely orbit about the Moon, on the other hand, and all the stars burning in the night above, Kimberly was certain that was real.

The orbit was beginning to decay. She could see the Moon's surface grow more detailed by the minute. Another city dawned on the horizon, and with the advancing hour came greater evidence of vessels snaking across the lunar surface or breaking free of it and ascending into orbit.

Mankind had inhabited the Moon for a while now. You couldn't just look up at it from the real New Allentown terrace on Earth and not see signs of human inhabitation peppering the lunar terrain on nights when the Moon rose full.

Mother and daughter said very little. They had no concept of time's passage, and in this ethereal realm, time probably didn't matter all that much anyway. What was there actually for them to do here in this illusion of their home city? Might as well just wait to see where on the Moon Athena intended to set down.

***

It wasn't too long after that Keith and Jeffrey appeared among them, themselves fully dressed. Kimberly looked over at Keith, beside her, smiled and asked, "When did you get here?"

He shrugged. "Awhile back. Wow," he said then, "that is one hell of a view."

"Let me guess," she said. "You and Jeff were in the apartment, the two of you decided to join us girls up in the City Top Terrace and you didn't feel like walking. So you just . . . blinked yourselves."

"I was still in bed, actually. Jeffy was sitting on the floor in front of our scenic window, just gazing at the Moon," he said. "He was dressed already. He said he called Athena in his mind and asked if she could whip something up for him right there in our bedroom; he didn't want to have to return to his own room and figure out what to put on."

"Oh, if he thinks it's bad now, wait till our little girl gets older." Kimberly smiled.

"Do you have to call him that?" he asked.

"Yes," she declared. "He's our daughter now; get used to it, hon. Athena chose that outfit for him?"

"Yeah," said Keith.

"And Jeffy was okay with that girly top? It looks like one of Frida's."

Keith shrugged. "He seems to be."

"He's accepting his new gender just fine." She chewed on that in her mind for a few silent minutes. "This blinking anywhere we want to be is kind of fun, isn't it, hon?" she said.

"Until the novelty wears off," Keith replied.

"She pick your outfit out for you too?" She asked then as a woman might who was concerned that another woman in her husband's life was getting a little too friendly with her man.

"No," he assured her. "I went to the dresser drawer and the closet and picked this stuff out myself and put it on. That I still could do on my own, and wanted to," he said of the brown Dockers and an off-white, almost brown knit pullover he had on with a pair of tan oxfords.

"Okay," she replied almost in a whisper. "Any idea where down there we're headed?" she asked of the bleak sun-bleached lunar surface below.

"We seem to be angling down for those mountains," Keith said. He thought about them. "The Northern Alps, I think they're called."

"Oh."

***

"Hey, brother!" Frida whispered, as she nudged up beside him. "Like it?"

He shrugged. "I'd rather it was our real terrace back home."

"Is that one of my tops?" she asked of his sweater.

He indicated with his facial expression that he didn't know. "If it is, I'm not wearing it on purpose," he said. "I just told Athena to get me out of that sleepshirt, and into my regular clothes." He glanced down at the rest of the outfit. "I feel like she met me half-way. Do I look like a boy in this?"

She giggled. "Do you think *I would* if I wore that?"

He glanced to her in the tights, striped shirt and suspenders. "No," he said. "You're too pretty to be a boy."

"Thanks, brother. So are you. You always were, but now, it's official."

"I think I'm still wearing panties, too," he said. "And knee socks under these jeans. Is this really all me doing this to me?"

"Oh, you know you love it. Being a girl is fun. Get over it. I always wanted a baby sister."

"Uh huh. What a big reveal that is. I've only heard you say you wish I were your sister since I was five."

Laying side by side on their stomachs on the grass beside their parents, Frida reached over to her brother and grabbing his waist pulled him toward him.

"I always loved doing that to you before," she said. "Now, it feels even more okay than ever."

"Frida, I'm a person, not a stuffed animal!"

"So? I love you, brother. I love having a brother like you. Hey, Jeff, I want to try something," she said then, whispering in his ear. And in her thoughts, asked, *Jeff, can you hear me?* She reached quickly for his mouth with two fingers and stopped him from answering out loud. *Think it,* she thought.

He nodded. *Can _you_ hear _me?_* he replied in his own thoughts.

She nodded, glancing over at her parents. They were oblivious to their kids and their telepathic antics. *Take my hand,* she said as she reached for him.

What are you going to do? he asked.

The city's not real, she said. *Let's you and me make it go away for a few minutes.*

No, Frida, wait! he pleaded.

The City Top Terrace vanished from around them. Frida could still feel

195

her brother's hand in hers, but it was as if she was now in a solitary orbit of her own above the Moon. "Say something, Jeffy," she said. "I can't see you."

"I want to go back," he said. "This scares me."

"It's fun," she replied. "We're all alone out here."

"Where's Mom and Dad?"

"Where WE ARE. We're just choosing at the moment to imagine we're somewhere else. Just enjoy it, will you? This is fantastic."

Jeffrey found himself adrift among the stars (and in the vacuum of space.) As he couldn't find or see his body, he supposed he should be grateful. Were he really out here without a life-belt, he'd be oxygen starved about now and icing up. In other words, he'd be very dead.

The Moon, its surface growing nearer, half-lit and half-dark, and a study in sharp ridges and cratered depressions, oriented itself directly beneath him. The experience resembled a Sensor Sphere visual.

He fixated on the view behind him and suddenly saw the pale blue disk of old Earth, very small and lost amid the starlight, its surface mired by cloud cover. It seemed an oasis in the dark, precious and fragile. That life had spawned upon it was hard to imagine. With every other world in the solar system so lifeless and inhospitable, it seemed almost intentional that Earth had avoided a similar destiny.

"Isn't this even better than the view from the City Top Terrace?" asked Frida.

Keith abruptly rose to a sitting up position. A thought entered his consciousness. He puzzled over it.

"What's wrong?" Kim asked, looking over. She heard it then too: she rose as well.

"COMMERCIAL TRAFFIC BETWEEN EARTH AND MOON ALERTED TO OUR PRESENCE. TRAFFIC REQUESTED TO REPORT ANY ANOMALIES. PROBABILITY IS HIGH THAT TRAFFIC WILL TRIANGULATE AND DETERMINE OUR COURSE TO THE NORTHERN ALPS MOUNTAIN RANGE. I WILL CONTINUE TO MONITOR ALL FREQUENCIES FOR THREAT OF POSSIBLE INTERFERENCE. END OF REPORT."

"Athena?" Keith asked, "You sounded almost like a computer just then. Why so formal?"

No answer.

"Keith?" came Kimberly.

"I was afraid of that," he replied.

"What?"

"That report we just received means he's still looking for us."

"Who?"

"*Randolph Phillips.* That bastard politician who wanted to wound me last night. Somehow, he knows we're heading for the Moon. We'd better not hang around up here in orbit too long." He glanced past Kimberly, then. "Where are the kids?"

Kimberly got to her feet and scanned the terrace. "Frida? Jeffrey? Keith, where'd they go?"

***

"Frida," called Jeff. "Look!"

A lumbering giant of a vessel pulled up from the surface. Several kilometers away yet and almost too distant to even be seen, nevertheless it seemed clear the vessel was huge. Its impending interception with Athena's orb was probably not intentional. The vessel looked a barge with engines.

"Are they coming for us?" Jeff asked.

"I'm not sure they even know we're here," Frida answered.

FRIDA? JEFFREY?! came their mother's voice in their thoughts, then; Kim sounded so clear to the two it seemed as if she were right there with them.

Abruptly, they were back with their parents in the terrace.

-2-

The *Julius Sigfry,* an ore barge from the Caucasus highlands regions, continued its climb into lunar orbit. Its two-man bridge crew, in the cramped and makeshift cockpit, were seated behind their instrumentation boards, watching the jet black sky above the lunar terrain for any unlikely traffic. Nothing of the sort registered on the sensors. There were no stars in the night above them, not yet, only the distant blue sphere of Earth, seemingly all alone out there. Their view of the terrain ahead was a humble, no-frills window, no electronic imaging gizmos, 3D or whatever, that could be tasked to enhance the image and bring back the stars. The culprit was sunlight bouncing off the moon's surface. So brilliant was its glare, it washed away, overpowered, the by-contrast, faint light of all those distant pinprick suns. Once the Moon's reflected glare ebbed with the advancing distance the *Julius Sigfry* put between itself and the Moon, the stars would again wax into view. Until then, it looked pretty grim and empty up there.

Phillip Trent, Rick Hegletter's second aboard ship, saw a blip and a furious spill of orbital data, paint across his main imaging board. "What in bloody hell is that?" he proclaimed in an almost deliberately contained voice.

Hegletter glanced over to Trent's board and read the report on the anomaly with him.

"It doesn't even read as solid," said Rick. The report estimated the object's size as no more than thirty centimeters round. "What IS that

197

thing?" Rick asked.

Phil Trent squinted his gaze out the view window in an attempt to see it with his naked eyes. No joy there. "It's definitely on a descent trajectory," he said. "It'll pass by pretty close."

Pass by, it eventually did. The two were no more enlightened as to what it was as it did so than they had been earlier. It almost seemed as if the energy ball (because that is what it resembled) knew where it was going, and purposely gave the *Julius Sigfry* a wide berth. The anomaly continued its descent for the Moon and for the distant rise of the Northern Alps range.

"I've been out here twenty years flying these supply routes between the planets," said Rick. "I've never seen **that** before. A charged ball of static electricity, you think? Like heat lightning?" "I don't know what that is," said Phil. "Dispatch is requesting a report."

Rick furrowed his brow. "On that?"

"They've been monitoring. They want us to divert our scans rearward and track whatever that is until we're out of range."

Rick understood. "Okay. Do they have any idea what the damn thing is?"

Phil grinned. Over his neural-com link he heard the dispatcher's response. Phil started chuckling.

"What?" (Rick.)

"That information is 'need-to-know.' We don't need to know. In other words, 'fuck off and do what you're told.'"

You got to love this job, Rick thought.

The *Julius Sigfry* continued on into orbit.

"Where **were** you two?" Keith asked.

Frida grinned weakly and shrugged.

With the entire Hagerton clan once again all in the same place upon the grass, in Athena's recreation of New Allentown's City Top Terrace, the four watched as the ore barge, *Julius Sigfry,* (its name was clearly visible on the vessel's hull, and yes it came that near) passed in front of them, so large it made the Terrace's overhead dome seem a snow globe by comparison.

Keith wondered. "Jesus, how tiny are we?" In the *Julius Sigfry's* cockpit window, Keith clearly saw the twin expressions of alarm and concern on its bridge crew. Obviously, the two men in the barge saw *something*. Athena's orb was not as inconspicuous as Keith assumed it would be.

"Shall we wave?" Frida asked. A second vessel, a ferry originating from a city in Earth orbit, appeared above them and angled its sleek, pointed self-Moonward, assuming an equally troublesome trajectory.

The scene in the overhead dome of the Terrace shifted, abruptly; there was no sound accompanying the maneuver. Both vessels fell out of sight almost at once. The Moon's contour flattened; the pitted length of the Mare Imbrium plain beneath Athena's orb's flight, fell away into the desolation of the southwest. Ahead was the northern ranges.

CHAPTER TWENTY-FOUR

-1-

Athena's orb entered the lunar Alps almost without fanfare. Whatever glory the range once might have had, it had lost it eons of time ago to countless micrometeorite collisions against its majestic ridges and terraces.

To Jeffrey they were like shoreline-sandcastles after several hours of erosion by bombardment of the surf. His parents had taken the family to the beaches of Virginia one summer a few years back, a rare treat considering how hard it was to obtain the excursion permits. Keith had been recording a visual for the network on a sand sculpturing contest held every ten years. When the judging was over, and the various shapes had been preserved on viewwafers, the tide was allowed to come in and reduce the sculptures to lumps of sand. Eventually, even the lumps disappeared, the beach becoming pristine once more.

The Lunar Alps seemed much the same to him—eroded by time and the elements. He wondered what they might have been like a billion years ago.

-2-

Athena's final intended destination within the Lunar Alps visualized in Keith's thoughts around the same moment New Allentown's recreated City Top Terrace vanished from around the four Hagertons. It was apparent once more that they were inside a ball of ethereal energy, the outer walls of which appeared to be like those of a soap bubble.

Keith reached out to touch it and watched the images beyond ripple as if disturbance patterns had been made on the surface of a lake. "So much for New Allentown," he said, "and our apartment. "It was only an illusion, a distraction, but it felt like we were traveling in style. Time to be reminded where we really are, why we're going."

"Keith?" called Kimberly of the scene ahead.

He nodded. "The Lunar Alps. Where we're supposed to end up, I suspect." The flight across the lunar lowlands was swift and hurried now; it was as if the orb now made great haste to get where it was going. Keith nodded again. "This must be it, kids, Kimmy. We're going in."

Kimberly faced in the direction he pointed. Far up a moon-washed ridge, little more than a pronounced rise in the dull, desolate terrain, she saw a fissure, a thing that from most angles would not have caused much in the way of curiosity. Even now the shadows of the surrounding hills caused its presence to appear unremarkable.

"It seems like, Kimmy," said Keith, then, "for the most part Athena's gone quiet on us." He nodded as if a bit of information was just then imparted. "This is only an extraneous avatar-like extension of her total being. She's been out here with us this whole time, enjoying the adventure as much as we. I don't think she gets to do this too often. The closer she gets to her true self, the less of her we'll perceive in this snare avatar of hers."

"Comforting," Kimberly could only respond to that. "What's the real her like then?"

He shook his head. "I guess we'll find out soon. Here we go."

Their approach was soundless. The Alps quietly parted to either side as the orb slipped easily past. The fissure itself was barely wide enough to allow a single very slender human being to squeeze past and only if he was less than five feet in height. One might imagine a child would find the way in easier to manage than an adult.

All four of them braced for impact. The fissure crack swallowed them whole. They were in as easily as that with no great fanfare. And to either side of them passed the mountain's interior walls. All around them now was solid rock; the fissure crack extended back several meters.

"Something up ahead," Keith observed.

Before them yawned a wide tunnel opening, a thing way too precise to have been formed naturally. The orb started down, descending what evidently was a very steep incline, and several meters across. They were descending into the bowels of the mountain, and below was only darkness. But to their sides came a faint purple reflected glow which told everyone that they were indeed inside an electrified orb. Keith peered down the tunnel's length for sign of its end.

A massive cavern revealed itself below, ultimately. In the dim light from Athena's orb, it looked dismal.

"Here we go," Keith told the others.

The orb reached the bottom and leveled off, creeping slowly then along the cavern floor in search seemingly of something specific, which it ultimately found: a crystalline mass about two meters wide and a meter high that only then began to glow as the orb approached it.

"Is that Athena?" asked Jeffrey of the crystal.

"Son, I have no idea," admitted Keith.

The orb hovered then directly above. The four watched as a twinkling half-sphere "bubble" formed and encircled the crystalline mass at a distance of about three meters. The four continued to find themselves hovering above the crystal mass, just a half meter above it, when suddenly they found themselves on the floor of the cavern, though still inside the "bubble." They faced back and saw Athena's orb as yet above the crystal, the four no longer its captives. It abruptly descended for the crystalline mass and was gone.

Ahead them in the faint glow from the crystalline mass, they could see they were indeed in a subterranean cavern, a scene of cold, formless Moon rock. It looked forbidding out there, more so than it probably was.

"What is this place?" asked Kimberly, walking over to Keith, her kids in tow and by her side.

Keith took a breath, studying the formations around him. "I'd say it was an old lava flow trench, probably formed when the Moon was still young, and still cooling down. That shaft we descended, though, from the surface, I mean; that thing was way too carefully formed to be natural. Somebody purposely cut that passageway."

"It did look too smooth," agreed Kimberly. "Too perfect."

Keith nodded. "These Barthonians must have really wanted to be isolated to burrow down this far. They must like being in subterranean tunnels. Maybe they're part mole."

"You think they're here, somewhere?"

"No," Keith said. "Athena was left behind to supervise the snare network."

"That's what I'm not clear on, Keith," she said. "What species was running this operation? The Barthonians or the Eleutions?"

"Good question. It's obvious the Barthonians can't leave their home solar system and go traipsing through the galaxy without the assistance of the Eleutions and their spiritual life essence to get around Einstein's *can't exceed the speed of light* rule. The Barthonians, while a lot like us, they're corporeal; where evolution is concerned they are way ahead of us, just not as far as the Eleutions. So, I'd say Athena and her kind are just helping them keep busy aiding inferior lifeforms like us so that we don't end up killing ourselves off before we have a chance to grow up."

"No welcoming committee then?" she observed.

"Doesn't appear to be one, no," Keith answered. "This place looks truly deserted, abandoned."

"And Athena lives down here?" cringed Kimberly.

"Almost feel sorry for her, right?" he replied. "Kimberly, kids, do you feel it? Something about us feels different? It's not just me, isn't it?"

***

He felt different, and after a few seconds thought he knew why. This was a real body again his "consciousness" resided within, no doubt by this point an energy to matter reassembly/ rematerialization. He could feel things about his anatomy, little things that people took for granted as the price they spent for dwelling in real-life bodies. His body seemed to be behaving as if its energy stores were low and needed "food." That sort of thing. One knows when the body is unhappy about something. Suffice to say that Keith recognized that he was a "real" person again, and not the imagined creation of one inside Athena's "mind essence."

202

His family felt it as well, that familiarity one had with their own physical bodily reality. Frida and Jeffrey, two young girls as it were, splayed their fingers before themselves, touched and grasped each other's palms, and felt things about their bodies that had been not present just a second before.

"We're real," stated Frida. "I can feel it. We're real again." She faced back to where the orb had last been and to the faintly glowing crystalline mass behind her. "What happened to Athena?"

"That wasn't the real Athena, sweetie," said her dad. "'Just an extension, an avatar extension that allowed her to roam beyond this cavern." Keith nodded. "The real Athena is down here somewhere."

"Then why didn't 'her avatar' self simply rejoin with her."

"I don't know," said Keith. He glanced to the crystal behind him. "I think it gets stored here until . . . hmmm." He cupped his chin with his thumb and forefinger and considered it.

"What?" said Kimberly.

"— stored here until it's recharged, perhaps, and sent back down to Earth to await. . . ."

Kimberly huffed. "*. . . Until the next unfortunate group finds the orb in the cave and gets scooped up in it and transported here!*"

He nodded. "That would be my guess."

Kimberly approached the bubble force field before her and pressed her hands against it. "What's this for? Are we prisoners in this?"

Keith glanced down at his waist. He was wearing the life/lift belt he'd fastened upon himself yesterday when he and Jeffrey first descended into the bowels of Crystal Cave. He glanced to his family and noticed that they too now wore belts as well, as if copies of his and Jeffrey's had been made for the four of them. He nodded to himself and smiled.

"What?" repeated Kimberly.

"Look what you're wearing," he said.

She glanced to her waist and noticed the life-belt. Frida and Jeffrey did the same.

The belts contained sensor devices that allowed one to read the atmospheric content of the environment beyond their influence. Keith reached down to his, withdrew the tiny neural-interface medallion stored in the buckle and affixed it to his forehead. He subsequently requested the unit do an oxygen content analysis.

"Yeah," he nodded. "We've air inside this force bubble." He glanced to the dark cavern beyond its reach. "Out there," he began. "We're on the Moon, remember? It's as airless as space itself. Nothing to breathe out there."

The life belt beeped in his thoughts and the following summation appeared as a thought bubble in his mind.

ANALYSIS OF ATMOSPHERIC CONTENT BEYOND

DETECTED FORCE FIELD ENCLOSURE:
Oxygen content: None
Mean Temperature: Minus Two-hundred degrees Celsius.
Life Support assistance required.
Unit activated and in standby ready mode.

"What does Athena want us to do?" asked Kimberly. "Go cave exploring and find her? How does she know we won't just try to leave here and get back to our own people?"

Keith grinned. "You're talking one hell of a walk to wherever the nearest lunar base or city resides." He shook his head. "I doubt her snare network would be that easy to outsmart anyway. No. We're supposed to find Athena ourselves and—"

"*And what*, Keith?" she pursued. "Voluntarily give up our lives as we've lived them up till now?"

He nodded. "I think so. I think if the orb could take us all the way to Athena, it would have, but this crystal seems like the end of the road for it."

Two brilliant orbs all at once evolved into being above the crystal mass behind them. His and Jeffrey's Light Sphere from their cave exploration and a second one, a duplicate of it. The two units took a position subsequently to either side of the Hagerton clan.

"Must be our escorts," Keith said. He grinned. "About time, guys."

"Oh Keith. . ." sighed Kimberly.

"Dad?" Jeffrey whispered, leaning over to him.

Keith dropped to his son's height. "What, son?"

"Where did the second sphere come from?"

Keith studied the two spheres and considered his answer. "Athena has the Light Sphere's molecular data pattern on file, Jeff. She could probably crank out as many copies of the unit as she wished."

Jeffrey looked at him. "You mean, she could make a room full of *ME*'s, if she wanted to?"

"Yes," he replied. "But I think turning you into a girl was cruel enough."

Jeffrey chose to ignore that one for the moment, not wishing to be reminded about that. "In a real human female body, the reality of it was even more . . . *strange.*

"Which one of the copies would be the *real* me, Dad?" he said, instead.

Kimberly issued a nervous laugh at her son's question. She eyed Keith, suspiciously. She didn't trust him to be sensible discussing such topics. Keith thought about his answer.

"All of them, and none of them, Jeff," Keith said. He faced all three of his family. "Technically, we all *died* the first time Athena dematerialized us to bring us here. From an esoteric standpoint, we're only copies, recreated from our original patterns."

"Keith, must you always do that?" chided Kimberly. "You don't just scare the *children* when you say things like that, you scare **me**. Are you proud of yourself? I'm still trying to wrap my brain around Athena's turning my son into my daughter."

Keith shrugged, and faced back down to Jeffrey. "Did you want me to lie to you, champ?"

Jeffrey only looked at him, and then at the second Light Sphere. He shrugged. "I guess not. And Mom I think I'm starting to get used to not being a boy anymore."

Kimberly smiled toward him and nodded, weakly.

"But don't sweat it, any of you," said Keith, encouragingly. "It's no big deal. We're all fine. In fact, think about it. From the day you were first conceived, your original essence has been retired and replaced by whole new versions of yourselves. People shed old body cells and replace them with new ones continuously. So you're not the you that you even began life as. You became a copy of yourself the day you were first conceived." He slapped his palm against his chest. "So, how about it? Shall we go learn where Athena wants us to find her? Life belts, everyone? Let's get them activated."

Kimberly glanced ahead to the darkened cavern, aided somewhat now by two intense Light Spheres casting a glaring light forward, and causing long running shadows to issue from everything in the foreground, running for the farthest reaches of the place. "Must we, Keith?" she asked. "Keith, you know how I feel about caves, and that's the ones on *Earth!*"

Keith shrugged and then smiled. "I've tried to break you in," he only replied.

She frowned and then nodded. "Let's do it," she decided. "Get it over with, before Athena starts to think we've stood her up."

***

The force field bubble surrounding the crystal abruptly dropped the moment the last of the four activated their lift belt units. The first thing all four of them saw was a sheen of purple energy formfitting each of their bodies—their cocoon shields, which protected them from the lunar environment. The cocoons fit them so delicately there was hardly any sensation at all. Only when one of them attempted to touch something did they notice the shield's presence, creating a sort of tingly coating between them and whatever they touched. The maintenance belts were a far cry from the cumbersome, environment suites their ancestors had worn back in the days of the Apollo moon missions.

Something about the environment in the cave became obvious to each of them, immediately. Their weights were reduced; each step was like trying to walk across the bottom of a swimming pool. Keith, over the com-link, said, "Oh, yeah, I forgot about the one-sixth gravity."

"Keith—" Kimberly moaned as she moved toward him and couldn't land. Keith reached out for her and caught her by the waist. He helped her come in for a landing.

"Can't the belts help?" Kim asked.

"No, they reduce gravity, not add it. Just give it time for you to get the hang of it." He tried to take a step, and felt like a man learning all over again how to walk after a long period of being bed-ridden.

The light spheres began to rise, finally, into the cavern and at the same time, raised their light levels until they reached near full output toward the ceiling.

The cavern splayed out all around them. It looked like one of the tourist caverns of Virginia, with only one difference; no water droplets. The stalactites and stalagmites draped across the expanses in the distance had obviously been fabricated, nothing like them would form here on the Moon. It was the deliberate creation, apparently, of the Barthonians. It was a colored wonderland of flow stones and drapery formations, pinnacles and snow cones. It was beautiful. No other evidence existed to suggest an intelligence had ever been here. Were it not, then, for this very definite incongruity about the cave's interior, one would never even suspect a lifeform had eve before been here.

"God!" Keith said. "Home away from home. Those little Barthonian buggers really <u>do</u> like Earth's caverns."

Crystalline formations in the distance refracted and twinkled the light of the two spheres back to them.

"It's gorgeous," Frida said. She and Jeffrey inched forward, gliding over to their father. He was moving off on his own, inching his way into the bowels of the cavern.

"Kids, don't go off like that!" Kimberly called. "Wait for me. None of us knows how to walk in this Moon gravity."

She eased herself over to them, like a diver on the ocean floor.

Keith paused to lend his kids a hand as they caught up to him. He then surveyed the cavern's many sectors in search of some clue as to why the Barthonians would create this place at all.

"This can't be all there is to it," he said. He looked back to the crystalline mass way behind them all now in the shadowy twilight. He wondered if the Athena avatar orb still as yet contained any of Athena's conscious essence, or if it even still existed once it entered that crystal storage unit. He wished a part of her essence was still around that he might ask her what they were supposed to find here. It was obvious some part of her conscious influence must still be in effect. Something powered the two Light Spheres and directed them to follow close behind the Hagertons.

"Hey, guys, I hope we find whatever we're supposed to soon," Keith said to the others. "These belts will last a pretty good while, but not forever."

Kimberly turned to glance back to the distant shaft that led back to the surface. "We can always walk away, try for the surface, one of the cities."

"You want to walk that far?" Keith queried again. "Hope someone finds us before we die of dehydration and fatigue?"

Keith glanced back. As if on cue a sudden purple mist—a force field—waxed into presence before the shaft's upward slant. "See what you did, Kim?" he pretended to accuse. "You got this place mad, with your talk about leaving here. Apparently, you . . . WE only got one pass to consider such notions. Two times and the system starts taking our thoughts about leaving here seriously." He nodded. "We're being observed, even now. Athena's essence is all around us, you can actually feel her."

Keith noticed then an unusually shadowed sector far to the rear. He started for it.

His family automatically followed. One of the light spheres also followed, darting quickly away from its mate. Keith stopped to study the sector. The sphere halted as well.

"Athena is definitely still running the show down here," he said.

Kimberly and the kids each nodded, one after the other.

Something definitely lay ahead. The Light sphere brightened even more, melting the shadows away.

A recessed area or cavity, formed by the presence of several limestone-like "column" formations, lay before them. It was about ten meters wide by five high. Its interior remained dark, shadowed. Keith couldn't figure why none of the light falling toward it penetrated its darkness.

"Keith, what is that?" Kimberly asked.

"I don't know. Something's not right about it, though."

The cavity's interior seemed to devour the light that struck it, the way perhaps *black holes* in space insatiably consumed light and all radiation into their bottomless depths.

They reached it finally. The Light Sphere stopped about six meters back, its light flooding the entrance to the cavity full strength. The cavity's inner reaches, however, remain unaffected.

"It looks almost alive," Keith said.

He could see the cavity's interior now, but superimposed over it appeared to be a membrane. It had an almost mottling or agitated nature about it.

It's almost as if it wasn't there at all, Keith told himself. He reached out his hand. "Damn!" he said.

"*Keith!*" Kimberly beseeched him. She grabbed his arm.

The membrane felt slippery. It rippled outward like a water sheen where he disturbed it, or actually like the field bubble of Athena's orb when one touched it.

The whole wall suddenly resonated. Keith backed away. All at once a magnificent fortress, a small *city of lights* appeared out of nowhere. It didn't look real. It floated in the middle of *nothing*, a nothing that went back forever. A red path of light ribboned away from it all at once and snaked it way toward Keith. It stopped just the other side of the membrane. He approached the membrane again. The ribbon was several meters wide. If the pathway was real, then the distance to the fortress was enormous. It would take hours to traverse the whole of that ribbon. But that was not possible. It snaked away farther then the Moon was wide. He had to be looking into another dimension, another universe.

He touched the membrane again. It had the texture of an inflated rubber balloon. All at once his hand pierced it—went all the way through. He pulled his hand out again and looked back at his family. They were at his heels. He turned back for the membrane.

"Keith, don't!" pleaded Kimberly.

"I have to," he answered. "You know I do."

He shoved his arm and then his whole body all the way through.

Kimberly gasped at that. He looked back at her from the other side of the wall. Then he looked around him. There was nothing to either side, no floor, no walls, just emptiness. Only the red "pathway" kept him from falling into what seemed a bottomless abyss. As he looked down at it, it made him dizzy. He gazed toward the city of lights, and suddenly felt a rush of red energy sweep up from the pathway and surround him in a *whoosh*.

"**Keith!**" called Kimberly, stunned, as it consumed him.

He barely had time to look back to her, when suddenly he noticed everything blurring all around him. He felt a rushing and then nothing at all.

"**KEITH! DAD!**" called Kimberly and the kids after him as he disappeared in a shot. The entire pathway retracted toward the city, taking Keith with it!

Kimberly and the kids were alone there, and the city disappeared.

CHAPTER TWENTY-FIVE

-1-

At first Keith didn't know what to think. He felt a breeze on his face; the sun's rays were warm, and he preferred keeping his eyes closed. He lay on the grass; he could feel its cool greenness beneath him, and the blades felt tingly against his fingers. A brook murmured off in the distance; he sensed a lake nearby, and the air smelled of spring. Opening his eyes, he saw he was upon the lake's shoreline, just upon a shallow bank, nestled in weeds and grass. The breeze shimmered the lake's surface.

He'd come here to rest, he reasoned. He did not know his location or the moment he decided to come here; he knew only that he liked it here. Hills rolled off to the horizons around him; he could stay forever, the way the peace of it all impacted upon his soul. He hated to think, to reason out the whys and wherefores of what it all was. But then far off in the distance and upon a drop off ridge overlooking what seemed to be a vast ocean, he saw what looked to be a cherry tree full of pretty pink blossoms, growing precariously off the edge of a tremendous drop off ridge. Low billowy steam clouds hung all about it, in red-tinted shades of the advancing sunset, and more such clouds hung everywhere upon the scene in the seeming approach of dusk. But the peculiar sight that made everything in his immediate area come into serious question as to its reliable authenticity was the flow of magma, of lava dripping from everywhere. It made no sense at all. It just made for a very provocative image and probably in the context delivered the point that it intended to:

Do you wish to see something cool in front of you? Okay, enjoy.

And the truth of that meant only one thing. This wasn't *Earth*; it wasn't anywhere he knew. He remembered the black abyss in the cavity, the city of lights beyond the membrane, the path of red light, and he remembered his family beyond . . . somewhere. He couldn't recall ending up here, and wasn't certain if he'd lain here for an eternity. And he really hated disturbing the peace he felt within him with all this foolishness about reality. But then he remembered the worry for *him* upon the faces of his loved ones, and he thought his peace a selfish one.

He rose then and considered just what it was he had got himself into.

This was it, wasn't it? he thought. Athena's capture domain. The world she fashioned for all her captured humans. A place of dreams, lovely or scary. As one might imagine Heaven, itself, had the capacity to be for whomever wished to see it as either one way or the other.

Even now despite that realization, his mind protested to the intrusion of sobering, intelligent ponderings. He wanted instead only to empty his mind again, to just leave thinking to people who needed it as a shield against their own loneliness. But . . . he had responsibilities, and he couldn't. He looked about the realm. Suddenly, in the blue sky above him, a shooting star seared across it leaving a jet trail in its wake and fell into the horizon beyond the next hill, somewhere amid all that cascading lava. He wondered what it had been. A fiery sheen lit up the hill and the blue sky above it. The light seemed to call to him. He rose and headed over for it.

He moved as naturally as he ever did on Earth, his movements among the weeds and grass as pleasant as any spring day romp he had ever managed to take beyond New Allentown. He felt the familiar pull of gravity challenging his ascent of the hill, and the anticipation of reaching its top. The city, or whatever, lay afire in a blaze of light so bright it hurt to look at it. And whatever the fireball had been that he'd seen streaking across the sky, there was no sign of it now in the distance beyond. Perhaps, it had merged with the light of the city.

Become ONE with it?

Now why did I think of that? he asked.

He didn't know; he couldn't quite get a grasp on what he was sensing or feeling.

He thought of his family. "Kimberly?" he called.

He looked about the valley for a possible sign of her, worried for her that she and the kids just might be stuck somewhere near that hot flowing lava. But there was no sign of her or the kids, anywhere. He was alone. *Where was this, really, this place?*" he wondered again. What type of domain, intended for what ultimate purpose? What had he passed through, a dimensional conduit of some sort, leading into Athena's very being? Perhaps, on the other hand, this time he really *was* dead. He might have fallen off the pathway, after it retracted, and perished in the abyss.

Then, would that make the city before him, *Heaven?*

"I'm not dead," he told himself. This made sense in a bizarre kind of way. If you were going to hold *captives* for an indefinite spell, and in a state that had no attachment to the physical universe, this might be what such a domain would resemble—a place of dreams.

A dilemma confronted him, ultimately. Should he start for the city, abandon his family back wherever they were, or search for a way back to the membrane? He faced the valley once more. God, but it was inviting. That lake. It lay in a stand of maple trees as cattails and other foliage idled in the wind. The only thing that looked wrong was the sight of those ridges in the distance with the lava flows cascading down from them. He should wish them away and quit spoiling the view. But were they? The sight of such a spectacle, as ridiculous as it was, was kind of invigorating.

That created another dichotomy within him. What did he want more? The peace of this scene before him, or to seek answers to the city of lights way off in the distance?

He wondered if the dear departed ever faced decisions like this in Heaven.

Kimberly and the kids remained before the membrane. She flushed her palms against it, shoving at it, hoping to rip it away, but it held taunt. Though as slick as an oily film on a window, it was as strong as any wall, and she couldn't imagine even a laser beam piercing it. She'd have loved to fire at it with a laser cannon, rip the lousy son a bitch membrane to velvet shreds. She was beyond level-headed thinking at this point. The force shield surrounding the exit tunnel, she noted out of the corner of her eye, had dropped behind her, but it quickly resurfaced, the second she glanced to it.

Kimberly looked around her to all the cavern-like formations. She gritted her teeth, and shook her fist at the cave. And then, "Athena, why? Why do you keep taking my loved ones from me like this? I thought we were okay, you and I. If you want the kids and me, then why . . . why is this damn entry of yours not working? ATHENA!! Are you even hearing me?"

She sat down in fatigue upon a nearby stalagmite, the general shape of a blunted snow cone. She looked over at her kids, and opened her arms to them. They accepted her invitation, directly. "No, Mom," said Frida. "I think she can't hear us. I think it's like when you leave your avatar and return to your own reality in your own body. It takes a while to get back into the reality of your real self. I don't think Athena means to be cruel."

Kimberly smiled, weakly, and reached a hand out to her daughter, which she then pressed up against her cheek and kissed. "I hope you're right, sweetie," she said.

"When is it our turn to go, Frida?" Jeffrey asked her.

"How should I know?" she queried, glancing to him.

"She's your friend, right?" he reminded.

Frida frowned. "So SHE says. To me, they were only dreams."

Kimberly looked back to the shaft entrance. The shield was down again. It seemed to be toying with her, taunting her to try and make a run for it back to the surface and to her own people topside in the lunar cities. She wondered what would happen if she and her kids did made a dash for it, caught it off guard. She wondered how far up the shaft they would get, or how far away was the nearest lunar city.

Jeffrey looked down at his life support belt. He pondered the membrane. "Maybe, Mom," he supposed of the membrane's surface, "It will open if real skin touches it. Maybe it doesn't like the feel of an energy shield surrounding us." He was fiddling with the control settings.

"Jeff!" she yelled. He froze and looked up at her. She got up and took him by his arm. "Don't you **dare** mess with that belt! We're on the Moon. There's no air. That belt is the only thing keeping you alive out here, you hear me?"

Jeffrey had teardrops misting his eyes. "I want to be where Dad is, Mom,' he uttered, lowly.

She cradled him against her breasts. "I know, sweetheart. So do I."

"Mom!" Frida suddenly called to Kim. Kimberly looked up. Frida was by the membrane. "Athena!" she pointed.

***

In the dark of this subterranean lunar cave the sight of such an incredible, ethereal presence was overwhelming. A halo of light encircled her, the glare from it so brilliant, it lit up the cave, overpowering the candlepower of the two light spheres. Athena, dressed in a long, white gown, which billowed and fluttered in an ethereal breeze, seemed to glide through the cavern beyond the cavity entrance and approach the membrane's edge. Her long blond hair in curls, cascaded down the front of her shoulders and draped her bosom. She seemed as if she were walking at the bottom of an insanely clear lake, and not so much walking but gliding. She certainly was a beautiful sight to behold. And she was smiling toward Frida so near to the membrane entrance at this point.

"Hi, bestie," she said to Frida. "You're awake for real this time. We're really here together. Come, I've been waiting for you to arrive. So much to do; so much to catch up."

"Frida!" called Kimberly storming forward for her daughter. (Not as easy as one might image, because of the Moon's one-sixth gravity. It was like walking across the bottom of a swimming pool.)

"Frida," she ordered, "get away from that membrane. "No, Athena. You can't take her. If she enters your realm it's with her family. All or none."

"Oh, Kimberly," Athena's beautiful voice uttered, her words seemingly filling the entire cavern, "will you trust me? Must you get so . . . *intense?*"

"*Bestie,*" Kimberly replied, as if mocking her, "you haven't seen intense."

Kimberly was only just a few meters away from her daughter now.

"Frida, NOW! *Get over here!*"

Obediently, the young girl began to move away, swimming in the reduced gravity, and trying to keep upright. Jeffrey, nearer to her than his Mon, extended his hand.

"I'm sorry, Frida," announced Athena, gently. "But that will not do. You must come with me. It's more important than you know."

Frida sensed a lift-belt activation warning fire off in her thoughts. She glanced down at her belt and then up her Mom. "Mom?" she began.

"Stop!" Frida then ordered of the unit. But it activated its levitation

212

circuitry nonetheless. It was an orbit class unit, and it was designed for work crews engaged in EVA in orbit above the Earth.

"Frida!" Kimberly called, reaching her but not able to take hold of her arm in time. Frida's feet left the floor and the momentum of her ascent sent her right up against the wall. She passed right through it as if it weren't even there. Athena extended her arms and Frida fell right up against her, into her awaiting grasp. A great explosion of light issued then, a searing surge of energy that ignited the entire cavern in a blinding white light. And with an abrupt flourish it died away. The two were gone that quickly. The membrane again was almost solid in appearance and blank.

"*Goddamn you, Athena!*" Kimberly swore. "She's **my** daughter, not **yours**. She's my kid. What about Jeffy and me? Take all of us then you *bitch!*"

She charged the wall, with Jeffrey in tow. The one-sixth gravity floated them smack up against it, and for them it repelled them like a brick wall. Kimberly began to pound the membrane with her fists. "Frida! Keith! *KEITH, where are you?*"

"Kimberly?"

Keith's voice suddenly filled her mind, Jeffrey's too, as she noted the acknowledgment in her son's eyes. It sounded utterly strange and distant, as peaceful sounding as she'd always imagined Heaven itself might sound.

"Keith?" she answered.

"Dad!" (From Jeffrey.)

All at once the city of lights reappeared far in the distance within the membrane and issuing from it a red ribbon snaked forward through this ether . . . this . . . whatever this membrane realm was. In her mind, Kimberly heard herself asking the thing to hurry the fuck up and arrive.

"It's fading again, Mom!" Jeffrey said of the city.

It was. Kimberly was certain the city itself was Athena and she was messing with Kimberly on purpose, for being so last-minute uncooperative, the only one who'd been, so it had seemed. She felt her muscles tense. Jeffrey felt her grasp tighten. His heart began to beat faster. They were going to lose Athena's city of lights, it was fading so swiftly.

It was almost gone, but the pathway (very vague in hue now) touched up against the membrane surface. Kimberly didn't give a hoot what nature or laws of physics explained a wall that a human body could walk through as if it were only partially solid. She just pulled on Jeffrey's arm and shoved them both through the membrane and onto the pathway. Jeffrey had no time to consider what was happening. He was in what he obviously realized was some different dimensional reality at once. It scared him, the total breath of it all around him.

Kimberly ordered in her mind for Athena to quit fucking with her and

Jeff. What did they really ever do, the two of them, to deserve to be treated this way? She demanded the distant city stop fading, and to take them both. Though barely even seen now, its diminishing seemed to answer her request and pause. Impatiently, she tried to walk herself and Jeffrey down the length of the pathway. It turned livid with light, exploded into a fireball around them, and suddenly, like a ball of heat lighting, charged away and for the city.

"Oh, ye of little faith," the two of them heard Athena say to them in their thoughts. "I had every intention of taking you. Your resistance just made it more fun."

In the sky above Keith all at once, yet another fireball screamed across the blackness. It wasn't in as much of a hurry as the first, he noted, vaguely, but one thing became clear: it was headed straight for him. With great difficulty he sought to awaken his lumbering thought patterns, but too late. The object was upon him and there was nowhere to run.

It missed him, just barely, landing instead at his feet. Kimberly and Jeffrey lay dazed upon the ground. Kimberly pulled her head up and abruptly saw the legs and feet of her husband. He was standing, staring at her and Jeffrey, open-mouthed.

"Kimberly?" he asked. "Jeffrey?" *That must have been how I arrived,* he thought. "Are you guys all right?"

Kimberly looked out upon the strangeness of the world she had landed within; she felt a warm breeze upon her face and the scent of spring in the air. And in the distance to her left: the high elevation ridge with all the rising steam clouds and lava flowing off it. She thought she was going to faint.

"Keith?" she called.

"You went through the wall, too, right?" he said, aware he was stating the obvious.

"What is this place?" she asked looking up at him. She eyed the lava flows again. "And what's going on over there? Is that lava?"

"Yes," he acknowledged.

"Why?"

"A new part of the island developing, I suppose," he replied, dryly.

"We're on an island?"

Keith shrugged. "Maybe. . . . Probably. I' m not really sure. I'm still trying to sort it all out in my head."

"You'll let me know when you do, right?" she smirked.

Keith grinned and helped her and Jeffrey up to their feet. "Jeff, you all right, champ?"

Jeffrey nodded, and then he saw the cherry blossoms on the lone tree upon the distant cliff, and all the lava flowing off the ridges for the ocean depths far below. "Oh, wow, Dad," he said. "Is that one of yours?"

Keith grinned and shrugged. "Jeff, if it is, it beats me how I conjured it."

"This is the real Athena realm this time, isn't it?" Jeff inferred. "Where she keeps all of us?"

"Yes, Jeff, that would be my guess. It kind of reminds me of what some people down the ages imagined Heaven might be. You two haven't even seen the best part. Look over in that direction," he said, pointing to his right and to the crest of the hill. Kimberly and Jeffrey looked. A bright haze on the far horizon suggested something immense on the other side of the hill.

Kimberly assumed an angry stance. "That's got to be Athena herself," she scowled. "I know it. And Keith, she took Frida!"

"She what?"

"Yes, snatched her right out of the cave. Why are you wasting time *here*, conjuring up pretty scenery? That's Athena, you know it has to be. Why aren't you trying to get there?"

"I was about to when you and Jeff arrived. Kimmy, actually I'm only just arrived myself. I'm still getting used to being here."

"You've been gone a half hour!" she said. "What are you talking about?"

He looked at her. "You didn't just follow behind me?"

"No!"

"Kimberly, take it easy. You trust Athena, don't you?"

"I want to," she replied. "But sometimes she displays a total lack of — what's the word I want — *Empathy*."

"Dad," called Jeffrey lowly all at once. Keith and Kimberly were staring at the crest of the hill and to the lights.

"Yeah, Jeff?"

"Can you hear it?"

"Hear what, Jeff?"

"*Over the River and Through the Woods to Grandmother's House we go?* It's in my head. Athena's telling me that's what we're supposed to do."

"I don't hear a thing, Jeff. What do you mean?"

"We're supposed to go to the light. Over the river and through the woods."

Keith looked at Kimberly and then back at Jeffrey. "Athena is telling you that right now?"

He nodded.

The two adults took a few steps upward for the hill's crest. "We will, son. Soon."

"Jeff, your sister will be fine," said Kimberly only half believing it. "She likes Frida."

"Mom? Dad? Do you know the story, *'Little Red Riding Hood'*?"

Little Red Riding Hood? repeated Keith in his mind. "It's old," he said, "very old. But yeah, vaguely."

"We have to start now, Dad, for the light. Right now!"

"Why, son?" began Keith. "Why do we have to start right—?"

Jeffrey's outfit had changed; he was now dressed in a Goth version of "little red riding hood," complete with the red hood and cloak, black maryjanes with a one-inch heel, fish-nets that tapered mid-calf and a very short matching burgundy red skirt with lacy black fringe, matching the fringe on the hood and cloak. "Oh. *Shit,*" Keith sighed in exasperation.

"Athena says so," finished Jeff. "Right now." He looked down at himself, at what Athena had dressed him in now. *Perfect,* he thought.

***

Now upon the hill's crest, they started for the descent down it again in the direction of the city. Keith took his wife's hand as Kimberly took hold of her "son's." Kimberly smiled and sadly shook her head at Jeffrey's predicament. "You make a cute 'little red riding hood,' honey," she said.

"Will Athena ever stop forcing little girls' Halloween costumes on me, Mom?"

"You wear them well," she only replied.

"Okay," said Keith. "Let's go find us a city of lights. . . . Hey, Jeff?"

"Yeah, Dad?"

"She could have dressed you as Dorothy from the *Wizard of Oz.*"

"Who?"

"Yeah, that was a bit before your time. At least you look cool."

The distant city of lights hung as if a tiny sun off in the distance.

CHAPTER TWENTY-SIX

-1-

Greg Phillips ambled over to the bedroom HoloView window panel in only his underwear. He had spent the night at his dad's place in Capital City. It was past ten. A fluffy bank of clouds hung above the distant horizon in the depicted scene.

He was half asleep. He'd put in a full day yesterday and the last thing he felt like enduring right now was a bright, sunny hologram scene.

"Go to black," he ordered the panel. He felt like telling it to go to hell, but he knew it probably wouldn't understand the command, much less be able to carry it out. The visual abruptly faded from the wall, leaving only a gray panel of nothingness. The room plunged into darkness. Well that helped his eyes out, but now he couldn't tell his head from his ass. "A little more light than *that* if you don't mind," he asked, gently. "Give me a midnight view."

Onto the panel evolved a night vista of the western skyline. A full moon washed the distant hills in a ghostly pale white. It seemed almost haunting. Greg looked up at the Moon image and was reminded of the Hagertons.

Poor dumb fools, he thought. He wondered if Athena had in fact gone to the Moon. If so, she should have landed by now. He wondered, as well, if anything strange over the Lunar Alps had been spotted. For his father's sake, he hoped so, and for the Hagertons' sake as well. There might still be a chance that they might be intercepted and rescued before Athena hauled them and all the prior captives away for ports unknown.

"Idiot," he called Keith Hagerton now. "You'd had a chance back there last night to let us help you free your whole family from that situation, and now . . . Shit."

Greg wondered why his dad had allowed him to sleep till so late in the morning. He'd be wanting the duplicate viewwafer, and only Greg knew where in his apartment he'd stashed it. He *had* to want Greg to catch the first shuttle out for New Allentown to retrieve it.

"Unless you already had Marion make copies of it before any of us, even Keith Hagerton, got here and spirited it away."

He wouldn't put it past Randolph Phillips to do such a thing. Not a bit.

***

It was getting on toward noon, already. Greg supposed he'd better call his superiors in New Allentown, soon, to let them know where he was and that he probably wouldn't be back at all today, at least not to report to work. He wondered where his father was; he then walked over to the door and departed the hallway foyer.

"Dad?" He entered the living room. Daylight blazed from the "HoloDeck" patio. It lit up the room.

No swath of sunlight on the floor, he noted, as he looked for one.

A real patio along the city exterior would cause a sunbeam upon the floor. This pretend one didn't. Neither did the sun's light warm him, as he faced it. The most he could say about the reproduction was that it looked like the real thing, but it lacked a real one's full impact.

The view faced the wilderness southeast of the city, the correct direction for that wall. His eyes adjusted to the light, and he looked again for his father.

"Hey Dad?"

He heard a movement in the kitchen. Someone got up from the table in there and started for the room's exit. "Dad— Hello, who are *you?*"

A man probably in his mid-thirties entered the room, dressed in standard bureaucrat issue attire: a "suit." It was actually casual-looking: blue trousers and a jacket with a collar that was reminiscent of what ministers once wore.

"Mr. Phillips," the man answered, absently, "your father sent me down to collect you."

"He did? Why, where the hell is he?"

"He had to step out. He apologizes for his absence."

(He had a meeting with the Commodore this morning in the old city.)

"The meeting in the old city with Commodore Stakely?"

"Yes. I'm to escort you to Sydney. Your father will meet you there tomorrow evening."

"He'll do *what?* What am I supposed to do in Sydney until tomorrow night? And where is *he* going to be?"

(Sydney, Australia. Earth headquarters for *InterWorld.*)

"My orders are only to escort you there. That's all I can tell you."

"Well, it's not as simple as that! He forgets I have commitments. I'm not some child he's getting excused from Instruc for a few days. I'll have to call New Allentown and clear an unscheduled leave with my superiors."

"Don't worry about that, Mr. Phillips," he said, dryly. "It's been taken care of."

"Oh." *Just like that,* Greg thought. "You can't give me a hint what's happening?"

He shook his head. "I don't know, myself. I don't have the level clearance."

Dad doesn't need me or my viewwafer, Greg deduced. *He never did. The arrogant bastard was only humoring me.*

Greg painted a smile on his face and nodded. "Have you been here long?"

"An hour," the man replied.

"Alright, give me time to get dressed, washed up? I'll be with you as soon as I can."

The guy nodded.

"What's your name, anyway?" Greg asked.

"Harrison."

"Did my dad leave any messages? Anything about my going to Pennsylvania, to pick something up I left there?"

"As far as I was briefed, you're not scheduled to make *any* trips back to New Allentown."

Greg nodded, vacantly. He smiled. "Okay, Harrison, make yourself comfortable." He backed into the foyer again and turned for the guest bedroom.

Government types. They never ceased to amuse Greg.

Randolph Phillips had been early out of the apartment that morning, and in truth he'd had little sleep the whole night. He'd been in secret contact with the World Council and *InterWorld*, pooling together all the material available about past UFO studies and research, and missing persons, as well as those who claimed to have had close encounters and lived to tell about it.

He knew to say little at the moment to his fellow associates here on Earth or the Moon because of the lack of convincing evidence, the same heartaches that had plagued UFO research in centuries past. So he had simply ordered the Think-Tank boys to come up with a few theories about plasma anomalies and ways to track them should they actually leave a residue of their having come and gone. By nine that morning they had come up with a few ideas, and had already begun to request experimental signal trace tests among the many orbiting cities, space stations and traffic above the Earth They hoped to detect some trace of the Hagertons' "orb" as it made its "presumed" voyage to the northern territories of the Moon. Naturally, half the people who agreed to work on this idiocy did so out of loyalty, curiosity, or service to Randolph. Without real proof, he was little more than an educated fool whose genius had probably slipped a few gears. It was embarrassing to work this way, but Randolph had to be fast to get anything on Athena and her ultimate mission here in the Earth solar system before she and her human captives vanished to wherever in the universe they were going.

"Okay, Chief, bring it up," Commodore Roger Stakely instructed

Security Chief MacIntire of the Playback/Time-Code from last night's security scans.

Onto the 3-D display table before him a model-like replica of D.C. Park (depicted now in bright and glorious sunlight) wiped off the screen, leaving it looking like little more than a glossy ping pong table with an intricate lattice-work design of crystal upon its surface.

Randolph Phillips stood patiently to the right of the display beside the commodore as MacIntire made the final inputs.

(Chief MacIntire had circles around his eyes. He'd only sacked out for a few hours after his watch had ended that morning. He was doing this at the personal request of the commodore.)

Washington D.C. Park returned to the screen, only this time in its night-time appearance, bathed in a multitude of artificial lights and the scarlet cocoon shields. There seemed only silence and tranquility amid the fountain displays; autumn leaves dropped and littered the many lawns and parks. Suddenly, a small purple orb emerged from the pyramidion tip of the Washington Monument and like a ghostly apparition wafted downward toward the monument's base and then across the Reflecting Pool. It climbed and cleared the Lincoln Memorial and ended by the banks of the Potomac near the Arlington Bridge. It stayed briefly, expanding in size to that of a human form, and there "appeared" Randolph and his son Greg. The orb shrunk back to its normal thirty centimeter size and began to rise high into the sky. It was gone a second later, streaking upward like a meteor would if it could leave Earth instead of fall for it.

Nothing of any great significance happened after its departure. The scene only showed the two Phillips men descend the bank for the river and their air car, parked just off shore.

Chief MacIntire took a breath, and Stakely shuffled his feet.

Randolph looked at the both of them. "Were you able to get a good close-up of that orb?" he asked the security chief.

MacIntire nodded and absently touched a menu screen; up popped Athena's orb in all its frightening form.

"Okay," nodded Randolph.

"It isn't much," thought Commodore Stakely of what actually had been recorded.

"I was there, Rog," he said. "Quite a lot happened, don't worry."

"I'm sure of that," the commodore said. "Incredible. That's the only word for it." He stood in awe of the image of the orb. Then, he turned to Randolph. "At least you got it on record. Although I doubt it will convince anyone to suddenly start believing we're being visited by alien intelligences."

"I'm working on that," he only answered.

"Uh huh," the commodore replied. "I understand you have your son to thank for bringing this all to your attention."

"Yeah, that's right," he replied, absently.

"So, what good will this discovery do you now, Randolph? Is there any trace of what that thing did after it left D.C.?"

Randolph smiled. "Alien sightings of any kind down the centuries have been notorious for eluding human tracking systems. I've put in a request with the Terran Fleet throughout the solar system to be on the lookout, but I'm not expecting a serious response to it."

The commodore looked at the image display again. The scene still hadn't changed from when he'd looked at it last. He nodded to the security chief, and Christ MacIntire shut the system down. The daylight version of the identical scene again resolved across the display's surface and within it came the tiny impressions of tourists walking amid the various attractions of the Mall and Park. The chief then removed himself to a corner wall where he extracted a copy of the archive extract he had just been replaying. It was stored on a crystalline wafer of a kind not unlike a Sensor Sphere viewwafer. He placed it in a tiny leather case and handed it to Randolph.

"Councilman?"

"Thank you," Randolph said as he pocketed the recording. "Well, I guess I'm off then. Thank you both for all your help. If anything else, this will make a good entertainment visual someday."

"Good luck," said the commodore.

Randolph nodded. "I'll find my way out." He looked about the small security facility, standing where the Pentagon complex once reposed. "Hard to believe what went on here once on this very ground," he mused. "Well, later gentlemen."

After he'd gone, the commodore looked over at Chief MacIntire. "I'd like to think he really gave a fuck about that poor family he claims were captured."

Chris MacIntire nodded.

"Give the (security) watch back to Ricolleti, Chief," the commodore said, slapping the man on the shoulder. "Go get some sleep, man. You've earned it."

Randolph Phillips entered the suborbital flight shuttle that was waiting for him beyond the main entrance to the facility. She was a sleek looking ship, with heavy duty magnetic drive engines, and she was fast. She'd make it to the Nellus Space Port in Nevada—the United States' main traffic port to the outer planets—in under an hour. No sooner was Randolph in, then the pilot lifted off and headed west.

The call alert on Randolph's gold communication pendant signaled. He gazed out at the rolling hillsides just under the shuttle.

"Phillips," he answered.

There was a small problem back in New Allentown, he was told.

"Everywhere?"

The response came in the affirmative.

"All right, I didn't want to put Greg in it, but no choice I suppose. Don't really need it, but if it's in his apartment, and he's not there, you never know, somebody else, the maid maybe, might find it. Even try watching it. Can't leave a thing like that behind, I suppose. I'll send Greg down for it. The place is clean, right? Good. You work out all the details on that end. . . . Very good. Phillips out."

"How's our time doing?" he asked his pilot.

"We're okay. The flight launches at noon. You'll be on it."

"It used to take three days once, did you know that? Three days just to go to the Moon."

"It was a bit before my time, I'd say." The pilot grinned.

Randolph nodded. "How's the Cassini end?"

"Foot and air crews are already traversing the Alps for any hint of the course. No luck so far. But they're giving it their all."

"I'm sure they are."

The Moon base in Cassini crater was only a few hundred kilometers south of the mountains, and made a perfect base operations point. He hoped to arrive there by the afternoon. He could only wonder what success any of this would bring.

He looked out the rear side windows to the vanishing profile of old Washington D.C. The Monument set within the brilliant blue sky, a perfect finger of white, vibrant against the aging morning light. D.C. looked so innocent this morning. He thought about what had happened here just a few hours ago in the night, and then he turned his attention to the broad length of the Appalachian Mountains of West Virginia just ahead the ship. He sat back and enjoyed the ride.

CHAPTER TWENTY-SEVEN

-1-

Greg was in the hot tube, enjoying the swirling hot water, in his father's master bathroom. No point, he thought, in rushing to get down to Transport only to sit around idle. His flight to Sydney probably wouldn't get off for several hours, yet. Besides, he felt just a wee bit rebellious and angry. His father had up and taken off on this Hagerton matter without him, leaving to underlings the servile task of seeing Greg safely to Sydney where he'd remain accessible, yet conveniently out of the way. It bothered Greg to be included in his father's endeavors only when it suited the man's purposes. He actually resented Randolph, resented his accomplishments, and wondered if he'd remain in his father's shadow forever.

"Mr. Phillips?" he heard a voice call, suddenly, from the other side of the bathroom door. It was Harrison.

"Yeah?" he shouted back to him. "Be out in a few."

"I have a message from your father, Greg."

"Unlock," Greg spoke softly into the air above his bath. "It's open," he shouted, then.

The door swished into the wall. "Sorry to disturb the bath," Harrison responded, absently.

"It's all right. What's up? Getting near shove off time?"

The man shook his head. "Change of plans. Your father sent word that he needs you to make a swing past New Allentown and pick up the article you left there. He said you'd know what he was referring to."

So he still needs it . . . and me, he pondered. Greg nodded. "I wondered when he'd get around to it," he said aloud.

"He's booked you on a flight out of New Allentown to Sydney, three this afternoon. He says that should you give you enough time to get back there and collect the item."

"Will you be joining me?"

Harrison shook his head. "I'm going ahead. I'll see you in Sydney when you get there. Your father said to lock up after you leave."

"I will. See you down under, then, Harrison."

The man nodded, and stepped out of the door. It closed behind him.

Greg slipped back down into the water. "The time please?" he called out softly.

"Eleven-thirty and twenty-four seconds," came an answer somewhere overhead.

He closed his eyes again.

Melanie Richards had gone to Greg's apartment in New Allentown around ten that morning. She had hoped to reconcile her differences with him, and maybe join him for breakfast. Neither of them were due in at work till noon. Already in the clothes she would wear to work that day, she had opted on a tight knit wool sweater, light gray, a dark gray, almost black mini-skirt smoky-gray tights and black pumps with a wide three-inch heel. As the turbo lift deposited her on Greg's floor, she glanced down to her outfit and wondered if Greg would find it "alluring."

Instead of finding Greg, she had stumbled onto a team of security men, searching through Greg's things and generally making a mess of the place. His home looked a shambles. Drawers and cabinets out turned, their contents lay spread out on the floors.

"And you are?" one of them had inquired of her as she entered the den.

"A friend of Greg's," she had answered. "What is all this?"

"Which friend?" the man pursued, checking down an imaging tablet of names. He looked up then, finding what appeared to be a match. "Melanie Richards? Transport Subsection B, Passenger Records Division?"

She nodded. "And who are you?"

He flashed a World Council Security emblem her way, and as quickly returned it to its pocket. "You were with Mr. Phillips last night when he found the visual, weren't you?" He read the report, then nodded to himself as he continued to read down the tablet. "Did he leave it with you by any chance?"

"How did *you* find out about that?" she asked. "Did Greg give you permission to trash his apartment, looking for it?" Melanie noticed Greg's entire ViewWafer collection spread out on the floor before the cabinet in the den where he stored them. She saw his Sensor Sphere, as well, lying like an old baseball upon the nearby sofa.

"The question I gave you, Ms. Richards," he reminded, "was *if Mr. Phillips left the wafer in your possession?*"

"I'm sorry, what?" she asked, abruptly. Her mind had been on the Sensor Sphere. "No, I wanted nothing to do with the visual or with Greg after he took it."

"So, then you wouldn't know where he hid it?"

"Why don't you ask *him*? Isn't Greg here?"

Obviously, he wasn't, she thought. *He'd never sit still for all this.*

"I wouldn't concern myself too much about Mr. Phillips, Ms. Richards," he lowly responded. "We do have the authority to be here, I can assure you."

I'll bet, she thought. The Sensor Sphere's innocent stance on the sofa continued to interest her, and suddenly she noticed one of its "command" headsets draping an armrest as well. She inched over to it, waited for the search team to be looking the other way, and deftly pulled it to her, concealing it beneath her attaché case.

"I have to go," she said. "I've a few errands to run before I start work today."

"Then, don't let us keep you," the team leader replied. He had not seen her take the headset, and offered what looked like a smile. "We won't need you for anything more. But, Ms. Richards, we *would* appreciate it if you don't discuss the contents of that recording with anyone."

She had nodded she wouldn't and quietly backed out of the apartment.

Fifteen meters down the hallway from Greg's residence, she stopped and leaned against the wall. She took a breath and knelt down so that she could lay her attaché case on the floor and open it.

She placed the headset within it, and quickly closed it again. Then, looking back toward Greg's apartment (as such making sure that she had got away clean) she got up, absently smoothing her very short skirt against her tights, and sort of using the tights themselves against her thighs to remove whatever imagined stress-elicited perspiration might have accumulated on her palms. She hurried, then, over to the nearest turbo lift.

Melanie's residence was one floor up from Greg's: level 146. She was breathing easier now, a whole floor above those men from World Council Security, but she still would not feel safe until she was back within her own place.

RICHARDS
APT. 2204, SECTOR 6
QUADRANT 1

She stepped quickly inside her door. Ahead in the living room she saw Samuel, her Himalayan cat. He was sprawled out on the narrow sill of the terrace-window and was looking out at the western vista of the Blue Mountains beyond the city. (Melanie left the HoloView circuits on during the day all over the apartment just for him.) The cat looked over, meowed, and got down off the sill. He trotted over to her. Melanie always wondered if a cat knew the difference between a real image of the mountains and a hologram. She wondered if it mattered. She picked him up and hugged his face.

"HI, Sam, you miss me?" She'd been gone only a half hour. She sat him back down on a nearby lounge chair, and walked over to the den. She took a breath and smiled.

No one had searched <u>her</u> belongings. Either they weren't planning to, or hadn't got to them, yet. That thought suddenly wiped the contentment from her face and made her hurry to her viewing chamber. She went inside and opened a storage nook on the other side of the entrance. She pulled out a recorder module. She fished around then for an empty viewwafer, and finding one, placed it into the record bay. The hard part came next. A *Command Headset, Sensor Sphere and Record Unit* were a "set." One unit from one set could not access the mechanisms of a unit from another set, otherwise people could easily accomplish what she intended to accomplish now: She was going to spy on the agents sent to rifle through Greg's apartment. She had his command headset, and even from this distance it would communicate with Greg's sphere, on the sofa in his den. But she had to get at the works of one of her record units to change its recognition code so that it would accept the inputs from Greg's system. Being good with computers as she had already proven on many occasions to be, she got her recorder down on her electronics workbench, and went about the alteration.

She placed a light probe between her teeth to free her hands, and went to work on her computer. She placed the computer's interface headset upon her head, and ordered her system to interface with the Transport Department's super systems she had access to in her work. Once in, she began a few access requests that went a bit beyond the boundaries of accepted computer ethics.

It took a while, but she got past the security codes of Sensor Systems Inc., the company in Los Angeles that manufactured the Sensor Spheres, and accessed the information files on its hobbyist and recreational division. She found Greg's customer file, using the serial number on the side of his command headset and matched it against the master file listings in Los Angeles. She copied down the information regarding his unit's interface encryption code. Then she called up the design specs on the Interface Communicator, and began to alter the code settings on her own system's record unit until it matched Greg's. When she did, she took a breath, shoved the works back in and screwed back the rear plate.

"All right!" she said. "It ought to work." She placed the unit in the record mode, and slapped Greg's headset upon her head. She closed her eyes, and suddenly all around her came the vision of Greg's den. It was so real that her anxiety level and her heartbeat began to climb all over again. The men were talking and joking to one another. Thank God it wasn't *her* things they were going through. They weren't being respectful of Greg's property at all. They only had a job to do and that was all that mattered to them.

She had really gone out on a limb for Greg this time, breaking into a major electronics firm's computer system to accomplish what she had. She removed the headset from her head; her computer room reappeared around her once more. She would let the unit record for a couple of hours.

She thought about Greg.

As angry as he had made her, what she saw this morning in his apartment made his offenses seem harmless by comparison. She wondered where he was. She requested a time update, and then went over to her phone.

Placing its neural scan headset atop her head, she formed an image of a colleague in Greg's apartment at work, and a moment later she saw the air above the phone's imaging disk come alive with gray static. A second later a long-haired, brunette attendant by the name of Loni Raphael visualized above the disk's metal pedestal.

"Mellie!" Loni greeted. "Hi! What's up?"

"Loni," Melanie answered. "Loni, do you know where Greg is today?"

Loni smiled. "Everyone is looking for Greg today, Mellie. The rumor is he left town suddenly. He only listed his destination as Capital City."

Melanie thought back to the events of the night before. She recalled the excitement he had had about reviewing that strange visual of the Hagertons. Greg's father lived in Capital City. She wondered if he'd gone there to see him about something.

"Loni, why is everyone looking for Greg?"

"You really haven't heard? There's some weird stuff going down, Mellie. Last night, Greg was in charge of locating a missing runabout air car."

"I know," she answered. "He called me about it. A father and son named Hagerton took off for Crystal Cave."

"I thought you didn't know what was going on? Do you also know they never returned?"

She nodded. "Greg had a search team out looking for them. He told me."

"Well, late last night he recalled it. That in itself wasn't so bad. What was, was how he just took off and left the city, without leaving word with anyone. Frank Cromwell is furious. Here's the best part. Greg's hot shot father got someone on the World Council to call Frank this morning and tell him to give Greg a break. Sandra heard everything. Frank was told not to make trouble for Greg, and to give him a leave of absence for the next couple of weeks. Just like that. Greg spilled something to his dad, I know it. And now with what else happened last night—"

"What?"

Loni smiled again. "The runabout that was missing? It came back last night . . . by itself."

Melanie felt a quiver ride up the back of her head.

"It's weird, Melanie. Someone in Craft Storage was walking through the flight garage and noticed the ship parked in its berth, all tucked away nice and neat, as if somebody put it there. Mellie, no one knows how it got there."

"Jeez," Melanie replied. "And the Hagertons? Last night Greg was really getting worried over them."

"He had good reason to. The mother and daughter are missing now also. They're nowhere. The whole family has disappeared."

Another ripple went up Melanie's back.

"I wouldn't go down to the garage, Mellie. I hear it's a nut house down there—federal agents, news people, all over the place interviewing anyone who may have known something about the runabout. Meliie, you don't *know* anything about what happened, do you?"

"Greg discussed the case with me, professionally, Loni, that's all. What I heard was just routine. What you're telling me now is making my hair stand up."

"It's the most fascinating thing to happen to this city in years. Everybody is abuzz over it."

-4-

Scout ships (air cars) and shuttles arrived and departed with droning regularity all around Melanie as the Citywide-Transport elevator deposited her in New Allentown's Intercontinental Flight Terminal.

Her curiosity had got the best of her. Not five minutes after hanging up with Loni, Melanie had taken off for the turbo lifts. The bustle of people commuting between the various island cities of the world, formed a backdrop of shapes and sounds all around her.

Loni's description of the concourses was accurate. People were everywhere, crowding the maintenance entry ways for a glimpse at the great mystery. A rope-cordon barricaded the main entrance to the hanger deck garage. The rope was merely for show. Several meters behind it an invisible force shield did what the rope cordon only pretended to do.

Melanie used her credentials to get past the checkpoints. She felt the mere curious and the gawkers among the civilian population of the city watch her in envy as Transport Security lowered the entry shields and allowed her to pass. She thanked them.

An angry voice cut through the hustle and bustle of the flight bay. Melanie's ears felt the assault clear across the main thoroughfare as she descended from a mezzanine. Doug Manning of Craft Storage and Maintenance was berating one of his underlings. Manning's eyes were bloodshot, he looked as if he'd been up for hours, and with a temper like his Manning didn't handle the stress of this type of confusion, going through his department, not well at all. Basically, his gripe against Al Nolender was that he had stopped his repair work on an excursion bus to converse with a news agency field representative. The newsman was a bigwig with the east coast affiliates. With credentials high enough to get him past the checkpoints, he had entered the flight garage, approached the sector where the Hagerton air car was berthed and had found the nearest body who would indulge his desire for information. The federal boys came close to having the newsman booted out. Most everyone else had had their fill of being interrogated. He had found Al Nolender an apple ripe for the picking. He'd talked Al into answering a few questions.

Manning had security escort the newsman the hell out of the garage, and then descended on Nolender with a vengeance.

Melanie shook her head in sympathy for the poor bastard.

She got within ten meters of the Hagerton craft and stopped. It was the Hagerton vessel all right. What little of the viewwafer visual Greg had allowed her to see last night, included a few scenes of the two Hagerton males as they prepared to board the craft, and later as they unloaded the ship and climbed the incline to the cedar cabin entrance to Crystal Cave. It felt funny to see the same vehicle now before her, seemed weird to imagine it the source of all this confusion. She wondered yet again what revelations had existed on the viewwafer-visual that explained how the visual had surfaced in the Hagerton apartment, long after the entire family had mysteriously vanished.

A stoic-looking male departed the ship's interior and Melanie recognized his instantly. He was the same gent who had been in charge of the group she discovered going through Greg's things in his apartment. He paused and talked with one of his underlings, and Melanie quietly backed away from the area, searching for the nearest walkway exit.

"Can I help you, Miss?" Doug Manning suddenly asked her.

She jolted and turned. The man stood there in his soiled overalls, an assortment of tools strapped to his utility belt. He looked as if he would bit the next person who gave him a hard time.

Poor Melanie. Doug Manning was a big man; he looked intimidating. Here she was about a meter and half in height, about a hundred and five pounds, and in that long, black hair, black miniskirt, tights, wool sweater and three-inch black heels. She looked cute as a button and easy on any man's eyes, including Doug's, but girth-wise she was a bean pole next to him.

She smiled. "Excuse me, I was just leaving."

"Who are you?"

She awkwardly extended her hand. "Melanie Richards. I'm in *Records*."

"*Records*?" he responded. "You're in Transport?" She nodded. "Greg and I . . . that is, Greg Phillips and I, last night were discussing this case, before all this weird stuff— that I've been told about since—happened. I just had to come down here and see it for myself."

Doug Manning smiled. (Again, in that outfit and with that face and her hair down to her shoulders, she was easy on the eyes.) "Greg Phillips, huh?" he said. He nodded. "You're a friend of that little shithead, are you?"

She threw her hair off her eyes. "Yes, I am, and I wish you wouldn't call   him   that."

"Well, that boy has some explaining to do. I wouldn't have been so quick to hand him a ship last night, if I'd known he was running the investigation. Stoddard and his team got back, and I looked at him and I said, *Reily, who the fuck* . . . uh, I mean, 'hell,' sorry, missy, *who the hell pulled you in?* And he said, *That Phillips boy, you know the one who's the son of that famous councilman?*" Doug Manning nodded. "That boy is up to something. Came into my hanger last night and demanded I hand him a runabout and shut my fuc— . . . my stupid mouth."

That's my boyfriend, she thought.

"He's lucky I didn't deck him right there, big shot old man or not. For good measure I should have put his butt over my knee and whacked him a few. Take that privileged attitude of his down a few notches."

Doug Manning noticed how antsy Melanie was, and how she continually darted her eyes back to the tiny air car and to the federal boys and their antics.

Melanie looked at him. "Uh, Mr. Manning, I mean, Doug, yeah. Uh, I . . . I'm due on my shift about now. I better get back." She smiled then. "Greg's not all bad, really."

Doug Manning grinned. "I hope you and he aren't mixed up in something together. You seem a mite worried about those G-boys over by the runabout. Do you know anything you shouldn't?"

"No. It's not what you think, and Greg and I are just friends. Excuse me, okay?"

She darted away, then. Manning shook his head.

Melanie thought she noticed the men by the ship looking her way. She never felt as relieved as she did when the turbo lift opened and she left the entire level.

CHAPTER TWENTY-EIGHT

-1-

Greg was in the air and eastbound by noon. The day was a gorgeous blue, and the forests below showcased the horizons in autumn splendor. This was the best week for Fall Foliage Festivals in this area and Greg was sure that below him amid the rolling plains and valleys were numerous group-and-individual-use Sensor Spheres roaming the countryside and being the eyes, ears, noses and touch sensors of a significant percentage of the human race. The fortunate ones—who had successfully obtained the advance "excursion permits"—were out there as well, roaming the wilderness on foot. The spheres were certainly safer; gone was the fear of encountering black bears or other wild life that resented man's intrusion. But the pleasure of becoming tired from all that hiking, or the seriousness of paying heed to where one went, was lost in the process. And it depended on how one felt about that which made the substitute of Sensor Sphere travel either acceptable, or a hollow imitation.

Greg almost hated to leave it all. The sun glinted off a dozen small lakes and streams, which he caught glimpses of every few moments as he passed overhead. He wished he could set the ship down on the bank of one of them for an hour, and enjoy the scenery, even if it would be an unauthorized landing. He could always insist he had engine trouble and needed to land. But he knew Doug Manning, the old fart, back in New Allentown, would never believe that one, and would in all probability log a complaint with the Global Aviation Consortium and try to have Greg's pilot license revoked. Manning would no doubt pitch a fit when his superiors inevitably told him to rescind the complaint and shut up, if he wanted to keep his job. Greg could get away with just about any such precocious behavior, and had done so, repeatedly. Manning had standing orders to hand Greg a vessel whenever he needed one. It drove the guy up the wall.

Even Greg admitted he sometimes abused the privilege, made a little too much of being Randolph Phillips's son, especially times like now when he really wondered if it meant much of anything to his dad at all.

The Blue Mountains of Pennsylvania crawled over the horizon; New Allentown's beacon lights winked into view as well minutes after, and gradually the entire city spread itself out against the east. It sat so high off the ground that the clouds fringed its dome at its highest point. It was a beautiful sight, sitting there so stately amid all that open land. It stood a grand testament to what man could do for the world and its precious resources when he put his mind to it.

Over his neuron receptor network, Greg heard the city's flight control center verify his approach vector. He answered them in his mind and prepared for his final course adjustments and landing.

Melanie Richards had reported for work after her talk with Doug Manning in the Flight Terminal. But after being at her desk for over an hour now she began to wonder if she'd have been better off calling in sick for the day. She couldn't concentrate; she'd barely done more than update and confirm a list of vacationers, attending an autumn event Friday in Vermont on the twenty-eighth.

She stared absently upon the phone imaging disk upon her desk. The noise of the day's business filtered lightly into her office, but she didn't hear it. She had tried to reach Greg in Capital City about a half hour before and had been unsuccessful. She had tried reaching him in his apartment, but there too she had received nothing. She couldn't keep her mind on work, and she wondered about the Sensor Sphere recording she had going back in her apartment. Not- knowing drove her crazy.

She decided to take an unscheduled break.

It was a little after one when Greg touched down in the city. He had about an hour to complete his errands before his flight departed for Sydney, Australia, and as all he need do was gather a few things out of his apartment and locate his copy of the visual, he had a little while to kill and so first he made his way to "Departing" to verify his flight and obtain his boarding itinerary.

The attendant knew him from the main "Admin" office and quite naturally she mentioned the events that had transpired since he'd left last night.

"The ship's *back*? They found it?" he asked, amazed, at the news concerning the missing air car.

She repeated the story that had circled the Transport Department numerous times that day, the one where a night shift maintenance worker had suddenly found the missing air car in its mooring berth, with no explanation on how it had got there.

Greg had only nodded, distantly. He'd thanked her for her assistance, and headed down for the flight garage. He couldn't pass up the opportunity to go down there and have a look for himself. He had to see it to believe it. He was relieved to find that Doug Manning had gone off duty about an hour before. (That the man had been on till this late hour meant that he would have been in an even fouler mood than was normal for the old geezer.)

The flight garage was enormous; he'd entered from a mezzanine that led to the huge floor area. Hundreds of private and commercial class aircraft lay parked about it, stretching on into the distance and looking like so many children's toys left unattended on a rec room floor. A labyrinth of storage bays and shelves decked the side walls, and in the distance he saw the source of everyone's misery: the ship the Hagerton men had flown to Crystal Cave. A rope cordon encircled it. Clearly, the ship was off limits. Even though the federal types had departed the area, it was clear they still wanted the ship quarantined until they were through with their investigation into its mysterious return. But that didn't stop Greg from slipping under the rope and making a closer inspection of the vessel. He approached the passenger side gull wing, and raised it. He climbed inside and looked around the cockpit. The ship felt like an old friend to him, what with his having had the sensory experience of having flown it twice. (The two times he had played the Hagertons' viewwafer.) He imagined old Kutztown, Pa. drifting past the cockpit window; he lived again in his mind the Hagerton men's journey into the wilderness.

"What are *you* doing?" someone asked him suddenly and very casually just beyond the rope cordon. "You *do* know what a rope like this one is here for, don't you, friend? Go on, get out of there!"

Greg looked over. "Sorry;" It was a Craft/Maintenance workman. Greg recognized the overalls and the department insignia. Beneath the insignia was the name Al Nolender. Greg didn't know him.

"I was in charge of finding this ship," he told the workman. "I was just curious to see it back. I hear you guys have had a time over this, today."

"Come on, buddy, just get out of there," the workman only repeated, a little less patiently.

Greg slipped his legs out of the hatch and pulled down the gull wing. He nodded. "No problem."

"Are you supposed to be somebody?"

"Hey look, Al," Greg answered, miffed, "I've already explained what I had to do with this ship's disappearance. That I should have to repeat it, or clarify it to the likes of you— My name's Greg Phillips. Administration."

Al Nolender got a troubled look on his face. "Oh," he suddenly' said. He knew the name for sure, and probably Greg's lineage as well. "You just got in, Mr. Phillips?"

Greg nodded.

"No offense, I hope. It's just that the G-boys made it clear we stay the hell off the ship until they were through. And if I let just anybody break that order, well you know . . . I didn't know who you were . . . and it would've been my ass."

Greg smiled. "Don't worry about it. I just wanted a quick peek." He crawled under the rope. "Thanks."

"Have a good day now, sir," Al Nolender called to him, then, as Greg departed the area. Greg waved his hand, absently, as he continued on. Greg wouldn't turn round to verify it, but he was certain the man was shitting his pants by this point—worried, that was, that pissing off Randolph Phillips's son (what with all these G-guys around) would get him in deep shit for sure. He continued his idle tour of the facility, eventually vanishing into an access corridor farther up the way.

After he'd gone, Al Nolender breathed deeply, fished out and swallowed a relaxer tablet. "I'll really be glad when this day's over," he mumbled. Eventually, he calmed down enough to continue his inspection of the shuttle bays.

Al saw a movement high up within a window of one of the offices. He thought a figure 'might have been standing there before it, surveying the activities of the garage. It made Al uneasy all over again. Manning, thankfully, was long gone, but by this hour Al imagined government investigators lurking everywhere, ready to hound him. It was making him paranoid. He looked back one last time to the rope cordon around the sequestered air car, and then up again to the window overlook. No one was up there now. He felt stupid. He continued on into the garage.

Al himself had had nothing to worry about. But in truth he had been more right about that window than he would ever have wanted to believe.
. . .

-4-

The first thing Melanie did upon returning to her apartment was check out the living room "window" to see what sort of day existed outside. The hills were ablaze with color, and the sky was so blue it seemed unreal. It had to be an imaging error in the hologram circuitry. Melanie couldn't help thinking that sometimes being stuck indoors, however much the city had been designed to alleviate the feeling, was a disappointment. She almost wished she could descend to one of the rarely used and off-limits "Exterior Egress" elevators which ran down the city's main support struts and out into the wilderness beneath the city. Just for a few minutes she'd love to go out there, to revel in the fading warmth of the season, as winter slowly began to overtake the countryside.

She shook her head, and suddenly felt Samuel rub across her legs and begin to purr against her. She picked him up and nuzzled his nose. She carried him into her computer room, plunked him down on the desk chair, and checked on the Sensor Sphere record unit.

She placed Greg's headset again on her head, and closed her eyes. She felt only blackness in her thoughts, which had to mean, she supposed, that the transmission had somehow terminated. She opened her eyes again and glanced over at the record unit. An indicator on the top of it listed several hours of record time left on the wafer. So the problem obviously wasn't a system-shut-down when the wafer got used up. The unit was still in the recording mode, in fact, still running, and the indicator verified that the link with Greg's Sensor Sphere was still in effect. She closed her eyes again and felt with all her senses. She nodded. The Sphere was operating in an enclosure. She could sense the room it sat within, felt the atmosphere or ambiance of it. What did it mean? There was total silence from the Sensor Sphere's end of the transmission. She traded headsets, the Sphere's for the computer's, and called up a directory for Capital City. She asked it for the phone number of Councilman Randolph Phillips. The readout visualized within her thoughts. She requested a key-in to the phone network, read the compliance affirmation in her thoughts, and looked over to the phone unit.

Greg, be there, she requested in her mind.

Nothing. She removed the computer headset and watched the static upon the imaging disk fade away. She looked down at her furry ball of cat, and pet his head. "Samuel, what do I do?" she asked him. "Go back to work? I don't know how else to reach him." She thought about the private communication channels and wondered where in the house she'd left her pendant communicator, seeing as how she wasn't allowed to wear it on duty. "Damn." She exhaled and tried the Sensor Sphere headset once more. She was about to shut the record unit down and file the viewwafer away for later. She heard something. Music. She pulled off the headset. It wasn't coming from her apartment. Returning the unit to her head, she again heard the melody. It sounded like the kind of mood music tune she'd heard Greg play on occasion.

She looked down at Samuel. "Be good, Sam," she told him. She was down the hall and in the elevator in under a minute.

Greg had taken his time heading for his apartment, and for the longest time he couldn't shake the feeling that someone was following him. He kept wanting to look behind him, wherever he went, to see who or what was there. He'd find nothing, but it made him cancel any further delay and move on to his business of locating the viewwafer copy.

It was One-Thirty in the afternoon, and yet he still had no reason to get worried about his flight taking off without him. That wasn't likely to happen. His dad's people would see to it that it did not. The flight would in all likelihood be held until he boarded. Inside his apartment now, he relaxed a bit, put on a music wafer, and began the business of filling his suitcase with whatever might be appropriate for Sydney. He heard the door annunciator go off, suddenly.

He looked up from the bureau. Who knew he was back besides a few personnel down in Flight? That uneasiness was suddenly with him again.

"Melanie!" he said at the sight of her, as gorgeous as ever, in his entrance doorway.

"Greg," she acknowledged. She smiled, but then as quickly looked concerned. She entered the room and couldn't believe the change, how neat and tidy it looked. "Wow," she said.

"Melanie, what are you doing here?" he asked.

"Greg, where are the Hagertons?"

Greg only stared. He was about to answer, when he thought better of it, and stopped.

"Greg, I don't know what they did, but I do know that something strange has happened and they're all mixed up in it. But it must be serious." She looked around the room again, and then slipped away for his den. "Yep," she continued, looking over the room, "it's serious, all right."

The den was immaculate.

"Melanie, what is this?"

"Greg, did you give someone permission to trash this place, to look for that wafer you stole from the Hagerton's last night?"

"Why would I do that?"

"Can you spare a few moments? I want to play something for you in my apartment. It's important. I think someone wants that wafer more than you do, and doesn't want you to know it. Where is it, anyway?"

He paused to consider what she was saying. He felt that clammy feeling again of being followed. "My bedroom . . . under my waterbed mattress, way under."

"Are you sure it's still there?"

They both went to go see. The bed was an antique, circa 1990, made of genuine pinewood with a vinyl bag to contain the 500 gallons or so of water. It had been a present from his father one "Winter," the year Greg had left Fort Lee and moved here to New Allentown. He liked it a whole lot better than he did floating in zero-g in a flotation bed.

Greg went over to the left side railing and pulled up the mattress as best he could considering how bulky and heavy it was. He indicated for Melanie to peer under it. The viewwafer was there all right. She picked it up.

"It's different," Melanie noticed, seeing no label. "It's not the same one."

Greg nodded. "It's a *safe copy*. The Hagertons got back the original."

She looked at him. "Did something happen last night?" She looked at his eyes, then, and nodded. "It must have." She looked at the wafer again. "The G-men didn't find it."

"Who?"

"World Council Security. I came here this morning to apologize for last night."

"You wanted to apologize to me?" he asked, releasing the mattress. He went over to her. "I'm the one who acted like a jerk."

She grinned. "Maybe, but you should have seen this place this morning. It had been ransacked. It's a wonder they could put it all back so perfectly. They said they wanted the wafer, Greg. They wanted to know if you'd given it to me. I was afraid they'd search my place too."

Greg studied her. She was so gorgeous a female, he'd believe anything she said, simply for the privilege to go to bed with her. But if he believed what she was saying, he'd have to believe that his father had pulled one over on him.

"No," he said, "my old man can be a rotten bastard, but not with me. He wouldn't dare."

"What are you talking about?"

"He sent me down to get this!" He held up the visual. "Why would he do that, if he intended to go behind my back and send Security types to get it?"

"Because maybe they couldn't find it? You should have seen this place, Greg. I'm not lying, and that's why I want you to come with me. I think it's serious; I can prove what I'm saying!"

He couldn't help believing her, and not just because he felt so attracted to her. Something else about what she said seemed to synchronize with all he'd been feeling since he'd awakened in his father's home this morning.

"What've you got, Mellie?"

"Maybe something that will dampen your trust in your old man a little. . . ."

"You're kidding?" he said a few moments later in the elevator. She'd told him how she had cannibalized one of her Sensor Sphere record units and interfaced with *his* Sphere. "I got to see that one!"

"You don't believe me?" she asked, softly.

"I know you're capable of it, Melanie, but I didn't think you'd actually do something extravagant like break into *Sensory Systems, Inc.*'s consumer files. Why?"

"So you'd *believe* me," she said, softly again.

He stared at her. "What's *on* that disk?"

She shrugged. "I haven't had time to play it back. Greg, are you going to kiss me or not?"

He pretended to look away as if to ponder it. "Maybe after we watch the visual."

She leered and grabbed his turtleneck sweater, pulling him toward her. He gently took hold of her shoulders, and lowered his lips to hers. She threw her arms around his neck and locked him against her to make sure he didn't simply give her a quick peck on the lips.

He didn't.

The elevator opened upon reaching level 146. Mrs. Lydia Patterson, an elderly neighbor of Melanie's, appeared before it' as the door panels parted. A bemused and surprised look traced across her face.

Melanie noticed her and disengaged from Greg. "Hi, Mrs. Patterson."

The woman nodded. "Hello, Melanie, how are you today?" She studied Greg, then.

Greg smiled, disarmingly.

"I'm fine, and you?"

"I'm very well, dear, thank you."

"Uh, Lydia, this is Greg Phillips, a friend of mine. He works for Transport, also."

"Aren't you usually at work at this time, dear?"

Melanie blushed. "I'm on a break, sort of. We both are. It's all right. "

"Well, that's fine, then, *if it's okay*," she answered in dubious sincerity. "Oh, my dear, if you can, do try to take in the view from the City-Top Terrace, today. It's a gorgeous day."

"I know it is. I will. Bye Lydia."

"Melanie," she answered. She eyed Greg again and nodded. They traded places in the elevator.

"Jesus!" said Greg. "Why do I feel like I've just been caught doing something naughty?"

"My neighbors worry about me a lot. I live a sort of free life, and this is a residential area. A lot of married people."

"Oh." He nodded.

"Greg?"

"What?"

Melanie saw a figure way down the hallway-only for a second. He disappeared so quickly to Melanie it was only a black blur.

Greg turned in the direction she was gazing; he too caught what had seemed a shadowy movement.

"Who *was* that?" Melanie asked.

He turned serious. "Let's see that visual you made, Mellie. This is starting to piss me off."

"What is?"

"Someone's been following me all over the fucking city!"

They reached Melanie's apartment and entered it.

-7-

Greg didn't seem to be taking very well the images Melanie had recorded. He had his arm around her waist. She felt his breathing rate change, and he gradually tightened his grasp.

"Greg, ease up," she said to him. "You're hurting me."

"What?" he called, suddenly aware of the dim images beyond his visor shield glasses. "Sorry, Mellie. . . . I don't believe this."

The government agents seemed all around Greg in the recreation in his mind, and he had to remind himself constantly that it was just a mental reconstruction and not a real vision, otherwise he'd want to jump up and strangle every one of them for the way they were so casually tossing his things around in his den.

Something grazed his arm in the darkness. He jolted. It wasn't Melanie, it was too small a mass. He was ready to strangle it, until he remembered Melanie's cat had entered the chamber with them.

Samuel must have decided, the way Greg was acting, that Greg needed a cuddle. Greg laughed and rubbed Sam's stomach a few times. He felt the cat edge its mouth against Greg's fingers.

"Your cat just scared the hell out of me, Mel," he said.

Melanie looked down below the visor and saw Sam's shadowy presence on the cushion. She reached for him. "Come on, Sam," she said.

Greg looked to the agents again. "It's amazing, Mel, you know," he said. "It's amazing those fucking idiots haven't broken anything!"

That very second one of them emptied the contents of Greg's antique bookshelf onto the floor. It held his prize collection: vintage copies of the complete works of Stephen King and Richard Matheson. The agent paged through them, haphazardly, hoping Greg might have hidden the visual in one of them.

"If I ever meet that guy," said Greg, "I'm going to take my volume of *The Tommyknockers* and beat the son of a bitch over the head with it."

Melanie laughed to herself and caressed his waist with her arm. "They put it all back," she said, lowly.

Eventually, the recording reached the spot where the agents in fact did that, and the Sensor Sphere itself at some point got consigned to its storage box and filed away within a closet. Melanie had to laugh at one point when one of the agents suddenly inquired, "Wasn't there a headset lying around here somewhere?"

"Why ask me? *You* were in charge of it. Isn't it back in the case?"

"No. You don't suppose that little bimbo friend of the Phillips's kid swiped it when she was here, do you?"

"Who are you calling a bimbo, DICKFACE?" Melanie answered.

"Easy love," Greg answered, caressing her waist, "I'm sure he meant it affectionately."

"Shut up, Greg," she said.

"Who'd want it?" the other agent asked of the command headset. "What good would it do her without the Record Unit?"

"Well, I can't find it, and according to the visuals we made before we started, it was here. We can search the girl's place."

"No, we're not authorized for that. If it ain't here, and if she took it, as far as I know there's nothing she can do with it. So leave it. Let the kid order a new one. He'll think he misplaced it, anyway."

The other nodded and closed the lid on the storage case. The sensory images went dark, but the audio remained, though now Melanie and Greg felt trapped within a cramped enclosure. Melanie felt that same blackness she had felt before, only this time it felt even more annoying with so much of the real world masked out by the visor/shield glasses. They both tossed them simultaneously to the floor.

"Computer," Greg called out, "enhancement mode. Reduce touch sensors and enhance audio."

"Right," again came the voice of the head agent," that's done it for the den." From the way Greg read the subsequent shuffling of their footfalls he deduced they were all departing for the living room now.

"We're almost finished in here, Frank," came the voice of yet another agent. "The old man won't like knowing we didn't find it."

"We'll have to tell him," the one called Frank replied. "He should be done with Stakely by now. He's probably already on his way to *Nellus*."

"*Nellus?*" asked Greg. He looked over at Melanie.

"The space port?" she asked.

"You guys pack up," this Frank guy continued.

Greg heard him re-enter the den. Then, much nearer, "This is Central," came still another voice. This one sounded as if over Greg's phone unit in the den.

"Kesler reporting in," Frank answered. "Patch me through to the councilman."

He was informed Councilman Phillips had already departed D.C., and had boarded the suborbital shuttle.

"That's all right," Frank answered. "Put me through direct to the councilman. I want an encoded transmission over his private channel. Okay, "

The line went silent.

Melanie looked over at Greg. "Where's yours?" she asked him of his pendant communicator. "I wanted to call you all morning."

He shrugged. "The apartment. I forgot it there."

"This is Phillips," Randolph Phillips's voice eventually acknowledged. "Sorry to report this, Mr. Phillips, but wherever your son hid the thing, he put it in a good place. We gave the apartment a thorough cleaning."

Melanie grinned and poked Greg one in the side.

"We looked all over."

"Everywhere?"

"All right, I didn't want to put Greg in it, but no choice I suppose. Don't really need it, but if it's in his apartment, and he's not there, you never know, somebody else, the maid maybe, might find it. Even try watching it. Can't leave a thing like that behind, I suppose. I'll send Greg down for it. The place is clean, right?"

"The boys are just finishing up now. Your son will never know we were here."

"Good."

"Do you still want the kid's copy removed to a more secure location?"

"Yeah, I think that's a good idea. When Greg finds it, persuade him to leave it with you."

"We'll take care of it, Mr. Phillips."

"Very good. Phillips out."

"All packed away sir," came an anonymous voice as it entered the den.

"Right, we're out of here."

A few more minutes of room noises, shuffling and the sort, people milling about the adjacent rooms to the den, filled Melanie and Greg's consciousness, until finally there was nothing at all. Greg could feel the logic circuits in the portable playback deck beside him obeying his prior command to enhance the sound levels. It raised them even higher to capture whatever ambient sound might be present.

"End Enhancement Mode," Greg ordered. "Stop Playback." He glanced over at Melanie. "You've really made my day, Mellie. Ignorance was bliss, you know."

"I'm sorry, Greg. What were they planning to do?"

He shrugged. "They probably were going to steal the wafer from me, once I came back here and retrieved it. It doesn't sound as if they want me involved in this situation at all." He shook his head. "Meanwhile, my father's heading for the Moon . . . without ME. If it weren't for us last night, you and me, he'd never even know anything about it! My old man!"

"Greg, what is on that visual?"

He fished it out of his shirt pocket. He looked down at the playback unit and ejected the other wafer. "What time is it?" he asked her.

Melanie looked up and called out, "Time?"

An electronic voice announced that it was Two-Thirty.

"I'm late," he said.

"For where?"

"My father wants to pack me away for safe keeping in InterWorld till he gets back from his business."

"Australia?" she asked.

He nodded. "Meanwhile, he combs the Moon looking for the Hagertons." He looked at her and then slipped the Hagerton viewwafer into the playback unit. He handed Melanie her shield glasses and pocketed his. "Forward normal," he called into the unit's voice circuit, and pulled off his headset. "I got to make a call."

Melanie felt the sensor images begin to fill her mind. She saw Keith and Jeffrey Hagerton down in the Transport flight bay loading their rented air car. She pulled off her headset. "*What* are you going to do?"

"Go ahead, Mellie, start watching it. I got to call the terminal, book myself a later flight, or at least let people think that I am." He went for the exit then. He had to stop and laugh as Samuel leapt and beat him out the door, disappearing down the hallway.

"Why do cats do that?" he asked her.

Melanie shrugged. "They're silly."

After he exited, she refitted the headset upon her head, adjusting it until the transmitter probes were directly over her brain centers. The Hagertons' Sunday excursion into the wilds of upper Reading, Pennsylvania, filled her mind once more.

CHAPTER TWENTY-NINE

-1-

"That's right," said Greg to the woman in flight reservations down in the terminal, "Greg Phillips on the Three P.M. to Sydney. I want to reschedule to a later flight. I don't care if they *are* holding it. Something's come up. I need a later one. What do you have for me?"

Greg was told there was a flight by way of London to Melbourne and Sydney at Eight-Thirty, Eastern Standard Time.

He nodded. "That's fine. I'm in no hurry." His father wasn't due in, supposedly, until late tomorrow evening. But that of course depended on whenever Randolph finished trying to snare the Hagertons and their space vessel. *Don't expect any more help from me,* Greg told his dad under his breath, as he waited for the attendant to confirm his new reservations.

When she did so, he thanked her and shut down the imaging disk. He got up, then, to exit the den, intending to rejoin Melanie in her viewing chamber. He saw a shadow, suddenly, cross in front of the exit.

"Melanie?" He went for the doorway. "Sam, don't you ever relax—"

"Your father won't like you interfering with his plans like that, Greg," a presence in the hall informed him, suddenly.

Greg froze.

-2-

The "aerial" shots of the Hagertons' air car —sailing above the hills of New Allentown— were nice, Melanie thought. And it felt weird seeing the very craft (that was now the subject of so much activity and controversy downstairs in the flight garage) so innocently being flown by a father and his young son out into the Pennsylvania wilderness and for the once famous tourist attraction, Crystal Cave in old Kutztown. But there had to be more to this recording than this, something that would explain why it was now of interest to World Council Security.

"Hold," she called, and removed her shield glasses. What was keeping Greg? He'd been gone now for a good ten minutes. "Mark position and shut down," she ordered of the playback deck. She pulled the headset off and went to the exit.

Samuel was standing in the entrance from the hallway, beyond the rec room. "Sam?" she whispered. She heard voices down the hall. He trotted over to her. She scooped him up and set him on a lounge chair. She crept then carefully out into the hall.

Greg recognized the man in the doorway at once. It was the guy he'd heard the other agents in his apartment call Frank. Frank Kesler. "Who the hell are you?" he asked, anyway.

"A friend of your fathers."

"Sure you are."

"Trust me on this one, Greg."

"Cut the bullshit and get out. You're in this apartment illegally. I'll have to call city security."

"I wouldn't do that, Greg." He held out his World Council Security emblem. "It would only cause an embarrassing scene."

"For whom?"

The man smiled. "Where's the visual?"

"I don't know what you're talking about."

The man took a breath. "You know you're supposed to be on that Three p.m. flight to Sydney. What are you doing here with the Richards girl? If you were diddling her, I'd at least have understood. You were watching visuals!"

Fortunately, anyone not wearing a receptor headset could not at all know the contents of what a person wearing one was watching, and therefore Greg did not have to fear Frank Kesler's having identified just what it was that he and Melanie had been replaying in the viewing chamber.

Greg smiled. "Are you sure that's only what we were doing? Those floor cushions can start to feel real cozy after a while."

Frank Kesler nodded, smiling. "You recognized me, admit it."

"How's that?"

"It's my job to read a person I'm assigned to follow. If that person knows me, my cover's blown. You had that look of recognition the minute you noticed me."

"I've never seen you before in my life. You're mistaken."

"I think that somehow your girlfriend managed to wire up that Sensor Sphere globe we stupidly left lying there in full view of us in your den. And perhaps that was what you were watching. And, if so, you probably know about a whole lot more than you were intended to."

Greg contained an impulse to respond to him. He smiled, again. "That's bullshit. My father sent me ahead to *InterWorld*. He left word he'd join me tomorrow evening. I can't tell you anything more than that without some proof that you have the proper level clearance."

The man shook his head with amusement. "I was kind of hoping for more from the son of Randolph Phillips. Okay. Greg, the duplicate wafer? You see, I *have* been briefed. Your father is on his way to the Moon, the lunar highlands in the North Country. There's been a change of plans. He wants your copy of the recording you made last night. He wants it for safe keeping. I promised I'd take care of that. I hope we didn't break anything in your apartment, but we really didn't have any choice. We didn't find the visual."

Again, Greg held his emotions in check.

The agent smiled. "Nice try. But I can tell you know. I really have to hand it to that girl. She's good. And she's quick. She saw the Sensor Sphere lying there on the sofa, and all she had to do was sneak the headset out of the room while we weren't looking, and figure out a way to break the lockout code. Come on, Greg, you know your father's got your best interest at heart. You're doing our species a good service with this discovery you've made. And that was an excellent bit of undercover work you and the girl did when you found that original viewwafer. The Hagertons have to be intercepted for their sake, as well as for what it will mean for our species and its future. Don't stop cooperating now."

"My father couldn't care less about the human race. His only interest is in himself. If I help him, if I give you the visual, then what? What about the Hagertons after they're 'rescued?' What will happen to them?"

"That's not your concern!"

"All right, what about Melanie and me? Do we just trot into the next shuttle to Sydney and behave ourselves? What happens to us?"

The smile left Frank's face. "Forget about the girl. You play your part and go to Sydney. It's unfortunate your girlfriend has got herself mixed up in this. She'll have to be *re-educated*."

"And so will I, if I don't cooperate, right? And what about the Hagertons? You'll re-educate them right off the face of the Earth!"

Greg suspected "Re-educate" was a government euphemism for being neurologically reprogrammed.

Melanie heard the conversation from its beginning. Peering from the edge of the rec room (where the viewing chamber lay), she recognized Frank Kesler the moment he entered the doorway to her den. When she felt safe that he wouldn't notice her milling about in the hall, she crept down and into her bedroom. Very quietly she went over to the nightstand and pulled out a tiny device she kept there to protect her lest in this age (though highly unlikely) some deranged fool decided to break into her home. It was a neuron beam projector. One only had to take aim at the intruder's body, and the unit would discharge a pulse signal that would have the same effect upon brainwave signals, surging up a person's spinal cord, as a pail of water had on a small fire. It caused temporary paralysis.

She checked it over. It was an ivory color. Very sleek and slim, contoured to fit easily in the hand. She activated the power-up regulator and gripped it snugly within her palm. She turned to leave.

"Aaah!" There was someone directly in front of her.

"I'll take that, miss," the man said, pleasantly, as he made a grab for her arm.

"Let go of me!" She squirmed. He was one of the agents that she had seen in Greg's apartment. He had both her arms now and she fell backward against the outer frame of the flotation bed. No way could she hold him off, and there were only seconds before he squeezed the stun unit right out of her hand. She felt along its length for the fire button. She pressed it. The man froze instantly, assumed a shocked and then vacant expression, and dropped slowly away from her. She slid out of the way and he fell into the manger opening, bobbing about then limp and unconscious like a twig in a lake within the sleep chamber. She took a long breath and looked up to the room's front.

Frank Kesler had heard the din down the hall and he made a run to Melanie's bedroom. He was there with a device of his own displayed and ready to employ just as his man went down; he moved quickly for her. He hadn't anticipated Greg coming up behind him and grabbing him. They began to struggle, Greg doing his best to hold the device in the agent's hand as far from himself as he could.

Most females, Melanie recalled from all the numerous, "old entertainment" visuals she'd scanned in the past, at this point usually watched helplessly at a distance in shock while her man fought bravely to win victory over his opponent. This man was a well-trained professional, and she had better things to do than play the damsel in distress. She checked the stun power level on her unit, got as close to Frank Kesler as she could (so that she wouldn't hit Greg) and released the trigger.

The beam shrieked blue and hit him square in his chest.

"You **little slut!**" he yelled, and his eyes glazed over.

Greg felt the man fall away from him almost immediately. Frank Kesler ended up in a heap upon the floor. Greg shook himself off and got up. He looked up at Melanie. "Thanks, Mellie."

"Are you all right?"

"Yeah. You?"

She nodded, breathing heavily.

Greg saw the "weapon" lying there beside the agent's limp hand. He picked it up and studied it. Then he looked at Melanie, who was eyeing him anxiously.

"What?" she' said, her heart racing.

"Kill setting. He meant to kill you."

She went up to inspect it herself. It was set on *kill* all right. At such an intensity a neural beam would cause a heart disruption: a fatal cardiac arrest. She looked at Greg. "Are these even legal anymore?" she asked. "A 'kill' setting?"

"You attacked a federal officer. You know law enforcers. It's an age old

246

tradition. They go for the good wound, and justify their excessive acts later.
"

"But so did you, this one," she argued of the man lying unconscious at their feet.

"Well, he works for my father, and . . . uh. . . ."

"Oh," she nodded, comprehending. "Uh huh. Your death he'd have to explain and answer for."

"Yeah," said Greg, sheepishly.

"What do we now?" she asked.

"How long will that last?" he asked of the paralysis.

She shrugged. "About an hour, I think. And I think they can still hear us."

Greg nodded and carefully backed out into the hall with Frank Kesler's weapon still in his hand, and deliberately reduced the setting of the device to a mild paralysis, like the more benign unit Melanie had. He checked out the remaining rooms. Melanie carefully padded out of her bedroom and into the hall.

Greg went up to her front door and called out "Vision." A portion of the door (halfway up) became filled with an image of the exterior in three-dimensions and Greg peered into it. There seemed nothing immediately outside.

"Looks okay," he said as he saw Melanie enter the room. "But that doesn't mean they're not somewhere out of view waiting for these two. We're lucky you had that thing," he said of the stun gun. "They probably wouldn't have been so lax if they'd known."

She nodded. "My father gave it to me."

"His gun collection?"

"Hobby, more like," she answered. "He said if I insisted on living alone at my age, he wanted me to keep it around, even if my having it wasn't exactly legal either."

"Yeah, well, you can bet that having it is the sort of technicality that types like these guys will use to put us both away."

"You mean put ME away," she said. "They won't touch you."

"I've defied my old man," he returned. "He'll deal with my acting up like this, probably. He'll see to it I'm way off the grid so that I don't cause him any more headaches. Just enough of a containment to make me realize how much being his son really sucks."

"It's made things cozy for you up till now."

"Well, not anymore."

"Really?" she asked, skeptical.

He nodded. "I've been thinking about it a lot lately. I'm not exactly proud of the way I've been using my old man's clout."

She smirked. "If I had to make an observation based on what I've so far seen here, I'd have to say he loves you more than you give him credit for. And as for hating the way you've acted, it's about the way most kids probably would react growing up the child of such a powerful man."

"I've had enough of it," he said.

"Why?" Her lips parted in surprise; she started to smile. "Are you doing all this *because of me?* Gregory Phillips, I think you're actually starting to care about someone besides yourself." She went up to him, and kissed him gently on the lips. "That's it, isn't it?"

He touched her arm. "Are you making fun of me?"

She grinned, and shook her head. "I think it's cute," she said.

"We have to leave the city, Mellie."

"Really?" she queried. "How?"

He placed his index finger against his lips, and indicated the agents in her bedroom. He whispered, "Help me drag those two into the bathroom."

Greg grabbed Frank's shoulders beneath his armpits and began to pull while Melanie helped with the man's feet. Kesler moaned, but was out of it. After securing him in the guest bathroom, they went back for the other one, removed him from the flotation bed, and did the same with him.

"Do you have a few extra rags or towels lying around?" said Greg. "I'm going to tie these guy's wrists and legs, gag them. Keep them quiet. There's no way I know to permanently lock the bathroom door."

"There isn't," she answered, and went off to get the items.

"That's that," said Greg as he pressed the room's door actuator from outside. It silently closed.

Melanie was about to speak and he hushed her again. He indicated the viewing chamber. Once they were both within it, he closed the entrance and turned to her. He took her arms. "It's okay, now. They won't hear us in here."

"They shouldn't."

The walls were soundproofed.

"How far do you think we can get, beyond the front door?" she asked.

He shook his head. "I don't know. Probably not far at all."

"And if we do make it, Greg, where do we go?"

He thought about it. "Outside; we leave New Allentown."

"Steal an air car?"

He shook his head. "We locate one of the lower level exits . . . and go outside. Haven't you ever wanted to try that?"

"Those exits are off-limits, restricted-access, they're forbidden."

"So?"

"We'd have better luck stealing a ship from the flight garage."

"You can do it, can't you, override the access codes?"

Melanie shrugged. "I won't know till I try. One of the first things they tell us in Instruc, when we're kids, is to never even fantasize visiting the city's old exits."

He nodded. "If we can make it to a turbo lift, without being followed," Greg only replied, "we can disappear into the city and work our way down. By the time they realize where we've gone, we ought to have a hundred kilometers of empty wilderness to hide in."

"And once we're outside, Greg, what then?"

He contemplated that. "We'll worry about that later. What about Samuel?"

She nodded. "I'll leave my mom a phone message to come get him. I can leave Sam a food dish and place the message on a time delay. Mom will get it sometime tomorrow."

He nodded. "Good, let's get on it, then." He glanced to the two stun units. "We'll take these along in case."

"Greg, the wilderness . . . outside . . . what about the Renegades?"

"We should be okay, shouldn't meet any, this far from the old land-based cities. I suspect the Wilderness Society, Mellie, is behind a lot of the Renegades' bad reputation, to dissuade us in the cities from joining them out there. Come on, let's do it."

"Wait. Will you tell me, first, what's going on? I think I deserve to know why I was scheduled to be _re-educated_."

"You heard?"

She nodded. "What happened to the Hagertons?"

He walked over to the center of the chamber, crouched down, and retrieved both their headsets.

"Here." he said, handing her hers.

Headset Placement Correct

. . . Came an image in his mind as he adjusted his own upon his head.

"Playback," he called, "skip forward, thirty minutes from image end."

Two electronic beeps issued from the playback unit. He looked at Melanie.

"Close your eyes."

She did.

"Oh wow," she exclaimed. "That's a part of Crystal Cave?" She opened them again, but the image remained superimposed upon the sight of Greg beside her. The sight of an underground lake, deep in the bowels of the earth, filled her consciousness, stalagmites and stalactites draping from a thousand nooks.

"No, if it were," Greg replied, "it would have been as famous and as desirable a tourist go-to in the old days as the caverns in Virginia."

"Oh, dear God!" she exclaimed then as the Sensor Sphere settled on the grotto where Athena's orb reposed and had for so long. "What in the hell is that thing?"

"You won't find a 'manufactured in America,' or anywhere else in the solar system on it, I can tell you that," he nodded.

Keith suddenly dematerialized from where he was sitting on a boulder in the middle of the lake.

Melanie glanced to Greg, again. "This is all real, right? Not an entertainment archive?"

Greg glanced over to her and laughed. "It's real, alright."

Jeffrey Hagerton bravely paddled his and his dad's raft, on his own, up the lake for the shoreline where he knew that orb reposed and possibly was waiting for him.

"That is one cute little boy," Melanie said, trying to ease the tension in the air.

Greg issued an amused grunt that caused Melanie to glance over at him. "Not for long," he said.

She wrinkled her brow at him, puzzled over that one.

"His father," narrated Greg, "the orb's already . . . well, you saw what happened. It transport-beamed him right off the boulder. The kid managed to pull his headset off just in time to prevent the same thing from happening to him. His dad . . ." Greg shook his head. "No."

"What does that orb do to that little boy?" Melanie asked in a whisper, fearful of Greg's reply.

"She has a name," he answered.

"She? **Oh, my god!**' issued Melanie once again at the sight of Athena's ethereal and gorgeous manifestation of herself. "What the hell is she?"

"Watch what she does," Greg said.

After several moments of pleasant requests to the young boy to trust her, Athena bestowed a "gift" upon him.

Melanie smirked, more out of surprise than amusement. "*And this is all real?*' she inquired again.

"It's like that old expression mothers are always told," said Greg. "*You're not losing a son, you're gaining a daughter.* Kimberly Hagerton has two now."

Melanie raised her visor sunglasses to eyeball Greg; he raised his as well. "That expression is for when two people get married!" she informed him. "You're *perverting* it. Oh, my god! That poor kid. That— whatever she is— she can do stuff like *that?*"

"There is probably very little she can't do. My Dad is a fool if he thinks he can go up against an entity like that. It's like us trying to stand up to God and naive enough to think we have a snowball's chance in hell of . . ." Greg grinned. ". . . not winding up there ourselves. . . . Stop playback and shut down," Greg said all at once. The scene disappeared from around them just as a now feminized Jeffrey was about to enter Athena's lair. Greg reached down and extracted the viewwafer from the playback bay. He pocketed it once more within his shirt. "We're out of time, love." he said. He kissed her gently on the cheek and motioned her out of the chamber.

Melanie finished gathering the things she'd take with her on the journey, making one final stop in the rec room to see her cat, as yet where she last left him on the lounge chair. She picked him up, cradling him against her breasts. "Be good now, honey," she whispered to him. "I'll see you soon." She gave him a farewell hug. She and Greg then departed for the front door.

Approaching it, Greg flattened his body against one of the walls beside the door and held the stun unit barrel-up before him.

Melanie looked at him oddly. "What are you doing?"

"I saw it in an old cop movie. It looked convincing."

"Jesus, Greg." She shook her head.

He nodded for her to open the door. She announced, "Exit."

The panel silently slid open. Greg slowly peered outside, holding the gun so that it wasn't immediately visible. He looked to either side. The corridor was empty. He slipped back inside. "Close," he called out to the door. It did.

"What?"

"It's clear, but I have an idea. I just thought of something we can do." He remembered the two agents holed up in the bathroom, crowded close to her, and whispered in her ear. "How good are you at forging Level Nine Excursion Permits?" he asked.

"Why?"

"They'll get us out of the city easier, and make a few other things I have in mind easier, too. Can you do it?"

"Yes, but under whose names? Ours?"

"Hell, no. I got it. Make us a VIP couple attached to *InterWorld*, Titan Division, Saturn. I got just the names too. I met them, once; nice couple: Fred and Wilma Davis."

"This will take a few minutes. I hope we have it. I don't know, Greg, the passes won't hold up to close inspection."

"I trust you."

Melanie went down the hall and to her den/computer room. She was interfacing with the main city computers almost at once. Greg watched her from the door in total amazement. Her talents were really going to waste, he thought.

Ten minutes had passed and the jitters were getting to Greg. He walked over to her by the work table. She had her computer headset on and she was really into it. Without a headset of his own, Greg could only imagine the readouts flashing into her mind.

"Greg, I hate to ask this," she said, suddenly, "but I need you to run down to the mall, to <u>Cosmic Electronics</u>, and pick me up a few blank data crystals of the type permits are issued on. I don't have any."

Greg looked at her. "I'd rather not leave you alone up here."

She shrugged. "I'll be all right. Greg, they may ask you why you need them."

"No, they won't. I'm an old customer. They won't care; they'll think it's business. I just hope our friends in the bathroom don't wake up."

"Do we have time for all this, Greg?"

"Trust me, Mellie, we better."

She nodded. "This is going to take me a few minutes more. Please don't get caught."

"I'll be fine. Be right back."

It was after three and the corridors in the residential levels were populated by only a few token residents. Greg was familiar with a lot of them, and as this was his own home area he felt at ease among them all. He felt all the more relaxed when he reached the nearest elevator, and descended to the intended level below. But his eyes became wide and suspicious of any shadowy movement the moment the elevator came to rest on the 104th floor and opened to the mall.

Beyond, in the great windows of these the City Top levels, he saw the countryside alive in its bright sunlight. The sun set around five this time of year. He and Melanie had to hurry if they intended to do much out there today. He looked to the shoppers below, walking the aisles before the various stores. He hurried on down to the electronics shop.

-7-

Melanie couldn't figure out at all what Greg really needed with the permits, but she trusted his judgement. With his familiarity with his father's affairs, he no doubt knew about things such as these special passes. A level nine would guarantee its possessor access to just about anywhere he or she pleased to go out beyond the city, and would allow entry to whatever exterior shelters and services existed out there.

She had it. The confirmation flashed across her thoughts, and she saw her and Greg's faces superimposed upon the bibliographies of Fred and Wilma Davis of Titan, the largest moon of Saturn. "Save," she requested.

"Compliance," came the response.

She rested her chin in the palm of her hand and exhaled. Then she looked back at the hall and pondered the two agents in the bathroom. She began to wonder about the other agents that she had seen with the two here, and she called up access codes that would allow her to scan all the new arrivals to the city that day, plus their ID's. She was idling for time, she knew, but if she didn't, waiting for Greg would drive her nuts. Her computer told her it was working on it. She heard the front door annunciator go off.

"Good, you're back," she said out loud. "Computer cancel." The machine answered in the affirmative, and she pulled off the headset. She got up to go to him.

"You made it, angel," she began. "I'm glad—"

It wasn't Greg.

"Yes?" she asked, trembling. She had left her stun unit in the computer room.

"Agent Smothers, ma 'am." He held out his I.D. and then his stun unit. "Please move over to that wall and lay flat against it."

"Why?" she asked. "This is my home. What do you want?"

"Please get over there and turn around." He pulled out a pair of handcuffs. "I'm sorry I have to do this," he said.

"You haven't told me why, yet!" she said. He took her wrist and fastened one end of the cuffs around it. He then went for the other.

"You're being detained," he said, finally.

"Ow! Will you take it easy with those things? You're hurting my wrists. . . . I have the right to know what I'm accused of."

"You have the right to remain silent, and a whole bunch of other things we used to have to say a long time ago." He turned her around. "Where's field agent Kesler?"

"Who? Who's that?"

"Over to the chair, ma 'am. And stay quiet." He pulled out a personal communicator.

Melanie tensed at the thought of his using it to call in more agents and ruin everything. She jumped up and went over to him. "Please, Smothers . . . talk to me, first? I'm sure we can straighten this all out. You don't need backup." She cocked her head to a side, allowing her long, brunette hair to fan down her shoulders. She smiled at him. "It's not necessary."

He threw her back to the sofa. "I told you to stay quiet!" he said.

"Somebody ought to teach you better manners around women!" said a voice suddenly.

The man turned instantly and drew his weapon. But he wasn't fast enough. Greg dropped him a second later.

"Thanks," Melanie said. "I'm glad you made it."

"Anytime, ma'am," Greg replied.

She sneered at him, and indicated the cuffs. "Will you get these things off me?"

They were code-locked. Greg would have to find the tiny key card and wipe it against the reader on the cuffs. He reached into the agent's suit jacket and fished around in the pockets until he found the man's I.D. He found what he thought was the code key with it. He touched it to Melanie's cuffs. They loosened.

She looked down at the agent, and then up at Greg. "Did you see any others?"

"No."

"The guest bathroom?" she asked.

He nodded. He handed her the blank data crystals. "Take care of' these," he said. "I'll take care of *him*."

She nodded and departed.

Greg looked down at the I.D. Then he looked at the agent, unconscious on the floor.

"First time in the city, Vincent?" he asked, as he picked up the man's arms and began to drag him into the hallway. "You'll be wanting to wash up, I suppose, before the little woman calls us in for dinner. So here, let me show you where the bathroom is."

CHAPTER THIRTY

-1-

Greg and Melanie sought one of the more out-of-the-way retail centers in the City Top district to purchase needed supplies for the journey. There they would be less likely to be recognized or identified as patrons so far from their own level and residential district.

***

Greg handed the proprietor of a sporting goods store (a good natured old guy, with only a smattering of white hair left upon his head) the level nine (Fred and Wilma) visas, after securing several small sundry items from the man's tiny shop.

"I have two life support belts right over here about your size," the man said, accessing the two young people in front of him. "You're both about the same build. I think a Small each would go round the two of you just fine."

Melanie glanced to a large wall in his shop that created the illusion of a patio view to the Blue Mountains of Pennsylvania beyond the city. "It's such a pretty day out there," she told the man. "I can't wait to get out there and feel what it was like for humans in the old days when we weren't all living underground." She glanced out the front door to a real overlook vista to the countryside below, ". . . Or aboveground like this city, or like Fred and me, living on a world whose atmosphere is poisonous methane and would kill us in an instant if our city's seals were to rupture and let it in. Outer space, Earth, the Moon, Mars, wherever, it's all the same: stuck inside." She glanced to the life belts. "Do we really have to take these along?"

"Folks took their chances in the old days," the old man said, "out in the open like they did, and had immunities built up that I'm sure you folks don't have, living out there in orbit around Saturn. No more than we right here surrounded by all that pretty wilderness right outside those windows over yonder," he pointed to the views outside the shop. "God-darn, just imagine such a thing. Crazy to believe, we people, we're scattered all over the bleeping solar system as we all are, anymore. Five hundred years ago. . ." He ignored his fake "View Wall" and glanced instead to the real thing out beyond the store in the City Top levels of New Allentown. "Can't say I'd blame you if you wanted to leave them damn fool things off. Might not want to go too long, though, breathing that good raw air out there. Nice as I'm sure it is. No telling what you might breathe in that will disagree with you a mite badly a time down the road a spell."

"He's right, hon," Greg replied to her in a low voice. "We can't go anywhere beyond the city without them."

"It isn't right, Fred, honey," she replied. "We come all this way."

'It'll be fine," Greg replied.

"You folks been on Earth long?" the man asked then. He scanned the readout, pausing at the words, *Tshshuman's Palisade, Titan.* "You're ARE a long way from home."

"Got in last night," Greg said. "Took us a week to reach Earth. Seemed forever. Wilma and I have been looking forward for over a year to a hike in the mountains. Right, honey?"

Melanie gave Greg a dreamy-eyed look and nodded.

The shopkeeper smiled. "You folks couldn't have planned it better. This is the week to be here, to watch the fall colors emerge. They'll be their best this week."

Greg nodded. "We know."

"What time does it get dark, this time of year, on this part of Earth?" Melanie asked, like a tourist.

"Five P.M., missy."

"Darling, shouldn't we get started?"

Greg nodded to her and kissed Melanie on her lips. "We should." He turned to the shopkeeper. "Thanks. Thanks for everything."

"You folks be careful out there now."

***

"I never said you could kiss me," Melanie told Greg as they left the shop. "You were enjoying yourself in there, weren't you? If the fantasy of being my husband tickles you that much, why don't you ask me to marry you?"

"You might say yes," Greg said.

She punched his shoulder.

"He won't get stiffed the spending credits, will he?" Greg asked of the shopkeeper.

"The account's legitimate, Greg, honest," Melanie replied. "I transferred a little of both our accounts. He'll be credited. . . . He was a nice old guy."

Greg nodded. "And trusting."

"Greg, how old are the Davis's?"

"Didn't it say on the file?"

She shrugged. "I wasn't paying attention. How old?"

He grinned. "They're in their seventies."

Melanie looked at him and began to break up in laughter.

They stopped in a nearby restroom facility to change, stripped off their city clothes and dressed in the hiking outfits they had purchased, strapping on the life belts last. Melanie slipped on a pair of pants, hiking boots, and a white, wool knit sweater over a denim shirt. Greg laughed at her in it. She looked precious. So did he. He wore somewhat the same. These were not the sort of clothes one wore to tour the city corridors.

They had paid for it all with their Fred and Wilma visas. It was a good opportunity to give the data crystals a tryout. They worked.

Quietly and without drawing undue attention, Greg and Melanie slipped through the flight terminal and walked a mezzanine that led to the garage. And quieter still they slipped down its cavernous length until finding a maintenance elevator that was reached off one of the side service hallways. Greg and Melanie looked carefully to make sure no one saw them enter the area, and Greg inserted his "Fredrick Davis" I.D. into the receptor slot beside the elevator door. What seemed endless seconds passed before the city's memory banks compared his name against a roster of names authorized to be in that area. This would be the first serious test of the data crystal's reliability, and, if it failed, an ACCESS DENIED wafer would light and a log of their attempted entry (plus their forged visas) would register upon the city's security computer banks. And then all hell would break loose.

"Fredrick R. Davis, Ph.D.: Identity confirmed," came a female voice before them. "Earth Visa permit #04673, Expiration: 01/10/16. Citizenship: Tshshuman's Palisade, Titan. Entry approval, dated: 10/27/15. Warning! Sensor scan reveals second lifeform in area proximity. Identity input required before access to elevator can be granted."

Melanie smirked at Greg and delicately handed hers over to him. He replaced his own crystal in the slot with hers. The summary was practically the same, identifying Melanie as Wilma Palmira Davis.

The elevator doors silently opened. Greg reached over for Melanie and kissed her one good on her mouth. "Sorry," he apologized for kissing her again. "You're the best."

They entered.

Neither of them had ever seen this part of the city. It was quite aged and not kept up very well. The elevator had opened to what seemed a dingy hallway, a hallway that stank of mildew and dripping condensation, a dank place with dull gray walls. The floor was wet beneath them, a layer of water about a centimeter high sheened across the hallway length at some points. They departed the elevator and entered it. Algae appeared to have painted murals along the walls, interesting patterns, none inspiring.

"Ick," commented Melanie.

Greg laughed, silently. "Yep, that describes it all right."

"Where's the nearest support strut?"

"There ought to be a floor plan on one of these walls sooner or later."

She nodded. "It's probably hiding under one of those fungus murals we just passed. Does anyone come down here ever?"

"Not often, I don't suppose. City maintenance, maybe. The fusion and environment generating plants are down here, carbon to oxygen converters and air purifiers, city water supplies, waste management, sewer treatment. Am I making you ill, yet?"

"YES!"

He nodded. "It's not just me, then." The smell made him want to puke. It smelled of waste treatment. "I hope we don't run across anything down here, or anyone. Too long down in this mess, and God only knows what it might mutate into. "

Melanie stopped all of a sudden and had to lean against him. She started giggling.

"What are you doing?"

"I'm trying not to laugh, damn you!" she said. Her whole body started shaking. She took a breath. "Greg, stop it. We have to find one of those struts soon, or I'm going to throw up."

"Do you want to activate the life belts now?"

"And miss breathing real, unfiltered air, once we get outside, if even for a few moments?" She glanced down to her belt, secure around her waist. "No. Fuck this thing. I'll activate it when I'm ready."

It was nearing Four P.M. They had walked the dank halls of this level for a good twenty minutes. They saw it finally just up ahead— a main Egress Elevator. It was at the intersection of about five different corridors. Greg thought he saw a form far down one of them and looked over at Melanie; he told her to creep behind him. They moved to the elevator, and pressed an old pressure plate "actuator button." The huge door was an overhead type, descended from above, was massive and of iron. This was obviously a service elevator (intended for heavy machinery), as well as one intended for transporting personnel and delivering building supplies back in the old days, and when its iron door opened, it created quite an echo. Let's just say it made a lot of noise, as if it really didn't care who heard it, who knew it was being activated. How often did it actually get to be used, why should it care? It once was of great importance in the days of the city's initial construction and outfitting, but that was many years ago, centuries in fact. This was its moment to be heard, and it wasn't about to squander the opportunity.

(So, we're in agreement, then? When it opened, it was loud?)

"Noisy son of a bitch!" Greg said under his breath.

As soon as the door lifted high enough, they ducked under it and entered the elevator bay.

"Do you still want me to whisper?" Melanie said under her breath.

"Yes!" he shouted above the din. "Smart ass!" He reached over to the inner pressure plate and pressed it. The door rumbled to a halt. In the falling silence that followed, Melanie eyed him in confusion. "Why'd you stop it for?" she whispered.

He shushed her again with his finger against his lips. He pulled out Frank Kesler's stun gun and motioned Melanie to hide beyond the edge of the door. He did the same on his side.

The silence was so complete they could hear each other's breathing despite a distance of six meters from the left side of the elevator opening to its right side. They looked at each other in the twilight darkness of the half closed door. They heard a footstep, then.

Melanie tensed and instinctively drew forward to peer out the opening. Greg waved her back and waited with the stun unit in hand.

A grizzled, old maintenance worker approached the fleet elevator. The poor guy hated his assignment down in the bowels of the city, and truth be told he was a little drunk. Stewed to the gills was more like it.

"Ah'm hearing things," Greg and Melanie heard him say as he came down the hall. "Ah aw'ways said this place was haunted. Who are ya?" He had a large pipe wrench in his hand. "You a ghost? I ain't a'scared of ya. Come on out."

Greg shook his head. *What a waste of a stun gun's pulse energy,* he thought. The guy could sleep for an hour even without being fired at. All he needed was a good right hook.

He was just about to enter the elevator. "Hey old man!" Greg called. The old guy froze, and Greg let him have it. The blue beam struck him chest high and the guy arched backward like he'd been run through from behind with a saber. He collapsed in slow motion onto the cement floor. Greg hurried to him, lest the poor old fool would hit his head when he hit the floor and kill himself. Melanie ran to him as well.

Greg shook his head. "He's out of it, all right." He checked the man's eyes. "I don't know if it's the ray gun or the booze that did it."

"He's filthy!" Melanie said of his clothes. "He stinks too!"

"He's had a hard life, probably. 1 wouldn't want to live down here. Can you help me drag him to the wall? He'll sleep it off. He'll have a hangover so bad, he won't know if we were real or the booze."

***

They re-entered the elevator and Greg released the HOLD button on the massive iron door. It rumbled back to life and completed its descent, clanging upon hitting the bottom. Greg then pressed the down button and slowly the elevator began to descend. They felt the vertigo effect of the elevator's descent; it left a queasy feeling in their stomachs and heads. Twenty-Fifth century city dwellers seldom experienced such in modern lift mechanisms. Turbo lifts usually ran smooth as silk. But not this old thing. It vibrated as it descended, gave one a nauseous knot in the stomach. They couldn't wait till it reached ground level.

Eventually, it reached the base of the strut, after what seemed an endless descent, and slowly the great door rose and opened once more.

The sunlight hurt at first, as it flooded into the elevator chamber, but gradually their eyes adjusted to it, and the day beyond stood before them in majesty. It was a gorgeous day all right, warm and filled with the rustic scents of autumn. They felt a breeze fill the chamber. Greg, remembering his father's ramblings about the air being dangerous to such pussy humans as humanity now was, automatically slid his hand down for his life belt. But at the last second, thought, *fuck it. I'll wait.*

The overhead door cleared their heads, but they remained there anyway. They were like kids experiencing a wonder never before theirs. The clang of the door against its moorings above them roused them from their trance, and slowly they entered the day. The weed and brush beneath them was high and brittle in the autumn sun as the summer receded. The countryside stretched on beyond for kilometers. Behind them the three other support struts rose as massive walls of concrete and metal, towering monoliths spaced across seven and a half square kilometers of land. It would take a good hour to walk completely under the city, if that were the route they intended. They looked upon the city high above. It seemed scary, all of it above their heads like that.

"And you say I never take you anywhere," said Greg.

Melanie moved out beyond the support column's obstructed view. "My God, Greg, it's beautiful!" She closed her eyes and felt the sun upon her face. She took a breath. "Wow."

Greg breathed in real air as well. A rarity for any "civilized" human living being on Earth these days, the Renegades non-withstanding.

The city was a good half kilometer above them atop its pedestal base; the city itself rose another two kilometers into the sky, and stretched almost five kilometers across the open plain. The sun hung low in the west against the northern foothills of the Blue Mountains which wove like a great brown and orange scar down for the southwest.

Greg faced them. "That's the direction I want, Mellie. Southwest. Don't worry, we won't have to walk far. If I've studied the region maps correctly, there should be a little forestry station about twenty kilometers toward the mountains. It should be abandoned right now, and it'll have just what we need. Is that all right?"

She looked at him. "Abandoned? You and me?" She nodded, inching her palms up his shoulders. "Oh, yes, it'll be more than all right."

Greg grinned at her motions toward him. "Mellie, honey, don't, not out here in the open like this." He looked up to the city, so huge right above him. Just the thought of that mass of metal hanging so ominously and so near like that, scared the royal piss out of him. "We better get on the move." He kissed her lips, very gently. "But I like the way you think."

He placed his arms, then, around her waist, and led her forward across the great open plain. They tried keeping hidden amid the trees as well as they could. They made progress, slowly, and yet one look behind them revealed the city as massive and imposing as if they'd remained as yet right underneath it. They continued up a shallow grade.

Melanie spread her arms in the mild autumn breeze; she heard a mockingbird in the distance about three-hundred meters. He was perched high up an evergreen, and performed a concert for an audience that remained unseen. In the world of the wilds, he was like a celebrity imitator, mocking everyone else. No doubt it was why they called him a mockingbird.

"Ummm," Melanie sighed. "People would kill to do what we're doing just once in their lifetimes. I could stay outside forever. I'm glad we did this."

"The world wasn't always like this," Greg replied. He looked back to New Allentown. "They say five-hundred years ago the ozone layer thinned so bad during the summer they recommended you not stay out in the direct sunlight too long. The exposure would give you skin cancer. They tried to alleviate the problem with sunblock, paint it on your arms, face, and any exposed skin. They had to keep increasing the protection factor. And then the air out here . . ." He shook his head.

"That was then, Greg," Melanie said lowly.

Greg nodded. "Back then the cities were a haven from the hostile elements. They're like a prison today, a self-imposed exile by the human race to make sure we don't ruin the planet again."

He smiled weakly and then took her hand. She grinned back. They continued on then for the mountains.

Randolph Phillips had joined the search teams north of Cassini crater on the Moon and amid the rising mounds of the lunar Alps. He was out this hour with the base commander as they moved on foot toward the crest of one of the southern foothills. His environment "suit" consisted of a simple pair of grayish-blue overalls, gloves, boots, and a maintenance life belt. The force shield cocoon molded against his body like a second skin, much the same as had the one he had had modified to breach the cocoon shields back in Washington D.C. Park.

The silence around Randolph was incredible. It was only bested by the way light draped across the cliff faces about him in stark harshness and clarity. It humbled any pretensions the Moon may have had about being grand. Only the Sun and Earth were visible in the jet black sky, high above Mare Imbrium to the west. It was full moon, the sun and Earth directly overhead. The great Mare Imbrium plain fanned out across the Moon a vast wasteland of orange in the distance.

The search for the secret destination of the orb so far had been unsuccessful. As mountains went, the lunar Alps were no great challenge, not like the peaks of Earth or even the volcanic behemoths of Mars. Randolph needed not worry too much about the teams getting lost or be in distress out there. The problem was the reports about the orb's path across the lunar terrain and its probable destination within the Alps. The commercial flight crews, who had forwarded the telemetry of the alien anomaly, understandably had been less than enthusiastic and quite nonchalant in the gathering and analysis of their data. Their data, nonetheless, had been a source of much surprise.

An impromptu briefing had been held in Cassini earlier in the day after the received data had been initially analyzed. Randolph had arrived almost just in time for the thing.

Gathered in the conference room of the base were its best scientific minds, and search team leaders who would lead the actual search out in the Alps. The moderator of the meeting was the chief administrator, a Mr. Ronald Isley.

"We'll be fixating the main search in the northwest quadrant, along these coordinates," said Isley. "We believe we're looking for a crevice so small that only a small dog might successfully enter it."

"I hope you're wrong about that," Randolph said. He'd caught the meeting at about that point, after coming straight from the flight deck.

The chief administrator nodded to Randolph, and said, "Councilman. Considering the size and nature of the anomaly in question, our consensus is that a very small entry point is more than likely."

"Meaning, you haven't located it, yet," Randolph surmised.

"No, not yet," Chief Isley answered him. "We're homing in, but it's quite a big area to comb through, and the opening . . . like a needle in a haystack."

"Have you ever *seen* a haystack, Chief?" Randolph replied, dryly.

The man smiled. "In archives. Not for real of course. I doubt anyone anymore would even recognize one if they saw it."

"Uh huh," responded Randolph. "Well, the sooner we locate the way in, the happier I'll be," he added.

Ronald Isley smiled. "We're giving it our all," he said in what had to be sarcasm. He shuffled uncomfortably on his feet at the head of the gathered assembly, and then bringing a fist to his mouth, he cleared his throat.

"We've reviewed the visuals you sent ahead from D.C. and New Allentown. That family, I'm afraid, Mr. Phillips. . . ." Ron shook his head. "I'd pretty much rule out a successful rescue. Drilling down into the depths of that mountain. . . . I shudder to think what's down there. What we'll find." He shook his head again.

***

"Can you do it or can't you?" Randolph had asked at the briefing. "I want that family back. I have reason to believe there are many more down there as well, have been, for centuries. There may be a whole community of people down there, descendants of the original captures."

"Frankly, councilman," said Isley. "Considering your Eleution 'orb,' we're all here a little leery about taking that Athena creature on." He shook his head yet again. "To be truthful, that bitch scares the crap out of me."

Randolph Phillips grinned, as if he were only humoring the man.

"She's a super advanced spirit plane lifeform who makes it possible for other lesser species to cross space through so-called wormholes. Apparently, without the assistance of these incorporeal entities, such as the one we're dealing with here, the lesser species would remain stuck traveling normal space, obeying Albert Einstein's relativity laws, taking centuries just to visit even the nearby stars. Our own predicament, curiously. That's quite a generosity this Athena and her species has bestowed on others."

"We think," Randolph replied, "these Eleutions limit that benevolence to that other species in their own home solar system."

"The Barthonians," had nodded Isley. "I played that archive you sent me that that family recorded. You believe these little purple 'elves' are the little critters behind all those UFO sightings half a millennium ago?"

"Possibly. It's hard to say which species is the brains of the operation." Randolph shuffled uncomfortably and impatiently. "This is all peripheral stuff, Chief. Do you have anything else?"

"We have the site where we think she tracks down into the Alps. That's a good start."

"Then, when are we launching?"

"Roll out commences within the hour. You're welcome to tag along."

"Oh, I'll be joining you, don't you worry about that. I have every intention of being a part of this."

"Well, then. . . . Oh, one thing," Ron Isley began then. "One puzzling question, councilman. Why did this Athena entity risk all this exposure, dragging your son and yourself all the way to the top of the Washington Monument? Why did she do that?"

"Personally, I choose to believe that was Keith Hagerton's doing, as revenge for my son and myself causing him all that grief." He grinned. "He was really hoping I'd climb all 900 steps of that monument."

"Yes, you say that in your summary, councilman," said Isley. "But do you really think this Athena would risk exposure, like she already has? The research suggests she's been snaring people for more than four-hundred years. She never took such risks, made such mistakes, in all those centuries. Why now? Unless she *wanted* to be discovered. If that's true, we're just playing along, a part of a scenario whose conclusion . . ." Isley shook his head, gravely, "that thought is even scarier than Athena, herself. What is her end-game . . . ? I'm not sure I would have selected a well-known park for a meeting like that, if I didn't want evidence of my existence broadcast all over the place."

"The park at that time of the night, Isley," Randolph informed him, "is manned by a skeleton security crew, only. Surveillance for the most part is all automated. The place is deserted."

"Still, councilman, she chose an area where the event could easily be documented. As I see it, it all amounts to the same thing."

Randolph nodded. "Will all this help your search teams out in the Alps, chief?"

Isley sighed. "Probably not. Throw a dark cloud over it, maybe. Like going into a battle you know you stand a good chance of not returning from." The chief administrator nodded, pensively.

"Well, alright then," Phillips only replied. "Let's get out there."

The lunar surface, Randolph thought now— hours after that meeting. The day was aging; that is, the "work day" for the men assigned to probe the Alps in search of a way in and down into the bowels of the Earth's lone moon. Time it would soon be for them all to retire from the long day of initial prep and deployment. As for proof that much time had passed at all since their arrival: none of any appreciable kind came. A day/night cycle? No. No such reveal, not on the surface of the Moon. Things happened, as even most amateur astronomers knew, in monthly phases where the Moon was concerned. Even the stars in the sky were no help. There were none to be seen. Not at present anyway. The full-on light of the sun was leaving the lunar surface "whited out." The human eye had to dilate in response, to diminish the glare, and thus while the stars of the night were certainly up there, they were made invisible by the glare.

And that wasn't the worst of it. In the vacuum of space, on the lunar surface, distances became visually corrupted. All the little identifiers people used on Earth to judge distances just didn't work on the Moon. It was easy to think a destination was just a few feet away when in truth it could be much more, even a kilometer, perhaps. And the Lunar Alps. They resembled not mountains so much, but eroded sand dunes. They were featureless, uninspiring mounds. Hard to believe they even contained rock. Everything on the Moon looked like a planet size version of a kitty litter cat box. The Moon was not the grandest planetary destination in the home solar system by even a little bit. But it was the closest to the home world.

Randolph glanced upward to the jet black sky in search of Earth's far away presence. It was the only celestial object bright enough, besides the sun itself, that it could be even seen with the naked eye.

And there it was, looking so very much like a tiny marble high up in the night above him. He took a moment to gaze up at it.

The eastern coastline of North America was just coming over the western horizon, at the extreme left edge of the planet. It was on the terminator between day and night. Direct on was the continent of Africa. It was Full Moon on Earth, which meant that the Earth was currently in orbital opposition to the Moon and Sun. Thus, only Earth's night side was currently visible.

It was approaching Five P.M. on the east coast. Night was descending. Soon Randolph might even begin to notice the night lights of the Island Cities as they rotated into view.

He wondered if his son had reached Sydney as yet, if he was safely kept ignorant of the activities that his elders were engaged in. Poor Greg. It was better for him to let experienced adults handle a situation such as this. Greg meant well, but he just didn't have the treachery to make a good politician or an undercover man. He wouldn't approve, probably, of the lengths his father and his associates would go to understand the true nature of what Athena was, and how her knowledge of the universe might benefit, maybe even slingshot forward, humanity's bold trek into the vast unknown. That was worth all the negatives, even if it meant sacrificing the Hagertons to do it. As for Greg's copy of the Hagerton visual, retrieval of the recording was not paramount in importance at this juncture, but Randolph couldn't help wondering why he hadn't heard from his operatives back in New Allentown. He wondered if everything was all right.

Frank Kesler was just coming out of his paralysis about then, and when he pulled his body up to a sitting position upon the tiled floor, he looked over at his other two agents and then looked up at where he was. He cursed the bitch Richards girl as he remembered what happened, and then almost as quickly grinned and shook his head in admiration. She was quick all right, someone who kept her wits about her in a moment of potential panic and who analytically approached the solution to a problem. She'd been ready for him no sooner than after laying out his assistant in her bedroom. He looked over at the man there now by the toilet. The guy was beginning to come out of it. Then Kesler saw his other man, Smothers, unconscious in the bathtub.

Kesler smiled. "When did you join the party?" he asked, lowly.

He felt the towels which bound his hands and feet.

No problem, he thought.

Mason, over by the john, was trying to sit up now. Between the two of them they'd be out of the restraints in no time. He got the man's attention and worked his way over to him.

-7-

Randolph got the news about an hour later. A full report by Kesler was waiting for him by the time Randolph left the search team and their preliminary prep work and descended for the main field operations land rover vessel. Randolph was tired. For a man his age and not used to such strenuous things, this search effort today, plus the trek for the Washington Monument the night before, was really cramping his muscles, and this despite all the available treatments to reduce that sort of discomfort.

Yet, tired or no, the report had just the opposite effect on him than he expected. He started to laugh.

"Greg, you're too much." How much his son reminded Randolph of the boy's mother, the same rash behavior, mood swings. According to Kesler, he and Miss Richards had an entire city to hide in. No record of their having absconded with a transport vehicle existed. They had to still be in New Allentown. Kesler had ended the communication with, "Your orders?" Randolph took a breath and looked down at the technician, manning communications. "Send this." he said. *"Take no hostile actions. Find them."*

CHAPTER THIRTY-ONE

-1-

The sun was setting behind the westward hills as Greg and Melanie began the climb for the nearest foothill of the Blue Mountains. They still had an hour yet of light before darkness swept over everything. The city was behind them as large as ever, and seemed to blot out the landscape to the north in the direction of the distant Poconos. Even now its beacon lights were beginning to grow stronger as the deep blue sky behind it began to darken to crimson blue. A hush hung in the air, the crisp feel of the cooling nights of autumn fell over the land like a reminder of the bitter season of winter that would soon come.

In the hour that had passed since they had left the city behind, they had advanced ten kilometers into the foothills of the Blue Mountains. They came across the remains of old roadways, which once winded into the hillsides, but now were only a few brief patches of asphalt every once in a while. Fractured and overgrown with weeds, they cut strange swaths through the land. They seemed so very odd, because they now no longer appeared to go anywhere, but instead flourished briefly, only to become engulfed once more in a world that did not require them.

The crunch of the maple and oak leaves that carpeted the banking forests of the rising lowlands was itself an eerie, new experience for them, a sensation no Sensor Sphere transmission had ever included. None had for one very good reason—Sensor Spheres floated through the air; they didn't have any feet.

A small band of crimson light hugged the horizon to the south and south west by six-thirty, and the stars were out now in full majesty above them. Still, New Allentown could be seen behind them, a great symbol of human ingenuity and intellect. It seemed one great domain of lights, casting its own glow upon the darkness surrounding it. And above in the sky to the east, the full and "harvest" moon rose above the tree line; it was as big as ever and the color of copper.

Melanie paused to gaze upon it; so did Greg, his arm around her waist as they simply pondered the tiny impressions of craters and plains upon it.

My father's there somewhere, thought Greg. *He's up there upon a whole other world, there in the sky. Can he see the Earth from where he is standing, has he a clear view of the sky above the lunar roil? What is he thinking about; doing, right this very minute?*

Melanie reached over and kissed Greg gently on the cheek. "Oh, Greg, why didn't we ever think of something like this before? It's so peaceful, so wondrous." She shook her head.

267

Greg nodded, faintly. "Mel?" he whispered, and he pointed her to the next wooded rise about a kilometer above them. "See it?"

She looked up in the direction that he pointed. A small wooden structure with windows all around its four sides lay supported upon a metal framework. It jutted out of a clearing high amid the evergreens, and stood in silhouette against the purple-blue sky. It seemed lonely and deserted, except for one thing: very faintly Melanie could see a faint scarlet haze completely surround it—a force shield cocoon. Greg gave the countryside a quick scan, and then gazed back to the distant structure. "We'll camp there tonight. It ought to be a great view."

She nodded.

A small maintenance shed squatted humbly before the base of the lookout shelter. The shelter itself hung large now against the starlight above them. The air was chilly, and Melanie felt herself grabbing her arms against it. The scarlet cocoon shield encircled it all. But Greg wasn't worried about that. He went over to the shed and looked carefully upon the ground before it. A small plaque-like memorial was there, angled, of marble, and with a gold plate upon it:

Forestry Station 019
Founded November 27, 2238
Wilderness Society
New Allentown division
In the commonwealth of Pennsylvania.

Below the engraving was a small inset for a data crystal, and Greg reached under his sweater for the one he had. He slid it into the inset and a repetition of the earlier litany concerning his identity and clearance softly spelled itself out in a female, computer-generated voice. The voice requested the second presence beside him do likewise, and when Melanie inserted her own, the force shield fluttered. It dropped then, blinking right into nothing. Greg nodded to Melanie and they continued past and into the area beneath the shelter's access stairwell. They started for it and as they did the cocoon shield pulled up and around the area once again. Its impact on the surroundings felt hardly any at all.

Nine-thirty and Greg was outside the shelter on the balcony skirt. In the moon and starlight the mountains hugged the world like great, black hulks, silent and wondrous. A breeze passed Greg and ruffled his hair.

(Within the shelter, among its many other instrumentation, lay a force-shield, cocoon-contour control. Greg had re-contoured the shape of the cocoon so that its influence extended now from ground level to only halfway up the skeletal framework. Otherwise, had he left it at full height, he and Melanie would have had no access to the night's breezes.) His view tonight of the wilderness surrounding New Allentown would be the grandest of all because it was real, not a hologram recreation, and because he was out within it.

He'd been out here now for about an hour, just gazing upon the stars with a blanket around him that he'd appropriated from the storage closet, inside. The shelter even had a few bunks. He and Melanie would not completely have to rough it upon the floor tonight. And down in the maintenance shed was camping gear. Hopefully, they'd even find a few other goodies, like a sled transport, maybe, for scooting across the terrain on an antigrav cushion, like bikers once did, tooling down the old land-based highways. Melanie exited the shelter eventually and nestled herself beside him as she shared the starlight with him in the silence of the evening. For the longest time she said not a word. Greg waited for her to speak, but was in no hurry to wreck the tranquility of the night.

"Kutztown is only a few kilometers south of here, isn't it?" she asked, eventually.

He nodded. "About fifty, maybe less."

Greg had left her for the last few hours within the shelter. She reviewed the whole of the viewwafer recording of the Hagerton men and their excursion to the caves to the south. He and Melanie had packed and taken with them a sensor globe, though so far they had not used it for more than a few quick recordings of the wilderness around them.

Athena's orb, buried for so long under the ground below her within this mountain range, left her so very much affected by the thought of it, and the dark night all around her merely added to the feelings of awe that hushed through her like the sound of distant thunder before a storm.

Aside from how cute little Jeffrey Hagerton looked in that *Alice in Wonderland* costume, she didn't have a whole lot to say about the recording in general. Nothing much was there to say. She felt she knew the Hagerton family very well now after viewing the whole of what they'd experienced last night. She had shared their departure from New Allentown for the universe beyond.

"I wish I'd gone with you last night, Greg," she said. She thought of what Greg had told her before about his and his father's adventure amid the landmarks in old Washington D.C. "Why'd you have to piss me off?"

Greg grinned. "I was a jerk. I knew I had an enigma with the original of that visual. I wanted to explore it, and I didn't give a hoot about the Hagertons. I didn't know them then, not like I feel I do now. I only cared about what I'd found; I wanted to share it with my dad. I wanted him to be proud of me."

"I'm sure he is in his own way."

Greg shrugged. "Maybe. . . . I won't be a jerk tonight, Mel. "

She looked up at him. "You promise?"

He nodded.

"Then, I won't act like a whiny, self-righteous little bitch, like last night," she answered. "Greg?"

"What?"

"Are we getting involved?"

"Are we?"

"You care about me, don't you?"

He grinned, and then nodded.

She smiled. "I care about you."

He held her tighter. "I don't know, Mellie. It looks like we might be hopelessly hooked on each other."

"Do you mean that?"

"You went way out on a limb for me today. No one's ever done that before. Now I'm worried about what might happen to you. My old man better back off, that's all I can say. He gives any further orders to have you handled, and I don't know, I'll. . ."

"Greg, don't. He's your father, don't say that."

"Well, he better not."

He leaned over and nuzzled her neck, tenderly. Melanie closed her eyes and then looked up at the Moon, even higher now in the night. She thought about the Hagertons somewhere upon it, and wondered what experiences they were a part of by now.

The stars inched to the zenith above them, and below within the forests, night creatures called to one another, and an owl hooted his solemn anthem. The night had fallen.

CHAPTER THIRTY-TWO

The following morning back on the Moon the teams were out and about again, combing the terrain of the Lunar Alps. The work continued as yet, locating Athena's orb's exact point of entry.

There was a knock on the door to Randolph's cramped cabin aboard the land rover. He had spent the most of the remainder of the preceding night sacked out in the tiny room, exhausted from the last two days and all that had transpired.

"Yeah," he called groggily as he pulled himself off the tiny bunk mattress, recessed into the metal wall. He worked his way through the tiny room to the hatch door and opened it.

It was a subordinate, someone he didn't know; an aid, obviously.

"Morning, sir," the man said.

Randolph nodded. "What's up?"

"Mr. Isley sent me down to collect you, Councilman Phillips. As soon as you're able, he requests your presence in the radio room. He says he has some news you may find interesting."

"Tell him I'll be right there," he answered.

"Very good, sir," the aid replied.

***

The radio room of the lunar land rover was a small compartment off the topside bridge. Randolph entered the compartment shortly thereafter, and made his perfunctory greetings to everyone within.

"Isley," he said.

The land rover was a massive vessel which made a good initial base facility for any new explorations or projects upon the lunar surface. Chief Administrator Ron Isley had remained aboard, assisting the vessel personnel in their orchestration of the resumed search efforts within the Alps. Mapped and logged were the regions where the ground teams were presently deployed.

"What do you got for me, chief?" asked Randolph, yawning.

Ron Isley smiled, weakly. "You been to the mess hall, yet? The cook's pretty good."

"I'll get to my personal amenities later. This sounded like something I needed to report here for before all that other personal care stuff."

"No offense intended by this, councilman, but if I may? You look like warmed over death."

Randolph yawned a second time. "Yeah. It's been a rough last few days for me. Just back from a conference in Sydney, Australia, my son knocks on my door and we're off on a foot trek across D.C. Park and up to the top floor of the Washington Monument. And now the Moon. Got to love it."

"Then, if I can amend my original statement: *you look like shit* . . . sir."

Randolph smiled. "Noted. So, what do you got for me, Chief?" Randolph asked once more.

"We think we've uncovered the route that energy ball used to enter the range. Take a look."

Isley was huddled over a three-dimensional display of the Alps Range. The hologram presentation reminded Randolph a lot of the one he'd seen in D.C. Park with its views of the Mall and its monuments. This one however accepted data from hundreds of sensor probes and spheres either hand-carried or seeded upon the range to aid the display in generating its detailed reproduction. Isley pointed to a small fissure break in a cliff wall. Randolph studied the simulation of the cliff face, intently. He requested from the technician nearby a neuralscan headset and put it on. The circuits read his request for dimensions, and in tiny green print the overall height and width of the slit splayed out beside it.

"Half a meter by one point five," Randolph observed. "Tight fit." He looked back at Isley. "Not bad, though."

The man nodded. "The line of entry toward it figures well, however, in our projections."

"We'll never squeeze any large equipment through that hole," countered Randolph. "It'll need enlarging."

"Agreed. But, you hired me to find it," said Isley, "not to vouch for its accessibility."

Randolph smiled, weakly.

"There's more." Isley requested Randolph's headset, and positioning it upon his own head, he entered a few commands of his own. The area of the slit enlarged and the majority of the Alps-relief disappeared off the sides of the display table. The mountain peak assumed a vertical shape that rose about a meter above Randolph's head, and the entrance slit inhabited a location near its top. Angling downward into the mountain core was a simulated shaft that appeared to enter a long, horizontal cavity beneath the surface.

Randolph studied the shaft's descent in interest. "How far down is that?"

"About two kilometers," Isley answered. "Long way down."

"And that horizontal area at the bottom?" he asked, pointing.

"About a kilometer in overall length, according to the initial reports. We think it may have been a lava bubble created during the days when the lava flowed hot through the Moon's core. When this portion of the peak hardened, there was a gas bubble, a pocket. It's since dissipated. That was a long time ago."

"And the shaft?"

He shook his head. "That shouldn't be there. It *could* just be an old lava vent, but there's no real evidence that that peak had a volcanic spout. The geology of the area is all wrong for that. That cavern down there must have fed the flows that filled and created Mare Imbrium. But not that shaft, its walls are too sheer, too accurate, to be a natural creation. Someone put it there. . . . There's one thing more, councilman," he said as an afterthought.

"Yes?"

"Something's down there. Energy output we're picking up confirms something unnatural is going on down there. The teams are down there checking it out now."

Randolph smiled. "Progress, finally."

"I don't know, Councilman. I have to ask again. *Why now?* Why are we so able to detect all this all of a sudden, and never before? Based on the archive documents you sent us, this other-worldly capture operation has been in place a long while." He shook his head. "It's puzzling."

"Isley, call your people at the fissure, and tell them you and I will be joining them in the next half hour. I want to check this out, myself."

"They're expecting us," he replied.

"Good."

Ronald Isley scratched his chin, pensively. "But it wouldn't surprise me if *my people* weren't the only intelligent life down there in that cave expecting us as well."

"Well, let's hope we're not walking right into a trap. Anything's possible." Randolph Phillips gazed again at the tiny slit up the rock wall, and then let his eyes wander the length of the shaft's descent into the Moon. "Amazing," he whispered.

***

The fissure crack could only be entered on foot. The tunnel that led back from it toward the descent shaft varied in width from as narrow as a half meter in some places to as wide as four.

Randolph and Chief Administrator Ron Isley followed the rope trail, hastily set up by the initial teams just a few hours before. Ten ground personnel accompanied them, leading the way. The ten were the latest group to descend for the subterranean cavern. The fissure crack tunneled inward several meters, and was quite fractured. The men walked the rope guide in a scene reminiscent of divers adrift in the ocean currents on the sea bed, the rope to ensure their course remained true. The rope disappeared far into the fissure. Maneuvering in one-sixth gravity, it should be noted, made the going easier. A Light Dog (the slang name for work crew versions of the Light Sphere crystal) took a position behind Randolph, and illuminated a scene of endless rock, walls so narrow sometimes a person just barely squeezed through. What a fortuitous thing it was that bulky spacesuits were no longer required in the wake of the life/lift belts. It would have taken a shoe horn to navigate not a few of the many turns and narrowing's.

"It doesn't get much wider," said Isley, gravely.

The next turn was only a half meter wide. "It certainly can't get much narrower," said Randolph. He tugged the rope, allowing the force of his pull to push his body along in the one-sixth gravity until he needed his feet to assist in the managing of the more difficult passages.

When the shaft finally came into view, it was of such a breadth in scale and posture that it literally floored them. The fissure tunnel opened to what was literally a long and angled descent that disappeared far into the Moon's interior. So far in fact did it descend that whatever light had been set up down in the distant cavern, did not manifest itself among the shadows below.

Randolph waited for the descent team to set adrift the other two Light Dogs they'd brought with them. The units were powered up; the shaft filled with light. Randolph saw the sheer, unnaturally straight walls drop into the lunar rock.

"It's five meters wide all the way down, councilman," said the group leader.

Randolph ran his hand across the floor of the shaft, and felt its machined smoothness.

Chief Administrator Isley assembled the group at the lip of the descent, and made sure all were ready to start down. "Okay, you guys, it's the lift belts from here down. Don't try to walk it; that floor is way too smooth and angled. Even in one/sixth gravity you could build yourself a nice amount of momentum if you started tumbling head first."

Isley looked over at Randolph, who affixed the neuralscan medallion to his forehead and then secured it with its leather strap.

Randolph nodded.

"Let's do it!" Isley called over his com-link transmitter. "Down the hole."

***

Two kilometers in length, the shaft took them about an hour to descend. Plans were already being discussed about constructing a ski-lift-type set up, but such would come later when something was done about enlarging the entrance fissure.

Randolph was not prepared for what he saw below.

Intricately detailed limestone formations hung from the ceiling or rose from the floor in what on Earth would have been acceptable detail for a subterranean cave. There was no logical explanation for such phenomena existing on the Moon. It simply didn't make sense from a geological standpoint.

He reached for a stalactite. "Have your people identified what their composition is, what they're made of?" he asked.

"Genuine limestone," Isley replied. "No doubt it was exported from Earth and sculptured to look this way. Someone went to a lot of trouble. There are other trace elements as well, and what generally reads as high energy output on an unknown wavelength of power, but for what purpose we still haven't determined. It's as if the entire chamber down here is a power field. Something really strange is going on down here."

"What's that thing?" Randolph asked of a very large crystal mass in the chamber room's center. It was aglow very dully, with a pulsing rhythm to the light output, implying the thing was alive somehow. Not alive perhaps, organically, although that was certainly something not to be ruled out too hastily, but alive in so much that it was definitely a power emitter of some kind.

Randolph moved his palm inches above and across its top. Even through his life belt's force field cocoon envelope there was evidence that the mass radiated an energetic force. "Any ideas on what it's for?" he asked, aloud, over his com-link transmitter. He glanced to all the personnel down here in the cavern. "Anybody?"

Most of the men in the area just shook their heads.

"Looks pretty, whatever it is," said Isley.

"Could Athena and her 'captives' possibly be stored inside this thing's crystalline matrix?"

'Yeah, we've all thought that as well," said Isley. "But there's no way to be sure."

"Could we try removing it?"

"The whole crystal?" asked one of the scientists nearby. "Without knowing what its function is, what's stored inside the lattices of its crystalline make-up? Very dangerous to even consider it. If our people, the ones that have been missing for the last five-hundred years, are being stored in a data storage configuration inside that thing, messing with it might be the equivalent of killing everybody who've been alive in that thing's memory all these centuries."

"Thank you," replied Randolph. "Your objections noted." He studied the man, then. "And you are?"

"Frank Henderson, PhD. Geophysics."

Randolph surveyed the chamber and just shook his head. He took a solemn breath.

"Like I said, councilman," said Ron Isley. "We're in over our heads down here."

Randolph faced him. "What *have* your men learned so far?"

Isley laughed and then nodded. "That we're in over our heads."

Randolph watched as a group of Isley's men probed the crystalline mass with various sensor instruments— magnetometers, metal analyzers, radiation probes, fatigue testers . . . .

"We won't dare pick at it with anything physical. Don't want to damage it." Ron Isley nodded. "She's down here. Can't you feel it? She's aware of us, this Athena entity of yours, and I suspect we're here by her invitation. She wants us to be here for some reason."

"Hardly a scientific statement, Isley," grinned Randolph.

The chief administrator faced him squarely. "You can feel the electricity coming off that crystal. I should point out, Mr. Phillips, that *electricity* also runs our life support units. We have to be careful what we do down here. Piss off this Athena entity of yours and she could drain our devices of every last joule of power. No life support, we're dead. This is the Moon, remember. A dead world, no air, pure vacuum."

"You don't know any of that for certain, Chief," said Randolph.

"Phillips!" he said, getting agitated. "I saw your Hagerton visual. I saw what this Athena did to that little boy. And that wasn't even Athena, but her avatar, an externalized part of her total essence." He faced the whole of the chamber. "We're inside her right now. All these fake formations and crystal masses all over. Jesus, Phillips, I don't know about you, but I've been as queasy as hell down here since I stepped off that long descent shaft."

"We're not leaving with no answers," Randolph declared. "You called in the best people on the Moon, correct? The best available? Human beings are trapped somewhere down here, in a reality they can't break free from. They at least need us to make an effort."

"What do you propose?" Isley asked.

Randolph glanced to the huge crystalline mass in the chamber's center again. "If we need to, we'll uproot that thing and take it to where we can run proper tests."

"But the people. . . ."

"You don't know they're in there!" he spat. "For all you know that's just a source of illumination for when they first arrive down here. Who's your best down here?"

"You met him, already. . . . Frank?" Isley called to the fellow who had argued to Randolph against messing with the crystalline mass.

"Yeah, Ron?" said Frank Henderson. He left the powwow he was conducting with his associates probing a nearby "stalactite" and sauntered over. He was a tall and lanky fellow, in his late forties, and liked to spend most of his time dressed in white turtlenecks and corduroy trousers. He'd lived most of his life on the Moon, hailing originally from Liverpool, England.

"Frank, the councilman wants answers."

Frank walked back and retrieved an imaging tablet. He took a laser pen and had it access his observations and conclusions on the crystal mass's configuration. "Take a look at this pattern, Mr. Philips," he said, handing him the tablet. "That crystal's structure is like none I've ever seen before .

. . on any of the moons, asteroids, all the cosmic junk we can actually land on and mine in this solar system of ours. For a crystal, I'd say it's organic in a way I can't even imagine explaining. There's evidence of elemental particles that would suggest a living cell structure, interlacing what would have to be an incredibly light and resilient material."

"So even now it qualifies as a living thing?"

Henderson nodded. "On some elemental level, yes. Trust me, councilman, that thing is alive. So much so, I wouldn't be surprised it's assuming the shape we see, deliberately. Piss it off as you keep proposing and it may assume a more sinister shape, jump up and bite you a nice one on your ass. Here's an idea. Ask it a question. For all we know it may even answer you."

He returned to his work, then, disappearing within the distant sectors of the chamber.

Randolph looked over at the chief administrator. "Isley, is he always that unprofessional?"

"Frank is the best, Phillips. Let's just say he knows your kind. Thinks very little of them too."

"We have to do better than this, Isley."

"Maybe we're here to see what we're up against it," thought Isley. "A test, even. To see if we're advanced enough, intelligent enough, to know when to just back off."

"Ron?" said Frank Henderson, returning. "Just letting you know. Your top man down here, what's his name again?"

"Boschovich," Ron Isley answered. "Stanley Boschovich."

Frank Henderson nodded. "*Asshole* probably works just as well as all that. Boschovich over there overrode my good advice, a few hours ago. There's the result. Take a note of that, Mr. Phillips." Henderson pointed to what remained of an industrial plasma beam cutter, sequestered off now to a side cavity. "One of our strongest antimatter-matter units. One hit with that thing, and most objects would be obliterated. Boschovich had it hauled down here, and was getting his men prepped to fire it up. He never even got close. That crystal sensed what that thing was. A beam shot out from it. For all I know it was an analysis beam of some kind. It probed our beam cutter. It only took that crystal a second to deduce what that device of ours was and what we intended to use it for. That's when a second beam issued and overrode the first one. That crystalline mass of yours doesn't want us messing with it. It's alive on some level all right. The beam cutter's been completely powered down, its antimatter pods emptied! That crystal literally sucked the energy right out of it."

"It sounds to me as if all you did was feed it," quipped Randolph, amused by his own statement.

Isley nodded. "Thanks, Frank, I'll have a talk with Stan."

Frank Henderson nodded and excused himself, returning once more to the further reaches of the cavern.

"I'd say your Athena is laughing her ass off at us about now," grinned Isley to Randolph. "Her devices spread out here in the cavern are designed to attend to their own safety. And that worries me. So far we've only tried Athena's patience. God help us if we get her mad. I'll say it again, Phillips. We're seriously out of our element down here. I wonder if you truly appreciate what you're tangling with. Half my men are getting antsy just being down here, period."

"How soon, then, can you get the excavators to widen that fissure, topside, cut a path inward all the way back to the shaft? If we can't do anything useful here, I want everything down here brought to the surface— send it out by transport to one of the high tech outfits south of us in Aliacensis. I would even have it shipped to Mariner Valley, give *InterWorld* a crack at it, if I thought it would help. "

"An operation like that," Isley returned, "will bring you a lot of publicity. You can't avoid it. The news agencies will jump on it right off."

"You think I'm worried about that? When?"

Isley sighed. "Noon tomorrow . . . maybe, if we put the wheels in motion now."

Randolph nodded. "All right, good." He turned to leave.

"Phillips!" Isley called to him. Randolph faced him. "Are you really sure you want to do all that? I don't think you appreciate the situation down here at all."

"Frankly, Isley," Randolph answered, "I think you need to get yourself more properly motivated."

Isley smirked and nodded. He left, then.

Randolph thought his sword play with Isley went quite well. He stared again at the crystal mass. It was refusing to cooperate with him, and so far he was powerless to get the better of it. He hated when anything or anyone managed such a thing. He cursed Athena, silently, under his breath. He pictured Keith Hagerton somewhere here, in this place, watching him; perhaps, directing Athena to deliberately defy Randolph. He cursed Keith Hagerton even more severely than he did Athena. He suddenly didn't feel quite so pleased, and for that he swore he'd make Keith Hagerton pay for it.

Randolph suddenly heard his son, Greg's, admonishment to him, yesterday. *Why the hate for Keith Hagerton? Your fight's with Athena.*

Or words to that effect.

Why? Keith was mortal. Him, Randolph could put a hurt on. Athena, on the other hand, scared the piss out of him. He hated feeling that way.

He had to take it out on somebody. . . .

CHAPTER THIRTY-THREE

-1-

"We're no closer even yet?" Kimberly Hagerton asked as she, her husband, and son reached the crest of still another hill. "Keith, what is this? We've been walking for hours!"

On the horizon, the glare that resembled the lights of a distant city remained as far away as when the three first began their journey.

Keith couldn't say how far they'd gone in search of the lights, or upon how many hill tops the same revelation had greeted them. Nor could he ascertain how long ago he, his wife and son left the lava flows to begin this journey. It felt to be hours they'd been out here. The entire experience was slowly beginning to seem more like a dream episode, where nothing was what it seemed.

Kimberly stopped by an outcropping and sat down upon it. She glanced back in the direction they'd come. "Do you realize that nothing back there even looks familiar? When did we pass that large oak with the yellow leaves? And I know I would have remembered that birch over there by the stream," she said, pointing.

Keith examined the objects she alluded to.

"And I thought we were on a volcanically active island? What happened to the fricking lava flows?" She faced back to him. "I don't recognize any of it, and I just *walked* through it! I know none of this is real but before, in Athena's orb, everything there at least *behaved* like it was."

Keith took a breath, and sat down upon the grass. He reached for a large weed in front of him. Jeff crept over and simply stared at him.

"It *is* like a dream," he answered. "And that light on the horizon. It's like trying to reach the end of a rainbow. You can't."

"Dad?"

His father glanced over at Jeff, decked out in that Goth little red riding hood outfit. Keith Hagerton sighed wearily. "Jeff, I got to tell you," he confessed, as he eyed his son in the little red riding hood outfit. "If Athena wanted to drive home the point that things are not what they seem here . . ." he pointed to Jeff's costume. ". . . *You dressed in that* would be enough to do it." He indicated then the countryside that surrounded them. "All this is not necessary."

"Maybe . . ." said Kimberly, approaching, and cuddling her son (daughter) in her arms from behind. "Maybe we're only where we think we are, or would like to be. Or maybe we're being deliberately prevented from reaching Frida because Athena knows that that's where we're trying to go."

"At least I'm still here, Mom," smiled Jeffrey up at her.

She glanced down at his red hood and pushed it off his hair, brushing his forehead free of any residual locks of hair. She bent down and kissed him upon it. "I know, sweetheart. And you're all girl, aren't you?"

"Don't remind me," he begged.

"All I know to do, Kimmy," Keith said, rising and getting again to his feet, "is keep on trying to get there."

***

They walked again for another half hour, after which Kimberly again collapsed upon the grass. "This is ridiculous," she decided. She lay her head back, closed her eyes, and allowed the autumnal breezes to waft over her long blond hair.

"We're going about this all wrong," she told Keith as she heard him settle beside her upon the grass. She looked over at him. He absently gazed upon the horizon. "This isn't real," she said. "I'll bet I can gaze out at that countryside and tell it to become whatever I want it to."

Keith grinned as he smoothed a strand of her hair off her eye. "You think so?"

Kimberly grinned, weakly and pondered her notion. "I wish there were mountains on the horizon, and not just any mountains, but the ones I loved as a child. . . ."

She was reminiscing about Shengele, her ancestral home in Sweden, thought Keith, smiling to himself. He continued to stroke her cheek, as she closed her eyes again.

He closed his own.

"Dad?" he heard Jeffrey, then.

Keith felt as if he had nodded off in that brief second. Jeffy's voice startled him. He opened his eyes. "Yeah, Jeff, I'm still here," he said.

Jeff was kneeling before him, and if he didn't know better he would swear the child before him was someone's beautiful nine year old daughter, her long brunette hair, red cloak and matching mini-dress, Maryjane's and sheer black hose, all screaming "Girl!" Keith looked up at him. He noticed the alarm on his son's face in an instant. Out of the corner of his eyes Keith noticed something else as well. Something was seriously wrong.

"Where's your mother, Jeff?" he asked his son. He looked back to where Kimberly had been resting beside him just a second earlier.

She was no longer there. . . .

Kimberly was positive she had lost herself too much in the memory of her Swedish ancestral home. The last thing she recalled was lying beside Keith on a hill. She wondered when she had got back up on her feet, because now she was standing. She glanced to the horizons and had her second shock. She found herself somewhere new, as if hours had passed and she were only now awakening to the reality of it. Her mind was in confusion. What had happened to her? Where was her son and husband? She was no longer atop the hill with them.

She looked around her. "Keith! Jeffrey?" She stood up. "Oh my God! Jeffrey, are you out there? It's Mommy, can you hear me?"

All she heard was her echo rolling off the distant hills. This was nowhere where Keith or Jeffrey would think to seek her out, and as she probed the valley terrain before her, she couldn't believe what had happened. The scene below was right out of a children's fairy tale. It was the dead of winter, the sky a sullen gray, and very large snowflakes sifted gently down from it. Far off in the distance, and losing themselves in the western skyline, descended the cloud-fringed Kjolen Mountains, hugging the Norwegian border. Mount Kebnekaise hung several kilometers to the west, snowcapped, and below in the gorgeous valley beneath the hillside upon which she reposed spread the rustic cottages of Shengele, Sweden, her ancestral home.

***

The cold hung upon her like draping sheets of ice, and she remembered the red, snow-bunny outfit she'd dressed in that morning. It was on her still, and whether this was an illusion or very real, she took comfort in its being there. It hung snug and warm upon her. This overlook ridge was no place to be caught out in during a snowstorm. She cupped her hands to her lips and breathed on them, rubbing them afterward, as she awed in the wintry scene below.

The old white church with its long, steeple-d roof was in the distance, and she heard its bell toll solemnly across the grayness. Kimberly stared to it in fascination. She knew this spot, and she knew the time of year. In the winter of 2393, when she was eight years old, she had come here with her family for the Festival of Light which had been celebrated in the town on the thirteenth of December. Kimberly remembered, because her older sister Julie got to play Saint Lucia, and bring hot coffee and buns to everyone that morning. It was the festival from long ago that celebrated the return of the sun (extra hours of sunlight) to the dark, Swedish winter. Mariatta and Ansel, Kimberly's parents, had been invited to celebrate the "Winter" holiday that year by Mariatta's family, "Wellenborg" in *Shengele*, the town of their ancestral birth. Every four years the restored, museum-town recreated a Swedish "Winter" reminiscent of the old days. The festival would run until the first day of the New Year.

Kimberly jumped to her feet and ran down the path she so fondly remembered, and before long she walked the snow-swept streets among the multitude of ancestral town dwellers and the sleigh bells of horse drawn sleds as they inched their way across the curving streets and wooden homes. She approached a few townsfolk and tried to talk to them, but they neither saw nor heard her. In fact, she ventured so precariously close to one advancing sleigh that, before she had a chance to react, it went right through her, and continued down the winding street.

After Kimberly's heart quit racing so much, she turned and tried remembering the names and faces of the town dwellers. It had been so long ago, and she so young. She found it near impossible, but quaint, all the same. She knew these people, or felt she did in her memories.

She looked farther down the street with its neat, gingerbread-like houses all alike one after the other with their slanted, shingled roofs, and smiled as she found the one that the family "Wellenborg" had chosen for their "Winter" gathering. She decided to spend some time remembering all over again. She thought of Keith and her children—her own family. They felt to be so far away.

"I'll only stay for a little while," she promised, and was soon slipping through the exterior walls of the cottage.

This was the past, all right, she noted at once. It seemed straight from her childhood memories. The din in the cottage was electrifying. Distant cousins, aunts, uncles were dressed in traditional garb for the holiday, passing around the brandy and singing the traditional holiday songs. She awed then at the sight of a much younger Ansel and Mariatta, her parents, back from their tour in Mariner Valley on Mars, back going on twelve years by then; in 2382, when her older sister Julie was born, and cavorting with family they hadn't seen in decades. Kimberly even remembered where she spent that wintry day in 2393. She Julie, Agnetha (her younger sister), and several cousins were out on the Shengele hillsides, learning how to ski, something not so easily accomplished anymore back in the U.S.A. (What with the people these days simulating just about every past sport of the species in hologram simulators). Most of the major ski resorts of the past centuries back in the states had closed ages ago. Nevertheless, during her mid-teens Kimberly and her sisters used to pine for the Vermont "Winter" holiday to get permission to leave "Waterbury," their island city in Vermont, and to venture out to the seasonally opened slopes. They were all avid skiers, a talent that poor Keith (Kimberly noted whimsically) tried desperately to master, but always came up a little rough around the edges when he tried to match Kimberly move for move down the trails. It gave her the greatest satisfaction to know that he could end up face down in the snow, after the way he'd poked fun at her over her fears of Whitewater rafting down the Lehigh River in Jim Thorpe.

As she stood atop a hillside watching her sisters and herself descend the shallow slopes, she wished she might do as much right along with them. God, she had looked so much like her daughter, back then. Same everything. It made her think of her offspring. Poor Frida. When it came to sports, Frida just didn't seem gifted. Frida did not take to sports at all, and in truth after only one session in the Poconos in Pennsylvania one winter a few years back, Frida had almost broke both her legs just going down the bunny slope. She'd had her fill of her mother's sport at that point. No, Frida was meant for something else, and it wasn't recreational sports. She was much too introspective, too serious; she seemed at times to not know how to enjoy herself the way most kids her age did.

The thought of Frida reminded Kimberly of her original quest to find her, and she knew she had to leave this all and resume it. She heard her younger self among her sisters and cousins cry out in elated hysteria as she made a particularly sweeping turn to avoid another skier. Kimberly knew she had to leave, and she swore she would . . . eventually.

When Keith and Jeffrey realized Kimberly had vanished, they immediately began searching the neighboring hills to find her. They were not successful.

They stopped to rest finally by a small stream. The sound of it was actually quelling. The shallow water trickled over a series of stones that created a tiny waterfall. Jeffrey was down on his knees in the short red riding hood skirt and hose, tearing green maple leaves into slivers and tossing the remains into the running water. Keith crouched down for the stream's bank, and drew his hand into the cool current. As he expected, the water was as pure as any he'd ever tasted, and better than most that had ever been synthesized back in the city. He saw a leaf stem sail past his nose, and land in the mirror-glass water. He looked at his son. Jeff seemed lost in a world of his own. Keith crawled over and sat down beside him.

"Why can't we find her, Dad?" Jeffrey said. "I only turned away for a second, and she was gone." He had a defeated, resigned look in his eyes. "Frida's gone, and now Mom. You're not leaving, too, are you?"

Keith rested his hand on Jeff's shoulder. "Not if I have anything to say about it. Hey, champ, come on. We started out as a team, remember? That's why we're still together, you and I! We work well that way, right?"

Jeffrey's lip crooked a wee bit, but generally he didn't want to be laid-back about the situation.

Keith turned serious. "Don't worry, we'll find our way out of this."

"Not that way, you won't, friend," said a voice suddenly farther up the bank. They both jolted and then looked in the direction it appeared to come from.

A figure in a pair of corduroy trousers, and a blue knit sweater worked his way along the bank toward them. He seemed an elderly gent, sort of stocky, good-natured, with balding, grayish-white hair fringing his temples, and bushy white eyebrows. He looked to be a real rugged outdoor type.

"A mite pretty daughter you got there, friend. What's your name, sweetheart?"

Jeffrey glanced to his father. He had no idea how to answer that question.

Keith rose and took a guarded stance above his son. "Who are you?" he said.

"Easy, friend," the gent returned. "We're all family here."

"We are? Where is *here*?" Keith said.

The old gent slipped under the low branches of the birch trees in the foreground and looked down to the two of them. He glanced to Jeffrey again. "Sweetheart, don't you talk? Cute costume. A Goth version of little red riding hood. You like that nursery rhyme?"

"Hi," Jeffrey uttered, finally. "Athena dressed me in this, and won't give me back my regular clothes . . . or my boy body."

"How's that?"

"His name is Jeffrey," Keith informed the gent.

The man smiled, knowingly, and nodded. "Oh. Well, Jeffrey, Athena allowed you to fulfill your fondest wish, I would imagine. You make a nice little girl, though not so much in that Goth get up."

And with that Jeffrey's outfit morphed back to what it earlier was: an off-white turtleneck, tan hiking shorts, brown leggings and tan hiking boots.

"Now that's more like it," said the gent. "Perfect for a walk out here. Those leather . . . I think they call them maryjane's you had on before must have been killing your feet. Not really suited for hiking in the mountains."

"Why can't I be a boy again?" wailed Jeffrey, frustrated. "Do I have to stay a girl?"

"Son, you can be whatever you want, here. Nobody judges. They just accept it as your personal fancy. You want to be a boy again? Do it.

"Would you mind, friend," he said to Keith then, "if I sit here beside yourself and your boy, for a spell? I could use the rest."

Sensing Keith's indifference, he took it as a yes and set himself down, listened then to the quelling shrill of a Varied Thrush nearby in the forest. He heard the stream trickle down the tiny falls. And glancing to Jeffrey again, one over, from his dad, and still trying to will himself back to masculinity, laughed and said, "Not happening, huh, son? Take the hint. You like being that way."

Jeffrey turned to his Dad. "Sorry, Dad," he said.

"Hey, at least now you're sensibly dressed for out here in the hills, Jeff," smiled Keith, patting his son's knee. "It's okay, son. I know it's still you under those tights." He turned to the gent, after. "As for you, *friend*, just who the hell are you anyway?"

"Name's Willard Somedale. And you're Keith, right?"

Keith wasn't expecting that one. "Yeah, how do you know that?"

Willard Somedale grinned, amiably. ""Those are sure pretty sounds, aren't they?" Willard commented on the sounds of the wilderness all around them. "Yes sir, you dream nice things, Keith; your wife, too. Kimberly's her name, isn't it? You have a beautiful family, Keith."

"You're jumping ahead of yourself, aren't you?" Keith replied, defensively. "You know who we are. I'm still waiting for you to explain how you know that."

Somedale grinned. "As I said, we're all family here."

"Who is family? Are we talking *my* family?"

"Certainly not." He smiled. "You folks just arrived. I'd go nuts with loneliness, if I had to wait all these years for you nice people to show up."

"How long *have* you been here?"

Willard raised his eyes in thought. "Oh, I don't know. I can't rightly say. Time doesn't pass here, as you've probably noticed." He looked up to the beautiful blue sky. "The day won't pass, unless you want it too. It wouldn't be authentic, though; it wouldn't be meant to be."

"Are you being deliberately evasive," Keith asked, "or are you fucking with me on purpose?"

Jeffrey gasped at his father's language.

Willard Somedale laughed and then nodded. "I didn't peg you for the foul language type, Keith, and in front of your boy at that. . . . It's all right, son, it's just words. No harm in it. You're right. I do tend to go on."

"Well now that we've established that, where the hell are we? What is this place?"

Willard furrowed his brow. "What do you mean? Athena's lair. You know that. I know you do."

"I mean . . . *this*," Keith said of the wilderness terrain before him.

"Well hell, son, you should know the answer to that one as well. You created this place." Somedale rose and strolled over to one of the birches; he fingered one of its leafy branches. "This is your place. You chose it. Your wife and son accepted it as real, and landed beside you within it, but in actuality you aren't really here. You're where the rest of us are." Willard looked off in the direction of the distant lights. They were hidden, however, by the bushes and brush.

"Inside Athena's mind essence?" offered Keith.

"Right. You're in Athena. So is your daughter. Your other one." He winked at Jeffrey. "Another beauty just like her younger sister, here. And so much like her mother, too, looks-wise, anyway. She's a pistol that girl. Right, Jeff?" Somedale gave him another wink.

"You know my daughter?" questioned Keith. "You've seen her?"

"Of course I have." He walked back to the bank, near Jeffrey, and crouched down beside him, grabbing a maple leaf from the grass. "Your wife, too. She's having the time of her life, you know, remembering a *Winter* holiday her family attended back when she was eight."

"*Kimberly is where?*"

Keith recalled Kimberly mentioning Shengele right before she vanished. He faced Willard again. "My wife wanted to find our daughter. What is she doing back on Earth?"

Willard laughed. "Only in her dreams, she is. She's still here with us, all of us, in Athena." He shook his head, sadly. "You folks entered a dreamscape fantasy setting too soon. You didn't even give yourself a chance to settle in. This is a real dimension, Keith. It can fashion itself as whatever you want it to be." He looked around him again." As I said, you dream well. I like this place. I'll remember it, next time I'm looking for somewhere new to go walking. But what happened to those lava flows? They were a nice touch."

"I forgot about them." Keith shrugged. "Now, about Athena."

"What about her?"

"She's an Eleution."

"Told you all about it, did she? Well, I guess she would. You folks are special. The last of the lot of them to come here. We'll *all* be leaving for Eighty-Two Eridani soon."

"What?" perked up Keith at the name. "Going where? Wait. I've heard that name before . . ." He turned to his son. "Isn't that where the *Stellar Quest* is going?"

Willard Somedale grinned. "Small universe, ain't it?"

"What is all this?"

"You see, Keith, it's this way. The Barthonians and the Eleutions both are interested in our race's survival. They've been tending to it since . . . I don't know . . . since the 1900s, I believe. You and your family are the last group to be herded up from Earth. I don't reckon there are any more after you. Things are happening. Athena's people will be recalling her soon, and us with her, especially now that they know the human race has finally sent a ship out to investigate Eighty-two Eridani. It's been a hundred years since Athena's people had the Barthonians send a radio transmission, deliberately, over a frequency they knew we were monitoring at the time. They knew we intercepted it; Athena says her people and the Barthonians have been wondering ever since why it took us so damn long to act on it."

Keith looked over at his son, and then back at Willard.

"Son," Willard asked Keith. "What year is it these days?"

"2415. October."

Willard nodded. "I've been gone two centuries give or take a year in that case."

"Were you taken from the cave in Pennsylvania?"

"I had a feeling you folks were from Earth," he answered, nodding. "Had that look about you. Earthers."

"You're from Mars, then," deduced Keith. "That's where Athena's other orb is supposed to be."

"I was on Mars, that's right," Willard nodded. "Wasn't born there. Hell, son, it's a long story. I'll tell it to you someday. We're going to know each other for a long time."

"How many of us here *are* there?"

"I hate to actually make tallies, myself; but several hundred, I say, by this time."

"And this snare operation has been going on since the 1900s?" Keith whistled. He furrowed his brow at Willard. "Why? Why are we being collected?"

Willard scratched his chin and frowned. "I wish I could answer that, I do. That is the great mystery of this place, you know."

"Are my wife and daughter all right?"

"Call to them. Ask them yourself."

"You mean, it's that simple?"

"Certainly. But really they both are quite preoccupied at the moment. I think first you'd be doing yourself a real service if you found out where you were. You really should have done that right off, you know."

"I can't imagine a species as evolved as Athena's. Incorporeal intelligence?"

"Yes, the Eleutions are a race that long ago evolved beyond the need for physical form. The Barthonians are not quite so far along. The Eleutions employ them as their arms and legs in the physical world where we dwell."

"Is Athena that distant light haze my family and I have been walking to for God knows how many hours?"

Willard Somedale's eyes widened. "Is that what you've been doing out here? Why, hell, Keith, you should have told someone sooner! Land sakes. I wish I'd known. I could have saved you a lot of aggravation."

Willard Somedale faced where he last saw the haze. "The haze is Athena's way of reminding you you're not really where you are. Some people get carried away sometimes and forget this all is an illusion of their own choosing."

"We've been trying to reach the light."

"Instead of going to *it*, son, tell yourself you're already there. That's the way you do it."

"It is?"

Without warning, Willard Somedale vanished. Keith and Jeffrey stood there alone once more.

CHAPTER THIRTY-FOUR

-1-

Keith shook his head. "If people in the real world, Jeff, could come and go like that, we'd save hours getting around. You spend your life believing that psycho-teleportation is fairy tale nonsense, and in here it's the way it's done."

Jeffrey stood, closed his eyes, and tried to imagine being somewhere else. All at once he sensed a huge sunlit plaza around him. He opened his eyes, and looked at his father.

"You all right, champ?" Keith asked, going up to him.

Jeffrey nodded. The sense of being there faded. "It was about to work, I think. I'm not really sure where I was, but if I leave, Dad, and you don't, we'll get separated."

Keith smiled, extending his hand. "Here, we'll hang onto one another."

"What if that's not enough?"

"Then don't worry, son, If we do get separated, according to that old fool, it's because that's what we really want. Come on." He bid Jeff take his hand.

Jeff did; the two of them closed their eyes. They both formed an image of what this Athena entity might be, and when they opened their eyes again. . . .

They were in a magnificent atrium, promenades and mezzanines winding and weaving high above them among brilliant and white corridor walls. Predominate was the sound of rushing water. There were fountain and waterfall displays throughout the plaza.

High overhead a glass dome ceiling framed a gorgeous array of fluffy clouds. People were everywhere along the walkways and mezzanines, and as in the cities of Earth many went from one level to the next using levitation platforms, silver-colored disks that one climbed on top of and rode like magic carpets. The city in many ways resembled Earth's island cities. No doubt it had deliberately been patterned after them.

There was one difference, however. As Keith and Jeffrey surveyed the atrium, they felt everyone's eyes on *them*. People studied them in interest.

"Now wasn't that easy?" came a familiar voice before them, abruptly.

Somedale. He was over by a huge fountain in the atrium's center. Within its ring of colored water spray ascended a crystal globe in the shape of a world.

The two Hagerton men abruptly joined him. He looked amused by their perplexity. "It's not exactly what you expected, is it?"

"It's a city," Keith observed.

"No, only a city plaza. It's as phony as that grove you were in before, but as real as everything else you'll experience here."

"I thought we were en route to see this Athena?"

"Well . . ." he answered, "that's as hard to as do saying you want to see the universe you live in. It's not an easy thing to do when you can only see a small portion of it at a time—from inside it. But don't worry. You're a lot nearer to enlightenment, now. You'll see."

The man was being evasive again, thought Keith. He decided to humor Somedale, at least for now. There were real other people here at least.

Keith glanced to and then studied the crystal globe being bathed in the fountain's colored water. "What about that?" he asked of it.

Somedale looked over at it. "Some say it's a representation of the Eleutions' home world, a sort of homage to Elieutia by Athena. Others insist it's Barthonia, because the little guys reposed within Athena, like we are now, in the years they were here with us in the solar system. No one knows."

"If this is just illusion for our sakes, why isn't the globe simply Earth?"

"Because it isn't. The land masses are wrong."

Keith reached his hand into the spray and felt the mist moisten his fingers. He touched the globe's surface. "Whose dreamscape is this one, Willard— of the plaza, I mean? Yours?"

"This is a group illusion, son. Athena, herself, contributes to it." He nodded. "Every so often we notice improvements: new technology, styles, architecture. We believe they reflect the changes that have been made back in the solar system. The Barthonians watched the goings on of Earth from here. Athena, we believe, continues that practice using her two sub-entities as remote viewers."

"Sub-entities?"

Willard nodded. "Her 'orbs.' The one you found on Earth, and the one on Mars. We think Athena intentionally allows us these small insights into the ways our race has improved over the years."

"Are most of the Earth humans from Eastern Pennsylvania?"

Willard smiled. "In a way. Most of them are what you city dwellers fondly refer to as those scoundrel renegades."

"Renegades? Here?"

"Oh, yes. Being wanderers on the surface of the Earth, they were more likely to stumble onto the caverns and Athena's orb."

"Are they civil?"

Willard started to smile. A few of the onlookers above started to giggle.

"Look up there," Willlard Somedale requested. "Do they look like they're about to lynch you, slice you up into juicy cuts of meat, boil you in a pot, maybe? Make supper out of what's left of your sorry hide?"

Keith felt thoroughly reprimanded. "No, call it my own prejudices," he regretted. "My apologies."

"Yeah, well, don't feel too bad about yourself," he returned, smiling kindly. "I had prejudices against renegades myself in my day. I believed all the horror stories, the propaganda that anyone who refused to live in the sealed cities wanted to be a primitive. But it ain't always so. They're some of the nicest folks, real land people, types who just can't stand metal and plastic all the time, and who need genuine grass to flop down in, not sensor-image illusions. They eked out a good living on Earth. There aren't as many of them as people imagine there are, and new generations one way or another make it back to the cities. The bad apples? Like everything else, you always hear about them first. They make the best news copy."

"Hey, old man!" called a female voice, suddenly, far above on a promenade.

"Melinda?" Willard called glancing up to her.

She looked twenty-something, brunette, and was dressed somewhat like a flower child, with a white rose in her hair against a yellow headband, and a yellow kimono which hung loosely from her.

"Hi, Keith," she called out, lowly, and sweetly. And then to Willard, "Hey, old man, how are you today?"

Willard nodded. "I'm fine, Mindy." In an aside to Keith. "Melinda Shepherd. We call her Mindy for short. Everybody does." And then to the female above him. "How's Michael these days, is he close?"

"No," she sighed. "He's away, unfortunately. He'll be so sorry he wasn't here to greet you, Keith, straight off upon your arrival. You and your family. He and I have been waiting for you guys to show up for four-hundred years, ever since we first dreamt of all of you back when we were still just kids in high school. You could say seeing your family in New Allentown, back when Frida and Jeffrey were still little kids on their first outing outside the city, sort of messed up our heads, Mike's and mine. It actually put us on the path that led us to here . . . *in Athena's lair.*"

Keith furrowed his brow and turned to Willard. *"When did all that happen?"*

Willard faced up to Melinda and smiled. "When *was that*, Mindy?"

The young lady in the yellow kimono gazed upward and pondered that. "Oh, God, that had to be 2014, April, I think. Frida looked about nine. And Jeffrey . . . couldn't have been more than five." She thought about it some more. "That's right. I remember realizing that it was for you the year 2410."

Keith nodded to himself. *Five years ago.* "I remember that outing," he told her. "The kids loved it; they'd never been out beyond the city before. They didn't even know people could do that."

"Mike never forgot it," she replied. "Both of us knew it was no dream. You guys were real people, and New Allentown is a gorgeous city. Mike can't wait to talk with you. Trade war stories."

"He's where, today, Melinda?" asked Willard.

"With my future incarnation, her and her friend Pam. They wanted a girl's only outing to the south of France, and I didn't feel like going. So Mike went . . . *as Michelle*. Yeah, he's at it again . . . profiling as Michelle. I swear he's been vacillating between female and male for four hundred years since we all first arrived."

Willard Somedale turned to Jeffrey. "You see, son. It's not just you. There are others who can't decide what gender they'd rather be, either. And her boyfriend, Michael DeAngelo? He's someone special. If Athena hadn't got to him when she did, back four hundred years ago, he might have gone on to supervise the construction of that dang fool Noah's Arc ship, *Exodus II*, and then we'd all have been up the creek, as they say, loading our entire civilization into that dang fool tin can and leaving the solar system for *Sigma Draconus Five*. And all for nothing. The system's already inhabited; the *Portendenites* don't like interlopers. Right Mindy?"

"That was a long time ago," she answered, smiling down to the three of them from her high perch up on the mezzanine. "Feels like ancient history."

"Exodus II?" queried Keith. "That ship never got off the ground. It was just a proposal."

"Keith," cautioned Melinda. "Don't tell Cindy that. Her and her friends are the last from her timeline, her universe, before it was erased. She remembers. For her that ship was real. *Exodus II* in her universe timeline was a very real thing, and almost happened."

Keith faced back to Somedale. "You've got people here from alternate universes?"

"No. Just Cynthia and her *adopted* family. Cynthia Bradshaw, she be. Nice girl, pretty blond like your wife, Keith." He glanced up at Mindy Shepherd. "Mindy's future incarnation, the one she'd have had if she'd stayed to live out her lifetime back then in her timeline. If Athena hadn't interceded, she would have, three hundred years later, and living just like you folks in sealed island cities. But that all changed. Athena put a halt to her Cynthia alternate timeline; it wasn't heading anywhere good."

"Wait a minute!" said Keith. "So this Cynthia is *her* in a future incarnation in an *alternate reality?*"

Willard Somedale laughed lightly. "Makes your head spin, doesn't it?" he replied. "And you thought this dreamscape stuff inside Athena was a mind-blower, right?"

"In Cynthia's universe, Keith," called Mindy down to him, "my Michael was a famous person, the inventor of the Arc ship that would rescue them from extinction. You should talk to Michael, when he's not pretending to be Michelle, all of us actually. Michael loves to go on about what happened back in the 21st and 23rd centuries. It's quite a mind blower. You might actually find it interesting."

"Mindy?" said Willard then. "Keith needs to know though before that happens. Are you like your renegade friends? Are you civil? Do you try to be well-behaved?"

She smiled. "You're an ornery old cuss, Willard, you know that? Dirty old man. As for me being civil. I try to be, especially around you."

"Myself, Mindy and her group, we're special, Keith," said Willard. "We weren't abducted like everyone else. I was needed for some excavating work on Mars. When it was done, I was allowed to come here. Athena leans on me a little more than I'd prefer, at times. The little Barthys first started messing with me when I was still a boy on Earth."

"Jeffrey?" Mindy called down. "Little boy, or little girl, if you prefer, hi. Did anyone ever tell you you were adorable?"

Jeffrey blushed. "Yes," he said tiresomely. "My mom and sister won't stop hugging and kissing me."

"Being a girl is fun, isn't it?"

"No, it's annoying," he replied.

Melinda Shepherd got a laugh at that.

To Keith, Melinda only winked.

"Well, bye for now, you three," Melinda said to the three in the plaza. "Keith, I'm looking forward to meeting Kimberly and Frida. We should all get together. It ought to be fun. I'm off to find my better half; whatever gender he chooses to profile as at the moment. AND Cindy, my other me. Four hundred years later, and that still feels weird. They'll be so disappointed they weren't here to greet you straight off. Oh well."

Willard grinned. "Friendly, ain't she?"

"So, the stories about two kids, disappearing on the day they were to graduate from high school back in the 2000s? It wasn't just a story?" Keith smiled. "I'm with the networks. Fluff pieces like theirs, even four centuries old, I come across them. Part of my job. I know the story of Michael DeAngelo. I just never understood until today what actually happened. His dad blew the family house to smithereens, did you know that?"

"Yes, I did. The old fart, hope he's rotting in hell by this point," said Willard.

"And that's Melinda Shepherd, his girlfriend," Keith mused. "Even in our timeline, Michael DeAngelo is known to have originally thought up the *Exodus II* arc ship. He just never lived to see its fruition."

"Thank Athena for that," said Willard. "Funny how things go, isn't it? All those alternate universes, wrapped all around each other, like a ball of yarn, event scenarios intertwining. Enough to make your head spin."

Keith looked the plaza over. "Is there a significance to this plaza? It doesn't lead to our rooms or something, does it?"

Willard laughed. "It can, if that's what you want it to do. Being the main group dreamscape, it's usually where newcomers first find themselves after arrival."

"We didn't," said Keith.

He nodded. "That was your doing, Keith. You chose to wake up on that make-believe volcanic island of yours. Your family went along out of loyalty."

"They why didn't Frida?"

Somedale nodded. "Yeah, I knew you'd want to get around to that, eventually. As soon as your missy shows up, I will. She ought to be done reliving her childhood about now."

As if on cue Kimberly faded into presence on the other side of the fountain.

"Ah, right on time!" said Willard. "Nice to meet you, Mrs. Hagerton. Your husband's told me a lot about you."

Kimberly looked up at him, dully. She glanced to Keith, Jeffrey, the fountain, and then the city around her. On her face was a mask of perplexity.

Keith looked over at Willard, irritably, and went over to Kim. "He's lying about that," he said to her. "His name is Willard Somedale, our tour guide by the look of him. He likes to hear himself talk. Likes to embellish too, I wouldn't doubt."

"Keith, that's harsh," said Somedale, overhearing that. "I resemble that remark, actually."

Keith furrowed his brow. "You *resent* it, you mean?"

"No, 'resemble.' It's wit, son. I'm messing with you. It's a clever, deliberate play on words. A bit before your time, I see. You two go on ahead and catch up. I'll be right over here."

Jeffrey ran to his mom. "Mom!" he called.

"Kimberly," Keith said, taking hold of her, "Don't mind the old guy. He's all right, I guess. Are you all right?"

She took a few moments to get her bearings straight, looked rather blankly upon the breadth of the plaza beyond the atrium, and upon the presence of her family, here as well, wherever here was. "Are you and Jeffrey all right?" she asked, blankly.

"We're fine. Are you?"

She looked at him. "Keith, I'm so angry at myself," she answered, with a glint in her eyes that showed more guilt than anger. "But I couldn't tear myself away; it was so glorious."

Keith nodded. "The Kjolen's. Yes, I thought they were something, myself, that year your parents invited us to bring the kids out there to your family birthplace. "

She furrowed her brow at him. "You *know* where I was?"

Keith indicated Willard now on the other side of the great fountain. "It was explained to Jeff and me. Are you all right?"

She nodded. "But I'm angry at myself! I got selfish and totally forgot about Frida. Have you found her? Is she all right?"

Keith faced back to Willard down the way. "Is she?"

"She's fine now."

"What do you mean, *now*?" worried Keith. He approached the man. "Come on, Willard, we've been through this. Answer a question, don't play with it! Where is she?"

Somedale's smile eroded as he pondered how to answer that. "You have to understand a little about the situation, Keith, old boy," he said. "Athena needed her for something special."

"She's just a thirteen year old girl!" insisted Keith. "Special, how?"

"It's beginning," Somedale continued, "the event we all were warned would happen when the time came for us to leave here. And it's sad. I feel like we all only arrived yesterday. Frida's all right, son, don't you fret over that."

"I want to see her!" Keith demanded.

"Well, you can, Keith," answered Willard, "and at the same time you can't." He quickly put his hands up in defense. "Now I know I'm answering in riddles again, but there's a reason. She's with Athena. You folks are special, yourselves, you know. You're the family of the chosen one. She's the one Athena's been waiting for. You should be very proud of her."

"*Why* has Athena been waiting for Frida?" demanded Kimberly, stepping up and into Willard's face. "Athena keeps telling us our daughter is special, but she won't say why."

"Willard's getting ready to explain it all to us. Isn't that right, friend?" Keith interjected. "You had something to show us?"

Willard nodded. "And unfortunately it will kill two birds with one stone," Willard answered. "Come on." He pointed into the midnight blue shadows behind him. Beneath the second floor promenade balcony came an area that one wasn't even aware of, until one chose to fixate upon it, and when one did, it chilled the spine. The blue just went inward, and kept on going.

The light around them appeared to come from somewhere ahead, but had no apparent source. It was a foggy blue and the corridor (or whatever it was) continued on down a distance. The mists billowing around them seemed more for effect than for any real reason to be present. It gave the place a funereal air.

Willard Somedale repeated to Kimberly everything he'd told Keith and Jeffrey. "Just prepare yourself," he requested now of all of them. "This is usually the disturbing part, the worst truth to swallow." .

"Somedale," Keith said, "do you have to be so melodramatic?"

"Some people have to be prepared for what they find. They don't take it very well."

The hallway ended finally in a very dark, midnight blue arena room, high-ceilinged, though lost in blue shadows, and filled with wafting mists. In the room's center, however, upon a floating slab of transparent crystal, reposed a human body.

"Frida!" whispered Kimberly, pausing in her gait to find her daughter lying there, asleep atop the slab. The slab, itself, faintly glowed yellow-white, bathing Frida's youthful feminine frame. She seemed at peace, the peace of gentle sleep, her golden hair fanning down from her white complexion and framing her angelic face.

"I thought you said she was with Athena?" said Keith.

"She is," Willard answered.

Kimberly ran to her daughter; she stretched out her hand to touch her.

"Ma'am, don't!" Willard warned her, too late.

Kimberly's fingers went through her daughter's body, as if Kimberly wasn't even there. Kim looked back at Somedale. "What is this?" she asked. "This happened to me in Shengele, but there I was just imagining the place. It wasn't real."

"It was only a dream," agreed Willard, "one you chose not to change, only relive. Therefore, you couldn't interact with it at all."

"I don't understand what's happened to her," she responded. She went up to him. "Tell me."

"Please, Mrs. Hagerton, don't fret. You are all fine, even the young one there." He faced into the shadows surrounding Frida's podium slab. "This spot was reserved for her. The rest of us are arranged in concentric circles, surrounding your daughter's slab, so that she is among her own, and can feed off their energy for support."

He nodded to them to follow him into the shadows. Kimberly and Jeffrey both preferred not to leave Frida's side so soon, but Keith only walked back to take Kimberly's arm. She and her son were gazing down at Frida's body, as if Frida were lying in state in a funeral parlor. She seemed so gone, no "presence" within her little body at all.

Kimberly took her son's arm, and let Keith pull her toward where Somedale waited.

In a stair-step formation, rising from ground level and continuing upward into the midnight blue reaches beyond, glowed over three-hundred other such slabs as Frida's. They were like amphitheater rows encircling the area that Frida's form solely possessed. Although there appeared to be no ramps, no steps, no footings, no way at all to allow Somedale, Keith, Kim or Jeffrey to ascend to the higher rings of slabs beyond the ground level ring, Willard showed them they need only put one foot before the other, as if they were climbing "invisible" stairs, and they all soon walked among the three-hundred or so bodies that inhabited the room. On the top tier they found the three slabs atop which their own bodies rested, and—like Frida—upon their faces and bodies went the peaceful image of deep sleep, a lifelessness which suggested that their true sentient selves were no longer imprisoned within their sleeping bodies.

Jeffrey went over to touch the tan sweater of his now female "real self" on the slab, and his hand only continued through into it. He pulled his hand back and looked over at his dad, who was immersed in the sight of his own form.

"You see," Willard told them, "unlike in the orbs, this membrane — that Athena herself has voluntarily allowed herself to be trapped within— is a real location, a dimensional limbo realm off our three-dimensional plane. We're actually not in Athena's essence at the moment."

"You mean, those are our *real bodies?*" asked Keith.

"Yes," he answered. He pointed straight up. "The way back to that lunar cave is right up there, on the other side of that black membrane you all fell through."

"I thought we were all reduced to data pattern storage," said Keith.

"In the orbs, but not here. Here, your bodies repose for real, for safe keeping. Athena, I suspect, objected to the idea of having to remember all your data patterns for five-hundred years. Can't blame her. That's a long time."

"We're not IN Athena's essence right now?"

"No, you can call what you're doing at present *astral projecting.* As for our bodies, for now, they're in suspension, for safe keeping. They won't age."

Keith looked to the bodies of his wife and boy, and then back to his own. He noticed affixed to each of their waists were the life-support/lift belts. They'd been given no opportunity to rise and remove them. He looked down at himself. His "astral" body on the other hand did not possess a replica of the belt.

Keith looked at Willard sullenly then. "Jeffrey and I were not the first to find that underground lake beneath Crystal Cave, weren't we?"

Willard Somedale shook his head. "No, you weren't. Was that important to you for some reason?"

Keith smiled. "When Jeff and I first saw Athena's orb, I thought we might be the first humans to ever penetrate that deep below Crystal Cave, and the first to find the orb." He shook his head. "My family and I were simply the last in a long line of others who've been abducted before us."

He glanced to all the lifeless bodies around and below him. He got a puzzled look on his face all at once. He glanced down to Frida's distant form in the center atrium. "Where's the way we came in?" he asked. "It's gone."

"You'll find it, again," the man said, "when we're ready to re-enter Athena's *essence.* You can't find it, because her realm isn't real. This is."

Kimberly faced Willard. "We're never going home again, aren't we?"

"Most people, ma'am, once they've been here awhile, can't imagine ever wanting to. What have you really left behind back there, that you can't have here? Life, Death?" He shrugged.

"And what about her orb? Does it go back to Earth now and wait for some other sad fool to find it?"

"No, that's where your daughter figured in all this," Willard answered. "She handled it. That's one brave little girl, you got there. Would you like to follow most of what's happened to her since she arrived?"

"You know damn well we would," said Keith.

Somedale pointed downward for the center atrium. And as they began to follow him, they saw him take the round way around and down to stop and gaze upon his own form, on about the third to highest row from the top.

"Sorry," he answered. "I do this every now and then." He shrugged. "I lived in that body for years. It's been a long time since I was in there. I like to gaze on it every now and then. It's sort of like nostalgia, I suppose. You folks have taken this all very well. I'm glad. Astral Projection. Many freaked out at first at the thought that that was what they were doing, until they got over it."

Kimberly looked back to the final row. "The top circle is completed," she whispered, "with us."

"Yes, you were the last group, fortunately, in light of what's been happening out in space."

She looked questioningly at Keith. He told her quickly about the *Stellar Quest*.

"Must WE be laid out so far above our daughter?" she asked. "We are her *family*. Couldn't that have been taken into consideration?"

Somedale grinned. "Mrs. Hagerton, you're not way up there, your body is. You're where I'm at, where everyone else is." He pointed to his body. "That's not me—hasn't been for years."

They were all once more down in the atrium and before Frida's slab.

"Athena will replay the images for you," Willard simply said to them, "some taken directly from your daughter's own thoughts. Just empty your minds of other matters, and let the images come. Okay?"

"Do we need to lie down or something to see all of that?" Keith posed, somewhat cynically.

Willard laughed, and looked up to the shadows where Keith's physical form reposed on its slab. "You are," he simply answered.

CHAPTER THIRTY-FIVE

-1-

Keith felt his surroundings change. He looked around him. It was the same spot where he'd been a moment before, the same room! Yet it was different. He was alone before the bottom atrium slab. Willard Somedale, Kimberly and Jeffrey were gone. Frida, herself, no longer reposed atop her berth, which floated now before him, dark and silent. It seemed to happen in the wink of an eye, although it left him disoriented, as if his mind could not be certain how much time passed, though time enough, perhaps, for things to rearrange themselves in the world around him.

He looked about the ascending tiers. They had not changed. Three-hundred or so forms still reposed atop the faintly glowing slabs, rising for the heights above him. But of his own slab on the top tier, he saw nothing. His body was not atop it.

He learned why a second later. Out of the emptiness above him, a single fireball of red light fell toward the outermost ring, descending for his slab. His form took shape upon it. It did not move once fully present and supine above it. So quickly it imitated the others around it in a posture of death. Directly above him, then, fell another, heading straight for him. He tensed and wanted to move, but the fireball slowed and became a round ball of energy directly above Frida's atrium slab. She materialized within it, and the fireball faded away. She too did not move. Keith wanted to reach out for her, but the mere thought of doing so suddenly made him aware that he wasn't a part of these events in even a semblance of physical presence. He was nowhere; he was consciousness only, a disembodied awareness of self. He stared at Frida's silent form for what felt the longest time.

A third fireball eventually fell for the outermost sectors of the arena chamber, and Kimberly and Jeffrey took form atop their slabs, before and behind Keith's.

Frida opened her eyes. She arched her body upward to a sitting position, her hands levering upon the transparent slab for support. She looked about herself, startled and in fear. Keith saw the faint sheen of the purple cocoon shield from her life belt as yet protecting her from what obviously just a few moments before had been the lethal vacuum of the Moon. She turned quickly and began to scan the surroundings, her mouth agape at the sight of the hundreds of other slabs that rose above her like arena seats at a sporting event.

Keith cursed this Athena entity for showing him only images. He could do nothing, as neither probably could Kimberly or Jeffrey, as well. Each of them, Keith imagined, bore witness to their own private viewing of these archive images, and the contents of what they "saw" went somewhat something like the following:

The last thing Frida remembered was Athena, her arms outstretched, entreating her to join with her in the membrane of the cavity. Only a moment had passed, the time it took for the shock to wear off and for the realization to dawn upon her that something unexpected had occurred. Her antigrav-levitation belt had activated and catapulted her toward the membrane.

"Where am I?" she asked. "Where is this place? Mom? Dad? Jeffrey? *Where am I?*"

Only silence answered her over her com-link transmitter. All around her she saw lighted table tops, floating slabs with no visible means of support, aglow and alit internally and rising upward into the blue reaches of wherever this was, as if magic carpets, hundreds of them, floating in concentric rings all around her. And she saw bodies lifeless upon them, and that frightened her. She looked down upon her own.

She raised her hand before her, rotated it for inspection, and felt that— so far as she could see— she was whole. She felt real enough, and hopped off the hovering table top to take a step away from it.

"Mom!" she called again. "Dad!" She searched for them above her. Her eyes drew her attention to the uppermost tier ring and she saw the three of them up there (Jeffrey as well), and confirmed that it was indeed them. She approached the bottom tier. Gazing up to the others and wondering how in heaven's name she would ever get up to them, she remembered her antigrav belt. She hadn't needed it up till now for anything but life support, and so she opened the forward compartment down by her navel, and removed the silver module with the leather strap. She raised it to her forehead, and fastened it there. In her thoughts she pictured what she wanted to do, and taking the courage to believe it would truly happen, she took the first step and felt herself float off the floor and upward toward the uppermost tier.

One by one she viewed them, as if in respect at their wake, for they seemed so much like the dead, laid out to be mourned. She had reached out for the face of her father, her mother as well, and by the time she reached Jeffrey's form, she realized that a force cocoon was being created by the slab's lighted glow, perhaps one to protect and preserve them.

She asked a question of the life/lift belt, "Is the air breathable?"

"*Atmospheric content: none,*" it answered.

She nodded, and looked down again upon the belts about her family. Theirs were in the off mode. She felt herself beginning to weep for them, because they seemed so much like they had died. She wanted to kiss her mother's forehead, and cursed the force field that prevented her from doing so.

She gazed back down to the atrium and upon the slab she had materialized upon. "Is that one mine?" she seemed to ask in general of whomever might be about. "Why all the way down there? I'd rather be laid-out here with my *family*! She felt her body again. "And why am I the only one alive? Are they all dead? *Where is this place?*"

"Frida, dear, do not go on so," came the by now familiar voice of Athena.

"Where are you?" she requested.

"Your family is not dead, only sleeping, and the force shield cocoons are there for their protection."

She looked up in alarm, and then probed the shadows for a form and face to go with the voice. There were none, and in truth it hadn't issued over her com-link and therefore could not have been real. It had to have come from beyond whatever this was. Which prompted her to ask, "What is this place? Am I in your *lair?*"

"No. Your family have been joined with me. But not you, not yet. Do not be afraid, dear Frida. You remain corporeal because I need you that way. Come, come to me and we shall talk. I need a task from you, but first I would have you draw nearer. So please won't you come to me?"

Frida swept the domain completely with her gaze. "Where are you?"

"I am here," Athena answered. The floor beneath the atrium suddenly turned foggy and milky, like the fog mists that hung and billowed all about her, and suddenly a blaze of golden light burst from it, hurting her eyes, but only at first. It became in seconds beguiling to behold.

"My essence, what I am, reposes in the field you see below you. It is as much a home as an interment for me, but one that I have engendered to myself willingly. Will you come?"

"How?" she simply asked.

The light of the field sent a ripple through everything around her, and suddenly Frida saw what she had seen from beyond the cave membrane—

. . . *Athena.*

"I am the guardian," Athena said. Her essence as before was that of a beautiful human female, in a flowing gown of wispy vapor. The gown billowed as if blown by a gentle wind. She approached Frida. "And dear Frida, must we go through it all again? We've done so with every visit you've made to me in the past."

"But I don't remember!" defended Frida.

"You do," Athena only replied. "You just have trouble accessing that which originates mostly in your subconscious mind. But you know me, and we have spent great time together. I am the guardian of the charges I have been remanded to collect and detain. The orbs, when they are touched, allow me to send my own consciousness to them and for a brief while escape the confines of this membrane. Thank the good fortunes of the universe that I have all of your people here with me to stave off loneliness. Five hundred years is a long spell to be alone with one's thoughts. I long for the day I can leave here."

"You're trapped inside this place?"

"It was a mutually agreed upon scenario of both my people and the Barthonians that I remain locked here that I might not be tempted to abandon this place and go wandering. For if so, it would surely distract me from the chore of keeping safe and secure all of you within my essence. I can only leave via the orbs and as an astral plane wanderer, a gift you possess as well. But to not to actually leave here. A half millennium is a long time."

"Can I touch you?" Frida asked. She reached out her hand for her. Her fingers contacted energy; it had a weird effect upon Frida's cocoon shield. The shield momentarily flickered, grew in power.

"I am not as you, little one," Athena said. We Eleutions evolved beyond the corporeal a long time ago."

"Is my family all right?" Frida asked.

Athena nodded. "They are fine. I have absorbed them, for now, within myself. Their bodies, however, exist within this dimensional limbo. I shall tell you the story, Frida, as I take you on a little journey. There is something I must show you."

"Why have you singled ME out?" Frida inquired.

Athena reached out to touch Frida's chin. Frida touched it with her, to feel Athena's energy emanations once more.

"My incarceration, as it might be called, requires the help of another to help me escape from it. And I have found the one I have chosen among your species to help me do that."

"ME?"

"You are special; I wanted your slab there in the center atrium to do honor to that uniqueness."

"By why am I special?" Frida asked.

"I say you are. Is that not enough?" Athena gently laughed. "I didn't just find you on my astral wanderings, little one. *You found me.* Search your subconscious memories. You have seen me before, before these last few days I mean."

"I've seen you in my dreams," Frida admitted almost in a whisper.

"You have gone on many adventures with me, while your body remained within your bed, have you not?"

Frida felt a chill go down her. She'd never told anyone of her night travels beyond her bed and apartment. On many nights, she had found herself leaving her body, breaking free of its bondage, a sensation very much like the live "monitoring" mode on a Sensor Sphere record/playback unit. She would rise to the ceiling, feel herself up against it, and descend again silently, studying her lifeless form in the bed. So much her body resembled a mere shell, in those times when she'd gone out of it, a mere container for her life essence.

She'd gone through all the rooms in her home, checked in on her parents, on Jeffrey, and felt certain the experience had been a real one, and not some immensely authentic-feeling dream episode. She'd even gone touring all of New Allentown and then burst through its outer wall and sent herself out into the wilderness where her very soul could roam free and uninhibited.

Athena nodded. She knew the course of Frida's thoughts. "And when you left the city on those nights you traveled upward into the stars, remember?"

"But I thought I had to be dreaming. Sometimes I thought what I was doing was real; other times I was convinced it couldn't possibly be."

"It was," Athena only replied. "What a clever little device your Sensor Sphere globes are," she said then. "So subtle a device to teach your culture the ways of the mystics who in past ages traveled beyond their human forms with only the power of their own minds and spiritual substance."

"Are you saying with practice I won't even need one when I wish to visit somewhere without actually going there myself? That's why they were invented."

Athena smiled. "Come," she said. "Where I want to take you, little one, you cannot go in that body. I need your astral skills to show you something."

Frida frowned as she glanced down the arena room to her slab at its bottom. "You want me to lie down and go to sleep?"

Athena smiled. "Do not think of it as sleep. Think of it as a release. Frida, you are special. Your family, and all you see around you, shield themselves instantly in dreamscapes, out of fear and inexperience. But not you. You know this state, and you know it well."

"Aren't any of these other people good at astral projecting? I can't be the only one."

"You're my friend, Frida. I've done this with you so often it is common now for both of us. Return to your slab and lie down. Release yourself from that human container. With my help you will be out of it in a second."

"Are my parents and Jeffrey dreaming right now?"

"They're in a beautiful valley. They think they are trying to reach you, to reach where you are. They do not know that they already are here. They are hiding in dreams, pleasant ones, but dreams. They will learn. I have tried to teach others here, when they wish to come here to this storage room and view their bodies. I must assist at such times their efforts to leave their bodies, once they leave my lair. But not you. You leave with such ease and grace that it's a wonder you don't stay out there for endless hours. So show me now, little one, how easy it is for you."

Frida instructed her lift belt to descend back for her slab at the arena's bottom. Once there beside it, she lay down on it. She felt her body almost immediately relax itself so thoroughly that in seconds she forgot it was even there.

"Now, wasn't that easy, Frida?" she heard Athena's voice gently tell her.

Frida didn't know what she meant by it. Nothing really had changed.

She was still in her body, so far as she knew. She opened her-eyes.

Frida looked down and suddenly below her the Moon hung large and pitted, vibrant and sunlit against the black reaches of space. In the distance she saw the small blue sphere of Earth, surrounded by a sea of stars.

"How did we get way up here?"

Athena smiled and placed her hand against Frida's chin. Frida looked down at her shorts and tights. There was no life belt upon her now. It was just her, Athena, and the universe all around her.

"You are so good at this," said Athena, "and I am so glad to have you here with me in the membrane. I can talk to you, and you shall remember, not forget as before."

Athena extended her hand, and Frida took it. Athena reoriented herself down for the Moon's surface, and suddenly Frida felt the two of them begin to descend for it.

The Lunar Alps. Frida saw the mountains rise from below. Athena stopped then several kilometers above the highest peaks. Below, upon the sun-washed soil, ground excursion vehicles, land rovers and Scoutcraft, maneuvered among the foothills. Frida saw people in force shield cocoons walking about the ridges and canyons.

They're looking for us, she realized. Frida grinned, because she knew where to look; the fissure crack they were seeking had thus far been overlooked.

"I'm afraid they will find the entry." said Athena. "They are very clever and determined."

"Can we stop them?"

"I cannot interfere in that way, not for now. Come, Frida, there are other things we must see."

Frida found herself pulled then away, into the sky and beyond the Moon. The stars surrounded her; the red planet, Mars, grew into a sphere of enormous size as it approached; its two moons, Phobos and Deimos, orbited Mars like tiny pebbles.

Frida and Athena entered Mars's atmosphere, and a sea of red desert soil and boulders hung below like a giant tapestry, an occasional massive mound of a mountain pulling up from the plains like it had been thrust up by some gigantic fist beneath the surface. Frida and Athena descended to the broad rip in the ground that was Mariner Valley. Soon she was in the continent-long trench and streaking along through it at a speed no Sensor Sphere had ever traveled.

"I did this yesterday," she told Athena, "in the Franklin Institute, its old Omnimax Theater."

"Do you know this next place, little one?"

"No," Frida said of a great sealed city some many kilometers beyond the rim of the canyon.

"Here is the headquarters of a place called *InterWorld.*"

"Oh, yeah. I know that outfit; I've heard of it. Is there something you want to show me here? Oh my God, look out!"

Frida tensed, but the impact was over in a second, and it was harmless. The two of them simply passed right through the walls of the city complex surrounding the InterWorld facility. They were walking the many plazas and departments of the city until finally Frida found Athena taking her to an art and natural history museum. It felt weird to Frida to find herself among a score of other museum patrons also here in the galleries, perusing and admiring the various works of art. It was funny, because she felt as real and present as they, and yet she knew she was not.

"Why are we here . . . viewing art?" Frida asked at length.

Athena had to giggle at that. "Because it's beautiful."

"That's what you wanted to show me?"

"No."

They departed the main art exhibits on the level they were on, and found themselves in a Martian history sector. It lay filled with various artifacts, canvases of the Martian terrain, rock samples, and various contributions by local patrons on Mars of some of the early utensils and artifacts the first settlers of the red planet had used almost four-hundred years ago. There was even an ungainly-looking apparatus that, according to the plaque, was built and launched from Earth, back in the 1990s. It bore the name Viking.

Athena stopped, ultimately, before a large sculpture, supposedly an example of local Martian art. It was bathed in blue lighting from overhead spots, inhabited a small anteroom all itself, and was protected by a purple field cocoon.

"What is that?" said Frida.

"That," Athena answered," is what I wanted to show you here on Mars."

"But, what is it?"

Athena smiled. "It is something pretending to be something it is not."

"That's not funny, not at all," Frida answered, wrinkling her nose at her. *"And not an answer!"*

Athena giggled again. "I know. You said that the last time we were here and you asked what it was."

"I wish I could remember those times."

"You will in time."

Athena approached the bejeweled artifact on display, then.

"It looks expensive," said Frida.

"Oh, it's valuable beyond comprehension," she said, "to me, anyway."

Athena released Frida's hand. She entered the security force field cocoon as if it were only a water spray, and gazed upon the crystal globe nestled atop its bejeweled metallic support structure. She extended her hands for it, then, as if feeling some unseen vibration issuing from it. When she finished, she turned and looked back at Frida.

"We can leave here, now," she said.

"Athena, what is that?"

"I told you. Something very special to me."

"But what, why you won't tell me?" Frida retorted, a somewhat hurt expression on her face. "What's so special about it? It's pretty, but what does it means to you?"

Athena smiled and glanced back to her. She extended her hand and bid Frida enter the force field with her. "I have every intention of telling you, Frida," she said. She smiled again and explained why. . . .

***

"Are we ready?"

Athena departed the field cocoon, and faced it one final time.

Frida was staring at it in awe, in lieu of what Athena had told her of it. She smiled and nodded. "Where're we going now?"

"Out beyond your solar system's farthest reaches. There is one last thing I want you to witness with me."

With a whoosh and blurring of walls and ceiling, Frida found herself suddenly above the Martian city, the red planet's soil so starkly agleam in the sunlight. Very slowly the planet Mars receded again into the star fields behind it. Soon, very soon, only the stars were around them, and the emptiness between solar systems yawned ahead.

CHAPTER THIRTY-SIX

The Stellar Quest Starship

-1-

A vessel appeared far ahead. Frida saw it among the stars, in the darkness of interstellar space. She looked over at Athena. They were pacing it. For a vessel traveling in normal space, it was moving very fast, so fast in fact that trying to spot it from a stationary position would be impossible. It moved almost as fast as a beam of light itself.

The cruiser was arrowhead-shaped, off-white, with window ports all across its hull, some very large and wide. The observation ports were almost useless at present, intended more for when the ship slowed and entered Eighty-two Eridani. At present, there were hardly any stars at all visible surrounding the vessel, thus for the most part the views out the portals revealed only black. Frida saw millions of stars around her; she wasn't aware of the vessel's near light speed optical anomalies.

Athena dropped Frida and herself down atop the ship's outer hull, amidships, and placed her arm around Frida's shoulders, prodding her to look directly off to the side of the vessel. Suddenly, all the stars Frida had earlier seen in the stellar night were gone; instead she saw a weird band of colored light, a "starbow" encircle the ship amidships, and dog the vessel as it proceeded onward toward a sky completely black.

Frida looked down the vessel's long, slanting hull to its stern. Its Electromagnetic "EM" Drive engines glowed a dull orange and silently propelled the vessel onward for its as yet distant and many light years ahead destination, ahead in the black night.

Frida in a moment of stunned realization looked over at Athena, and said, "I know this ship! Oh, my God, I don't believe it. I've actually seen this thing before, pictures of it. Am I really here, seeing this?"

"Of course you are," said Athena. "It's the ship your people call *Stellar Quest.*"

"But that left the solar system five years ago!" Frida answered. "It's on its way to Eighty-two Eridani in the Eridanus constellation."

Athena nodded. "Yes, I know, Frida. That's my star."

Frida's mouth gaped again. "You sent that radio signal a hundred years ago?"

Athena smiled. "It's about time your species did something to acknowledge reception of it."

"So, your people and the Barthonians know we're coming?"

"Oh, yes, we know. This tiny craft doesn't look like much, but it's on a straight line from your star to mine, and it's interfering with the subspace channel my people use to communicate with me. They've decided to do something about that."

"Did they say anything else?"

"Yes, they wanted me to be here today, any way I could be. I asked them if I could take a friend. There's something here I have to do. Something is going to happen."

"What?"

"Let's go inside," Athena smiled, "I have a surprise for you."

Frida only looked at her; Athena took Frida's hand again and led her forward for the huge viewport on the vessel's bow. Athena looked down at the metal hull beneath her. Frida looked down with her, and suddenly the two descended through it as if it were made of air. Frida and Athena dropped right into the *Stellar Quest*'s bridge, and Frida immediately felt herself gape in shock at what she saw.

Inside were assembled the entire crew complement. Captain Mitchel Samuel Katill was over by the navigation console, hovering above his navigator/communications officer, Lieutenant Commander Monica Jessica Cressler. To his side was the first officer/pilot, Commander Douglas Lawrence Bahner.

Behind them and toward the back of the bridge was Lieutenant Commander Dexter Rudolph Zeigler, ship's engineer, who was monitoring engineering status indicators from his bridge display. The civilians present were Angelique Belinda Bonnachelli, food and agriculture specialist; Charles Howser, Environmental specialist; Rita Katherine Knowler, Linguistics and Archaeology expert; Serina Cruthers, Zoology; and Harry Michaelson, expert on planetary systems, orbital mechanics.

They were moving in slow motion, half speed of normal as it seemed. They were staring in various poses of alarm at the forward spectrum-adjusted images which superimposed themselves over the view of the portal window it fronted.

Within that image projection, the stars that formed the constellation of Eridanus were vibrantly represented and rendered. Something small and purple-hued inhabited the image's center. It looked a cloud-thing directly ahead which masked the pinprick star dot that represented Eighty-two Eridani.

Frida approached the bridge officers. She watched them for endless seconds. She turned then to Athena. "I read on the news that the crew went into hibernation immediately after leaving the solar system. Why are they awake?"

Athena smiled. "We did that," she confessed. "We woke them up. Somebody had to."

"And why are they like that?" Frida asked then of their slow motion movements. "Are they all right?"

Athena nodded. "They're fine. You're witnessing the effect of *Time Dilation,* little one. The Stellar Quest is moving at ninety percent light speed. At that speed, time passage slows inside the vessel. They're alive, but they're advancing through time much slower, compared to us; they only appear to be moving in slow motion."

"They don't look real," said Frida. "They don't act like they're real people." She approached handsome and young Doug Bahner, the commander. With his two meter frame, blue eyes and blond hair, Frida could tell he was a ladies man. But even he at this moment seemed worried over matters for more threatening than rivalries between jealous lovers.

"Athena," Frida began, timidly, "what are we doing here?"

"Witnessing," she simply replied.

Frida looked to the tensed expressions of the entire crew. "They look scared."

"They are . . . *of that.*" Athena pointed to the view screen.

"What is that?"

Athena smiled. "Brace yourself, little one. I'm about to slow us down to match them."

The inhibited antics of the crew began to quicken. Their lips pursed and formed words that were actually legible, though mostly guttural in tone, but their vocal ranges soon climbed the pitch register until they began to sound like normal people again. Before Frida even realized it, the crew was acting normal, and all hell was breaking out aboard the bridge of the *Stellar Quest.*

"We definitely have company!" shouted Monica Cressler over the alarm claxon. "Mitch, will you turn that noise off? I can't concentrate!"

Mitch Katill looked over at Doug Bahner and nodded to him to go attend to it. Doug flashed him an acknowledgement and went over to his helm console. The room abruptly died of its warning alarms.

"It's an energy mass, type unknown," said Monica. "It just suddenly appeared right in front of us, stopped and now it's pacing our progress forward." She glanced up to the anomaly presented in the image. "It's as if it's escorting us forward to the solar system." She glanced down again to her console. "No, now it's deliberately decreasing its rearward thrust to fall back toward us. Affirmative, if it keeps that up, it's going to smack right into us."

It was as round as a small moon, and nebulous— a huge wall of energy!

***

"Memory banks find no match ups at all?" asked Mitch.

"Negative," said Monica. "Mitch, that thing's alive! It's putting out patterned energy. The wavebands are nothing the computers have ever encountered, but they're clear evidence . . ." she scanned her instruments and then glanced at the anomaly . . . *"that it's a lifeform,* hundreds of individual signatures. Mitch. . . That's a colony."

"Of what?" he dreaded to ask.

"Of whom, you should be asking me, and I don't know. But there's enough charged material in that thing to burn us and the entire solar system to cinders. My God! Oh, shit, it's accelerating its forward approach!"

"Commander," said Mitch, facing helm station, "Evasive action. Ten degrees starboard. Now."

"Complying, Mitch. Not sure the ship can move out of the way fast enough though."

"He's right," added Dexter Zeigler, ship's engineer, leaving his bridge displays. "Not enough time."

"Then can we reverse direction? All ahead back? Slow us down. Slow that thing's approach?"

"Mitch," said Zeigler, "we're not that kind of starship. We're not the *Enterprise.* That would take time. We're moving too fast. It's going to take us hours to lose our forward momentum."

"They know we're out here," said Doug Bahner. "They're matching our course changes, Mitch. They wants to hit us. They're pacing and approaching us at the same time. That thing better not be solid. If it hits us, there's going to be one hell of a fireball, us going up in flames in a millisecond upon impact." He shook his head at the thought. "Shit. We're about to make contact with an alien life form."

In seconds, the ball of light grew enormous and blotted out the entire view ahead. All nine aboard felt the vessel lurch as the mass smacked right up against the ship. Suddenly, all ship's power fluctuated. There was a brief shutdown, and the spectrum-adjusted view screen image faded to black.

The entire bridge remained on emergency lighting and power from that point on, and very faintly Harry Michaelson noticed it first: Without power to run it, the forward viewport's hologram overlay dissolved and very slowly Harry began to notice faint points of light out there in the skies before the ship.

"What the hell?" he asked.

Angelique noticed it as well. The purplish cloud had thinned almost completely beyond visible influence as it engulfed the ship.

"Come on," Angelique said to Harry. They ran down to the alleyway, slid down the hatch ladder to the level below, and headed for the observation room. Out the many windows they saw the same image.

"Mitch, this is Harry. Angel and I are in the lounge. It's the same thing out this window. I don't believe this. We're not moving; full stop. The stars are normal out there again."

"Confirmed," said Monica, "all forward motion stopped. Auxiliary power. Primary systems off-line. Mitch, we're dead in the water."

"I thought you said slowing down would take hours, Dex," said Mitch to his engineer.

"I'm not Scotty from that old TV series," he answered. "All I can say is, *I don't know, captain*. But we're stopped, totally zero momentum."

Mitch Katill eyed status readouts on Monica's console in the dim red lighting. He looked up at once to the viewport. A strange phenomenon was beginning directly in front of it upon the bridge. As Mitch discerned the forms slowly coalescing into presence before him, he glanced back down to Monica's console and spoke into communications. "Harry," he said.

"Captain?" Harry Michaelson answered.

"You and Angel get back up here, now!"

"What's going on?"

"Just get up here."

Harry and Angelique looked at each other, and did as they were ordered. When they reached the bridge, they froze in disbelief. The entire crew stood aghast. Before them were ghostly apparitions of a little earth girl and this entity that looked to be an earth woman, but seemed a whole lot more. There was an ambiance about her that suggested she possessed far more substance and potential than the meager image of a human female implied.

"Who are you?" said Mitch, approaching the ghostly specter of a woman, apprehensively.

"You may know me as Athena," she said.

The words she spoke seemed in his mind, not spoken words so much. Mitch looked down at the little girl, then.

Frida grinned and gave Mitch a little wave. "Hi, I'm Frida Hagerton. . ."

So too did Frida's words: thought impressions, not actual speech.

". . . From New Allentown, in Pennsylvania," Frida continued. "That's on Earth."

Mitch nodded. "I've been there. What is this?" He approached her, and stuck out his hand. It passed right through Frida's form.

She smiled; it didn't even phase her.

"I don't believe in ghosts," Mitch said.

"She's not a ghost," Athena answered. "She's having an out-of-body experience. You're witness to it."

"I don't believe in them, either," he answered.

Athena smiled and shrugged. "That's too bad."

Mitch looked at Frida again. "You're with her?"

Frida nodded.

"She's not human. What is she?"

"An Eleution . . . from Eighty-two Eridani. One of them." Frida pointed at the purple energy mass in the forward viewport.

The entire crew glanced over at Athena.

"Why have you done this to us?" asked Mitch.

Athena turned and faced back to the viewport. "I've been told to meet you and speak for my people who are holding just beyond the ship."

"What is it you want?"

She faced back to him. "You've been out here a long time trying to reach my star system. Frida and I are from back in *your* solar system. You intercepted a few of my transmissions that I tried to send my people in Eighty-two Eridani. You've no idea what a nuisance your ship has been."

"Are you here to rid yourself of that nuisance?"

Athena grinned. "In a way. Your voyage is over. In your own Earth vernacular, we're extending a courtesy . . . we're giving you a lift."

"So kind of you," said Monica.

"Haven't you ever wondered," she began, suddenly, "why the stars are so far away?" Athena smiled. "They aren't. They only are to beings like you. Your species is one not far enough along yet, spiritually. You are on the Earth and in the three-dimensional universe because those are the rules as spirit entities you agreed to live by. Your people chose those limitations. It's no accident that the speed of light is the cut off speed, or that all conventional means of travel as you know it in the solar system is impractical for star voyaging, considering how far away even the closest stars are to your own. Your species, as long as it is in its current stage of spiritual development, is not meant to travel through the galaxy, not yet, or even leave your solar system. You won't earn that right, until you have the proper growth, the wisdom, that comes when you also learn how to exist in higher states of dimensional existence."

"Sounds like a lot of metaphysical nonsense, if you ask me," replied Mitch.

"She didn't," smiled Frida.

"Your species considers Hyperspace travel a fantasy. It isn't, but no object that exists in your three-dimensional universe can survive entry into other dimensional states. To do so one must become liberated, shed physical form. There is only one state in the universe that is constant through all the dimensions, and that is as pure energy, the energy of spirit. And in such a state, the energy traveler must be proficient in moving about as such, to go at will amid and through these higher dimensions, to not become imprisoned in any of them or be held accountable to their laws, if he ever hoped to again return to the dimensional plane he calls his own.

"These corporeal limitations exist for a reason. Your species with its violent history by now would have declared war on practically every species you met in the galaxy had it the freedom to go where it wished. But do not feel bad. You're not alone. There are many other aggressive species like yours in the galaxy, and they too aren't going anywhere beyond their home stars until they gain wisdom and maturity."

"Thank you," said Mitch, perhaps cynically, he was being too coy to actually tell, "for that lesson in spirituality and quantum mechanics. That was quite a speech. Are all of your people so *long winded?*"

"You're being rude," Frida spat at him.

"It needed to be stated," defended Athena, "so that you know the situation as it is and the impossibility of what you're attempting to accomplish."

"Then, If we're still so primitive and backward as to not deserve to leave our home system, why are your people so interested in us?" said Mitch.

"Because your people are on the threshold of a spiritual metamorphose. You are changing, shedding the warrior within you. Your species is the manifestation of spirit forms who have incarnated as earth beings many times over the course of human history. The novelty fades eventually. Your peaceful trek to my people's star is to us evidence that you have grown. We are going to help you, help you to grow more. You nine are to be the first; many more will follow. My people await. Frida and I will take our leave of you now. Be well."

Athena turned to Frida, and bid her take her hand. The two vanished from the bridge.

Seconds later they were several meters beyond the vessel, and Frida looked around her and saw the totality of the Eleutions and their energy mass surrounding the ship.

The *Stellar Quest* slowly vanished. Athena faced the Eleution enclave before her, and held what seemed to be a silent conversation with it. She nodded.

The energy cloud coalesced itself into a far more tighter band, and suddenly headed out into the starfields. It was en route back for Eighty-two Eridani.

"It's time to return to the Moon, Frida," said Athena. "We must make the final preparations."

Frida looked up at her. "Your people are coming back, aren't they . . . for everybody?"

She smiled and nodded. "Eventually. Your people, Frida dear, exist in a state of arrested development. You should have advanced to a higher level ages ago. Your own planet is suffering from your reticence. Your people require a little nudge. Come, we have things to do back home. There is work I must do, and I need your help to do it."

Athena looked back to the distant image of the sun, so faint and pale among the millions of other stars. "We've been gone a long time," she mused. "I'm sure Randolph Phillips has found the cave by now."

There was a rush of star light, and the sun slowly grew in size amid the night.

At the Mariner Valley *InterWorld* facility on Mars, a steady stream of largely autonomic telemetry from the *Stellar Quest* continually reached it. The contents had to be time-compressed for legibility, two and a half hours of signal had to be reduced to one hour to achieve meaningful legibility, and sadly what was being received at present left the *Stellar Quest* when the ship was still only two light years out from the home solar system, over two years ago. The signals had been traveling back at light speed as the *Stellar Quest* trekked another two L.Y.'s even further into the dark voids between stars.

Said telemetry received by *InterWorld* monotonously reported the good news that all was fine aboard the vessel, the crew as yet in suspended animation for the long twenty-three year trek to Eighty-Two Eridani. There were no anomalies, no problems as of two years back, at any rate. No one at any of the many facilities interspersed throughout the solar system would suspect any difficulty or problem at all. For all any of them knew, as recently as two years ago the Stellar Quest was on course for Eighty-two Eridani, and all was proceeding well.

She would now have been four light years away in space. That meant whatever was happening aboard the *Stellar Quest* that very day would not be known by Mariner Valley and *InterWorld* for another four years. It would take another four years, in other words, before anyone on Earth even knew the ship was no longer on course and doing well. And one thing telemetry would never tell them, when it abruptly stopped, was that the crew of the Stellar Quest had just arrived at its destination—

***

. . . sixteen years early.

PART FOUR:
SUMMONS.

CHAPTER THIRTY-SEVEN

-1-

Tuesday morning. It was very early, at least so said Randolph's pendant communicator when he asked it. He was in the cramped mess hall aboard the land rover, parked in the Alps range, having spent the night in his tiny bunk that passed for a VIP cabin aboard the vehicle. He took a sip from his morning brew, the twenty-fifth century equivalent to coffee, a concoction that had practically the same texture, and went down the same, had the same kick that was, but was synthesized from a chemical a lot nicer on the anatomy than caffeine.

A long viewport possessed the wall to his right in the mess hall. Only a few personnel, mostly ship-board members, were in there with him, having their breakfast. Most of the others were at their stations aboard the rover. Randolph looked out at the long window. In the foreground he marveled at how desolate everything now looked in the sun-washed bleakness of the lunar terrain. It was bleak because the land rover was one of only a handful of vehicles still remaining in the area. Seeing as how the search had proven productive the night before, the search crews had gone back to their normal duties in Cassini and its neighboring facilities.

The viewport also looked out at the Mare Imbrium plain as it met the Alps, and above in the sky and almost totally blotted out by the glare of the sun, was old Earth, its night face as yet in view above the lunar terrain.

Ron Isley's crack scientific team was still in place down in the cavern, doing what probably amounted to meager to nothing of any use to anyone, and so far as Randolph had been briefed nothing new had revealed itself during the night. For the most part, despite the presence of high energy output readings among the transplanted limestone formations down there, nothing else had really been discovered. Randolph's plans, thus, to remove all the alien artifacts located therein in the cavern, once the excavator crews arrived and started widening that fissure crack up the cliff face, were still on the books for some time later that day.

He'd just returned from the radio room. New Allentown officials, in their cooperation with Randolph's security team back on Earth, had pieced together a clever deception perpetrated, they were certain, by his son, Greg, and Melanie Richards. The two had left the city. New Allentown security was certain of it by this point. Their likenesses had not turned up on any monitors all night, and there was no sign of them in either of their apartments. In its attempts to detail, thus, how the two might have left, city security had stumbled upon Carmen Demero, a city sewage and waste treatment underling down in the city's basement level. He claimed to have seen two young people late yesterday afternoon down in the basement, fooling with a maintenance elevator. Another worker had stumbled upon Carmen's unconscious form and had sent for a Medical Alert unit when Carmen insisted he'd been stunned with a weapon of some kind. Evidence to substantiate his claim was later detected upon his body, but his superiors suspended him anyway for being stewed to the gills on cheap whiskey while on duty.

His story was eventually checked out. Access logs were pulled. To everyone's surprise, one of the fleet elevators had been entered and activated yesterday afternoon. Rarely were the things ever used anymore, not since the city's early construction days. The elevator, they learned, had been accessed by a married couple in their seventies, who according to the summary, were vacationing on Earth.

Randolph assured New Allentown officials that, had the Davis's planned an Earth voyage, he'd have known of it in advance. Subsequent inquiries verified Fred and Wilma Davis were as yet on Titan, Saturn's largest moon.

Still, accessing the logs of I.D. readers within a hundred kilometers of New Allentown, it was revealed that Gregory Phillips and Melanie Richards (posing as Fred and Wilma Davis) around sundown used their level nine excursion permits to access the cocoon shield of a forestry station south of the city. They had in effect trekked across the wilderness on foot.

Randolph laughed to himself. The next time he was on Titan he'd have to look up old Fred and mention Greg's little antic to the man. Fred would get a belly laugh out of it. Between Greg's ingenuity and the Richards girl's expertise with memory storage, the two were quite a pair.

The radio man, as he listened in on all this at Randolph's invitation, couldn't help laughing. Randolph just looked down at the guy and shook his head.

"I'd say your boy was in love, councilman," said the radio man.

Randolph had sighed and nodded his head.

Gregory Phillips awoke that Tuesday morning, just as the sun climbed above the eastward foothills and filled the interior of the forestry station in its light. Against the northward skyline and only now faintly visible above the hilltops, a cloud-fringed New Allentown hung, its highest levels red-tinged as the sun's first rays caught them in its radiance. He and Melanie had made roughly twenty kilometers of travel across the rising terrain of the Blue Mountains, and yet among them at this distance, the city still made a significant presence, though now it seemed wispy-looking, soft-focused with distance, as the morning haze slowly prepared to burn off with the dawn.

Melanie as yet lay asleep beside Greg on the floor. (They'd settled for the floor over the tinier cots, butting two of the mattresses together in the middle of it to facilitate the two of them.) Greg reached over to the Sensor Sphere carry bag and removed a "command" headset and the playback/record unit. He affixed the headset to his head and cued up the monitoring mode on the record unit. He immediately felt a sensory displacement, as if he'd suddenly lifted out of his body and had relocated his very awareness to somewhere else, somewhere currently dark and confining. Melanie moaned silently in her sleep and then nestled her head against his chest. Greg blinked his eyelids twice, forced his awareness back to where he lay on the floor, and then looked over at the carry bag. He commanded the Sensor Sphere to levitate out of it. He lay flat, then, staring up at the ceiling, enjoying the way Melanie's long, silky hair draped across his chest and navel. The imagery from the Sensor Sphere invaded his thoughts once again; he felt in two different places at the same time: beside Melanie, against her soft, supple curves; and over by the east side windows with their stunning views of the countryside. Both locations had their advantages.

He closed his eyes and took a deep breath, slipping himself as much as he could into an altered state of consciousness. The sphere transmission soon swept him away, and when he no longer felt beside Melanie, but adrift before the windows, he willed his consciousness out to the balcony railing and found himself suspended fifteen meters above the hill. He took off then for the countryside in the direction he and Melanie had come the night before.

He went weaving through the evergreens, conscious of all the morning sounds that issued from the forest cover. He stumbled upon a doe in the underbrush, drinking absently from a stream. He sent the sphere down for her. He could hear her pad, gently, upon the brittle grass and weeds. She turned and looked up at him, but she didn't run away. She only watched the ten-centimeter crystal globe remain adrift there, until she eventually turned and vanished in the underbrush.

Greg searched the terrain within a forty kilometer radius of the forestry station. He found no evidence that a search team had gone out looking for them. He directed the sphere back to the station.

Melanie sensed something watching her. She opened her eyes and almost screamed. A Sensor Sphere unit hovered about a meter above her and Greg. She quickly looked down and noticed Greg wore a command headset. She realized the truth, palmed her chest and exhaled. She then smirked and glanced up at the sphere, again.

"Shame on you, Greg Phillips!" she directed toward the sphere, knowing his consciousness was centered within it. "That is kinkier than a mirror on the ceiling. You frightened me half to death. I thought it was a surveillance sphere sent by city security."

"Melanie," she heard him answer, weakly, beside her. She faced down to his almost lifeless face. Greg's lips barely moved. "I feel like I'm one with the universe, free to roam it at will. I sent the sphere out to survey the terrain, make sure no one was following us. It looks all clear, but now I'm having a hard time getting back inside my own skin. It's like I don't want to, or I've forgotten how. It's like I'm a milkweed seed, adrift in the wild. Pull the headset off me, please, hon? I can't find my fingers."

She started to giggle, silently.

"That's funny?"

She saw him smile, and she kissed him. She then removed the headset.

Greg suddenly looked confused. The tranquility on his face evaporated.

Melanie gently lowered her lips again to Greg's and gave him a passionate full mouth kiss— a long, lingering one, kneading her nipples as she did into his own upon his bare chest. Eventually, she felt his hands rake the back of her thighs and caress her tiny rear. She inched her arms under his neck and began to twirl her sexuality in little circles about his manhood. Unfortunately, little to nothing was going on down there—the curse of impotence that in recent times now plagued the human race.

Greg moaned; he opened his eyes and kissed her back. "Is this a new revival technique I haven't heard of?" he asked her, then.

"Greg, shut up and make love to me," she replied. She began to writhe her body up against him and his sexuality.

"We forgot to bring the sex sensories," he told her of the virtual reality recordings from the past people used to compensate for what Mother Nature had taken from the human race. "Nothing much is happening down there."

"Shush," she said. "We'll manage just fine," she promised.

***

The two had dressed, indulged in a nourishment package (which gave the body all the food nutrients it needed, plus fooled the mind into thinking the body had eaten) and gathering all their stuff together, descended the tower stairwell for the maintenance shed. The morning was cool and autumnal in texture, low humidity. Upon a neighboring bank, yellow maple leaves wafted in the wind, like great snowflakes, and Melanie looked out to the north upon New Allentown above the tree line.

Greg took hold of her waist and pulled her up against him. He kissed her, the bright glow of the dawn, the rolling hills of the Blue Mountains, flanking them in a golden, yellow splendor.

He walked her over to the maintenance shed and opened it. "We'd better make progress getting away from here."

"And go where, Greg?"

He looked south. "Across the mountain range . . . to Crystal Cave, maybe. There's something in the cave I want to check out."

"But, Greg, there's nothing there now. The orb is gone."

"Yes, but it also returns. It's done it before. I don't know, maybe because I've seen the cave so much in the last two days, I feel this urge to go there in person."

He then keyed the lights in the shed. Inside was a low-ceilinged and dimly-lit interior, narrow aisles weaving like a maze between metal shelves and racks. Cartons filled with boxes of optic cable, first aid equipment, auxiliary food packs, and a host of other junk lined the shelves which the Wilderness Society personnel (this was a forestry station, remember) might need when traveling beyond the city.

Far back to the left, rear wall sat a levitation sled. It looked (for want of a better description) like an old-style snowmobile, metallic blue with black snow runners. Greg took Melanie's hand and led her back toward it, past the racks of equipment.

"Ain't it pretty?" he said of it. It was a two-seater. "It'll be more fun than a lift pack."

He climbed into the driver's seat and tested how comfortable he'd feel behind the wheel. It had an old-style bicycle steering wheel, and (by twenty-fifth century standards) a primitive display board. It was all touch-activated, not neuralscan wired. He'd actually have to steer it. He positioned his hands on the handle bars and got a feel for what driving it would be like.

"This is the *only way* to explore the great open spaces," he said.

"How did you know this was here?" she asked.

He pointed to an ID plate beneath the dash. "*New Allentown Transport.* Our department is in charge of the equipment."

She nodded and studied the rear, black leather-upholstered seat.

"Mel," Greg said, "see if you can find a few lift packs, preferably equipped with repelling fields, back there along those shelves." He pointed over to the right rear wall. "We'll want them within the cavern."

"I'd love to take some of this stuff back to the city with me," Melanie said. "It's like an electronics junk store in here."

"I've a geek for a girlfriend," Greg sighed.

"And you love it, too," she answered. "We'd never have got this far, if one of us weren't."

He nodded, then punched the "taxi mode" wafer on the sled's dash and watched the sled silently rise a third meter off the floor. He climbed out of the seat and leaned over, grabbing the handle bars. He started pushing it out into the sunlight, carefully inching past the narrow rows of shelves. The handle bars didn't really work in this mode. He could see the runners styling to the right or left a bit whenever he wheeled the handle bars, but as to piloting the sled while in flight, moving the bars translated into a command to reconfigure the mag-force beams which propelled the ship. Since the system was not active in taxi mode, to turn the sled, he had to push it in the direction he wished it to go.

He edged it all the way to the door and then powered it down so that it gently eased itself back to the ground. He checked the fusion packs to make sure his department had serviced them recently, and they were one-hundred percent reliable. If they weren't, he'd have someone's ass for it, the next time he reported for work. He squinted his eyes up to the sun and to the blue sky of the morning, took in a breath of air, and then walked back into the shed to help Melanie round up all the supplies they would need.

***

A half hour later, the sled packed and ready, Greg and Melanie took their places. Greg brought the fusion packs on line and powered up the dash. He keyed the in-dash GPS display and had it file down from its world map to a local one of the Pennsylvania countryside. He "zoomed in" on his and Melanie's current location south of New Allentown. The GPS satellite array in geosynchronous orbit above in space was able to resolve the live image of himself and Melanie with such precise detail that he could actually count the hairs on the back of his head had he wished to. It was almost disturbing. He couldn't resist the urge to look up to verify the recording camera was in fact hundreds of miles up and orbiting the planet and not just a few feet away on a high perch somewhere.

He zeroed the display in on the old Kutztown, Pennsylvania area, and then fine-tuned it for Crystal Cave. (The cave was just west of the old town limits.) When he data-entered that the cavern was his intended destination, the display gave him a course vector, and literally informed him how much of an angle to put on the handle bars to set the sled on the proper flight path. It would do that for him all the way to the cave's entrance, if that were his wish. And looking south toward the mountains (which winded off into the cloud-be speckled horizon), he nodded to himself that there was no way he'd know how to get there without a map. He grabbed the white helmet off the dash and put it on, adjusting it for a snug fit. Then he secured the seat belt, and looked back to Melanie, to assure that she'd done the same.

She had.

"Okay!" he said to her.

The handle bars had leather grips at their ends which twisted clockwise or counterclockwise. The right one controlled lift. Twisting it forward stylized the levitation system so that the sled rose; rearward (toward him) caused it to descend. Greg twisted it frontward; the sled abruptly lifted off the ground.

Melanie glanced down. They'd climbed halfway the height of the forestry tower. The ground looked way below. She put her arms around his waist, and hung on.

The left handle bar grip controlled acceleration. Greg glanced to Melanie, nodded, and then twisted the grip forward. The sled lurched into the wilderness. Greg's display graph advised him of how much pressure to apply on the bars and how many degrees off the desired course he presently was. He made some minor adjustments, and the sled abruptly sailed above the tree line and made a great arc to the south. He applied more forward pressure on the left grip. As the wind kicked up against his helmet and ears, he faintly heard Melanie hoot in excitement.

"Like it?" he called to her.

"I love it I Greg, watch where you're going!"

He looked frontward, twisting the right grip just in time to avoid the top crown of a tall evergreen. He angled the sled into a climb and it gradually began to ascend the first of a long line of tall peaks fanning down to the southeast. They shot into the morning clouds and soon lost sight of New Allentown completely.

***

Greg sent the Sensor Sphere ahead of them. Not him, personally, of course. He had to steer. He landed the sled, briefly, to allow Melanie to locate the unit and the playback/record deck from the storage compartment, power up the record unit and don the headset upon her head. Then they were in flight again. Melanie held the tiny sphere in her right hand, and as if it were a milkweed seed, she released it and watched the sphere sail off into the wind. She commanded it to climb and move off some hundred meters ahead, and only when she was sure it was safely away, did she take a deep breath and thought-input the command for the sensor imagery to invade her thoughts and spirit her off the sled and into the clouds. She was as if a bird in flight, the four horizons beneath her, and the land rolling off to them in majesty.

She searched the sky for the sled; it lay several meters ahead now; it was departing rapidly. She chased after it, and found herself eventually alongside. She looked over and was awed by the sight of Greg and herself atop it. That felt weird—was she there behind him, or floating free several meters away? She saw the expression of peaceful bliss upon her face and was awed yet again.

Greg saw the sphere approach from below; it matched the sled's speed and flight path. He craned his neck back to gaze upon Melanie.

"Hey!" he called to her above the wind.

She jolted, and opened her eyes to him. "That is wild!" she exclaimed. The sensor imagery continued to intrude upon and confuse her.

"I told you it was addictive," he said.

"It is!" She closed her eyes again, enjoying the wind screaming past her face and hair.

He saw that she was again merging her thoughts with the data from the sensor sphere. He looked over, therefore, to the unit and pointed his index finger down for the hillsides below.

"Check things out downstairs, okay?" he said.

He felt her hands upon his waist gently knead into his skin, and then saw the sphere drop toward the Earth, swooping in an arc toward the tree line as the sled continued on into the mountains.

"Not too low, now," he called to her. "And try not to get too far behind the sled."

Melanie simply kneaded her fingers against him once again in response. His voice felt as if it were accompanying her as she journeyed in spirit down for the ground.

She sailed among the treetops, basking in the glory of something that hitherto felt only the stuff of dreams, astral dreams of flying amid the wilderness.

***

They reached Kutztown and Crystal Cave about an hour later. Greg brought the sled in from the westward valley and very carefully parked it upon the crest of the hill. The spot was once a scenic overlook, so christened as such by the Crystal Cave management, one that gave tourists views of the Blue Mountains to the west. The long sloping hill descended back for where the rear parking lots and buildings once stood.

"Are you sure this is the spot?" Melanie asked him.

"Sure I'm sure," he said. "It's down the slope, and up that other incline, over there." He pointed off to the right.

Among the distant oak trees Melanie very faintly made out the cedar wood cabin.

"It looks clear, so far," she said.

He nodded.

"So, what are we bringing down with us?"

"The lift belts, water, food capsules, a few lights and stuff, I don't know. The usual stuff."

She looked at him. "Are you hoping the orb is down there?"

He shrugged. "Possibly."

"Do you want to become its captive, also?"

"I want to experience these things for myself. Melanie, if we're running, we might as well be creative. Where can we really run to—another city? They'll identify us, and want to know how and why we came to be outside, unlawfully. We're buying some time at least."

She nodded, distantly.

Greg handed her a lift belt; she put it on. He withdrew from the storage compartment a fusion reactor pack, a light sphere, and a small bag the size of a throw pillow, which contained the inflatable raft they would need to retrace Keith and Jeffrey's water journey back for where they found the ship.

They began the trek down the long incline for the other hill.

CRYSTAL CAVE
Discovered A.D. 1871,
Formerly in the
County of Berks,
In the commonwealth of Pennsylvania.

Though it seemed to him a reprisal of the images he'd accessed in Keith Hagerton's visual, he paused and read the marble marker before the cedar wood cabin. The lighted bar lay beneath it, and before it a scarlet cocoon faintly shimmered and prevented anyone from entering the cabin.

"I feel like I was here only yesterday," said Melanie.

Greg nodded. "What we're doing they once called a *sequel.*" He inserted his Fred Davis visa.

"Gregory Phillips. Identity confirmed," came the report. "Resident: New Allentown. Entry approval, dated: 10/28/15. Warning. Sensor scan reveals second lifeform in area proximity. Identity input required before shield cocoon can be lowered."

Greg removed his card; his hand was shaking. He looked at Melanie. "They're onto us," he said. "They know about Fred and Wilma."

Melanie looked at him and then inserted her card.

"Melanie Richards. Identity confirmed. Resident: New Allentown. Entry approval, dated 10/28/15." The red bar below the input slot faded to black just as simultaneously the cocoon shield dropped from the cabin.

"Shield will remain lowered until entry," the voice continued, "or until such time as new approachees enter sensor area."

"They'll know where we are," she said.

He nodded. "It's too late to do anything about it now, though. Our entry has been approved. That may mean they know, but they don't care, anymore."

"Or it's their way of letting us know they're onto us."

"Go on in, Mel," he said of the cabin. "Start setting up reactor power. I'm bringing the sled down. No use hiding it on the hill anymore."

CHAPTER THIRTY-EIGHT

From the doorway of the cabin, Melanie watched Greg trek back up the long incline. She felt the cool autumn air, and heard a flock of geese honk by overhead. She caught a glimpse of their formation through the branches of the trees. A wood thrush did excavation work on a tree truck nearby. She heard his rhythmic tapping, while elsewhere a wren filled the woods with its song. She looked up to the sun, filtering through the forest cover, and closed her eyes to feel it all upon her.

Perhaps, she supposed, had humanity not taken the world for granted centuries ago, it would not have been so necessary for humanity to swear off the land entirely, or for her, unbeknownst to Greg, to risk being out here with her life support field momentarily deactivated. But to experience authentic life out in the wild. The likelihood of any real harm was probably slim with such short exposures to the natural air, and as far as Melanie was concerned it was worth the risk. Being out here like this was a once in a lifetime treat.

She took a breath and caught the aroma of the cedar wood all around her in the cabin. Greg was halfway up the other long incline by that point. Melanie turned and reached down for the utility box which held the fusion reactor and the light sphere. She opened it, touch-activated the top panel, and withdrew a neuralscan headset.

She looked behind her to the exposed wall of the mountainside, and to the stairway that vanished below into the depthless black of the cavern. Placing the headset atop her hair, she looked back to the box. Like a sorcerer, she ordered the Light Sphere to levitate out of it and to descend for the cavern. Seeing it vanish into the darkness, she then sent it a power up command. Crystal Cave and the stairway suddenly burst into light below her. She inched down the steps, and recognized instantly the slit opening that Keith and Jeffrey Hagerton had used to descend to the lower levels. She neared the opening, and eyed the white flowstone rock—resembling cake batter tossed against a wall— before her.

She looked back to the topside entrance, and wondered how long Greg would take to get back. She decided she had time to explore the cave, and soon found herself following the old tourist path underneath the massive, collapsed limestone block which now formed a natural bridge tunnel.

"There you are," Greg said, fifteen minutes later, as he emerged from the shadows.

She'd reached the back of the cave, and was above him, her arms draping the railing of the overlook area, as she vacantly contemplated the formations before her in the overhead light of the Light Sphere. "I forgot you needed light to see," Melanie replied.

He shrugged, and climbed the stairs for her. "I managed."

"It's not the grandest cave in the world," she answered. "I've seen nicer."

"You saw on the Hagertons' visual how beautiful it is farther down." He shook his head. "It's hard to believe it's that impressive below us."

"That's the creepy part," she said. "We're going to follow the same route Keith Hagerton took, aren't we, to where he found that collapsed rock wall?"

"Which leads to the subterranean lake," he added and nodded.

"Greg, before Keith Hagerton, the only people who even knew the lake was down there was the Athena's other victims."

"I know."

"Are you sure you can find his route?" She looked around her and grabbed her arms. "Caves, I forgot how damp and creepy they can be. I've already jumped a few tiny bats with that light sphere."

He grinned. "Keith Hagerton never left the cave the same way he entered. He left a trail of these things. . . ." Greg showed her a marker beacon. "When we get back to the entrance, I'll have the reactor access the power-up frequency of Hagerton's bunch and light them. We'll just follow them down."

"You think of everything, don't you?"

"I try." He nudged her forward and down the long, divided stairway.

The exit route went along the left side wall, and eventually went over top of the collapsed limestone block. When they reached the slit opening to the lower levels, he indicated her lift pack.

"Set it for about the Moon's gravity-one-sixth of Earth's. It'll make the descent easier. Living our whole lives in the city doesn't exactly make us rugged cave explorers."

"Spelunkers," she corrected.

He nodded. "Whatever. Oh, and if you catch any bug out here because you keep leaving your force shield off, don't give it to me."

She stuck her tongue at him and then set her belt buckle control pad for "gravity-reduction-only," tweaking it then down for the one-sixth setting. Greg requested proprietorship of the neuralscan headset, and Melanie promptly removed it and handed to him. He retrieved the utility box from where he'd left it beside the stairway, and with the command headset now snugly in place on his head, he formed the image in his mind of the tiny marker beacons below. He requested they be powered up. He heard a beep from the power pack, and the confirmation response clouded his thoughts. He then commanded the Light Sphere to descend into the fissure, and proceeded to follow it, easing carefully along the jagged crevice, trying hard not to jar the utility box too much as he descended. Melanie, recalling the faces little Jeffrey kept making as he went the same route, found herself in an almost identical position. She found that amusing. She entered the slit, then, after Greg.

"Did you ever think it might be easier to reach Athena's orb from the *other direction*, the other entrance?"

"You know where it is?" he inquired. "I don't. It's up on the surface somewhere, by a shallow brook, but that's all I know about it. We'll be all right."

They soon came upon the first lighted marker, and thereafter found one about every twenty meters or so. It felt eerie watching them light the route inward, bathing distant rock walls. The markers stood as a testament to another's having come this way before them, someone who never returned to retrieve them again.

Eventually, they found themselves in the tiny passage that just sort of gradually narrowed until Greg and Melanie were reduced to crawling on all fours. Greg knew what to expect, and so he didn't need to send his light sphere on toward the break in the distant wall. He simply stumbled onto it. Suddenly, the light sphere—which he'd by that point dimmed to almost candlelight-bathed two vertical walls to either side of him. He thought he noticed a drop off ahead, and he paused.

"What?" said Melanie.

"Hold up," he said.

He noticed the tunnel ceiling ended just ahead, and so he ordered the light sphere to drift out beyond it and to rise several meters. He saw the drop off before him for sure now. It was about three meters away. He ordered the light sphere to intensify its output. His universe suddenly became one huge and wondrous chamber room, full of pinnacles and twinkling flowstones the likes of which did not exist above in the main chamber of Crystal Cave.

Glinting mirror-like just down the way and far beneath him was the subterranean lake. He crawled out to the edge of the drop off and looked down. He heard Melanie come up beside him. She looked down as well.

"That's it, huh?"

He nodded.

She drew her legs over the drop off edge, and studied the distant shore. "Do we just hop off the edge and float down?"

He smiled. "In the buckle of the belt is a tiny medallion on a strap. Fasten it around your forehead and switch the mode select on the buckle to thought-controlled navigation."

They both made the proper adjustments on their belts and then very slowly slipped their bodies off the edge. They wafted down to the rocks, Melanie steering her descent so that she landed upon a clear section of floor. She approached the shoreline, then, and looked down at it. In the distance she heard the faint plopping sounds of tiny limestone droplets as they fell from the ceiling and into the lake. Except then for the occasional ripple across its surface, the lake appeared invisible. Reflected stalactites seemed instead to be stalagmites, rising up from the floor.

She looked down the waterway. "It took the Hagertons two hours to paddle down the length of this thing," she said of Keith and Jeffrey, "and they didn't always take the correct tunnel offshoots."

Greg unstrapped his back pack and retrieved the tiny pillow size bag. He pulled out from it a crinkled mass of synthetic material, and pulled a concealed string. The inflatable raft began to hiss and expand. "I'd *love* to try one of the other offshoots they didn't take," he said of the waterway tunnels, "just out of curiosity, to see where they would lead. But we might only get into more trouble than the Hagertons did."

He pulled out a paddle and started sectioning it together.

Melanie smiled and then sighed a tiny moan.

"What?" asked Greg. "Why are you smiling for?"

She looked at him and then approached. "A raft trip down this underground lake, just you and me? . . . It seems almost romantic."

Greg grinned, pulling the raft over to the shoreline; he loaded it with their few provisions. "Shall we do it?"

Melanie looked one last time to the drop off far above her, and to the wondrous formations surrounding the lake. She nodded and stepped into the raft.

Greg pushed it all the way into the water, waded in a few meters with it and then hopped in. He began to paddle.

Melanie watched the overhead formations approach and pass at times only centimeters above her head. The Light Sphere, now having been set to hover three meters behind them and light their route forward, very deftly worked itself under or around the pointed columns.

Greg was idly rowing the boat, staring out at the pristine water, and listening to the distant plip-plops of dropping limestone solution. He felt a movement in the raft, and suddenly he felt Melanie's hands up his arms.

"Tell me the truth," she said. "Did you plan all this, hire Keith Hagerton to fake that visual, get your father's men to invent that little charade back in your apartment, just to get me in a boat down here where we couldn't possibly run into other human beings?"

"No, but I wish I did," he answered. He started nuzzling her neck.

The raft continued down into the caverns.

***

Two hours later Greg recognized the familiar landmarks from the visual that told him he was nearing their shoreline destination. He saw the huge boulder, which Keith and Jeffrey had sat atop, jutting up out of the water, and the hanging "Drapery" formations, like so many towels hung in the sun to dry overhead. He spotted the distant stretch of landfall where

Jeffrey had come ashore, once deciding to continue down when his father disappeared. Greg angled the raft over for it.

Melanie grasped his arm and nervously tightened her grip upon him.

"Yeah," he said, "we're almost there. This is where it all went down. It gives me the creeps, too."

He gave the water one last pull with the paddle and then, detaching from Melanie, moved to the front of the raft, as it glided the last few meters to shore. He leapt off and pulled it the rest of the way, parking it right alongside of Keith and Jeffrey's raft.

Melanie climbed out after him. The first thing she noticed in the other raft was tiny points of lights scattered upon its floor.

Greg noticed them too and looked up to her. He walked back to the raft and flipped the lid on the fusion pack utility box. He shut down power to the Hagerton marker beacons. The few in the raft blinked off.

The Light Sphere followed them onto shore, obeying Greg's prior command to remain behind them. The caverns ahead filled with light. Pinnacles, buttresses and draping formations of many types, shapes and colors were showcased before them. It was both glorious and eerie.

Greg took Melanie's hand, and led her onward into the caves. "I don't think the orb has returned, yet," he said.

"Why not?" she answered.

He shrugged. "It just doesn't feel as if it's here. And besides, our Light Sphere isn't acting crazy like Keith Hagerton's did with his son."

"It could mean," she answered, "this Athena entity doesn't need to persuade us to find her orb. We're doing it anyway. If it is there, Greg, are you planning to let it capture us?"

"I don't know," he said.

Melanie looked back at the rafts. She wondered if she'd ever see either of them again.

The grotto with the lone stalagmite jutting upward toward the low ceiling and splattered in glistening white flowstone became illuminated in the distance by the Light Sphere's light. Melanie noticed it first and nodded over to it.

"Uh huh," acknowledged Greg.

They took a few steps more, got closer. It soon became obvious the orb had not returned. Melanie felt relief over that fill her. She was about to look over at Greg to comment upon it, when suddenly the Light Sphere's illumination glinted off a strange deformation in a part of the stalagmite up near the top.

"Greg?"

"I see it," he said.

He took her hand again, and quickened his pace to the grotto.

"What is that?" Melanie asked.

"It looks like a crystal embedded in the upper part of the stalagmite,"

Greg only replied. "But it looks dead inside as if something inhabited it that's gone now."

Embedded near the top of the stalagmite nestled a beautifully polished crystal globe. It was as if the rock of the formation's top had been heated enough to jam a large crystal globe into the side of the thing, so that it would remain there when the rock hardened once more.

"I didn't notice it before in Keith Hagerton's video," said Melanie.

Greg nodded. "Neither did I. The light blasting off Athena's orb might have caused us to miss it. But if it's what I think it is, it was always here. We were just too busy staring at the orb to notice."

"But what is it?" she pursued.

"A resting place, maybe," he mused, "for the orb as it waited all those years for people to come down here. I don't know. If anything else, it's proof that an alien race put it here. No human would go to this much trouble to jam a crystal globe into a stalagmite like that, and especially display the final product all the way the hell down here. I need a better look," he decided.

He reached down to his lift belt and extracted the medallion; affixing it to his forehead, he glanced to Melanie. "Back in a tick," he said. He lifted off the floor, rising to where they crystal reposed in the limestone column. An invisible cocoon shield halted him as he reached out to touch the globe. "Huh; that's interesting."

Melanie joined him several moments after, reached for the globe, herself, and felt the contour of the shield. She looked over at him. "Is it alive? It gives me the shivers."

"It doesn't want us messing with it. But I'll bet anything this is where Athena's orb rests until it detects one of us approach." He turned away and faced the caverns. "Melanie, oh shit, wait a minute. . ." He faced back. "I know this. I've seen something like it before. I know I have— or read. . . ."

"Where? You couldn't have; it isn't human made, you just said so. You saw something that reminds you of it, you mean."

"No, I saw—" He thought about it some more. "Willard Somedale. Oh shit, you're kidding me!" He faced her and the crystal again and smiled a wide smile. "On Mars. Of course. In that museum! with my dad! . . . When I still just a kid." He looked at her then. "He and I were told yesterday about the abduction legends in this area. There was another snare trap on Mars, like the one that Keith Hagerton found here. Something happened to it— a cave in. And somehow the other orb became inaccessible. The alien race who built them convinced one of us, Willard, to go to Mars and find it." He nodded. "Willard Somedale."

"Who?"

Greg smiled. "Just an old someone who died about two hundred years ago. Yeah. Somedale insisted the twin of this crystal was an authentic alien artifact which he claimed he found in the rubble of the cave in. He had it mounted but never revealed who had done it for him. He tried to pass the piece off as something otherworldly, then later backed off on that claim. But the museum curators loved it so much they showcased it anyway. The dumb fools have it on display, and they don't even know what they have. I think you and I were meant to come here and see this. I know that sounds crazy, supernatural, but I can't shake the feeling. The one on Mars could be a fake, but not this one. Something's going on here."

He pointed to her lift belt. The two of them were bobbing in the air before the top most tip of the monolithic flow stone splattered stalagmite and very much looking as if they were in Earth orbit and in zero G. He directed his finger downward and nodded to her. She nodded back. The two slowly descended back for the bottom of the tall stalagmite formation and the cavern floor.

"But what can *we* do about it, Greg?" said Melanie of the possible other orb. "Say you went to Mars, and proved they were identical, then what?"

He nodded, and put his arm around her waist. He studied the crystal globe, silently. "What if we did go to Mars?"

"Are you serious? Greg, this . . . whole thing, it's . . . do you know what you're getting us into? This stuff is . . . *unearthly*."

Melanie walked back for the rafts and the shoreline. She saw what she imagined were faint signs that further up the river's run sunlight from the surface faintly found its way down to this point. Greg came up behind her.

"You made a joke, Melanie," he said.

She started to smile. "It was strictly to relieve the tension. You're going to make my pee my panties."

"Will you help me see this thing through?"

She looked back at him.

"Nothing like this has ever happened before to anyone. Melanie, the whole human race, from Venus to Pluto, is bored to tears."

"So we should consider ourselves lucky that you stumbled onto the Hagertons' viewwafer? That wasn't supposed to happen, was it?"

"But it did. If anything else, our involvement in it all has justified our taking a trip to Mars, just to verify that I'm not imagining things. I'd like you with me. It's not everyday people like us have an excuse to tour the solar system."

She shook her head. "What about your father?"

He smiled. "Dad gets to tour it whenever he wants."

She wrinkled her nose at him. "Stop joking, Greg, you know what I meant."

He nodded. "Don't worry about my dad, or anybody else. We'll be fine."

"How do you know?"

"Look how far we got, with no one trailing us? They know where we went. Someone should have intercepted us by now. But they didn't. And our phony cards have been re-entered with our correct identities." He nodded once more. "We're all right. We're far enough south already, Melanie, to be nearer to New Philadelphia than to New Allentown. I think when we get back to the surface and leave we should try for it."

She nodded, absently.

"Melanie?"

"I wish we didn't have to get back," she said. "You've never paid me so much attention before. Greg, either we're getting more and more like brother and sister or we're really starting to like each other's company."

He caressed and kneaded her shoulders and forearms. "I'd never play with a sister this way."

She smiled. "Lucky me."

Greg felt his affection for her building once more within him. He took hold of Melanie's chin and drew it toward him to kiss her.

Soon after, they returned to the lake, secured the mooring line of the Hagertons' raft to their own, and started back for Crystal Cave. Three hours later they were in the sled, heading south for New Philadelphia and for a future neither of them could ever imagine.

CHAPTER THIRTY-NINE

-1-

Frida opened her eyes and saw above her a dark emptiness. Then, glancing down to the topmost row of the arena tiers, she found her entire family asleep atop their slabs. It had been so long since she had actually been with them, shared words and laughter with them. She missed their company.

She rose to a sitting position and slid her legs off her atrium slab. She felt her chest to make sure she was whole, and in her mind saw again the *Stellar Quest* starship and its fate far beyond the solar system. She wondered what great discoveries awaited the crew in Eighty-two Eridani.

"I'll know soon," she thought. "Athena is going to take us there next."

But first Athena needed to be liberated from this membrane, and for that she needed Frida. Why she couldn't just leave, herself, was a safeguard built into the snare network by her Eleution people and their cohorts the Barthonians. It was believed that even a "voluntary" incarceration, attending to the gathering and care of over three-hundred snared humans from Earth, would wear on an individual's patience after even only a half-millennium of time passage. Athena couldn't leave the membrane, physically, she was trapped within it. In order for her to be liberated from said confinement, it would be necessary for a chosen "human" to personally "escort" her two externalized segments of herself — *the avatar orbs*— from their lunar prep facility in the lunar cave (the central mass of crystals) and return them to Athena for refusion within the membrane.

And that's where I come in, she thought. Me.

"Athena?" she called.

"I am here, Frida," came Athena's voice all around her. But Athena so far did not appear in an image form. Frida only felt her presence below and within the arena room.

"We made it back," said Frida.

"Yes, we did."

When Frida and Athena had returned to the Moon, they had stopped off in the lunar cave. As invisible astral presences they had witnessed the busy activities of all the Cassini personnel in and around the cavern's central mass of crystals.

"We have been found," had said Athena. "Randolph Phillips and his cohorts located the entry fissure much sooner than I'd hoped."

She sensed, hoped at any rate, she said, that the humans here in the cavern would soon grow despondent at the lack of real information they could obtain from the scant artifacts present in the cave. The cave's refusal, in fact, to yield any of its secrets would discourage them even more. She was confident they would soon give up and depart, allowing Frida to leave the membrane and complete her task with Athena's Earth avatar orb.

***

Frida activated her lift pack. The command medallion was still fixed to her forehead from the last time she'd used it. She ordered the belt to lift her up off the floor; the arena room fell away beneath her as she headed for the blackness above. Frida gave her mother, father and brother one last lingering gaze as they and the top tier slipped below and grew small with distance. The black of the void where Athena's essence dwelled surrounded her once more, and very soon she saw the tiny opening that led back to the lunar cave.

Frida saw a great light on the other side of the membrane. The lunar cavern lay awash in light spheres, a whole slew of them, now. She heard many voices. A life-belt-cocooned human suddenly walked past the cavity nook, only a few meters away from her. Frida saw the insignia, Cassini Base, upon his shoulder patch.

The other voices were background chatter which her com-link transmitter picked up from personnel far up the entrance shaft, and from beyond on the lunar surface. She had no real way from this side of the membrane to determine how many people actually inhabited the cave at this hour.

She felt Athena's presence behind her and turned. Athena once again manifested herself in the human female guise she had assumed before. Frida smiled. The look seemed to fit Athena's personality wonderfully.

Athena smiled back. "I wish I were able to exert more control beyond the membrane," she said, "but I currently am not. I cannot help you. You do face a danger, I won't lie to you about that."

"I know," Frida answered. "Do you know if it's clear out there, yet?"

"It will be . . . soon. When you approach the crystal formation, Frida, summon the avatar orb still reposing within it from snaring yourself and your family and make sure it knows that it is no longer required to snare any more victims below in the Earth cave, that it is time for the refusion with my total being. Tell it all I have told you about the Stellar Quest and your role in my refusion. The orb will know what to do from there."

Frida nodded.

When the Lunar cave felt to be as quiet and deserted as Frida thought it ever would be, she very carefully inched her body forward until she felt the membrane. She pushed against it, felt her arms slip through. The rest of her, she shoved through, slowly. It had the effect of slipping through two tight and overlapping lengths of rubbery sheets which she shoved out of the way.

She stepped beyond the entrance (which now seemed only a shadowed area in the bowels of the cave), and eased around the stalagmites about it. She listened ever so intently for the sounds of anyone in the area. So far as she could see, the cavern was deserted.

She very carefully tiptoed back toward where the ship lay, and after a while realized how stupid that was, because sound did not travel in a vacuum, and the only things anyone anywhere on the Moon would hear of her would be anything she shouted or caused to register over her com-link transmitter.

She approached the cavern's crystal array, marveling all the while now at the plethora of technical sensory equipment attached to it, and the ancillary equipment splayed out amid the chamber all around the other pretend formations.

"And with all this equipment," she thought, "they still learned next to nothing useful."

She shook her head.

No one could hear Frida's footfalls in the vacuum of the Moon. Unfortunately, the same was true for her. She didn't hear when security man, William Saunders, who'd been busy in a side nook of the main chamber room came over to her and grabbed her arm.

She turned and let out a scream.

A voice filled her life belt transmitter. "Hold it right there, missy. *Where did you come from?*" She tried to run. He held tight. "Now, now, no one's going to harm you."

"Let me go!" she said, squirming. "Athena needs me to do something. I have to talk to the crystal mass."

"Talk to it?" Security guard Bill Saunders glanced back to the mass of seemingly meaningless— though pretty to look at— crystals, its myriad array of colored protrusions all alit and resembling a "Winter" season holiday display. "You can do that?" he asked her. He considered the implications. "I'm sorry," he simply informed her. "I can't allow that. But I'm sure others will want to know how that's possible."

He pulled her along (which was not hard to do in one-sixth gravity) over to the ancillary equipment by the forward wall opposite the crystal mass. He keyed the base station communicator.

"I'm just doing my job," he told Frida. "Mr. Phillips was hoping one of you might turn up."

Randolph's last report on his son and Melanie Richards had them logging in at Crystal Cave. Randolph had to laugh all over again, as he sat alone this time in the radio shack of the land rover.

"They do get around, don't they, Frank?" he said to his man, Frank Kesler. There was a one-and-a-half -second communications lag between the Earth and the Moon, and so Randolph had to wait three seconds from the time he finished speaking until he saw his man react.

Frank Kesler nodded and grinned. "Oh, Mr. Phillips, I'm sorry to report I'm having a few problems with the people here in New Allentown."

"Oh?" Randolph wearily asked. "What sort?"

"Your son's boss for one, a Mr. Frank Cromwell, is pretty riled at how Greg and the girl up and left Monday. The fact that you authorized Greg an extended leave to go to Sydney only pissed him off more. He's ranting. He says he's tired of that little piss ant son of yours and his big-wig, big-shot father making his department a hell to get work done at."

Randolph grinned. "That's a problem, Frank? Ask him how he'd like being dismissed from his job. I'll have him scraping bird shit off the city walls so fast, it'll make his head spin."

"I told him, councilman, his attitude allowed no room for negotiation."

Randolph laughed. "Good. Anything else?"

"The Wilderness Society is angry. They don't like people forging level nines and leaving the city at will. The city fathers want to bring charges against your son and the girl for tapping into city computers and creating phony visas. Mayor Battini is calling for their immediate termination from Transport, and wants to send a security team out to round them up. He's not happy you arranged for their level nine authorizations. He also wants to know why you've put a lid on the Hagerton case. He says it's his jurisdiction." Frank Kesler smiled. "He says, the controversy over their disappearance and the missing vessel returning to the city empty like it did, has turned the entire city upside down. I think he's a little flustered."

"Good," Randolph answered. "Somebody ought to deport that fat asshole back to Italy, anyway."

"That was the old days, sir. Earth's a global community now. We don't do that, anymore."

"I know, Frank, but it's a damn pity."

"I thought you liked the guy, councilman?"

"Politics, Frank." Randolph waved his hand before him. "Look, you know the routine. The Hagerton case is now under the jurisdiction of the World Council, and if that asshole doesn't like it, he can file a complaint at the next general meeting. As for Greg, tell Battini: the councilman would appreciate it if he calms down. Tell them all to relax. Tell them my son's in love; he's not thinking with his head. Didn't any of them ever do anything stupid when they were young? Tell them the councilman really appreciates their continued support, and would like them to drop all charges. My son and his girlfriend obviously wanted a few days alone in the wilderness. They earned it. And Frank, from here on in, have everyone leave my son and the girl alone. Contact whomever you have to to make it so."

"Yes sir."

"In fact, if you boys are done sweeping up down there, I'd like you to take the next flight out for Cassini. I could use a few more hands on my side up here."

"You got it, councilman."

"Good." Randolph nodded, and closed down the secured channel; he motioned the radio man to come on back in, now. He was finished.

"Councilman," the man said, as he passed Randolph in the narrow corridor, "Mr. Isley's looking for you."

"What about, son?"

"He's waiting for you in the launch bay; he has a two-man prepped and ready to take the two of you up to the fissure crack. He says security tagged one of the Hagertons down in the cave. The little girl."

Randolph nodded, tapped the young man on the shoulder, and was about to head down to the launch bay, when he turned and faced the radio man. "The daughter?" he asked.

"Yes sir."

"Which one?"

The young radio operator looked confused.

Randolph smiled. "Never mind. Not important."

"Yes sir."

Randolph was gone a second later.

Most of the scientific crew, relaxing on a noon hour break in the land rover and its few attendant vehicles, were called into service with the chief administrator and Randolph Phillips. They all very excitingly slipped their forms through the narrow fissure tunnel, and hurriedly descended the shaft for the cavern.

Frida and the security man were waiting by the equipment table, and the two of them turned as the personnel began entering the room from the shaft. Frida very angrily pulled at Will Saunders's hand as he continued to grasp her wrist.

"Little Frida, I presume?" Randolph Phillips asked as he approached. He seemed in very good spirits. He looked at the security man. "Saunders?"

The man nodded.

"Good work, you caught one of them." He glanced to the crystal mass. ""Did you see where inside that pile of meditation nonsense she emerged from . . . or how?"

"She didn't exit the crystal mass, Mr. Phillips," the man said. "I was here by them when I saw her enter the area. I'd say she had to come from somewhere back there." He indicated the rear quadrants of the cave.

"But you didn't see where?"

"Not from where I was, no. She was heading for the crystal, though. She said something about this Athena entity needing her to do something with them."

Randolph turned to Frida. "Okay, Saunders, I think you can release her arm— give her a break. We're not animals, after all. Right?" he said to Frida.

She didn't respond. She didn't even want to look at him.

"We've been all through this cave, missy," Randolph said. "We've found no evidence of any hidden sectors leading to anywhere. Our instruments would have detected something. You came from somewhere down here. Where?" Frida remained absolutely stoic.

Randolph smiled. "We're very much concerned for you and your family, Frida. We want to help."

"Liar," she finally said. "I know what you want. You want to make my family disappear, take all the credit for proving intelligent life exists in the galaxy besides us humans. You can't, it's not how you think it is!"

Randolph Phillips knelt down beside her in a guise of cordiality and extended his hands, palms up. "I very much want to know, then, how it really is, Friddy. May I call you that?"

"No."

He laughed that one off. "You and I need to have a long talk, Frida. But I'd rather you and your family were all back with us and safe. I'd prefer to speak to your pop. Won't you take us to him?"

She turned away, tight-lipped.

"All right, Chief, will you have one of your men escort her topside, back to base, make sure she's in good health, that she's suffered no ill effects from her adventure? Frida, it would go better for you, a lot better—we'll treat you well and all—but it would go a whole lot better if you took a few moments to show us how you suddenly appeared among us. Is there some secret to it?"

"It wouldn't work for you, even if I told you. Athena knows who you are, Mr. Phillips. She doesn't like you."

He considered that one and then nodded. "You were going for the crystal mass. Why?"

Frida grinned. "Do you want me to show you?"

Randolph caught that one, immediately. "Only if I'm holding your hand at the time. I'm not that much of a fool, you know."

"My dad thinks you are."

Randolph heard Isley and half the men in the cavern over their com transmitters grunt a laugh at that one. He looked back at them; he wasn't amused. He turned back to her and smiled, then, that same politician's smile, and nodded to have someone escort her up to the surface.

The Geologist, Henderson, volunteered himself and took the little girl's hand. Frida let him, at least momentarily. She saw the others interview the security man Saunders and press him for any details he may have overlooked as to where Frida might have emerged from.

She considered her options. If she could touch the crystal mass, it would know immediately by accessing her mind that Athena had sent her to collect the Crystal Cave orb for refusion with Athena. It would protect her immediately and push away via repelling energy fields anyone who tried to interfere and raise a force shield around itself and Frida to prevent any further attacks upon her or it.

She would have to somehow break free of this Frank person (so he said his name was in his desire to be her friend) and make a dash for the crystal mass before anyone else had a chance to get hold of her. The last thing she would try was to head back for the membrane and Athena's lair. That would reveal to all gathered in the cavern the secret of where Athena *physically* resided. That she would not risk revealing.

So. My only options are to either go with them topside and hope Athena sends a rescue party to get me, or hope the orb and the crystals can help me. But how do I get over there quickly?

She remembered her lift belt and the medallion affixed to her forehead. She formed an image of the crystal mass, and had the lift circuits calculate the right combination of lift acceleration and course parameters.

It was a crude series of inputs from someone with no experience attempting such things, but the unit communicated to her that it understood what she desired, and told her it was ready to implement the maneuver as soon as she gave the "commit" command.

She slowed her pace as Frank escorted her back toward the angled shaft. The way back up to the surface went two kilometers. That meant a long walk, to be sure. She pretended to want one final look back. Frank wasn't sure just what she was doing, but paused to be cordial, and as they both paused for a glance back, Frida initiated the mental "commit" command, and suddenly she shot out of his hand and out of his reach in a flash!

"Little girl, **don't!**" he called after her.

His voice over the com-link frequency was intercepted by everyone present in the cave—even Randolph Phillips.

Randolph saw Frida jet packing toward the ship, and he snapped into action. "Somebody stop her!" he ordered. He reached into the outer pocket of his parka and removed his stun unit. He aimed and caught her just as she was almost upon the crystals, and going in for a landing.

Ron Isley saw him. "Phillips, **no!**" he called. Randolph fired. The blue beam hit Frida's cocoon shield around her torso, a direct hit, and shorted out the belt mechanism. There was a shower of sparks from its belt buckle and she bounced off the crystal array, head first. The lift circuits malfunctioned, careening her toward a cavern wall so that she hit it, her head and neck taking the full impact of it, her back smashing into it a second later as her body did a somersault against it. In the slow motion descent of the Moon's weak gravity, Frida's limp body wafted to the ground and settled there, like a maple leaf dropping lazily to the ground.

An ashen gray color crept across her face and complexion, and to all practical appearances she looked dead.

"*Warning!*" a droning machine-voice from her lift belt unit transmitted via com-link to all nearby receivers. *"Belt unit #91526B, sixty seconds from full life-support failure. User in extreme danger!"*

Randolph only then remembered the force field cocoons and the vulnerability of these units to disrupter beams. He was about to go over to her and check to see if he had killed her, when suddenly he felt something catch him from his left side and plow him into the protruding array of crystalline rods. The mass of crystals read him as an authorized intruder and threw up a repelling field which caught him just before impact and threw him back. Frank Henderson began beating the royal shit out of him—or tried to.

Hands came down on Frank, to pull him back.

"Frank!" Ron Isley called. "Are you out of your mind? Besides, you're not going to do any damage to him with his shield cocoon on-line! One of you men go check on the girl! Get Medical down here, now!"

Randolph slowly pulled himself up off the floor. He looked at the geologist with empty eyes. "You ought to show more restraint, Frank. I know I made a mistake. You don't have to try to kill me for it."

Frank Henderson wanted to lunge at him. Ron Isley interrupted and stuck a finger in Randolph's rattled face. "Fuck off, Phillips!" he said. "You're lucky I don't kill you, myself!"

"Those crystals recognized her. They repelled me but not her," he said. "She was going for it. I couldn't allow that. We'd lose everything."

"You may have lost it anyway!" one of the others called from beside Frida. He had a new life pack affixed and activated around her. He was probing her with a medical scanner. "She's had a massive blow to the brain stem, fractures in her neck, and there may be severe spinal damage as well." He shook his head. "She may not even live long enough to make it back to base."

"Where's that evac unit?" Isley called.

They were just now clearing the descent shaft that moment. They headed over to her and quickly assessed her medical needs. They set her in an evac stretcher, and activated the force beam restraints which would prevent undue movement in her now fragile spine and neck. The evac team leader, as he watched her be floated off and upward the shaft, only looked back at Randolph and Isley, and gravely shook his head.

"Will she make it?" Randolph simply asked.

"I may have to get Hesterbraun from Copernicus One to come out and work on this one. I don't know. It'll take some time to get him here."

"What can you do for her in the meantime?" Randolph replied.

"Make her as comfortable as possible," he answered. He looked up at the man, at his condition. Cocoon field or no, Randolph had suffered some bruising when his shield cocoon grated against his skin in the impact with the crystals' repelling field. "Shall we have a look at you as well?" the med-tech asked.

"I'm fine," he said. "Take care of the girl."

The team leader only nodded, and left with the remainder of his men.

Ron Isley looked back at Randolph, and simply nodded. "Nice work, Councilman."

"Do you think I wanted that to happen?" he asked. "Are we squared away here for the present?"

"Yeah, I suppose so."

"Then, we'll leave a security team in the area in case any more of the family shows up. I want every millimeter of this place checked. That girl emerged from somewhere, I want to know where!"

"Are you heading back with the girl, to make sure she's all right?"

Randolph stood there, pensively, and after a second's consideration, said, "My presence won't help her situation. I can be more useful here, for now. You and me both! I'm still waiting for the excavation crew to arrive topside!"

"They're finishing up on the south rim, Phillips, I told you. They'll transfer as soon as they can." Ron Isley looked back toward his men. "All right, people," he said, "there's a hidden entrance to somewhere down here. We know that now, and you're the experts. It's your job to find it. So *find it.*"

"Anything else?" said Stanley Boschovich, Isley's on-site coordinator. Isley turned back for the crystal mass and all the equipment littered about the cave. "Phillips wants the wrecking crew down here by nightfall. It won't take them long to widen the fissure. Let's start tearing what we don't need down and pack it away."

"You got it, chief," Boschovich said.

Isley shook his head and left.

CHAPTER FORTY

-1-

Frida was evac'ed by the fastest route possible out of the Alps and back to Cassini crater. Her vital signs were stabilized as well as modern (on-site) medical techniques would allow, and Senior Base Physician Millan MacCruthers had already radioed ahead to have the Trauma Unit put on ready status.

"I just hope there's time," he said to the two technicians beside him and his patient, as the evac shuttle traced across the lunar highlands and eastern fringes of the Mare Imbrium. The Alps were already kilometers behind and dwindling fast against the horizon.

"Hanson," he called to the shuttle pilot in the cockpit.

"Yes, sir?" Hanson checked the readout displays atop his board, and then looked back.

"What's the latest on Hesterbraun?"

"Copernicus is still trying to locate him. He's off -site at present. Someone took a fall from the crater ridge, busted himself up pretty bad. Looks like a bad day today for accidents. That's two of them already."

"This one could have been avoided," MacCruthers said, reaching down and wiping Frida's forehead. "It shouldn't have happened at all."

"The trauma unit called back and requested our arrival time," Hanson replied. "They said they have the whole team in place."

"How far out are we?"

"About fifteen minutes away.

MacCruthers nodded, solemnly, and looked down to Frida's lifeless body. "I just hope there's time," he repeated.

***

The Trauma Unit, with Millan MacCruthers leading up the team, worked as hard as it could to stabilize Frida's condition as much as possible. Dr. MacCruthers immediately had to go in with a laser scalpel, and relieve tension on Frida's severed spine. In the end the consensus was to place her in stasis, reduce all body functions and metabolic rates to almost none, and preserve the body until the experts arrived on the scene to do whatever could be done to repair her.

"What a pathetic mess," Millan MacCruthers simply mumbled mostly to himself in the O-R, as he finished hooking the necessary feeds.

Faint murmurs of agreement filtered up from everyone assisting him in the room.

"I'm astral projecting again," Frida thought, "I must be." She felt aloof, detached. Everything was strange to her. Something had happened.

"Where am I?"

The question seemed to drift in the air in front of her. She had only a sense of floating, like before with Athena, beyond her body, in her safe and unencumbered *astral* body, and it felt so wonderful, so free. She thought she heard people talking in very hushed tones, somewhere off in the distance. It sounded like the quiet chatter one might overhear in a funeral home or a hospital waiting room.

She glanced down from her position upon the ceiling.

"How curious!" she told herself, conversationally, eyeing the scene below her. It was a hospital scene.

The room was a solemn blue; instrumentation and readout displays glowed in red along the wall, and upon another, a huge, status graph of a human form turned in three-dimensional simulation in a long black rectangle.

"Is that a representation of *me?*" she wondered. It looked to be a diagnostic.

She recalled her having crashed into something, a something hard and glass-like, and she remembered the pain of impact. There was no pain now, and she felt guilty about that, that she could simply declare, "No, I'm not going to feel the hurt, endure the pain. I'm going to leave my body." And do so whenever it suited her.

She was afraid, however. She knew her body must be in terrible misery. She was afraid to find it, and verify that suspicion.

An intensive care unit lay beneath her, three meters from the diagnostic wall. She saw a lifeless figure atop it, supine and quartered beneath its protective force field.

"No, that can't be me," she told herself. And from this angle, covered as the little blond-haired girl was with all the status/life support equipment, it was in fact rather difficult to glean who might reside underneath it at all.

She floated down to the floor, and stood beside the lifeless face of the little girl. She nodded, solemnly. "Me," she admitted to herself, lowly.

How queer it always felt to her to gaze upon her own physical presence! Frida wondered if the dead or near dead did this often, left their bodies prematurely, or after they'd died, hung around for a while, like a faithful dog, refusing to leave the site of his dead master's grave.

She was reminded of her parents and Jeffrey back in Athena's arena room. She had imagined herself a mourner at their wake. How queer it felt now to stand vigil at her own deathbed. Her instincts kept insisting she should say a prayer or something for the soul of the poor creature reposing beside her.

"But why? I feel fine. And really, my body doesn't look so bad. So why don't you just wake up, Frida?" she called to herself.

Her body never stirred. If life did remain within it, it lay faint now and fading. A red sterilization field fluttered atop and about it, and a series of red energy beams were directed from a tri-beam unit to her forehead. She was connected to a host of life support equipment; lighted tubes, energy cables angled away from her with internal streams of red light.

She felt bad for the people who were trying so hard to save her. They really wanted her alive. A nurse entered the room, eventually, and Frida watched her go over to the I.C.U. table and check the readings on the displays beside Frida's form. She keyed, then, with a laser light pen the information into an imaging plate that she'd brought in with her.

Frida smiled to her, as she watched the woman work. "I'm fine, really," she told the nurse. "Don't look so sad."

The nurse just sighed and touched the little girl's cheek. The woman shook her head, then, and departed.

Frida left the room, herself, eventually. She didn't want to stay there beside her body, become depressed as others paraded past and mourned her body. She wandered into the other sectors of the hospital. She'd been taken, she realized, to a medical facility at some installation upon the Moon. She spied on the hushed conversations of the hospital staff, as it went about its work. Finally, she found the corridors that exited the medical wing, and as she wandered down them for what could have been hours she finally found one sector that entered upon a great observation plaza. She drifted (not walked) just above floor level, and ahead came a mezzanine or balcony railing. Beyond it was this steeple-shaped, three-sectioned glass wall that looked upon the Mare Imbrium plain far in the distance to the west.

There were hardly any stars above Mare Imbrium, washed out as they were by the reflected glare of the sun's light, bouncing up off the lunar surface. "Oh, stop," she told herself. "I have better sight now. Let me see the stars." And out they came in full stellar glory upon the sun-washed lunar soil out beyond the glass window.

She looked to all the small craters and fractured lengths of soil that marked the grayish-blue land beyond. It was Full Moon or thereabouts on Earth, and she remembered all the hours in the City Top Terrace she used to lie down in the grass up there and just watch the full moon above her, high in the zenith, beyond the city's glass bubble.

The lighting in this sector of the moon base was probably subdued to allow the lunar landscape beyond the windows to be grandly displayed. Off-duty personnel were below in the plaza and upon the red lounge chairs and sofas. They chatted idly and in low tones as they gazed out at the plain, and watched an occasional shuttle or transport bus distantly journey across the lunar terrain.

Frida paused before the railing of the mezzanine. Here, she decided (through the huge glass wall before her), was as good a place as any to exit whichever Moon base this one was. And so she simply advanced into the balcony railing, walked right through it, and found herself suddenly in mid-air again, suspended several meters above the off-duty people in the plaza.

It felt fun to be floating again, and so she arced her body forward and spread her arms, as if she were adrift upon an idle breeze. She let herself float like an apparition straight for the steeple-d glass. She melted right into it, and was on its other side as if it were nothing. She turned, as if a swimmer under water, and looked back to the people in the lounge. She smiled at them. They never even knew she was there.

Standing now out amid the cold surface of the Moon, she awed in the knowledge that she no longer had to check to make sure she'd activated her life support belt, or for that matter wonder if she could manage the lesser gravity of this new world she was on. As she pulled up and beyond the massive base facility nestled in this monstrous lunar crater, she saw mountains on the horizons.

She wasn't sure which mountain range was the Alps, which direction was north. She so wanted to return to the cavern, to make everything right as it was before by sailing on the wings of forever with Athena to the four horizons of time and space. But this session of astral projection was proving to be difficult. Her mind wasn't functioning as clearly as before. She felt befuddled. The thought that her human body was about to pass on bothered her, brought terrible distress to her. She felt real sadness, a sadness that resembled tears upon what felt to be a real complexion and face. She felt grief that she'd been separated from her mother and father, from Jeffrey, or that she might never again see Athena.

It was just a body, she told herself, and she felt fine. Why, therefore, was locating the mountain range, and the cliff face with the fissure crack so difficult?

She sensed the cause, she thought, a second later. She sensed . . . her body's life energy take a steep plunge. She looked back upon the thin silver cord— that snaked away from her astral presence, angled back to the Moon base, and to where her body as yet lay. If and when the cord snapped and recoiled for her, she'd know in a heartbeat that the end had come. She would then have "passed on." She would no longer be a living presence within all this.

Lo and behold in the sky suddenly burned the most peaceful light she had ever seen, one even more wondrous than even the sun, and unlike the sun it didn't hurt to gaze upon it. (It was a lot like gazing at a Light Sphere while monitoring a Sensor Sphere transmission.) But this light *sang*, or maybe she only thought it did. Maybe, it was only the power of the emotion the spectacle of it precipitated down upon her.

One thing was for sure, it beckoned to her. It wanted her to come; it offered her everlasting peace.

Frida wanted so much to enter and revel in its domain, forever. But she remembered Athena far away in the mountains. Frida had failed her. "I'm sorry," she felt herself call to the mountains. "I'm not going to be able to do what you wanted of me, and I'll never see you or my family again. I can't stay anymore and I let you down."

She faced away from the mountains and looked up again to the light. It was nearer now; she herself had gravitated upward for it, as if either by instinct or like a moth homing in for a flame.

A voice called out then, from the distance. And amid the mountains she saw a vague vision of a wondrous presence, a light almost as wonderful as the one above her, and just as pure. She recognized it.

"Frida," it called to her, "you haven't failed me. I knew your powers would allow me to help you, were things to go wrong, and I am able to reach out to you in this state, for you are strong with the skill to travel in this fashion. And you are strong of will; you will not expire your corporeal form so soon in defeat. I will not allow you to die doing this for my needs. Tend to your life, Frida, hang onto it; fight for it! I will find a way to salvage it for you, and allow you to yet complete what I have sent you out here to do. I will not desert you, I promise that."

Frida stood there. Her "higher self" or heavenly light tunnel" began to fade and retreat. She thought of her body, and knew to send to it the healing energy it would need to sustain itself until the thing that Athena was attempting manifested itself in the course of the next few hours.

Security man, Will Saunders, sat before the bank of ancillary equipment in front of the crystal array that inhabited the cavern's center. He was staring at it, ponderously, musing over how it had allowed the little Hagerton girl to approach it while repelling Randolph Phillips. He envied Randolph Phillips, his resolve, his dedication to what he believed in, no matter the cost or consequences. He got up and approached the pretty Christmas tree colored crystals in the array and wondered how far he'd get. He soon discovered. An invisible wall rose up in front of him, as if a glass shield had suddenly dropped between it and him. He played all ten of his fingers against the shield and pressed them into it, testing just how strong it was. Eventually, the shield tired of his impertinence and sent him an electric charge which made it past his life belt's cocoon shield and gave him quite a jolt. He backed away and seriously wanted to find a blunt object among the many articles the teams had brought down into the cavern, that he might grab it and smack the wall, pay it back for shocking him like that.

"You pain in the ass motherfucker," he swore under his breath. "Give me the chance and I'll grab a shovel and smash all those silly crystals to dust. Pain in the ass motherfucker!"

He sat back down at his security console and scanned all the readout screens.

A call had come over the com-link several minutes before from G-O-T One (Geologic Off-site Transport One.) That was the official title, of the huge land rover topside. The science team had been called to the surface, and the one other security man, Chris Farrell, down here with Will had also been called topside on some unspecified matter. That left Will Saunders all alone down here.

But he didn't mind. He'd been alone down here before, and the sacrifice— no matter how spooky it felt being the only human in this dark cave, with an alien entity hiding somewhere amid all those fake limestone formations and crystals—was worth it. He'd found and apprehended the little Hagerton girl, and had received an accommodation from the Earth councilman for having done so. He didn't feel a lick bad by what Randolph Phillips had caused to happen to her. The man was just doing his job. Saunders did feel concern, possibly even guilt, over one thing, however. He couldn't help wonder if, were the little girl to die as a result, he, himself, might be morally at fault. He took a breath, and listened absently to the low chatter over his com-link frequency. The others, he grinned, were halfway up the tunnel, and still debating what in heaven's name could have occurred topside to warrant their abrupt recall. He shook his head, and glanced again to his displays. No change in any of them.

A single Light Dog hung above and slightly behind him at a very low setting. He looked off to his right and to the far other end of the cavern, in the direction, he was convinced, the little Hagerton girl had earlier emerged from.

He took a second look! He saw something—he thought he did, anyway. Way against a wall back there, was a recessed area that seemed strangely to always be in shadow no matter how many lights shined toward it. It was thought it was an effect created by the way the formations and cave structure were set up. It was dismissed as nothing.

He thought he'd seen a *shimmer* across the front of the shadowed area. That was crazy. He looked to it again, and this time he felt his heart skip a beat. The hairs on the back of his neck bristled. There was a ripple effect upon the face of the cavity and what appeared to be a light burning from beyond it, *an internal light.*

"What's going on?" he wondered. Randolph Phillips had ordered security carry stun guns in case something unexpected occurred. Half the civilians who'd heard him bark that order had thought Randolph Phillips was a good example of why wearing side arms while on duty had been largely discontinued as a real practice for lo these many generations. Randolph Phillips was considered something' of a throwback, a Neanderthal. But the order had been carried out, and at this point Will

346

Saunders was glad. He felt the stun gun. It was on a special utility belt. (The belt and weapon had to be attached after activating the force cocoon, or else the cocoon would have molded around the gun, making discharging the weapon deadly . . . *for him*.) Will was ready to pull it should something unexpectedly shoot out at him from whatever was going on back in the cave. He slowly got up to check it out.

Fat and squatting stalagmites jutted up from the ground in the area before the cavity. Will was really nervous about all this as he approached the area. Those fake cave formations formed a sort of open-ended stall; when the light caught it wrong it was easy to imagine all kinds of ghoulish apparitions amid the weird shadows of its interior. Even now, Will thought it peculiar that this entire structure before him was made of transported and fake limestone columns. It hadn't formed here through a natural evolutionary process, but was more like display exhibits in a natural history museum back on Earth.

The Light Dog had tailed him and he ordered it from his neural scan headset to increase its light level output. It did, and the rear walls behind the front of the cavity became filled with light, and he just shook his head at his foolishness. Perhaps, he'd only been seeing things, after all. The lights had to be playing tricks with his eyes.

He paused there for a while and simply studied the rock beyond the cavity entrance. Suddenly, the scene within it darkened once more, and he turned quickly to the Light Dog to see if its light had dimmed. It had not, nor had it shifted position, and when he turned to peer back into the cavity's interior . . . the hairs on his neck bristled once more.

A ghostly specter of a beautiful woman, her gown billowing in an unseen breeze, silently gazed upon him. She said not a word and remained several meters back, too far back in fact; the back of the cavity nook did not extend that far.

She seemed to be assessing the man, mournfully, pityingly, as if she felt sorry for the man. She tried to keep a sympathetic, hopeful glint in her eye toward him, but it was clear she had nothing to say to the man. Saunders even wondered if she *could* speak, if she was even real. He was too shocked to think anything at all; he'd never seen the likes of a thing like her ever. He reached down for the stun weapon, to make sure, it was there on its clip, and then touched his life support belt to make sure its com-link circuits were on and the mikes unobstructed.

"This is Saunders!" he called into it, trembling. "There's . . . something here! You . . . you better get back *down here . . . right now!*"

"Will, what's the matter?" answered Chris Farrel, his partner, way up beyond the descent shaft. Chris was wedging his body through the fissure tunnel by this point, along with the science team.

A flurry of other voices topside answered Will. They demanded a more detailed and sensible report.

"This is Boschovich in G-O-T One," came the on-site leader from the topside land rover. "Saunders, are you *down there ALONE?*"

"Yes. . . ." he answered.

"Where's the *rest* of the team?"

"Nearing the surface."

"What idiot authorized *that?*" asked Stanley Boschovich.

"You did. . . . We all heard you, Mr. Boschovich, even the science team."

"I haven't been near the radio room in over an hour! What is this, Saunders?"

"Really, sir . . ." answered Will.

Chris Farrel voice's came over the com-link, answering the on-site leader. "That's an affirmative on that, Mr. Boschovich. It was your order."

"What the fuck are you guy's talking about?" shouted Stan Boschovich. "What's going on down there? Henderson, Chestleton, what are you people doing *topside?*"

Will Saunders was way too fascinated by the sight of Athena and her beguiling presence in the membrane to be distracted any further by the topside chatter. The "shadowed area" before him had the semblance of a drawn curtain. He ran his fingers down its length, and tried to press them into it.

"Saunders, are you still there?" came Boschovich.

Will glanced down to his com-link. "Affirmative, G-O-T. Sir, this is amazing. It's the woman. That alien woman, what was her name? I've never seen anything before li—"

A hand suddenly reached out from the other side of the membrane and grabbed hold of his! He looked back in terror, just as the hand jerked him right through the membrane.

"Holy Christ! *Haaaaaaaaaaaaaaaaaaaaaaaaaghh.*"

A second later he was gone.

***

The land rover topside and on the surface suddenly became filled with chaos as men poured into the small radio room and fought Boschovich for available space. Boschovich watched the radio man attempt to re-establish contact with Saunders.

"*Say again!* Repeat your message! Do you **read** us?"

Apparently not.

A shadowy figure emerged from the other side of the membrane. He very quickly surveyed the cavern, and with the power of his mind, directed the Light Sphere to follow him over to the crystal array. It did, and then without any hesitation (because already he saw flickering shafts of light in the descent shaft) he called to the array and identified himself. It allowed him to approach. He walked right for it, feeling it probe his thoughts, searching for it what it sought: authorization from Athena. It gave him permission to proceed; he continued forward and melted into its mass, disappearing an instant later within its myriad colors.

When the science team and security man Farrell arrived a few minutes later, they found the cavern deserted; they began an immediate search for William Saunders.

They never found him.

CHAPTER FORTY-ONE

-1-

Dr. Wilfred Hesterbraun, Ph.D., of Copernicus Memorial arrived within the next hour. German in ancestry, although he'd lived his whole life upon the Moon, he was a rather stout individual, rather wide of girth, short, with a somewhat longish shock of black hair and a goatee. He was fond of traveling in the traditional white, medical frock that people identified easily as worn by esteemed members of that time-honored profession.

He'd looked in on his patient once already, and was assembling an O-R team this very moment from among the available and quite capable talent that worked in Cassini Medical. He was tired. He'd only an hour before managed to stabilize the condition of the excavation personnel who'd almost fatally injured himself out on the rim of Copernicus. The poor man's fellow workers had only watched helplessly as he descended for the crater floor in what seemed slow motion. The sun high in the night sky, he had light all the way to the bottom. By the time he'd made impact, however, he'd accumulated quite a bit of speed. It was a miracle he hadn't died, although Hesberbram wasn't so sure the poor man would ever be the same ever again.

He'd finished his preliminaries on young Frida Hagerton. The most he thought anyone could hope for was that her vital signs could be stabilized, and eventually she might be detached from full external life support. In all probability, however, she'd be totally paralyzed, would never walk again, and with her brain stem damaged as it was, she no doubt would never regain a level of conscious thought adequate enough to even allow her to manage a few vague syllables of slurred speech. That also would be too much to hope for.

Randolph Phillips listened to all this in the background. He and Ron Isley had left G-O-T One after learning that the science team in the cavern had uncovered no new clues as to the whereabouts of the Hagertons or where their secret hiding place might be. As for the excavation crews out on the south rim of Cassini, it would still be several hours yet before they'd completed their very delicate operations.

The two men had elected to return to the Cassini base to check on the little Hagerton girl.

"Haven't you any *good* news?" Randolph irritably demanded of the neurologist. "This isn't the dark ages, doctor. Medicine has come a long way from the butcher knife technology of your ancestors."

To which the physician had only responded, "Was this your doing? Who is this man, anyway?"

His O-R team gave him a quick overview of what had transpired. He nodded.

"Have you notified the girl's family?" he asked the councilman. "They should really be here. They'll be needed to authorize the work I have to perform."

"You'll have your authorization," Randolph assured him. "Don't trouble yourself over that."

"I don't understand. Where are the girl's parents, her family? Are you telling me they are nowhere near? Surely, they're on base. What's the story here, councilman?"

"That information, doctor," Randolph replied, "is strictly on a Need-To-Know basis."

It sucked. Frank Kesler, one of Randolph's best field men, was still en route to Cassini, having departed the Nellus Space Port with his team several hours ago now. They weren't due to arrive for another hour yet at least. Randolph had to endure the brunt of this alone. He didn't like it.

"Okay," Hesterbraun said, "let's get the girl prepped and ready." Hesterbraun was notified an orderly had been dispatched and would be transporting Frida to O-R any time now. The doc nodded his approval, and dismissed the team members to get scrubbed and prepped, themselves.

Randolph was alone in the administrative lobby outside the Trauma/Examination Center where Frida reposed. He rested his elbow against the long, curving reception desk, as a nurse busied herself with various imaging tablet files on other patients. A side elevator door opened and a rather stocky and tall man appeared within it, standing behind a white, antigrav-propelled-and-levitated stretcher. He pushed it out of the elevator interior and wafted it over past the reception desk, where he stopped and proceeded to show the on-duty nurse an imaging tablet.

She asked him, "The Hagerton girl? Room B."

He nodded, gave Randolph a congenial look and then a nod.

Randolph nodded back, but couldn't take his eyes off the man. Something about him looked familiar.

The orderly disappeared into the red shadows of the facility.

Randolph smiled, pleasantly, to the serious-demeanored female behind the desk, and turned to stare down at the floor.

"If it would make you more comfortable," she suddenly said, "I can have someone call you from the waiting room down the hall when they take her in. There's beverage there, hot brew, and a food dispenser."

"No, thank you, I'll be quite fine." He smiled, graciously, and walked over to a hard-backed chair over by a wall and next to a healthy and green hibiscus. He looked across at it, and to its leafy branches.

Another gentlemen came into the room, and walked over to the desk. Randolph, from where he sat, couldn't see who it was. (He saw only a part of the man's back.) He saw the nurse show the man where Randolph was. The man turned. Randolph stood up. "Isley," Randolph acknowledged.

"Phillips," the chief administrator responded.

"Anything new to report?" asked Randolph.

"How's the girl?" Isley was more interested in knowing.

Randolph shrugged. "It's not good, whatever the outcome. But Hesterbraun is encouraged. He thought, given her condition, he was surprised she lasted long enough for him to get here. He called her a fighter."

Ron Isley nodded. "There has been some news from the site."

Randolph glanced to the nurse, who didn't seem to be attending to their conversation. He nudged the chief administrator into the shadows behind the hibiscus. "What?" he asked.

"Saunders was on watch down in the cavern. . . ."

"The guard who caught the girl," Randolph said.

Isley nodded; he paused then. "All we know is G-O- T One got a call. Saunders was clearly agitated, I believe the term that best described how he sounded was *rattled*. He mentioned seeing this Athena. She made an appearance. He requested assistance."

"He was down there alone?"

Isley shrugged. "I'm still trying to find out why. How that happened? We lost contact with Saunders. We have no idea what happened down there."

"Where is he?"

"I don't know. When my people finally reached the bottom of the descent shaft, they found nothing, no body, dead or otherwise. They did find a Light Dog over by that crystal array, but as for Saunders . . . ." He shook his head. "He's gone."

"The Light Dog . . . Did your man maybe try to mess with the array somehow?"

"There's no evidence to support that. According to the monitors, the last thing he did was head for the rear of the cavern."

"Where was his back up, the science team? We agreed to keep a full team down there until the excavators started taking the place apart."

Isley nodded. "Apparently, they got a call from my on-site chief to return to the surface. Stan never made that call, Phillips. There's no record of it, in fact, in the library banks of the G-O-T computers."

"So who made the call?" requested Phillips?

"No one knows. It was just one of those things. The crews were hallway up the descent shaft before any of them even began to question the order. They claim they don't know what came over them. Why they all just dutifully began ascending the exit shaft. I don't have an explanation for you, Phillips. Use your imagination."

Randolph scratched his chin and nodded. "I'd prefer to stick with empirical evidence," he said.

"We have coverage of Saunders heading back for the rear sections of the cave," Isley repeated. "Something must have happened back there, we're not sure what. When Saunders got about halfway, the visuals went blank, as if the cameras were deliberately blackout from that point on. Somebody wanted us to know he was not heading for the crystals at the time."

"Hagerton," Randolph nodded. "He's come for his daughter, or ME." He pondered it, then. "You better have your men keep on the lookout out there for anyone bearing his description. Your men have it, right?"

Isley nodded.

Randolph nodded back, and looked down the red-tinted hallways leading back into the trauma centers. "He may try to steal a shuttle, make his way to here and . . . he's her father. There may be an opportunity to. . . Huh," he paused, as a thought occurred to him.

"Phillips?" queried Isley. The man, Ron Isley thought, seriously looked beset by something.

"Excuse me, Miss?" Randolph called abruptly to the desk nurse. He furrowed his brow and faced her straight on. "Did that orderly head back this way, the one wheeling the Hagerton girl to the O-R? "

She glanced down the hall, leading to Frida's prep room. She shook her head.

"Is there another exit, another way out of I.C.U. for the operating theater?"

She didn't have to answer. Randolph read it on her face. To leave I.C.U. one had to go right past her desk. His face went very pale. "Aw shit, you're kidding me!" he declared.

"What's wrong?" asked Ron Isley.

Randolph started running for the Frida's I.C.U. room.

"What?" Isley called after him.

"Come on!"

Isley ran down it after him. He signaled to the sentry sitting directly outside Frida's I.C.U. compartment, and all three stormed into her I.C.U. room.

Frida was gone.

Randolph turned to the sentry. "Did you let an orderly in here?"

The man nodded. "He said he was here to take the girl to surgery."

"Where are they?" Ron Isley asked.

Randolph pounded the door frame with his fist.

"What?" said Isley.

"That was no orderly! That was a man who *died two hundred years ago!*"

Ron Isley simply stared at him.

Randolph nodded. "His name was Willard Somedale."

After taking out the security guard, Saunders, by the membrane, grabbing his hand and flinging him head first straight into Athena's lair, Willard had left the membrane himself and approached the crystal array, aware that very soon the rest of the on-site personnel— who had fallen for the ruse of being recalled back to the surface— would complete the long two kilometer trek back down the descent shaft and return to the cavern. He had to quickly call to the crystal array, identify himself and allow it to file through its memory and recognize in addition to his brainwave pattern the authorization code that told it his entry was sanctioned by Athena herself.

It located his pattern and logged it in its memory, then scattered his molecules, or more accurately it disintegrated them and him, logging the reconstruct pattern for future retrieval. Once now a part of its identity matrix he waited as the unit analyzed the report Athena had downloaded into Willard Somedale's consciousness.

The crystal mass acknowledged that it had witnessed Frida's injury, but was under standing orders to not interfere with transportees once off-loading them here on the Moon. It was in fact awaiting word from Athena to again return the Earth avatar orb to Earth and Crystal Cave. From Willard's mind, it also learned that little Frida was the one who would carry the orb's essence into the membrane for refusion. The time for that event had come.

Frida's survival was in the hands of twenty-fifth century butchers, who in the end, would consider their work a success if the girl survived their surgery. No, that couldn't be allowed, not for Frida. She was too important to the crystal array itself, the avatar orbs and Athena. Frida Hagerton needed to be brought back here, and there was only one way to assure that. Send Willard with the Earth orb, take the thing on one last off-site assignment.

Willard had not experienced orb transport in what felt forever, but the exhilaration of it came back to him in an instant. He was consumed in a field bubble and was wafted up out of the crystal array and over for the descent/ascent shaft. With lightning speed, the orb shot straight up the shaft, meeting the descending cavern personnel on their way back down, and doing so at speeds near that of light itself. They never even suspected its passing. If anything the most they would have sensed was a too brief fluctuation in the light all around them, easily dismissed as the light spheres causing changing patterns against the walls as they descended the shaft with the returning men.

Willard and the orb were out of the fissure crack and back out over the Lunar Alps in no time and soon was tracking across the Mare Imbrium plain for Cassini Crater. The Earth avatar orb found a window port close to the ER trauma wing of the Cassini facility and with a "pfffft" maneuver, it was right through the glass and into the facility. One might wonder why it didn't just enter Frida's trauma facility. Too complicated a procedure when Athena, the crystal mass or her avatar orb didn't know the schematics and layout of the base facility and owing to Frida's diminished mental state could not distinguish Frida's brainwave signature from the hundreds of other that inhabited the lunar base. That was why Willard was needed and where he came in.

Willard, from his years as an excavator/construction crew personnel, knew his way around most bases. He'd participated in the construction of the InterWorld facility on Mars, and in his day had even walked this facility here in Cassini. The place hadn't changed all that dramatically over the last two centuries. He directed Athena's orb to enter the base through the portal window already described, once peering in and assessing that it was a safe area to enter. Using Willard's consciousness "signature" as a homing device it would track his progress through the facility and when he was ready and called to it, it would show up at the right location, arriving at the last second so not as to invite detection.

Now in the medical ward of the Cassini base facility, Willard went to work quickly, assessed the itinerary regarding Frida's emergency care, and found the name of the orderly who had been tasked with taking her from I.C.U. to the O-R. He had begun a conversation with the man, and with the subtle powers Athena had given him prior to leaving the membrane, he'd simply put a hand to the guy's shoulder and watched him gently collapse to the floor, whereupon Willard borrowed as much of the man's outer garb as would fit, and assumed his duties as Frida's transport orderly.

***

What a little angel Frida looked, so much like her mother, a smooth, white complexion, small nose, tiny lips. She looked like so innocent and young for all her thirteen years, her waist length hair, golden and silky, fanned about her like the billowing robes of an angel. She was adorable.

He had little time to waste. He pressed his outspread right palm onto Frida's chest, and watched the yellow energy pass from his essence and into her own. It spread as a reddish shimmer across her entire form, and she immediately moaned. It hadn't cured her of what was wrong (he'd have to get her back to the crystal mass for that), but this would allow him to pick her up and detach her from external life support, temporarily.

She was in a white hospital gown, and her long, thin legs draped out the end of it from above her knees. He reached down to pick her up off the sterilization table, after shutting down its sterilizer beam and most of its life support feeds. She moaned again as he settled her into his arms and her head against his shoulder.

"It's okay, baby," he whispered to her. "The cavalry is here, you're going to be fine."

It was at that moment he heard people shouting and footfalls getting louder down the hall. He called to the orb. It dropped from the ceiling in a millisecond and descended atop the two of them, consuming the two within itself. Diminishing again to its normal thirty centimeter round size it again took off for the ceiling and for the nearest window out the moon base and for the Mare Imbrium plain beyond.

Not a minute later, Randolph, Ron Isley and the sentry burst into the room.

"He must also be one of Athena's captives!" Randolph said of Willard Somedale, "although like Hagerton, I'd say he was more a willing captive than a reluctant one, based on his bio sheet. There are hundreds of unaccounted-fors like him, probably being held against their wills. They've been there for centuries, and if we're lucky they're all still here on the Moon. We've a rescue we have to launch, Isley. Call your men at the site! Have them set up tight surveillance around that crystal mass. Use whatever arsenals you have on hand! We have to take command of the situation!"

"Are you really doing this for them, Phillips," Isley suddenly inquired of him, "or do you just want to somehow thwart whatever it is this Athena has in mind?"

"Are you suddenly turning soft on me, chief?" Randolph spat at him.

"I'm ordering my men to hang back," Isley said. "I'll have them observe, take a watchful stance, but I won't risk any more injuries. You've done enough damage, as far as I'm concerned. Besides," he shook his head. "Do you remember the story of Moses and the liberation of his oppressed people from bondage in Egypt?"

"I don't have time for this," he sighed. "What about it, bearing in my mind that no real proof exists than an Israelite named Moses ever even lived," Randolph replied.

"So you have heard of the story?" Isley verified. "Real or not, the point can still be made."

"Which is?"

"The Egyptian Pharaoh, Ramesses II, actually thought his army could beat the God of the Israelites. And if you know the story, you know what happened."

"Are you saying I'm Ramesses II?"

"I'm saying *God* handed Ramesses his rear end for thinking he was

God's equal. Athena's going to hand you yours and enjoy herself while she's doing it."

"I'll keep that in mind," Randolph replied.

"Quit while you still have one," Isley begged, "a backside I mean."

Randolph's pendant communicator started beeping. He pressed it. "Phillips here, what is it? . . . I urge you to be careful, Isley. You're putting your career way out on a limb irking me like this."

Ron Isley couldn't help laughing over that one.

"Mr. Phillips," came a voice over his pendant communicator. "It's Kesler. My team and I are here in the terminal. We just got in."

Randolph grinned. "Frank, it's good to hear from you."

"Yes, sir."

"You and your men get ready to shove off. We have an emergency situation in the Alps Mountains. I want the entire team ready to go in the next ten minutes."

"We can do that, councilman."

"Phillips, out." He looked up at the administrator. "You're welcomed to come along, chief, and if you and your men want to sit back and watch professionals do their job, you're welcomed to do that, also. We're going to get those people back, even if we have to level the entire Alps range to do it."

"I thought men like you became extinct four centuries ago, Phillips?"

This time Randolph laughed. "We did. The solar system's been going downhill ever since."

CHAPTER FORTY-TWO

-1-

Frida Hagerton felt herself bobbing in zero G . . . in her manger bed . . . in her family's apartment . . . in New Allentown. She'd awakened; she felt fully rested. Her sleep had been long and extremely beneficial. She felt great, re-energized, and ready to face a new day in the city. The dreams she'd had about an evil man who actually had the temerity to fire a stun weapon at her . . . *on the Moon!* She wanted to giggle at that. How absolutely absurd dreams can be some nights. What could she, a little nobody, thirteen year old girl, from a largely hick island city along the Atlantic coastline, ever do to warrant being shot at?

Yes, it had been a relaxing, beneficial sleep. She glanced down at her kitty cat nighty, and cute young, slowly developing into full womanhood legs and body turning the shape of the nightshirt from a dull straightness to the curves of a young girl on the cusp of womanhood.

She grabbed the left edge of the manger bed and in a maneuver reminiscent of being on the shallow end of one of the swimming pools in one of the spas on the recreational levels of New Allentown's City Top Terrace, she bobbed her body upward and swung her legs around to push them over the manger bed's edge and off and over it. Once that maneuver was done, she pulled herself forward till her rear end was scrapping the edge as well, and she hopped out of the bed, her bare feet and toes hitting the red and white Native American pattern on the throw carpet surrounding the bed. She padded over to where she'd evidently draped her clothes at the foot of the thing, and started rummaging through her closet and dresser drawers for a new outfit to climb into.

Once dressed, she yawned once or twice and in her flats padded her way down the wall to the living room in search of the rest of the family. When she hit the living room that was when her serenity shattered.

The Mare Imbrium plain on the Moon revealed itself in the terrace view window, and there was a rather large, strange and stocky man, napping on her living room sofa, facing away from her and for the terrace window.

Oh my God, she thought. "I'm really on the Moon," she said aloud in barely a whisper. "And this is . . . has to be Athena's Earth orb avatar again."

The image of Randolph Phillips firing his stun weapon at her and causing a shower of sparks to issue from her life/lift belt hit her square between the eyes. It was the last real image she recalled before the onset of . . . all the dreams, hallucinations, really crazy images of astral projecting, leaving a moon base I.C.U. bed and taking flight out a great steeple-shaped view window in a lounge center in this moon base facility somewhere and venturing out into the air above the sun-washed moonscapes of pitted craters and bleak, white sand dune-ish mountains in the distance, the dull, really not all that attractive land features of the Earth's lone satellite.

The man napping on the sofa heard her approach, and rose, looking somewhat weary-eyed himself after what must have been several hours of uncomfortable repose upon the sofa.

"Oh, hello, there, Frida. Are you feeling okay?"

"Who are you?" Frida inquired. "This isn't my apartment, my real one, back on Earth, is it?"

"No. My name is Willard Somedale," he said. "Athena sent me to rescue you from the butchery of 25th Century witch doctor rituals. We're lucky we got you in time before those savages cut into you even more and tried to fix you back up . . . *their way*."

"Is my family all right?" she asked.

Willard Somedale smiled, getting up off the sofa and going over to her. "I'm sure they're fine. How are you doing?"

She told him she felt fine.

"You rescued me?" she inquired.

"Yes I did," he smiled.

She glanced down at herself. For all intent and purposes she looked unscathed. "This isn't my real body, it's just an image construct."

He nodded to that. "We're in one of Athena's avatar orbs on our way back to her lair."

"Is the other one still on Mars?"

"Yes, in fact it is. Athena informs me she already has set plans in motion to recall it, to send chosen ones out there to retrieve it." Willard Somedale chuckled to himself. "I bet if Randolph Phillips thought he could launch a timely sortie to Mars, he could try to grab the other orb from Athena's retrievers before they had a chance to secure it. What the poor misguided fool would only find, if he tried it, was the orb taking out his entire sortie, even killing them if that was what it took. That man is determined."

"Was he trying to kill me when he shot me?"

"He wanted to stop you, little darling," said Willard, going up to her. "He didn't want you dead. You were leverage . . . against Athena, at least that was what he was hoping to have. Didn't work out that way."

"Why did he shoot me?" she pondered. "How could he do that? Fire at another human being like that. Why?"

"Men like him want what they want. You getting injured was what was once called *collateral damage. It means—*"

"I *know* what it means!" she told Willard. "It means when civilians are accidentally injured or killed in a military engagement, innocents who get caught in the crosshairs and are taken out anyway. Acceptable loses. He's a monster."

Willard nodded. "In some ways that he is. Actually, a throwback to a more despicable period in our species' evolution, a period we would like to think we've outgrown. I guess not all of us can say we have . . . or even want to."

"I want to hate him like you wouldn't believe," Frida confessed.

Willard smiled, wistfully. "He did stay with you at the hospital. He was worried for you. The man is not all bad. And if he's an example of the worst of what our race can currently achieve, then we're probably a lot better off as a species than we once were. At least he's not a cold blooded killer. He just wants what he wants."

"Selfish thing," she answered. "That's from Alice in Wonderland."

"Uh huh," he smiled. "That he is."

"How long have I been asleep?"

Willlard Somedale shrugged. "Hours, I don't know. Athena said you needed it after what you went through."

"But that puts the cave and all of us in Athena's lair in danger of that man going back there and doing even more bad stuff down there."

"Hours to us, little missy," he said. "Actually, Athena has all but frozen time. I think she called it one second of real world time equaling for us an hour. In space normal time, we'll be back to the cave in only seconds. It just seems longer to us."

And as if in proof of that, Frida detected the sight of several craft out in the distance over Mare Imbrium, seemingly frozen in midair. Frida approached the terrace view window and marveled at the sight of it all. "We're frozen in a single moment of time."

"You needed the time to recover," he answered.

She ran to Willard then and threw her arms around him, hugged him as tightly as she could manage for a man as stocky built as himself. "Thank you for coming for me," she said. He hugged her back. It was as if she'd never even got hurt. "They said I was dead," she told him. "I heard them around me say that the only thing keeping my body going was their equipment, but that my brain activity had stopped. I was on the ceiling, looking down at them at the time!"

Willard Somedale grinned down at her. "I've heard many folks talk of doing that before, folks who for a while were considered clinically dead. They used to call it a *Near Death Experience*. On the ceiling, you say you were? You must have been very surprised by that discovery."

"No," she replied, lowly, "I've been up there before."

He nodded, knowingly. "Heard tell of people who had that ability as well. Claimed they could travel wherever they wished out of their bodies, and to hell with them fangled Sensor Sphere globes."

Frida smiled. She liked Somedale's manner of speech, the way he talked. He was a friendly old guy. She felt she could speak freely with him at length.

"You know Athena well, Willard?" she asked.

"Sure do, missy."

Frida told him about her astral adventures with Athena to Mars and the Stellar Quest starship.

"It sounds like you two had a busy couple of days," Willard answered.

Frida smiled. "She said she met me for the first time when I was out of my body, down on Earth. She had my father take that trip to Crystal Cave that he always wanted to. She picked me to . . ."

". . . To take her orbs into the membrane with you," he finished for her, nodding.

"It's only been eight seconds," she reiterated, "since we left Cassini base?"

He nodded. "That's right."

She gleaned the presence of the Lunar Alps still many kilometers off in the distance to the north. "Can we leave this extended seconds things, and just get there? I'm anxious to get this over with, the joining of her orb with Athena."

"Athena says as you wish," Willard replied.

Immediately, the frozen space vessels depicted in the terrace view window assumed normal life again and travel speed, and the flight of the orb across the Mare Imbrium plain speeded up to an instantaneous transverse across its length. Seconds later, the fissure crack upon the face of the Lunar Alp mountain peak yawned right before them, and in no time after that, the orb was darting quickly down the two kilometer long, dark descent shaft to the cavern.

"Athena talked to you just then?" Frida asked her.

He nodded. "Yes, why?"

"Why won't she talk to me?"

"She's feeling bad for the danger she put you in. She's not happy about what Randolph Phillips did, her inability to do little more than watch from the other side of the membrane while he damaged you. You were beyond her ability to come to your rescue and heal you before you had to suffer all this subsequent stuff you went through after."

"Tell her I don't blame her."

"She'll get over it, little Frida, don't you worry over her. She's a big girl, and used to things not always going right."

The Hagerton apartment scene vanished from around the two, halfway down the descent shaft, and there was now just the two of them alone in a field bubble the size of a small spherical room perhaps no more than two meters round. At least it felt that size to them. In truth the bubble was the size of the orb itself, thirty centimeters round.

The orb reached the bottom of the shaft and entered the cavern. Frida immediately saw personnel assembled in the chamber surrounding the crystal array. The orb wafted into the cavern and descended right on top of the crystal mass, merging with its essence. And for a moment the scene before Willard and Frida was a blue misty foggy one of the cavern beyond with a sheen in front of them that appeared as a protective wall between the outside reality and theirs.

"Does my family know what happened to me?" Frida asked.

"Athena thought it best to wait until after you were safe."

Frida glanced to the room beyond. "The orb is ready for refusion . . ." She looked at Willard again. ". . . but we both have to exit and become real people again for the process to begin."

"Yes, Frida, I know that," he informed her. "I'm ready when you are."

"Is it safe out there? We'll be vulnerable at first, until it happens."

"The crystal array will protect you, sweetheart, with its force shield until you complete the process. I think we'll be all right. And as far as that lowlife who almost killed you. He was alerted to what we were doing. But trust me, Cassini Base is at least a half hour away by transport. I think we'll be all right. Frida, dear, Athena said not to hate Randolph Phillips; he's just not as far along in his spiritual growth. He misses the days when people lived for the conquest, had worlds and empires to conquer. He finds this century far too tame for him."

"And how do you feel about him, Mr. Somedale."

"Well . . ." He grinned. "Best not to get into that one. There are words I can use to describe how I feel about him that your delicate ears don't need to hear." He laughed then. "Are you ready to do it, go out there?"

"I'll need my real body," she said. "It got damaged. How can I use it?"

"Frida, Athena turned your brother into your sister. And just between you and me, he's happy over it. He likes being your little sister."

Frida grinned. "I know. I like it too."

Willard Somedale smiled. "So, replacing a damaged body with a new one is no sweat for her. She still has data patterns of you from before, before you were injured. She'll just do a pattern search and replace. You'll be as good as new."

"Then let's do this, Mr. Somedale," she said, staring forward at the cavern and all the personnel there assembled.

"Let's do it," he agreed.

They took two steps forward and were immediately beyond the crystal array, still enveloped by its external force shield that allowed no outside intrusions. Frida glanced down at herself. She was whole again, corporeal, her body brand new as if it nothing bad had ever happened to it. A life belt resided around her waist that would keep her from experiencing oxygen asphyxiation in the Moon's vacuum.

"Is there a reason," she asked Willard, "that these allegedly intelligent men and women never thought to seal the shaft and pump an atmosphere into the cavern?"

Willard laughed. "What a thing to be thinking about at a moment like this," laughed Willard. "They tried, I'm sure, but that would damage the formations Athena's people set up down here. Oxygen has a tendency to have a corrosive effect on things over time. She probably put a stop to those plans straight on."

***

About eight men and women were in the cavern and surrounding the crystal array. They were keeping their distance, though they watched the two of them, intently. Willard looked down to his life belt, and checked to ascertain that its com-link was in the active mode. He smiled to everyone beyond the crystal array.

"Hello," he said. Several light spheres hovered about the area and brilliantly lit the place up. "Don't mind us. The young'un and I are just passing through."

Frida, over her com-link transmitter, heard several of the base personnel marvel at her restored appearance. She looked up at them; she recognized Frank Henderson, the Geologist. He stood behind a bank of monitors and other instruments. He had a neuralscan headset on his head. On his face was written the word "amazement." Frida could see it on him. The last he'd seen she'd had a shattered spine.

Frida smiled, waved to him and whispered, "Hi."

Henderson looked over at Willard. "What happened to her?" he asked, over his com-link. "She was . . ."

Willard smiled. "Technology. Ain't it something what they can do these days?"

Frank Henderson smirked. "You're a funny old guy, aren't you? It's okay. You don't have to be afraid of us. We won't interfere with whatever you're going to do. After what happened, we wouldn't, even if our boss hadn't made it an official order. But hurry. We're told Phillips, is on his way. He hasn't given up yet. If he tries to stop you again, he's going to die this time."

"That won't be necessary, friend," said Willard. He took Frida's shoulder and moved her forward, away from the array as they now exited its force shield's influence. The group gave them room, and then Frida turned and faced the array.

"I'm ready," she whispered.

"What's she going to do?" Frank queried.

"Watch and you'll see," Willard answered. He nodded to Frida and left her side.

Frank Henderson heard a beep from his instruments. He glanced down to them, and then scanned the neuralscan images flashing across his thoughts. An interference pattern ripped across the com-link frequency.

Athena's avatar orb from Earth rose out of the crystal array and hovered in the air above, sparking and crackling with energy. It looked like

363

a thing to be feared, an energy ball, something that might do one serious damage if one got too close. Frida closed her eyes and smiled upon it. It rose even higher and tracked its way over to her.

Willard backed even farther away. Frida held her ground; it hovered then directly over her head, and as it did her hair began to flutter as if blown in the wind. Strands of it lifted and then spiked. Frida felt static charges snap and tingle above her head. She tensed and with her eyes still closed, held her arms beside her, fingers splayed. The fireball descended then and vanished within her very essence.

For the longest time she stayed there, as if no longer human, or as something perhaps infinitely more, and then she turned. In her eyes blazed a depth of intelligence the likes of which gave Willard (still the nearest to her) the shudders simply to behold. Everyone in the cavern, no doubt, had the same reaction. There was a sheen, a white glow upon her entire body, one that overwhelmed her life belt cocoon. She smiled then to everyone present; she looked over at Willard, and extended her hand. He took it. She led him slowly for the cavity where the membrane entering into Athena's lair resided.

Frank Henderson and the others watched her, keeping their distance, yet following, as she and Willard reached the cavity opening. They all saw the mouth of it develop a black that was completely unnatural, given the lighting in the area. They saw then, far down the blackness within it, Athena's ethereal form wax into presence in the black void of the membrane and slowly come forward. "Please don't be mad at me, Frida," Athena implored of her. "If I could I would never have allowed that to happen."

"I'm not," insisted Frida. "You're my friend."

She smiled in return and extended her arms.

Chris Farrell, Stan Boschovich and the science team all turned to one another in shock and trepidation. Sally Chestleton, an archaeology major at Cassini Technical, grabbed Frank by the shoulder. He looked over at her. Her knuckles were white. The light issuing from Athena within that cavity overwhelmed even the power of the orb entity that had fused with Frida's essence.

Athena came within inches of the membrane's presence and enticed Frida to come forward. She smiled.

Frida looked up at Willard; he looked down at her. She nodded and they stepped into the membrane. They slipped through what should have only been a shadow, dropped right into Athena. There was a scintillating explosion of light that caused everyone in the cavern to turn away and protect their eyes. And when it eventually died down, the membrane was again dark.

A few members of the science team ran from the scene. It was too much for them. Larry Canova, radio-spectrum-analysis specialist, walked up to the membrane, reached out for it and awed in its actually being a solid substance before him. It held taunt like a form of synthetic and unbreakable rubber. He tried to push on it harder.

The membrane right under his fingers began to fade and the area of the cavity again resembled just a shadow caused by the lights in the room upon it. Larry found himself falling forward into the shadows of the cavity. He picked himself off the floor and got out of there, simply turning to stare in wonder upon what they all had just witnessed.

Keith Hagerton blinked open his eyes. The archive images disseminating the travails of his daughter's activities beyond Athena's lair faded from his thoughts. Frida and Willard Somedale entering the membrane and becoming one with Athena remained with him for some time.

"Willard," he began to speak, "whose dumb ideas was it to send a thirteen year old girl out there anywa—" He looked around him.

No Willard, or Kimberly or Jeffrey, either.

He felt a cold surface beneath him. He didn't understand what was happening. He looked down. He was atop his preservation slab in Athena's arena storage room. The three hundred other humans who shared this domain with him encircled him, all the way to the floor where he again saw Frida's body upon its atrium slab. He wasn't sure what had happened. The last thing he remembered was being down in the atrium with Somedale, Kimmy and Jeff. Willard Somedale had just invited Keith and his family to access the events of what had occurred to Frida during the course of the last whole day.

Keith slid his legs off the slab, and immediately felt the departure of an energy field from around him. The slab cocoon shield dropped. He looked down at his body. His life belt was on. He felt his chest.

"Am I really awake?" he asked himself.

He saw Kimberly and Jeffrey on the two slabs opposing his own. They remained unconscious like everyone else around him.

"I don't understand," he said aloud, and wondered if Athena heard him. "I've seen what has happened. Why have I been allowed to awaken? What is it you want of me?"

The floor of the center atrium far beneath him became milky, a light glowed from it. Keith recalled Frida's witnessing the same phenomena at the beginning of her "adventure." Almost unperceptively the arena room dropped. It collapsed onto itself, becoming a blue sphere beneath him which slowly fell away. Only the light remained, and it too began to shrink with distance. He looked around him and saw that a depthless darkness surrounded him, the same one he'd entered when he'd first stepped through the membrane back in the cave.

Athena once again took form before him. "Attend, Keith," she told him in his thoughts.

Over his com-link transmitter he heard voices. He turned; behind him was the membrane and the way back to the lunar cave. Keith willed himself toward it. The membrane seemed only a flat orange panel adrift in the dark of the void. It reminded him of a mirror. As he neared it, he saw human figures within it. One in particular caused his fists to clench.

Randolph Phillips was livid. Some thirty minutes after Frida and Willard had re-entered the membrane, he and his group, with Ron Isley, arrived in the cave. First thing, Randolph ordered the science team to drop whatever everyone was doing and be ready. "We think the little Hagerton girl," he told the team, "and some old fossil who helped her escape might turn up."

Frank Henderson smiled. "You're too late, councilman. They've been here and gone."

"Gone *where?*" he spat.

Stan Boschovich approached Randolph and his team. "Councilman, I'm the man you want to talk to. Ron, let me show you and the councilman here what went on."

"That's an excellent idea, Stan," said Isley.

"I have another good one, Ron," Boschovich said. "Councilman, I don't wish to be rude, but there's frankly little for your security team to do down here now, and I'd very much appreciate you're telling your men to hang back, let my people work."

"Pull your men back, Phillips," Isley said.

Randolph Phillips eyed Ron and the on-site coordinator, obstinately. He looked over at Frank Kesler and nodded. Frank smiled and began speaking. He and his team had switched to another frequency. They returned to the shaft.

"I take it they can listen in on us," said Isley to Randolph, "but not vice versa. You really get off on that intrigue stuff, don't you?"

"They're professionals."

"*. . . professional assholes,*" Frank Henderson mumbled over his com-link, forgetting it was in transmit mode. Everyone looked over at him.

"I'm surrounded by children," Randolph said.

"You have to realize," said Isley, "hurting the girl the way you did, even if you hadn't planned on it, was reckless, and left a bad taste in everyone's mouth. If that kind of desperation is standard among our politicians, the human race is in serious trouble."

"I thought your man had something to show me? Or do all you people do is make speeches?"

"Right," Boschovich began. He pointed to the crystal array. Giving Ron and Randolph his eyewitness account of what transpired, he led them ultimately over to the recessed area way to the back where the phony cave formations created a cavity nook.

"It formed a physical membrane," he continued, running his hand across the front of the nook. "We all witnessed it. It was incredible."

Randolph listened patiently to it all.

Boschovich called to the archaeology major. "Sally, do you have a dupe made yet of the visuals?"

Sally Chestleton nodded. "I was about to transmit Cassini a copy when Ron showed up," she said. "We just now finished editing a summary." She pressed an indicator on a portable editing deck, and out of it in barely a second popped a viewwafer. "Is one copy enough?"

"It's fine," Stanley said. "Bring over two headsets and a playback unit with it."

She nodded, pulled the required items, and brought them over. "Here you go, Ron, Councilman," Chestleman said, handing them the equipment. "It won't take you long at all to get through it, and under the circumstances you'll understand why doing nothing was probably the smartest thing we did."

"Uh huh," Randolph answered her, distantly.

Folding chairs were brought over. Randolph set his down to the left of the cavity nook. He placed the headset and visor upon him. Ron Isley did the same. He looked over at Randolph. "You ready?"

The man nodded.

"Image start," called Ron.

***

When it was done a few minutes later, Randolph Phillips removed the visor and headset and glanced over at the cavity. He entered the nook, and looked around inside. Seeing nothing, he turned. Boschovich and Isley were at the mouth of it.

"Are there any residual traces of what happened here?"

"None," Boschovich replied. "We've run all the usual scans—no anomalous energy emanations, gravitational vortexes or even locally disrupted gravimagnetic field aberrations. Even heat scans show nothing at all. Everything reads normal now."

"What about during?"

He handed him an imaging tablet and a laser pen. Randolph filed through the various charts and graphs.

"Things went nuts. We read disruptions in local gravity fields, power emanations like you wouldn't believe— broadcasting beyond any known frequencies of the spectrum. As you can see here, wave spikes indicate an abrupt activity rise precisely the moment the void was first spotted, followed by the appearance of that light anomaly within it."

"Her name's Athena, Stan," Ron Isley reminded him.

"Yeah, I meant 'her'," Boschovich replied. He keyed another set of graphs from a second pen. "And here is where the readings made a dramatic down swing, once the little girl and that old geezer went through the membrane. It was the damnest thing I ever saw."

Phillips turned from the charts to face him. "And the girl was completely healed?"

Boschovich nodded. "Nary a scratch."

Phillips nodded back.

"We're not dealing with a technology so much here," said Stan, "as we are a living entity, alive in that vortex, which no doubt can subdivide itself and transmute its form into whatever shape is needed."

"Such as an avatar orb or a crystal array?" nodded Randolph to the mass of crystals in the other sector.

"Yeah."

"Figured out why, yet?" grinned Randolph.

Boschovich shrugged. "Perhaps for the sake of whatever parasitic lifeforms use it for transport."

"You mean us?"

"To an entity like what we saw, no doubt we would appear that way. We're certain the entity, itself—"

"*SHE!*" corrected Ron. "For god's sake, Stan!"

"Fine, Ron," he responded, comprehending the reprimand. "We're certain the entity, *herself* . . ." he smiled over at Isley, ". . . derives her sustenance from an unknown type of power probably stored in the crystal lattices, interspersed among the limestone formations. They may look pretty, but they have a genuine other purpose. We believe they're what generates and maintains the dimensional void little Frida and that old geezer entered. And from what I gather they don't take kindly to someone wanting to pump an oxygen enriched atmosphere into their midst, as evidenced by that crystal mass over there constantly laser blasting our attempts to seal up that shaft opening and get an atmosphere going down here."

"Yeah, well. Small steps," Randolph replied. "We're making progress at least."

"We are?" queried Stan Boschovich.

"Yes, we are. Finally. Frank?" Randolph called over the com-link to his team leader. Frank Kesler started over, as Randolph faced the on-site leader once again. "Boschovich, that notion has occurred to me too, the one about Athena's source of power, those fake cave formations, and if you're right, we have a leverage here."

"What do you mean?" asked Ron Isley.

"Frank," said Randolph again as the man arrived, "did those excavators show up, finally?"

"They're topside, Mr. Phillips, standing by on our order."

"Tell them to start blasting that fissure, and I want two men down here now with portable cutters."

"What?" said Boschovich. "I tried that approach once already with the crystals, and it failed," he said. "That collection of new-age chakra energy sticks destroyed my cutter in a heartbeat. Bringing more down here is a stupid idea. It'll just make those crystals mad all over again, or worse, *this* *Athena!*"

Randolph ignored the man's protests and looked the room over. "Frank, I want all these fake formations catalogued and removed, *carefully*. We'll reconstruct the whole of it, elsewhere, in an environment we can control."

"Now wait a minute!" Ron Isley interjected. "We've been over this before, Phillips!" he barked. "The unaccounted-fors. . . ."

"What about them, chief?" Randolph said.

Isley turned to face the cavity. "They're here, all of them, you know they are! You disrupt whatever field is maintaining the void environment they exist in, and you'll probably kill them."

"*InterWorld* thinks it's worth the risk."

"Well, *InterWorld* can go fuck itself!" Ron Isley replied. He eyed Randolph straight on. "You really are a barbarian, aren't you?"

Randolph turned to the on-site coordinator. "Your people are through here, Isley. Tell them, I want them out in the next half hour. We're going to start blasting that opening topside. I don't want anyone down here at the time. There's no telling what might happen."

"And if we refuse to leave?"

Randolph glanced over to his right hand man. "Frank?"

The man looked up from his powwow with his team. "Yeah, Mr. Phillips, we'll take care of it."

Randolph simply smiled. "We're all good here," he said to the chief administrator.

CHAPTER FORTY-THREE

-1-

Ron Isley's science team were escorted out of the cave and were now nearing the surface. The two excavation personnel around the same moment emerged from the descent shaft and entered the cavern. Frank Kesler called to them. He immediately began giving instructions. One of the two commenced inspecting the stalactite formations in the cave, surrounding where the crystal array. The other carried his portable beam cutter over to where Randolph Phillips was, far to the back of the cave. Randolph explained what he wanted, and directed the man's attention toward the cavity nook's interior. The man entered it and started setting up.

Ron Isley had deliberately lingered behind, after his people were ousted. He dared Randolph or any of his men to try to evict him. He followed the excavation man over to the cavity. He faced Randolph. "I can't allow this," he said. "I have a man in there!"

"Saunders?" answered Phillips, sighing to himself over the interruption. He faced Isley. "Are you sure of that?"

"How sure are you that I don't?"

"Short of pleading with this Athena entity to return him, I don't see what we can do about it at this juncture. He'll just have to take his chances."

There was an arc of light. The excavator had the beam cutter aimed at one of the tiny stalagmites in the cavity nook. It began to turn red. . . .

-2-

Keith Hagerton watched from the other side of the membrane, seeing the man with the cutter approach the cavity nook and begin his work.

"I cannot permit this!" Keith heard Athena in his mind report, suddenly. He turned to find her, but there was no one there.

"What will tampering with all your formations do to you, Athena?" Keith posed.

"Allow me to leave here," she answered. "But you and all the others . . . These men threaten the lives of other members of their own species. I cannot believe they care nothing for them!"

Believe it, thought Keith.

"I must preserve the void, but I do not wish to harm those people in the cavern!"

"Athena?"

"Yes, Keith?"

"For four centuries no one even knew you were down here. All those men out there are here by your invitation. Can't you just *un-invite them?* Throw them the hell out?" He sensed Athena's was considering his suggestion. "But if you do," he added, "I have one request. . . "

Ron Isley watched the light erupt from the cutter. He wanted to kick the thing out of the man's hand, but he knew he'd be restrained by Randolph's team in an instant. His men were hovering all around. Suddenly, overlaid over the sight of the man at work inside the cavity, the membrane returned and within it:

Athena looked singularly displeased. She glanced right at Randolph with a total look of outrage and displeasure. She glanced then at the technician and his work the beam cutter. There was a blue flash, and the guy and his beam cutter just up and vanished!

"Oh, shit," fretted Ron. He looked at Randolph.

Randolph glanced back at Athena.

"Ron?" came a distant voice over Isley's com-link.

"Stan?" he answered Boschovich, topside.

"We have an emergency situation up here, Ron! We've just spotted someone about fifty meters beyond the fissure crack, free floating toward the valley. He suddenly materialized before it. I think it's one of the excavation guys!"

"Can you verify that?" Ron Isley requested.

"We already have. It's a guy named Jackowitz, according to the personnel roster. We got a rescue party lift-packing up to him now."

Randolph, hearing the exchange over his own com-link, glanced back at Athena. She was very stoic in her demeanor and finished with indulging the man.

"Where's his beam cutter, Stan?" asked Ron Isley to his distant on-site coordinator.

"Right alongside of him," said Boschovich. "It's also on its way to the valley."

Ron Isley looked at Randolph Phillips. "Happy?" he only asked. And then to Athena: "I'm sorry," he said to her. She glanced to him. "This isn't my doing," he said.

Athena glanced to the distant crystal array far to the front of the cavern. She stared intently upon it. Ron Isley stared over to it; he felt in his bones somehow this was not going to be good. There was a sudden static surge over the com-link line. All at once a huge fireball of blue light erupted from the crystal array. The effect was blinding. All the pseudo limestone formations within the cavern starting shooting blue bolts of energy toward one another. The entire cavern became as if one huge dynamo generating an unknown form of energy. Ron Isley barely had time to react and shield his eyes.

Moments after, he and everyone else still present within the cavern . . . *vanished.*

-4-

Frank Henderson and Stanely Boschovich, topside, suddenly saw twenty tiny forms, and a whole bunch of machinery, materialize twenty meters beyond the fissure slit opening. A kilometer of dead space existed between the fissure crack and the lowlands before the great peaks. One by one gravity started to pull them downward, until they all came out of the shock of it and started activating their life/lift belts.

The rescue teams were ascending to them as quickly as they could. No one really wanted another incident like the one that had occurred the day before in Copernicus when that poor maintenance worker on the crater rim slipped and kept on going until he reached the bottom.

Stan Boschovich, using a pair of high-powered binoculars identified his chief administrator among the falling individuals. "Ron," called Stan over his com-link, "are you all right?"

"Yeah, I'm fine," Ron answered. "This is really weird." He looked out at the lunar highlands all around him. "I've never taken the time to do this before. I got to say, it's really beautiful out here."

"What happened?"

"We got the boot. Athena just kicked us out. About time, too."

Stan Boschovich laughed to himself and shook his head. He continued to watch his superior drift slowly downward. He breathed easier when he saw one of the rescue personnel reach Ron and help him descend to the makeshift base in the valley.

Teams from the base had reached the vicinity of the fissure and were homing in on it like a swarm of bees. "Hey!" came the voice of one of them over the com-link line, *"The opening's gone!"*

"Ron?" came Boschovich again.

"Go ahead, Stan."

"We just made a count and a facial I.D. read of all of you. Phillips is missing."

Ron Isley began looking around the many floating bodies in his vicinity. "What do you mean? He wasn't ejected with the rest of us?"

"It doesn't look that way. What do you want us to do?"

Isley looked back to the fissure crack (where it used to be, at least). The topside excavation crew, who at the time had been assessing the proper way to set the explosives, themselves had been jettisoned with the others. They were attempting to lift pack back to where the slit used to be, and appeared as if to be moving their demolition equipment into position.

"It appears a rescue is already under way," Ron answered as he observed their progress.

A purple force shield in the form of a half sphere suddenly winked into presence before the former slit opening, and everyone ascending for the fissure who was within range went flying. They were catapulted away, like dandelion seeds blown from their stem. To Ron it looked almost comical.

"So much for that," he said lowly into his com-link.

"Ron?"

"Frank?"

(Frank Henderson.)

"Yeah, Frank, what's the matter?"

"Ron, all our long range scans from down in the valley now read that the shaft isn't there anymore. That doesn't mean it isn't, it means we no longer read it as there. Which is consistent with how we used to read it before today, before we discovered it."

"It's as we speculated all along," nodded Ron. "The only reason we found it was because Athena let us."

"Athena's been humoring us like children, you mean," answered Frank Henderson. "Obviously, we crossed the line. We've been told to stay the fuck out from now on."

"And Phillips?"

"I'd say if he's still in the cavern she has some terse words for him. I don't envy him . . . at all."

Ron Isley still had another fifteen minutes at least before he reached the valley floor. He watched the lunar lowlands rise from below ever so subtly. He thought of Randolph Phillips. He wondered if there'd soon be a vacancy in the World Council. He didn't like the guy, but somehow he almost felt sorry for the poor son of a bitch.

CHAPTER FORTY-FOUR

The energy pulse had gone through the cavern like a wind storm. Randolph Phillips had no time to comprehend what was happening. It swept everything in its path—people, lights, monitoring equipment, everything. As the only light remaining in its wake, Randolph watched the blue fireball as it flung itself toward the descent shaft and slithered right up it. A faint gleam of blue lingered on the shaft's entrance for endless seconds after, retreating farther and farther up the tunnel until even it finally dimmed and was gone.

Randolph was alone and in darkness.

Ron Isley, Frank Kesler . . . they had all been swept away in the tide of whatever that thing had been. Randolph was afraid to move.

Eventually his eyes adjusted, and he began to notice an eerie light all around him. The pseudo- cave formations glowed indigo. He looked down at his feet and very faintly saw the cocoon shield as it engulfed his body. All these tiny sources of illumination did not however add up as any real benefit to him. He still stubbed his foot on the uneven floor the moment he moved.

"Frank?" he called into his com-link.

He looked down at it. The belt buckle was aglow in purple, deliberately, to indicate the belt was active.

"Belt #967321 A, reset transmitter," he called to it.

Since he wasn't wearing the medallion on his forehead, the machine had no way to communicate its response textually. It therefore beeped twice.

"Frank? Frank, this is Phillips. Are you out there? Can you hear me?"

He fumbled with the belt now and extracted the medallion. He placed it on his forehead.

"Display com-link status," he said and thought.

The image that flashed in his thoughts was: "Com- link status: active."

"Transmit mode status?"

"Engaged."

"Perform full com-link diagnostic."

"Performing. All systems nominal."

"Fine tune to an active frequency."

"Non-compliance. No active frequencies detected."

I'm cut off, he surmised, finally.

He decided to grope his way to the shaft. If anything else he'd crawl the two kilometers back to the surface if he had to. In the myriad colors of the rainbow issuing as yet from the crystal array, he found the exit shaft and sensed a rise in illumination behind him, and he very cautiously froze and tensed his fingers.

He faced back.

The cavity was full of light.

He expected to see Athena again, returned no doubt to negotiate his terms of surrender. But no, Athena it was not. Randolph turned fully now toward it; he did not approach it, however. A black shape (backlit by the light behind it, Athena herself perhaps) suddenly appeared and slipped itself out beyond the cavity entrance. The form was clearly that of a man. Randolph was almost positive he knew the man's identity. The guy wore the same casual outfit he'd worn several days before in the Washington Monument.

Randolph inched his hand into his parka and searched for his stun gun.

(Since the cocoon shield was active around him, it had been necessary for Randolph to activate it first, and then slip on the parka over the cocoon field. That way he'd have access to all the pockets of the parka. Otherwise, had he done the reverse, the parka would also have been surrounded by the field, and thus he'd have no way to gain entry to its pockets. In this fashion, he could secure the stun unit, and even fire it, without fear of puncturing his field cocoon envelope.)

He reached into the pocket now for the stun gun, and couldn't find it. It was gone.

The silhouetted figure before the light mass went up to Randolph and whacked him one hard across the face with his fist. Randolph fell in slow motion in the one-sixth gravity to the ground.

The figure rubbed his knuckles. Attempting to inflict pain with life cocoons in active mode, hurt the perpetrator as badly as the victim. Randolph, as if floating at the bottom of a pool, bobbed his body slowly onto his stomach and got to his feet. He massaged his face where the cocoon field grated against the figure's cocoon-protected hand.

"I know you didn't mean to harm my kid," came the voice of Keith Hagerton over Randolph's com-link, "but you've been reckless with that stun gun ever since I first met you."

"I suppose I did have that coming," Randolph said.

"I asked Athena to strip you of the gun, when she threw everybody and everything else out. I asked her to leave you behind, purposely."

"So you could beat the shit of me for harming your kid?"

"Because the human race needs a man like you the way it needs another outbreak of plague. You're bad news, Phillips. By now I'd say your weapon and all your men are halfway down the side of the mountain. Hopefully, the gun will bury itself in the sand, and never hurt anyone ever again. You're worse than an old west gunslinger with that thing." He pointed to the cavity nook behind him and the light mass therein. "Athena would like some words with you," Keith said. "This was all I had."

"*Randolph Phillips,*" Athena called to him, gently. Randolph squinted as he beheld her. "What is it you hope to obtain?" she asked of him.

Randolph looked to the backlit profile of Keith. "Is this really necessary?" he asked Keith.

"Can you be civil even a *little bit*?" begged Keith. "Athena could crush you like an insect. But she sent ME to reason with you."

"Tell her, *I simply want to advance humanity's knowledge of the universe.* That has been our species' quest since it learned how to think."

"Tell her yourself, Randolph!" Keith barked. "If I can hear you, she can hear you. And quit with the rehearsed sound bites, okay, councilman? You sound like you're trying to get her to vote for you."

"Randolph Phillips," she called again, "had you successfully dismantled this cave and its artifacts you would have killed hundreds of human beings who have been remanded to my care."

"You mean *taken hostage!*" he answered. "I might be more sympathetic, if I could hear it from every one of them that they actually desired their captivity."

"This is not confinement, this is no punishment. You do not understand. Speaking with you upsets me terribly."

"Really?" he answered, amused.

"Phillips, are you really that closed minded?" asked Keith. "Even if the others were not happy about their situation, how could that justify killing them . . . for nothing?"

"I wasn't sure I would kill them. Transporting this cave's contents to a location where I could analyze it, was a risk I was willing to take."

"Why? You'd learn nothing. This Eleution technology is way too advanced."

"Then, I suppose I'd learn *that*, wouldn't I?" Randolph answered, coldly.

"You really are a cold hearted bastard, aren't you?" Keith said.

"Keith," called Athena, "do not react to his words. Instead, see through them to their hidden meaning. This is his way of punishing your species for leaving behind the sins of its youth. He still wishes the human race thought as it did centuries ago."

"Is she right?" Keith asked Randolph.

Keith saw only a blur. Next he knew he was sailing in slow motion into a stalagmite. Randolph had taken a swing at him. He was coming at Keith again. The Moon's lesser gravity slowed Randolph's movements, considerably. Keith had ample time to recover and get out of the way. He did. Randolph simply bounced off the stalagmite.

Keith kicked and caught Randolph in his groin. The man fell on top of Keith, then, and the two began to wrestle. Randolph went for Keith's neck, smacked Keith's head against the rock several times, and started squeezing. The force shield might make physical contact impossible, but the shield was pliant enough to not prevent Randolph from strangling

Keith.

"You want to blame someone for what happened to your daughter?" Randolph said to Keith. "Blame yourself! You should never have sent her out here *in your place!*"

Keith kicked outward with his foot, using the Moon's gravity to propel him and Randolph into the air again. Randolph's grip loosened as he was thrown off balance.

"Phillips, the truth!" Keith shouted as the two drifted to the ground, meters apart. Randolph struggled to regain equilibrium. "Why did the *Stellar Quest* leave for Eighty-two Eridani? Just to reach another solar system, to search for other life in the galaxy, or was it something else: colonization, and tough shit for whomever lived there already?"

Randolph wanted none of it anymore. He only wanted to hurt Keith. He went for Keith, again.

Enough!" Keith hollered, backing away. "Phillips! *Athena's people* sent that transmission from Eighty-two Eridani a hundred years ago, the one that got you all fired up about going there in the first place. It's *their* solar system!"

Randolph paused. "What are you talking about?"

"You think all of this, their snare network, is just a coincidence? Come on! They're *interested* in us. They have been for centuries. They intercepted your *Stellar Quest.*" He nodded. "Yeah! They took it! It's gone!"

Randolph stood there, breathing heavily, and debating if he should take Keith Hagerton, seriously.

"It's over, councilman. Your dream of conquering the galaxy. The Eluetions won't allow it. There's a reason the speed of light exists, a reason the stars are so far away. We're not supposed to leave our home star until we've grown up. Get over that hopeless dream of yours, councilman, and get on with your life."

Randolph latched hold of a rock, and catching Keith off-guard, he came for him, smashing the stone against Keith's head. The blow sent Keith reeling, and in slow motion Keith dropped to the floor.

Randolph was beyond feeling any compassion for Keith by this point. He seriously believed this Athena was going to dispose of Randolph anyway, or at any rate never allow him to escape this prison he no doubt was in, cut off as he was from the rest of humanity. Thus, surmising all this, and feeling the rage that he did, he was about to hit Keith with the rock again, not at all concerned if the second blow killed him.

Keith, very much injured by the first blow had only time to look up and see Randolph come after him again.

Randolph went in for the kill.

He never succeeded.

A hand suddenly grabbed Randolph's parka and yanked him back and around.

"*You?*" Randolph said, glaring at the stocky old gentleman who had him by the collar.

"Haven't you done enough, yet?" Willard Somedale asked the councilman.

Randolph glared at him and raised his knee to kick Willard in the groin. Willard twirled Randolph just enough so that the knee arced through empty air and missed.

Willard released him, letting him float to the ground. He went then to check on Keith.

"You doing all right there, son?" he called.

Keith looked past him. "Willard!"

The man felt the blow to his neck, stooped over at the brunt of it, and then hopped off the ground to give him distance from his attacker.

(When Willard originally entered Athena's domain, he'd been a man in his early sixties. Thus, he may have been elderly, but he was still as strong as a horse, and the blow Randolph wielded to Willard with his fist hardly even fazed him.)

Randolph, realizing that, came after the man once more. He leapt off the ground for him. Willard caught him by his shoulders, and then delivered a blow to the man's stomach. They started struggling, and finally with his massive forearms, Willard twirled Randolph around and kicked him hard in his rear.

Randolph went soaring for a wall, colliding with it head first. It was not a pretty sight.

In slow motion Randolph settled to the floor in a heap. He did not move again.

Willard took a deep breath. His heart was racing a mile a minute. He shook his head, and looked over again at Keith. He went over to Keith, then, and did what he could to help Keith regain his equilibrium.

"Think you'll make it?" Willard asked then.

Keith squinted up at him, wincing at the pain. "I don't know. I feel light on my feet."

"Well, hell, you're on the Moon, son. What do you expect?"

Keith laughed. "You're really something, aren't you? Are you all right?"

"I spent forty years in the off-Earth construction business. Son, you can't easily hurt an old horse like me." He looked back at Phillips. "The councilman, on the other hand, he took that wall pretty hard."

Keith scrutinized Randolph's condition. "He's not moving," he said, springing to his feet. He went over to him. "Damn, I think he may have broken his neck when he hit that wall."

"Land sakes, you mean I killed him? Can't really say the world will be worse off without him."

Keith suddenly froze as a sight on the other side of the cavity membrane caught his glance. He grabbed Willard's shoulder.

"What now, son?" Willard innocently asked. He looked over to the membrane. *"God almighty!"*

In a heap beneath them was the crumbled body of Randolph Phillips. On the other side of the membrane –in Athena's lair— was *another* Randolph! The second stood and looked unhurt. He was gazing back at the two men and his own body as if too numb to respond.

Keith and Willard only looked at each other.

Randolph (the astral image of him in the membrane) uttered not a word. He wasn't even wearing a life belt. He felt the great light of Athena behind him, and turned to face her. She was calling to him.

CHAPTER FORTY-FIVE

-1-

"What happened to me?" Randolph asked Athena. "Am I dead?"

"Your body," Athena responded as she neared him, "suffered severe injury and shut down."

Randolph reached up and felt his chest. He suspected what he felt and saw of himself was illusion only. He'd died; he looked back to the cave, and to his lifeless form.

Keith and Willard remained on the other side of the membrane. They stared at him and Athena with deep shock and interest. That amused Randolph in some morbid way.

I'm a ghost, he thought to himself. He was still too shocked by the abruptness of it all to fully understand what it meant to him. He turned back to Athena.

"Why am I in here with you?"

"I rescued your life essence, Randolph; I prevented it from leaving the earthplane in the normal way Earth entities do as they prepare for their new incarnations. It would have been the end of your awareness and life as Randolph Phillips. Although that may in fact be your destined karma, I will not be the direct or indirect cause of your earthplane demise. Randolph Phillips, so long as you remain in this domain under my protection, your life as Randolph Phillips will continue."

"And my physical body?"

"It is only a vessel; it can be easily repaired."

"The way you repaired the Hagerton girl?" he answered.

"Yes. You, however, have a very important decision to make in that regard, Randolph Phillips."

Below him suddenly he saw all three-hundred occupants of this domain, asleep upon their transparent slabs. He saw little Frida Hagerton at the bottom of the concentric tiers, asleep upon a slab all her own. He suspected Frida was someone special to Athena.

"Will you remain here and join these others in the fate that awaits them, or if not, are you prepared to accept that your lifetime on Earth as Randolph Phillips has ended?"

Randolph looked down to the top tier row of slabs. He pictured himself unconscious on a new row all his own. "Those are my only choices?" he asked.

"You know that I cannot simply return you to your former life. At present, for reasons I sense you are acutely aware of, you know that I am vulnerable. You are a danger to me. Until I am completely reintegrated with my remaining segment, I cannot leave this membrane or complete my mission."

"Someone has to go to Mars, you mean, and retrieve your other segment. If I gave you my word that I'd no longer interfere?"

"You'd be lying. You live for opportunities— to gain the upper hand. I know the pattern of your mind, Randolph Phillips, and it saddens me, because for not only my safety and those I protect here in the membrane, but for your race's benefit as well, does my better judgment tell me that I cannot simply allow you to resume the normal course of your present lifetime. It depresses me to take such a harsh stand. I offer you continuance, but on condition."

"And if I consider the condition unacceptable?"

"Your life as Randolph Phillips, and all conscious memory of it, will end. You must depart the membrane as a disembodied spirit, and accept the fates that await all in your earthplane when they die."

He nodded. "Where I come from a man only gets one shot at life. When it's over, it's over."

"You know I have the power to make a mockery of that supposition."

"Which brings us back to your one condition again."

"Randolph Phillips, you persist in the sad belief that there is a future for you in the solar system and in your present time, but you are wrong. The way of life you wish to see become reality will never come to pass. You have been told of the *Stellar Quest* and its fate, but I sense you do not believe it. I'm going to share with you visions young Frida Hagerton and I witnessed in our sojourn into and beyond the solar system. . . . "

Randolph felt his consciousness sway. The membrane and Athena's presence before him blurred. He saw Frida Hagerton and Athena on Mars, in Mariner City's art and history museum. He smiled as he saw the two pause at a uniquely presented art piece, a simple crystal ball in a bejeweled, platinum cradle mount. He'd been intrigued with it, himself, for years, and always made a point to visit the history museum to stroll past it whenever he visited the *InterWorld* facility on Mars. Athena and Frida then departed the solar system. He saw the *Stellar Quest*; he saw his old friend, Mitch Katill, and the remainder of the crew, many of whom he'd only begun to get to know in the months before their ship left on its voyage. It felt strange to be seeing them again.

Four years before, when he shook each of their hands, and told them how proud of them he was, Randolph was sure he'd never see any of them ever again. If they returned to Earth at all, it would probably be years after he'd passed on.

He watched the crew of the *Stellar Quest* bravely attempt to cope with the fate that was sweeping toward them. He watched Athena's people consume the starship and take it with them back to Eighty-two Eridani.

The images cleared. Only seconds had seemingly passed, and he was back again before the membrane.

Randolph turned back to Athena. "It's true, then," he simply replied. "You have my people. Is what you told them about faster-than-light travel also true?"

"What does your common sense tell you, Randolph, about humanity's desire to explore the universe it sees above it at night?"

Randolph smiled. "Since Albert Einstein first published his Relativity theory, most level-headed thinkers have known that faster-than-light space travel is hopeless fantasy. The stars are so far away their presence at night above mankind is like a cruel taunt. The stars will always remain beyond reach. You really know how to quench the fire of men's dreams, don't you?"

"The cosmic consciousness does not desire to be cruel, Randolph. The stars are there to entice you, to inspire you. Can you not see that the attainment of your dream to travel to them will come when you have reached a higher plane of existence?"

He laughed. "Instead of a brave crew setting sail for distant ports, we'll be a legion of angels, adrift on the cosmic currents? I'm no heavenly choir boy. I'm not what you might call a helping spirit to younger races in need of spiritual guidance. Where is the fun in that, the thrill of exploring the universe?"

"You would visit them instead in proud vessels boasting colors of conquest and colonization, wouldn't you? You would imitate your Earth ancestors who sailed Earth's seas in ships of wood and sail, making for new and exotic shorelines. You would then invite the natives to enter into an alliance with you, or suffer the penalty of war and subjugation."

"What is the point," Randolph argued, "of incarnating as a human being at all, if there's no adventure in what one does, no struggle, no quest? The human race is bored to tears. It has no new worlds to conquer. We conquered them all centuries ago, when the Earth became a global community."

"Yes," she answered, "you understand the problem, but interpret it as a barbarian would. Your race must remain quarantined in its home system, and there learn how to transcend the thirst for conquest. The cosmic consciousness, that your race refers to as God, designed the earthplane universe this way that you would learn the lesson, not postpone and evade it by visiting other societies in other solar systems and inflicting aggression upon them."

"I see," he simply said.

"Surely you a man of science can see the intent behind your universe's limitations? They deliberately preclude space travel."

"You took from me my one chance to defy that limitation when you ended the *Stellar Quest*'s mission sixteen years early. It could have made it to Eighty-two Eridani on its own, you know."

"Of what use would that accomplishment have been to you or to anyone back on Earth?"

"It would have given me satisfaction," he rebutted, "to know that this Universe could not defeat me! I'd still get what I wanted, if only symbolically!"

Athena smiled and shook her head. "Randolph Phillips, the time has come for your race to leave its cradle, to enter a higher plane, to grow up. Your race has taken its enjoyment of this plane to its extreme. Like an entertainment visual, rerun one too many times, the majority who reincarnate upon the Earth have now grown bored with it. Most of your people learned in the last few centuries, on a subconscious level, why travel to other worlds was never a reality. It caused them to make peace with one another, to cease the silly bickering's of their ancestors, the posturing, the proud rivalries, and the foolishness of quarreling with one's neighbor solely for the adventurous sport of it."

"I knew there was a reason I was bored," he answered, "besides losing my ability to procreate on my own."

"That is because you resist the work you must accomplish, the spiritual work of attaining final perfection, perfect harmony, the oneness with all that is. As for the other reality, your species' loss of potency, Mother Nature usually finds more drastic solutions to a species whose numbers grow too much. Your species is fortunate that your newly acquired impotence happened at a point in your technological advancement that you could affect viable, artificial 'work arounds.' There are as yet a dozen natural catastrophes, however, that might befall and extinct your species. Anything from a cosmic collision with another celestial body, a massive seismic event or a volcanic one, reducing your species to a distant memory. Another reason why we Eleutions need to help your species move on to the next phase in your evolution. Sooner or later something will happen on your world that will wipe out your species. And you are not a species that deserves so common and tragic a fate."

"If it happens it, it happens," Randolph retorted. "Who are you to decide otherwise where our fate is concerned?"

Athena sighed. "You make me so very sad. I hope you do not require too many more earthplane lifetimes before you tire of evasion. You have so much to offer both yourself and the universe. There may be time left for you to manage a few last lifetimes here in the Earth system. The three-hundred here with me have much to learn from us Eleutions. They will live many lifetimes on my old world until they have finished with their attachment to the earthplane. When they are ready, they will enter a higher plane. Most have spent years already disembodied and within MY essence. I doubt the lessons they must learn will take too long. They are eager, all of them, for a new level of reality."

"And what about the rest of us?"

"The three-hundred will return to Earth and tutor the rest as we have tutored them."

"Well, just how long are we talking?"

Athena grinned, weakly. "I need your answer, Randolph Phillips. Your body requires restoration. I already sense some tissue breakdown. Think of your son. There is a possibility you may yet see him again, before we embark for Eridani."

Randolph saw in the blackness beyond and above the arena room the faint presence of the entry membrane leading to the cave. "Greg's a good boy," he said. "He'll do all right. . . . As long as my body's on the other side of the membrane, you don't have a hold on me, do you? I'm free to select my own fate."

"Would you choose oblivion?"

He looked down again at the arena slabs. "I'm not one of your chosen, Athena, you know that."

"I cannot stop you."

"And I won't beg you to reconsider repairing me and sending me back home."

He found himself once again before the membrane. He saw Willard Somedale and Keith Hagerton noticing him there again. He grinned to them. He faced back. Athena was right behind him. "There's one final thing I'd like to know," Randolph said.

"Yes?"

"My crew aboard the *Stellar Quest*, what will happen to it now?"

"They are on my home world, and have been given makeshift ground shelter among the ruins of our old and long abandoned cities. They are being prepared for the arrival of the three-hundred. They will join with them in the learning."

"The learning?"

"The disciplines and rituals to aid in ridding themselves of all last earthly attachments and enticements, and to soar as more perfect entities."

"Okay, then," he replied. "At least I know they have fulfilled their mission." Randolph nodded and walked all the way to the edge.

"I hope your path to your own final perfection is a rewarding one, Randolph, whichever path you choose. I'm also positive I shall know of you in the future. Though you won't remember, perhaps, I will tell you of yourself in these days."

He faced back one last time, smiled, and then pressed his astral substance against the membrane. He felt himself slowly ooze through it.

Keith and Willard watched his astral presence come through the cavity membrane. It had only been a few minutes to them since Randolph had injured himself fatally in the cavern. They still hovered as yet above his body. Randolph approached them; he grinned. "You two actually see me, don't you?"

"Spending time," answered Willard, "immersed in Athena's higher essence develops our own psychic sensitivities."

Randolph nodded; he reached down to touch his deceased real body's shoulder, only to see his astral hand disappear within the shoulder and reappear as he swept it back out again. He looked at Keith and Willard and shook his head. "This solar system belongs to people like you now. It's no place for an old throwback like me, anymore, I suppose."

"Why not stay with us, Phillips?" asked Keith.

He laughed. "Because one of us, Hagerton, would strangle the other before too long."

Keith nodded. "We'd both get the boot, then."

Randolph looked down at his lifeless body. "I made one hell of an exit," he said.

"Do you know what will happen to you now?" asked Keith.

Randolph Phillips looked heavenward.

A great and beguiling light suddenly appeared above them upon the ceiling. Vaporous entrails of it snaked down for Randolph and began to flitter across his astral form. He felt the power of it, and was humbled. He looked back at Keith and Willard.

"I guess this is it. If either of you ever runs into my son, explain it to him, will you? Tell him, I'm sorry I couldn't stick around. Tell him . . . I know I never really liked to say things like this to him, but tell him . . . I was always proud of him. And tell him . . . his father loved him."

The light encircling him from above was quite profuse by that point, and suddenly Randolph's astral light merged and became one with it. The heavenly light retracted for the ceiling, swooped right up for it, and faded away.

The cave fell into silence once more.

Keith and Willard simply stood there. Keith looked then to the membrane. He saw Athena staring at the spot on the ceiling where Randolph and the heavenly light had been. She seemed very despondent.

"Keith," she called, lowly, "you were injured in your altercation with Randolph. Your body needs care; you've both done everything you can out there in the cave."

They returned for the membrane, and when they were in and a part of Athena once more, her light shrunk in diameter within the membrane and faded until it was gone, entirely, and the cavern returned to darkness.

CHAPTER FORTY-SIX

-1-

It was late in the day, Tuesday, October the twenty-eighth. Ron Isley and Stan Boschovich had supervised the dismantling of the topside base facility in the valley before the cliff wall. It became apparent Athena did not want them to attempt any sort of re-entry into the fissure. All endeavors to breach the force shield were repelled. Boschovich had proposed several scenarios where frequency beam compatibility could be used to enter the force shield, much as Randolph Phillips had breached the shields in D.C. Park. But even when they attempted to fine tune their own force shields to match up, the fissure field simply altered its configuration. When about an hour of trying resulted in no success, the entire operation was considered over. Ground Off-Site Transport One slowly raised itself up off the lunar soil and began the trek back for Cassini.

Ron Isley remained in the area for another hour; he'd sent for his personal runabout and he parked it upon the valley floor in full view of the peak. He was expecting Randolph Phillips to hopefully appear in the fissure crack, and to signal that he needed rescuing. Or at the very least, Ron hoped for some kind of signal from the man over his life-belt com-link line. He heard nothing. Ron Isley departed for base.

-2-

The backlit Earth hung above the lunar plain as Mare Imbrium stretched away to the west. Ron was in an observation lounge in the off-duty, residential sectors of Cassini. He'd tried to sleep that night. He'd only had to get up again, dress and walk the residential corridors in his civilian attire. He'd ended up here, with a textual imaging tablet in hand, so that if he felt like it he could choose a good book to read, and try to endure his bout with insomnia.

The hour was around two A.M. Wednesday morning. He was all alone in the lounge. He wished he could fall asleep where he sat, knowing damn well by morning he'd be as stiff as a board and would ache all over. The sun-washed soil of the Moon in the steepled-glass overlook would have been an irritant, had he had to endure a sunlit scene at so late an hour in his "day/night" schedule. Cassini crater and the Alps would not be given a break from the sun for another week yet when the Moon passed its third quarter stage, and the terminator between light and shadow crept westward over the Mare Imbrium plane.

Ron, however, did not have to endure a daylight scene out the observation port. A night view, regardless of what the conditions were outside, could be created by asking the environmental computer to darken the glass surface, to match the twilight ambiance of the lounge.

He found himself staring out at the dark view of Mare Imbrium and simply reviewed everything that had happened the day before. He looked down then at his imaging tablet, and keyed it to display the next page.

Suddenly, as he read, the print faded off the screen. Ron wondered if the thing had shorted out, or if the tiny power cell was defective and had inexplicably depleted itself.

He re-keyed the on button; all at once, letters began to form and spell out words.

To Ron Isley, Chief Administrator, Cassini

Please be at the fissure crack in the Alps
By 0300 hours and await pickup. Come alone in
A small vessel. Tell no one, and ensure that
Henceforward after you no one ever returns
And disturbs the site.

Ron hurried to the flight deck and informed Maintenance he was taking a runabout out for a brief flight. Before anyone had time to press him for further details, his vessel cleared the deck and was out and away.

Ron had no idea how or why the message had been sent to him, or who had sent it, since it obviously could not have been sent by conventional methods. When the words had first began to form, the shock of it had almost caused him to drop the tablet and run.

The hour was indeed nearing three A.M. by the time he returned to the Alps location. He was before the cliff face and hovering a half kilometer from the tiny fissure. The force shield around it seemed gone again. He squinted hard in the harsh, flat sunlight for signs of someone waiting within the crack. There were no shadows being cast, since the sun was directly overhead. The dark thread of a line that was the fissure crack snaked across the sun-washed face of the cliff like a rip in the fabric of the universe, itself.

He keyed the neuralscan and inched the ship toward it, turning the vessel then to butt its side egress panel against the cliff wall. He brought the vessel all the way up to the wall and felt it bump upon contact.

Ron Isley then left the pilot station, and secured around him a life belt. Activating his force shield cocoon, he walked up to the exit door then and keyed it to open. A force shield arose within the doorframe, preventing the air from escaping into space.

Security guard, William Saunders, stood in the doorway, at the edge of the fissure, and in his arms was the lifeless form of councilman Randolph Phillips. He approached the force shield and walked right through.

Ron Isley opened his mouth in shock as he recognized his man, Saunders. He registered even further shock when he realized Randolph Phillips was dead.

Ron never did get a whole lot of sleep that day. The news soon spread via the interplanetary news services that Randolph Phillips had died. It was reported only as an accident that had occurred while the Earth-World-Council and *InterWorld*-member had been on a field excursion into the lunar highlands. The entire solar system soon learned of it, and reacted. An outpouring of shock and remorse swept through it. Randolph may have been envied, hated even, by his contemporaries and rivals, but everyone admired his drive and dedication, and his charisma.

Dr. Wilfred Hesterbraun, still on loan from Copernicus, performed the autopsy—an advanced MRI-type sensor scan of the body to officially log the cause of death.

He shook his head. "These things always did happen in threes," he told the staff later at Cassini Medical. "My father told me that when I was a boy. He said it was an old, a really old, saying. I wish to God it was only a silly superstition." He gazed down at Randolph Phillips's remains. "I wonder what the poor fool was doing when he bought it. I see evidence that the man had been in a quarrel with someone. There's another old saying, *What goes around, comes around.*"

He pulled the body blanket back over the head. "If this keeps up I'm going to put in for leave time back on Earth."

By noon that Wednesday, Ron Isley was on a VIP shuttle en route for Earth. Will Saunders had relayed an assignment: *"Find Randolph's son. Deliver what I'm about to tell you to him, personally. . . ."*

Ron Isley slowly watched the blue and night lit ball of Earth slowly grow in size in the forward viewports. He'd get to breathe real air again, he thought— for a few hours, at least.

He'd been informed that Greg Phillips was in New Philadelphia. Greg had got in the night before. Ron had known through Randolph's conversations with his operatives back on Earth about Greg's escapades with his girlfriend beyond his home city. He hoped the boy had stayed long enough in the city to hear the general reports of his father's death on the news services. That would make Ron's task so much easier.

He still wished he wasn't the one who had to take Greg the news of his father's death. He hated being the harbinger of such ill tidings. He thought the only thing he needed to complete the guise was a hooded black robe and scythe.

If anybody on Earth, he thought, requested his name, he'd list it as, "Ronald David Isley, a.k.a. the Grim Reaper."

CHAPTER FORTY-SEVEN

-1-

Greg and Melanie, after leaving Crystal Cave and the Kutztown, Pennsylvania area, had reached New Philadelphia sometime in the late afternoon on Tuesday, October twenty-eighth. They had steered the sled straight for New Philadelphia's flight deck, and at the last moment opened a channel on the sled's communicator. Greg had identified who he and Melanie were and requested permission to enter the city and land.

He'd only had to make way and allow a shuttlebus from Pittsburg to enter first. The bus had already been on final approach. But the two had been granted permission to land with nary a word of explanation. They were simply vectored in for a private-class landing bay.

The head of Philadelphia transport operations had summoned them immediately upon touchdown. He assured them no official interdepartmental hearing would be convened to bring charges against them. The man simply told Greg that had anyone else pulled a stunt like his and Melanie's, they would have been in hot water for years, probably would have found themselves reassigned to a land reclamation site in Savannah, Georgia (hell on Earth in its own right), cleaning up the damage left by nuclear breeder reactors—that old nightmare from back in the 1900s.

Greg had his father to thank, he was told. The man had ironed out all the messes for Greg. His father had also wished Greg all the best with Melanie, and had seen to it that the two had access to do whatever— and go wherever— they wanted for as long as they wanted.

"Is this the same man?" Melanie had asked

"My old man," Greg had only answered.

-2-

They got married the next morning. It was an impulse decision; they had still been in bed when they made it. Greg looked over at Melanie and asked her how she felt about marrying him. Melanie's mouth opened so wide, it surprised even her.

"It might be fun," Greg had then added.

"Are you saying you love me?"

He got serious. "I'd have killed for you, had it come to that." He nodded. "I really do. I love you, Melanie. It took me long enough to find it out. Do you love me?"

She smiled. "Yes."

"So, do you want to?"

She reached over, hugged him, tightly, and then kissed him.

They checked in for a day at the New Philadelphia Holiday Inn after the small ceremony, which they requested held in the Terrace View Park, just them and a justice of the peace. The hotel was on a level near the top of the city; their room faced the city exterior, and gave them a wonderful "real view" of the east coast. Though New Philadelphia was based in old West Chester, from way up here one could very faintly see the William Penn statue atop the city hall building in Historic Old Philadelphia far on the horizon, and behind city hall spire— though still some distance east of it— began the Atlantic Ocean, weaving across the state's old eastern border, sadly substituting the thin blue ribbon of the onetime Delaware River, consumed now by the ocean.

They'd spent the entire day exploring the city, taking in its cultural and entertainment treasures, and by nightfall checked into their suite. That was when Ron Isley showed up.

"You're who?" Greg asked the man as he appeared at the entrance.

"Ron Isley, chief administrator at the lunar facility in Cassini crater."

"You're from the Moon?"

Isley nodded.

"Has this something to do with my father's business up there . . . in the Lunar Alps?"

"In a roundabout way, yes."

"Come on in," Greg said.

"Thank you."

"How many people know about that by now?"

"News is spreading fast, Greg, believe it or not, among the *InterWorld* people, at any rate."

Melanie entered the room at that point. She'd come from the bedroom, had just taken a bath, and was in a bathrobe, a sexy one.

"Hello," Ron Isley said to her.

"Mr. Isley," said Greg, "I'd like you to meet my new bride, Melanie Richards*."

*(No misprint. By the twenty-fifth century married women had long since reclaimed the right to keep their last names.)

"Hello," Melanie said. She looked at Greg, questioningly. He repeated Ron Isley's identity to her. She nodded.

"Ms. Richards. Oh, yes," said Ron, smiling. "I've heard a lot about you. You're a whiz at memory banks from what-I've been told."

"She is," Greg answered.

"Married, huh? Congratulations you two. Maybe we can celebrate your coupling over a bottle of Chablis tonight or something. I don't know."

The man looked troubled, Greg noted. He could tell Isley's visit wasn't an entirely friendly one. "Why are you here, Mr. Isley?" he asked.

"Ron."

Greg nodded. "Ron. Why would you come all the way special from the Moon to see me?"

"Then you don't know?" he said, saddened by the reveal. "It's been on the news channels all day. I was hoping you'd have heard by now."

"Heard what? Melanie and I have been out celebrating. What's this about? It's about my father, isn't it? He's located Athena's secret lair?"

"Your father's dead, Greg," Ron answered, sighing. God, he hated doing this. "He died sometime yesterday afternoon in the Lunar Alps. He was in a fight with someone whom I think you met. There was an accident." Ron shook his head. "It's a long story, and not an easy one for me to tell."

Greg was too stunned to even move, to be sure he was in the same room, the same universe, anymore. He felt his body shuddering. "Dead? My father's dead?"

"Oh, Greg, I'm so sorry!" Melanie had whispered as she went over to him and hugged him.

Greg led her over to the sofa. He indicated to Isley to take a seat. "Tell me about it, anyway," he told the man. "I. . . ."

Ron nodded. "I know, Greg, it's hard. You've no idea how I hate to bring news like this."

Greg wiped his palm up over his eyes and forehead. He shook his head, and then looked up again at Isley. "This guy you mentioned. Were you talking about a guy named Keith Hagerton?"

Isley nodded. "From what I was told he was a party to the fight, but didn't, himself, cause your father's death. The man, in fact, who did was trying to save Keith Hagerton's life at the time. Your father was about to crush Hagerton's skull with a rock."

Greg sighed in disbelief. "Did he have a name?"

"Who?"

"The other guy."

"Does that matter?"

"I want to know!"

"I told you it's a long story. But if you want me to cut through some of it—Willard Somedale."

"Who?" said Melanie.

"You're kidding?" said Greg.

"You know of him?"

"He was one of the last subjects my father and I discussed the day he left for the Moon. The man's been dead for two centuries!"

"—*thought* to be dead," Ron corrected.

"Maybe you had better start from the beginning," Greg said.

Ron took a breath. "I'm really sorry, Greg. I can't say I liked your father. A lot of what he did, or tried to do in the last few days wasn't right, ethically, in my opinion."

Greg nodded. "My father was notorious for stretching ethics when he wanted something."

"Yes, Greg, but I think under the circumstances none of that matters anymore, and to tell the truth, I've met worse people. . . ."

-4-

Greg and Melanie put their wedding-vacation plans on hold. They listened to Ron Isley's summary of the incidents in the cave on the Moon, and the events surrounding Randolph Phillips' death.

The following morning, they made a hasty return to New Allentown, gathered some stuff together for an extended journey, and Melanie made a belated visit to her parent's home to give them the news of her and Greg's spur of the moment marriage. Her parents were both shocked and elated for the two, and hoped they would be as happy together as they were.

It was an awesome step, Melanie's father had told Greg, shaking his hand. "I'm proud of you, son. She's a good girl."

"I think so," Greg had answered.

Melanie begged her parents to hang onto Samuel, her cat, for a little while longer. She told them about Randolph's death, although they had already heard of it by then. They conveyed to Greg their deepest sorrows.

He thanked them.

Melanie told them that Greg had to go to Cassini to attend to the burial, and that as his wife she insisted on going along and paying her respects.

It had sounded quite sensible to them, her parents had answered.

Melanie kissed her father and mother, and gave her cat one final hug. She was plagued by the feeling it would be the last time she might ever see any of them in this lifetime ever again. It troubled her immensely.

-5-

Ron Isley was waiting for them down in the flight deck. He had them all booked on a sub-orbital shuttle for the Nellus Space Port in Nevada, and they would all be returning to the Moon to attend to Randolph Phillips' interment. That was the official story. What Greg and Melanie were really heading up to the Moon for was a private matter between them and Ron Isley.

Ron told them about Will Saunders, and everything the security guard had said of what existed down in that lunar cave. Ron said he purposely waited until they were all safely away from Earth and en route for the Moon to speak of these things.

Greg glanced to the tiny view portals, and saw the bright blue and white sphere of Earth blaze like a brilliant jewel in the depthless black of the night. He felt Melanie take his hand as she looked over and studied the vista with him. He smiled to her.

"I haven't told anyone, Greg, Melanie," Ron said, "about the private message I received on my imaging tablet."

Greg faced back to him on the other cabin sofa. They were in Greg and Melanie's private accommodations aboard the lunar-bound shuttle. Greg grinned. "It sounds like you made a wise decision."

Ron Isley grinned in response. "I thought I was heading out to the Alps to pick up your father, Greg. I never dreamed it would be my security guard. I asked him on the way back, *'So, why did this Athena give you the boot? Was it simply because she needed someone to carry Randolph's body all the way back up the shaft and for the surface?'*

"He said he chose to leave. Actually, Athena felt he didn't quite measure up to the Eleutions' criteria. She conveyed to him that leaving was in the best interests of all parties involved."

"Ouch," smirked Greg.

"And he didn't take offence to that?" queried Melanie.

Isley shook his head. "Saunders told Athena he wasn't ready for the afterlife just yet. As far as he was concerned the three-hundred were dead and had gone on to that great reward in the sky."

"Wow," Greg and Melanie replied, shaking their heads.

"I asked him if he'd sent that strange message I picked up on my imaging tablet. He said it was Athena, herself, who sent it to me."

"She has that much power?" said Greg.

"She's extended herself, Greg, all the way to Mars. I'd say, even incomplete as Saunders claims she is, she has powers. Receiving that text from her liked to scare the shit out of me, I'll tell you that much. I thought at first, when the words started appearing on my reader, that it was the dead trying to communicate with the living. . . . Anyway, Saunders also said this Athena entity knew you had been to Crystal Cave. You found something there you didn't expect to. She said you knew where its mate on Mars was. You'd seen it before. She wanted you to go talk to it. She said you'd know what that was all about."

"I have a pretty good idea," Greg replied. "Dad wanted his remains spread over the Mariner Valley canyon, so I was going there anyway. It's really funny sometimes how things work out, isn't it?"

"Yeah." Ron nodded, cynically. "A fucking riot. . . . Pardon my language. After all I've seen in the last few days I'm kind of burned out, if you can understand that." He clearly didn't find the irony of it all amusing in even the slightest bit. "This Athena gave Saunders some instructions for you for when you got to Mars," he continued.

"She did?" answered Greg.

"Yes."

Ron Isley proceeded to tell them what they were. The shuttle, meanwhile, continued its leisurely voyage to the Moon.

CHAPTER FORTY-EIGHT

A Scoutcraft journeyed across the long trench that was Valles Marineris (Mariner Valley). Longer than the United States in length, the valley was the planet Mars's answer to Earth's Grand Canyon. The extended troughs that comprised the trench were thought to have been formed by Mars quakes, seismic events that long ago ripped the surface open, allowing internal stress to bleed off.

Greg Phillips didn't care how the trenches came to be here, nor was he flying over them to simply enjoy the view. In his father's early years at the *InterWorld* facility here on Mars, Randolph Phillips had gone hiking in the canyon. He'd spent many a night camped out on its rim, gazing up at the stars, and dreaming of explorations to unknown worlds in distant solar systems. It was Randolph Phillips's wish to have his ashes laid to rest here within the canyon, and Greg was here to honor that request.

It was Tuesday, November forth. Six days had passed since he'd got the news of his father's death way back on Earth— eighty million kilometers back in the direction of the sun. That fact alone had an impact on his sanity. He wasn't used to traveling much at all beyond the cities of Earth, and here now in the last week he'd been to the Moon and the planet Mars. His body's biorhythms had not yet adjusted to the time and environment changes. People still called it JET-LAG, although no one really bothered to question the origin of the term.

-3-

Randolph Phillips had wished his remains ritually cremated, which was his right to request, as opposed to their simply being incinerated and then disposed of. With Melanie and a few of Randolph's closest friends and associates flown in from Earth and other ports on the Moon in attendance with Greg, he had seen the ceremony performed at the moonbase in Cassini crater.

Greg and Melanie then booked Randolph's ashes and themselves onto an out-going supply ship, and promised the officials at the *InterWorld* headquarters on Mars that he and Melanie would arrive in plenty of time to attend the memorial service slated to be held in Randolph's honor the following Monday.

The ship arrived on Mars and in Mariner City late Friday afternoon (New Allentown time). Early Monday morning, the memorial got off on schedule, and Greg was asked to say a few words in his father's behalf.

***

"I never got to know my dad as well as I would have like to," he'd begun. "I was even mad at him for what I thought he was going to allow to happen to me and my new bride. I never thought my father really cared about anybody but himself. Then, I learned about everything he had arranged for my wife and me, and the good things he'd said of our relationship, and I felt terrible and guilty. My only consolation is that I didn't start feeling animosity toward him until *after* he left for his destiny on the Moon.

"My father never knew, then, that I started to question his love for me. And you never really appreciate what you have until it's gone. When I saw him last, he and I were the best we'd ever been together in all the time I knew him. We'd just come from one of the strangest experiences either of us had ever had. Some of you may know of it. It was in D.C. Park."

Greg paused to remember the quiet time they had shared in the air car as it drifted downstream on the Potomac, and the walk across the park grounds for the Washington Monument. First he started to smile, and then felt tears begin to well up in his eyes. He took a breath and did his best to continue.

"My father felt out of place, bored, in the twenty-fifth century. A lot of us feel boredom, but not the same kind Randolph Phillips did. Some may fault him for that. Dad worshipped the more adventurous times of our race's past; he couldn't reconcile the cultural advances that our race has experienced since the start of this then new millennium over five-hundred years ago. He had high hopes for the *Stellar Quest,* even though he knew the mission was a dubious one. He knew we might never hear from its crew, or if we did, couldn't do much with the communication once it arrived. It would take twenty years before their first messages reached us, and another twenty after that before ours reached them. We'd all be in our graves before the signals finished walking back and forth across the galaxy.

"I think, had he been younger or free to, he'd even have gone with them. Theirs was the ultimate adventure, to explore the far horizons and learn what was out there.

"My dad. I loved him. I didn't always say so in so many words, and didn't always believe it. It troubled me that I could never measure up to him, his accomplishments. As much as I admired the man, I envied him. Wherever my father is today, I hope he has found peace. . . ."

-4-

A signal alert flashed in Greg's mind from the neuralscan unit. He was approaching the spot along the long Martian canyon that his father most especially loved, and had camped out at on several occasions. Greg would be over the coordinates in another minute.

He acknowledged the navigation alert and glanced to the eastern rim for a place to set down. He angled the tiny vessel over to it.

Greg landed the ship by a clearing about fifty meters beyond the rim of the canyon. Having secured his life belt, he stepped out onto the red soil of Mars, the small container with his father's ashes in hand.

Greg walked all the way to the canyon rim, opened the canister, and stared for a long time at its mouth. He took a breath, finally, and emptied the ashes into the air. They wafted downward for the canyon floor, almost six kilometers below.

"Goodbye Dad," he whispered.

CHAPTER FORTY-NINE

-1-

"He was a good man, Greg," said a voice over Greg's com-link as he returned to the scout ship. Greg looked up and saw a second vehicle parked alongside his own.

Mr. Alfred Winfry, African-American in origin and chairman of the entire *InterWorld* membership, was outside his runabout and smiled as he saw Greg look up. He was a man in his mid-fifties, on the stocky side, but not really obese—hairless except for a few remaining strands on the sides around his ears, and had a very congenial, but business-like air about him. He came from tough stock, so it was said. His family was originally from the poorer and black sections of the old land-based Camden City in New Jersey.

"Mr. Chairman," said Greg, reaching him and extending his hand, "why are you out here?"

Alfred Winfry looked up at the red sky and squinted. "The same reason as you— to pay my last respects." He glanced to the empty container Greg held onto. "You made your peace with old Randolph, I take it?"

Greg nodded. "He's where he wanted to spend eternity, if he had to remain trapped here in the solar system. He never could stand life on Earth."

"I came out here with him once in a while," said Winfry, "camped out, and gazed up at the galaxy. What you said last night about him was right, Greg. Randolph Phillips wanted to be up there, a starship captain, a real one, not like Katill and the *Stellar Quest*. That ship is no real interstellar vessel. The *Stellar Quest* is more like a rusting old barge being dragged upriver by a tug."

"You sound cynical," said Greg.

"It's not my idea of what travel through the stars should be like." Winfry grinned. "That was a nice eulogy you gave for your father, Greg."

"Thank you, but I can't believe you came all the way out here just to tell me that."

Winfry smiled. "I didn't always see eye to eye with Randolph on everything, but he was well-liked in the membership. People always used to wonder where he found the ambition to be both a part of *InterWorld* and also a high ranking member of Earth's World Council."

Greg smiled. "My father once referred to himself as what was once called a type-A personality. Type A's, he said, were always on the go, they couldn't sit still, were overambitious."

"And what about you, Greg?"

"I envied him for what he could accomplish. . . . I don't anymore, though. I've seen what too much power can do to a person, how it can go to a person's head, muddy his outlook on humanity. I'm actually happy doing what I do on Earth."

"Working as a clerk in transport?"

Greg studied the man. "You keep informed, I see."

He smiled. "Your father's an old friend. I knew you when you were this high." He leveled his palm around his kneecap.

"I remember," answered Greg, wistfully.

"What do you know about this Lunar Alps affair, Greg?"

"What do you mean?"

"Well, from the sketchy reports I've received from the Moon." He shook his head. "There was some mean stuff going on in those mountains."

Greg shrugged his shoulders. "My dad kept me out of it, once he left Earth. I really don't know what went on up there."

"A Mr. Ronald Isley flew all the way to Earth to tell you about your father, didn't he?"

Greg nodded. "You are informed."

"Why did he do that, Greg?"

"I don't know why. Out of respect to my father, maybe. I was my dad's only offspring."

"Well, you see, Greg, the problem is that Mr. Isley and his staff at Cassini haven't exactly been open about what went on down there. The details that surrounded their attempts to find where the orb went are almost nil. I hoped maybe you could shed some light on the situation."

"I see," Greg answered. Now he knew why the man was here. "How?"

"Your father's men went back to the cave in Pennsylvania to investigate the site where the Hagertons found the orb. A Mr. Frank Kesler sent the images on to your father—the only copies, as I now understand it. What happened to them?"

Greg shrugged. "I never even knew to ask Mr. Isley about them when I went through my father's things at Cassini."

"Recorded on the visuals, Greg, was supposed to be evidence of some strange artifact in the caves, according to Randolph's field agents. The reports got forwarded to us. With the visuals gone, though, we can't substantiate that report, and subsequent trips to Pennsylvania in the last week reveal there's nothing down there."

That news stunned Greg for a second, but he covered the surprise of it as well as he could. He didn't think the man noticed.

"Well," Greg answered, "all I saw was a weird ball of energy, I think they used to call that heat lightning in olden times."

"Heat lightning?" the man inquired. "Are you purposely trying to downplay the whole thing?"

Greg shrugged. "Wouldn't you?"

Alfred Winfry took a breath. "There are reports, Greg, that you re-entered Crystal Cave the day after your father's men did."

"Melanie and I did return there. That's public record."

"Well, did you see anything or not?"

Greg smiled and then shrugged his shoulders again. "Where specifically in the cave would you mean?"

"You tell me."

"Mr. Winfry, this is very much beginning to feel like an interrogation. What is it you want from me?"

"I want to know what you saw down there."

"I saw exactly what your teams saw—nothing. Really, I don't know what Kesler and his men told you, but I didn't see anything but limestone."

"And you have no idea where the visuals your father received got to?"

"No."

The man nodded, pensively. "I've had the opportunity to obtain copies of your father's visuals from D.C. Park, the night you and he met the Hagertons atop the monument. But there was also the Hagertons' visuals from the cave—even you just now alluded to them."

Greg nodded; "Keith Hagerton managed to get them back. Believe me, Mr. Winfry, how he did it is a very long story, and I'm sure you know most of the details by now."

"I was told, Greg, that you made a safe copy of the visuals."

Greg smiled. "I did, but in the hustle of leaving Earth, it accidentally got ruined. It's totally unplayable."

"Greg, what happened in the Alps? There are rumors of a place where humans have been held captive for four-hundred years, and rumors that they've been heisted not only from that cave you found in Pennsylvania, but from right here in Mariner Valley. I've actually scanned news reports of people visiting here in Mariner City who suddenly turned up missing, and no one could explain how it happened."

"Once again, Mr. Winfry, you're asking someone who never got that involved in my father's investigations into all this. I haven't been to these Lunar Alps. I don't know."

"And you aren't aware, then, that a security guard from Cassini is rumored to have become a temporary member of that abducted bunch and was later released?"

"Yes, I am aware of that, but only because Mr. Isley was quite open on the subject, while my wife and I accompanied him back to the Moon. I take it you're planning an investigation of your own?"

"If we make the attempt it may be too late by the time we're able to initiate it. Greg, what I need from you is information I believe would help us buy time, allow us to delay this rumored departure from the cave that this entity is alleged to reside in, and figure out how to break through that shield that supposedly is blocking the way back down to that cavern. I'm having trouble believing you came up here to Mariner City simply to pay your last respects to your father."

"I had a choice," Greg answered. "*InterWorld* was holding a memorial to my father on Mars, and Earth's World Council was holding one the same day on Earth." He shrugged. "I couldn't be both places, and besides I had to spread my father's ashes in the canyon. Space exploration, Mr. Winfry, not Earth politics, was my father's first love. I chose to come to Mars. I've always wanted to return here, in fact, since I was a kid. I really don't see where I have to justify my motivations to you or to anyone. If you'll excuse me, my wife is waiting for me back in the city."

"You *are* your father's son, Greg," Melanie concluded later over communications as Greg called her from the runabout. He'd been airborne near a half hour by then, and in his rear scanners he could find no trace of the *InterWorld* chairman. Greg had apparently taken another route back. He finished telling Melanie about his talk with Alfred Winfry.

"Randolph Phillips would have been proud of you, Greg," she continued. "You bend the truth probably as well as he ever did. Are you sure you're not interested in petitioning for his seat in the council?"

"Don't be mean," he begged, "I've had a rough morning. It's been hard enough as it is these last few days, deliberately steering clear of the museum complex, to not bring suspicion to what we're really here for. Melanie, do you think you might take one of the tours through the museum to verify that the artifact is still there?"

"I can do that," she replied. "You have no intention, I take it, of telling Winfry about the *Stellar Quest*?"

"And confirm that I got that information second hand from Saunders through Isley? No way. Winfry will find out eventually that the *Stellar Quest* isn't out there anymore. It may simply take a few years."

"At least four," she only answered.

Greg wasn't due back until noon, Melanie thought. She and Greg were officially slated to remain on Mars until the next day, Wednesday, November fifth. As per Greg's request, she took the tour of the Art and History Museum. A young, blond-haired woman, a tour guide from Mariner University, led Melanie's group through all the major art departments that boasted the most recent of Martian work that had been crafted in the last three-hundred or so years, since colonization of Mars had got underway.

When Melanie found herself entering the history section of the museum, she had to keep her face neutral, especially when the group finally went past the pedestalled art piece affectionately called "Merlin the Magician's Crystal Ball."

"This is a very interesting piece," the young guide had said. "The author is an unknown. He claims he didn't create it at all. He found the top piece, the crystal ball in the rubble of a cave in, dusted it off and had it mounted in this beautiful bejeweled mount. Rumors over the years have even surfaced that it's not a work of art at all, but an artifact of an alien culture. Scientists, attempting to do spectral analysis of the sphere have said that they can't find a match to any crystalline substances known to man. This piece is definitely an import— from where no one is exactly sure."

"Could it really be from an alien race?" asked a mother of two young kids. The two were at her side, squirming and seemed way too young to care what was being said about the object. "It's not proof, then," the mother continued, "that there was a race of beings on Mars before we got here?"

The guide smiled. "No, we're certain little green men from Mars didn't make this thing. We believe those fanciful stories were just an attempt to perpetrate an elaborate hoax."

"Uh," Melanie had timidly raised her hand to ask, "You say you don't know who the author is?"

"We're not sure. We think it's the man who brought it to us."

"Who was he? Where did he claim he found it?"

"He was a local man, I believe, lived here in the city. I really don't know too much about him, I'm sorry. He lived a long time ago, and claimed he was exploring the trenches in the valley, and he just found it. He left it with us." The guide touched its sphere. "It's a gorgeous piece," she continued, "and the museum loved it so much they decided to accept it as a gift, and display it, so here it is."

"You wouldn't know, would you," Melanie had gone so far as to ask, "Who the man was?"

The guide pulled out her laser pen and inched down her imaging tablet. She scanned the readout. "Yes, it's here. A Willard Somedale in 2287, donated it to the city."

"Oh," Melanie nodded, lowly. In reality, the hairs on the back of her neck were spiking, and she felt a ripple travel down her spine. *Willard Somedale*, she whispered to herself. *My God, Greg was right. Somedale found what the Barthonians and Eleutions asked him to.*

Later, after the tour reached its final stop, Melanie lingered in the area. She let stand the unspoken notion that she was viewing some of the more obscure pieces that the tour— being limited to viewing only a few in the hour it was held— had not been able to visit. She found herself back by the artifact, and looking surreptitiously to the walls to make sure that no one was in the small gallery at that moment, she walked up to it, and very gently touched her fingertips against its crystal sphere.

"My name is Melanie Richards," she whispered to it, gently, again looking the chamber over to make sure no one would enter and wonder who in hell she thought she was talking to. She looked back to the crystal. "Athena sent Greg and me. You'll meet Greg tonight. Athena said don't take any more people. Greg and I are to bring you back to the Moon for the refusion. You're being recalled. But I think we're being studied, watched. Other people have some knowledge of the abductions, and Greg and I suspect they might know about your mate on Earth. The Earth-artifact is gone. I'm told it's re-fused with Athena. Do you understand what I've told you?"

There was a sudden milky flutter of light that winked on in the sphere. Melanie, startled, backed away.

A pin-prick-thin beam of red light all at once struck her head, and made her dizzy. Melanie, after it dropped away, felt as if her thoughts had been probed. A thought then filled her head:

Message understood and testimony
Validated.
Once re-fusion with Athena verified,
Vessel repository no longer needed.

The sphere all at once strobed! A single flash of light lit up the room. And then the sphere darkened again.

Melanie thought she'd seen a shadow in that instant against a rear wall. She swore she was being followed. She slowly backed away from the artifact and left the gallery.

CHAPTER FIFTY

"You think you may have been followed?" Greg asked Melanie, later that day.

"Even when I was with the tour group in the museum," she replied, nodding, "I had the feeling that I'd seen someone following me around the city, off and on. It's like in New Allentown, again. Greg, I think they know something. I think they might know that Athena is waiting for someone to take her Mars segment back to the Moon one last time, so that she can leave here."

"The sphere actually communicated with you?"

She nodded. "I saw the words in my head, like a neuralscan readout."

"It understood, then, why we're here?"

"We *have* to do it tonight, Greg," she said. "We're due to leave Mars, tomorrow."

"We're not breaking into computer systems this time, Mellie, or someone's apartment. Even if it's just our paranoia, and no one is really suspicious about us, the museum after hours, all the pieces will have cocoon shields around them."

She nodded.

***

One section of the city top terrace in Mariner City was reserved for an outdoor restaurant-villa. Greg and Melanie had dined there as the day slowly waned. Mars had a day/night rotation near identical to Earth, though its sidereal period, its orbit around the sun, caused its year to be almost twice as long. Thus, nightfall commenced around the right time in the course of a human's twenty-four hour "day."

As eight o'clock in the evening came around, Greg and Melanie headed down for the Art and History Museum. A staff member at the information booth informed them the museum was closing in another hour, and that it might have been better had they come here earlier.

"That's all right," Greg had only answered. "I've been here enough times. Tonight I wanted the quick-tour— just a few select pieces."

As they walked away and entered a lift-tube, Melanie looked over at him. She placed her lips to his ear. "You've only been to this museum once before in your life, right?"

He smiled and looked at her. "I know."

She shook her head. "Such a liar!"

Purposely avoiding level six, the level the artifact was on, at eight-thirty the two finally boarded a lift-tube and exited onto it. They still did not seek out the orb. Instead, they headed for a storage nook that Melanie had said she'd found that morning when she'd gone back after the tour and scoured the level for just such a place. She'd jotted down the general directions to it on a small imaging notepad. She pulled it out and keyed it with a laserscan pen. They found the nook, eventually, and entered, careful, all the while that the museum patrons still perusing its galleries at that hour did not see them.

The storage nook was about ten meters long and wide, and was filled with dust and cobwebs. (The critters [spiders] managed to find some way to follow humanity off the Earth and to its exotic other-world locations.) Greg and Melanie found a corner behind some old twenty-first century items that had been transported to Mars by its first explorers in the very, very early days. Greg crouched beside a seventy-inch, 16:9, High Definition TV which was probably someone's older set even when it was shipped over. God, what an antique!

Melanie plopped herself down on the floor beside it, and removed a small sensor device from her pants pocket.

She put it down beside her, and lifted up her blouse, revealing a life belt. She unfastened it, tucked in the blouse, and wrapped the belt around her waist again. She looked at Greg, then. He'd been in a trance, staring at her. "You *are* going to do the same, aren't you?"

"Yeah," he said, snapping out of his reverie. "I guess I just love looking at you."

"I should have a doll of me made for your office. And I know right where I'd put it."

"Where?"

"Atop your phone-imaging disk, so you can ogle me all the time, not just when I phone you up."

"How do you know I do that?" Greg smiled.

"Why do you think I give you so many full-body shots?"

She smiled also.

He reached over and grabbed her. "I have the real thing now; I'd rather play with *it*." He kissed her, and then pulled his shirt out from his pants revealing his own life belt. He did the same as Melanie had.

"Attention," came an announcement, muffled, from beyond the closet and out in the galleries, "the museum will be closing in ten minutes. Will all patrons please finish up your tour of our exhibits and prepare to depart? The museum will open tomorrow at nine in the morning sharp. The building will close precisely nine p.m. Security systems will immediately and automatically be activated. We thank you for being with us today, and hope to see you in the future. Thank you."

Melanie looked over at Greg. "We better do it now," she said.

They activated their force shield cocoons, the purple haze erupting around them. Immediately, Melanie began to adjust the settings on the portable remote. Faint white diamonds of light sparkled along Greg's and her force cocoons.

"Almost there," she said, her voice now being transmitted over the com-link line. A red alert wafer flashed on her sensor device. The unit also buzzed. "Got it! Harmonics established. Our body functions are now completely masked. They won't even pick us up on heat sensors."

She leaned back against the HDTV, and sighed. "I guess we wait now."

"I'd say about a half hour," Greg said.

She nodded.

**

The portable sensor Melanie carried enabled her to detect the presence of all force shields and adjust her and Greg's cocoon fields to penetrate all others. Talking was no problem. The museum was also equipped with primitive audio detectors, which meant they had to be careful not to bump into anything, but so long as Greg and Melanie had their cocoon shields activated, talking itself should not be recorded. The cocoon fields were designed to be fully reliable in zero air environments like in space or on the Moon. Activating the fields made it necessary to be on internal life support, because the things sealed out the outside world (including breathable air) that thoroughly. Exterior sounds only faintly filtered through the force shields; interior sounds leaked out just as poorly.

**

Prior to the memorial services on Monday, she and Greg had visited the local libraries and pulled all the design records available on the museum. Her check of the storage nook that morning was mostly to verify that it was accessible to them.

As with the Washington Monument back on Earth, no elaborate trip-beam detection system was really needed in the museum, because most people weren't proficient at replicating the type of devices first Randolph Phillips and now his daughter-in-law were able to assemble. Once through the major force screens in any level, no other deterrent devices existed to prevent intruders from disturbing the art treasures, except that each of them also were protected by individual or group-wall shields.

The storage nook had been very near the location of the artifact, and all Greg and Melanie had to hope was that there were no video cameras present in the area to catch them. Fortunately, they didn't have far to go.

Greg gasped. The orb solemnly sat in its indigo force shield. A spot of faint gold light flooded it from directional lighting on the ceiling. The artifact, itself, like the one in Crystal Cave, was roughly a thirty centimeter globe, the only difference was that this one was mounted in a platinum support structure interspersed with red jewels. It looked exactly as he remembered it. It inhabited the tiny gallery nook all itself.

Melanie paused and pulled out her sensor unit again. She began reading the force shield characteristics and adjusted the settings on the ones being generated by hers and Greg's.

She received a "lock on" confirmation, and nodded to Greg. They stepped into the force shield, cleared it and walked to the sphere.

"Hi," said Melanie, "I'm back."

The sphere remained dark, as if all it ever were was an artwork, after all.

Melanie became concerned. She looked at Greg. An idea occurred to her. "Tell it who you are. It knows me, but not you. Tell it, Greg."

He did.

The sphere suddenly burst into life, a low sheen of energy lit up the chamber.

Melanie looked up instantly and scanned the walls. She saw what she feared the worst, and calling Greg, pointed to a flashing emergency light. She deactivated her force shield; a general alarm wafted ominously across the museum level. She faced Greg and began to speak.

Greg saw only silent lips. He shut down his force shield, imitating her. "What?" All at once, as the field dropped, the sound of the alarm claxon filled his ears.

Melanie nodded. "I wanted you to shut down your force shield to hear that. We set off an alarm." She glanced down to her sensor device and scanned for other life signs. "Shit, they're coming already!"

"Intruder alert!" came an announcement over the address system. "Intruder alert in level six, section B127."

"We have to hurry!" said Greg. He turned to the sphere. "Take us to the Moon, now! Athena wants out of that membrane!"

"You!" came a voice suddenly behind him, as the lights in the room came on.

Melanie and Greg turned to see guards enter the tiny anteroom. The security men were repelled immediately by the artifact's force shield.

"Somebody call central!" shouted one of the guards. "Tell them to shut down the shield in Sector B127, level six! I don't know how they did it, but they're through the shield!" He looked at Greg and Melanie again. "You folks just come on out of there," he said.

"Greg Phillips," said a familiar voice, then. It was Alfred Winfry. "I had a feeling you might show up here. Your wife's been nosing around this crystal all day, asking about it, too." He glanced to their life belts, nodded and grinned. "You used the same tactic your father did to breach the shields in D.C. Come on out, Greg. You and your wife are in a lot of trouble. Your father could get away with stuff like this, but until you acquire the influence he had, you two can't. Now come on out of there. You've nowhere to go."

"Why isn't it working, Greg?" Melanie asked as she turned back to the sphere. The sphere was brilliantly aglow. "Why isn't it taking us?"

Greg had no answer, not at first, for why it would not begin the abduction sequence. Then he remembered the scene in the Hagerton visual where the Sensor and Light spheres were inching toward the force field surrounding the Crystal Cave orb. The moment the two made contact, Keith Hagerton and the two spheres were pulled inside, even though Keith was several meters up the underground lake and upon the ledge with his son.

"Melanie," he called to her, "touch the globe. Touch it!"

She touched it. Before he did so, himself, he turned back to the *InterWorld* chairman. "I'm sorry, Winfry, I can't. This is far more important than you can know— *far* more. If it's any help, I'm going to tell you something that I hadn't planned to. This artifact and the avatar entity within it hails from the Eighty-two Eridani solar system, and the people you launched for that star four years ago are already there."

He touched the sphere, then, and all hell broke loose. The entire artifact began to glow and a shimmering flutter infected every inch of it. It exploded then into an incredible fireball. Greg and Melanie were immediately consumed. The light was so bright, Alfred Winfry and the security men had to turn away and shield their eyes.

"Son!" called Winfry then, trying to look back. He saw the immense fireball rise off its pedestal, hover briefly in the air, and then in a flourish smacked right up against the ceiling. With a low "phfwt" sound, it went through the ceiling and was gone.

Alfred Winfry stared at what had just happened in shock. He turned to the guards. He thought about alerting the general security network that worked in behalf of the entire race throughout the solar system. He imagined it was already too late to launch some sort of intercept squad for the Moon. He was certain he'd seen the last of Greg Phillips forever.

"I said this before, when I heard his father died, and I'm saying it again, damnit!" he said to the men with him in the gallery. "What a waste. . . ."

CHAPTER FIFTY-ONE

-1-

It was ten p.m. in Mariner City, but back in Cassini Crater on the Moon it was early morning. Ron Isley's and his base's day/night schedule was situated such that for him and his base personnel it was six o' clock a.m. He was just about to get up for the day. He turned over in his bed, and glanced to his window.

The window had a neutral density producing substance in a layer of the glass that—like the one in the observation lounge he'd stared at before—could filter incoming light and darken it. Before turning in for the night Ron had adjusted it so that only a twilight washed into the room. Outside, and facing the east, he saw in his oval window frame a dark representation of the sun-washed surface of the Moon. Though still unseen beyond the horizon as yet, the day/night terminator was moving slowly to the west, and in just a few more days would sweep over Cassini crater, and give it a break from perpetual daylight.

Ron glanced up then at the ceiling. He wasn't even sure what compelled him to do it.

An ethereal substance drifted near the ceiling. Ron furrowed his brow at it, curiously. It took him a few seconds to realize that the sight of it was not a naturally occurring phenomena. It took his rational mind, in other words, a second or two longer to suddenly shout, *"Hey, what the hell is that?"*

He tensed and froze.

The cloud mass became an image of a little blond-haired girl— Swedish by the look of her. She was smiling at him and was dressed only in a free-flowing negligee that looked to be made only of ethereal light, like she was.

Little Frida Hagerton! he told himself.

The apparition of Frida never said a word, but Ron heard spoken words in his head, impressions perhaps of someone else's thoughts. The message she conveyed was, *"Find the fissure crack, and be in the cave in an hour, or you'll miss it. Hurry. . . ."*

Her image slowly dissipated. She was gone.

Ron had to ask himself if he hadn't only dreamt he'd been awake all this time. The experience of witnessing little Frida's astral presence above him felt too unreal to have been anything he'd actually seen.

Nevertheless, the message rebounded again in his thoughts. The words sounded as real as if someone had spoken them. He decided to heed them. He jumped out of bed, and got dressed. He laughed to himself. The last time he'd headed down to the launch bays on the spur of the moment, he'd scared the piss out of the maintenance crews on late-night duty down there, and shocked them even further when he returned a few hours later with Will Saunders and the late Randolph Phillips. He was about to pull another stunt like it on them once again.

Another thought made him laugh. *What would they do if he never returned?*

Greg and Melanie, moments before they left Mariner City, had had no time to think about what was about to happen. One moment they were cornered against the pedestal and the orb in the Martian museum, and the next they saw the room fall away beneath them, their very powers of reasoning beset by what could only be described by them as being in a numb detached state. They had grabbed for each other's hands, or at least believed they must have because they felt like they were holding onto one another as yet. A bubble-like membrane seemed to exist just a few feet in front of them and to all sides.

Oh wow, thought Greg. *I'm in one these again.* This felt a repeat of the moment he and his dad realized they were suspended high above the Washington Monument and near its pyramidion top weeks earlier in old D.C. Park.

Melanie and Greg felt themselves shoved through the ceiling, and blurring past the level above. The next level and the one after it followed so quickly it seemed a mere formality. Eventually, they caught a fleeting glimpse of the city-top terrace, where they had dined that evening, and felt themselves propelled through the city's protective shield bubble. In seconds, the red soil of Mars was taking shape beneath them, and began to contour into a planet. The continent-long scar that was the Mariner Valley trench loomed below them as a wondrous creation of nature. It was genuinely impressive.

Phobos and Deimos, Mars's two pebble-like moons (both for the most part too small and useless for anything commercially exploiting) hung in the night above the planet's surface, and the stars gradually began to dawn upon the heavens above them as the glare from the planet's surface waned with the planet's size as it dropped away from them.

They didn't know if they were real as yet, or disembodied entities. When Greg pondered the future the Eleutions promised the chosen few within the lunar cave, and then the future he and his new bride had to look forward to on Earth, or anywhere in the solar system, he really felt that a life with the three-hundred in the membrane was far more enticing.

***

Eighty million kilometers separated Earth and its moon from the planet Mars. The trip was over almost as soon as it began. Suddenly, there was the Moon, its shadowed and pockmarked shape racing for them from out of the star fields. Greg and Melanie were getting a treat that was indeed rare. The Moon was in orbital opposition with the Earth and Sun. The side facing them, therefore, as they approached the dual planetary bodies of Earth and Moon was the far side, that hemisphere of the lunar globe that the Earth never saw.

Greg swore the ride he and Melanie were taking was only a "thrill-visual" created by a modern-day special effects team. Neither a spaceship-mounted-sensor-sphere, nor one sent aloft on its own power, however, could streak across the lunar sky as quickly as this. One second the Moon's far side was drawing near, the next the Moon slipped below them as they headed for the day/night terminator.

The Lunar Alps arced into view all at once. Mere oversized mounds of Moon rock, they resembled to Greg the withering remains of sandcastles on a shoreline as the tide little by little eroded them to nothing.

Athena's Martian avatar orb deliberately slowed as it dropped to the valley floor before the cliff. Someone was down there, only now departing his private runabout, and only now leaving its egress panel.

Ron Isley stared, open-mouthed, as he watched the tiny ball of purple-blue energy waft down the lunar mountains and settle only a few meters beyond him and his runabout. All at once the thirty centimeter round ball of energy expanded to three meters, and within it an ethereal likeness of Greg and Melanie appeared.

Greg took a few steps forward and extended his hand toward the outer perimeter of the spherical cocoon. He grinned to Ron Isley. "Want a ride?" he asked.

Ron Isley felt the hairs on the back of his neck vibrate. This was way too much for him. He grinned back to Greg and took a breath. He took Greg's hand and stepped into the glowing sphere. Melanie took his other hand as the sphere shrank back again to its normal size.

The three turned to face the small runabout, and then felt a vertigo effect as the orb levitated up off the lunar valley floor and up the face of the cliff to the fissure crack. It approached it so slowly, Greg almost thought he was lift-belt-levitating to it himself. His instincts were to reach for the neuralscan medallion, place it on his forehead, order it to set him down on the fissure ridge, and just let him walk the rest of the way.

Instead, the forward motion slowed and he, Ron and Melanie were eased into the crack, and were saved the trouble of slithering through the oft-times incredibly narrow sections of tunnel that snaked back and into the mountain peak.

They could see. They sensed they were deep in the bowels of the mountain, and yet in a weird type of twilight, like a moonlit night, everything around them was visible to them. The orb itself seemed to be affecting the incoming light frequencies, enhancing them to allow sight.

They reached the wide descent shaft, and felt themselves lofted down its two kilometer length. There was a great haze of light at the very bottom. Its glow wafted quite a ways up the sheer walls of the shaft. The three almost instantly reached the area where the glow began, and only a few seconds after that they were at the bottom of the tunnel.

The cave looked exactly as Ron Isley had seen it last, the day he was abruptly ejected from it. He had shown Greg and Melanie segments of the visual log his staff had recorded down here as they worked. Thus, to the two of them, the place likewise possessed a sense of Deja vu.

Several Light Dogs were dispersed about the cavern, going all the way back to where Ron recognized the cavity nook. These, Ron thought, must have been clones of the one Keith originally brought with him to Crystal Cave on that first momentous day. Athena must have deployed them throughout the cavern length purposely for this occasion.

Her Martian avatar orb was about to touch down in the exact same spot where the other one had done so— directly above the myriad-colored crystal array in the cavern's center area.

The new arrivals were not alone in the cave; they had a welcoming committee. Keith Hagerton, his wife, son and daughter, were before the touchdown area, and they were joined by Willard Somedale. They were all smiling and wide-eyed as they watched the fireball waft downward, dropping a meter above the cavern floor and right before the crystal mass.

Keith and Kimberly held their daughter's hands as she stood between them. Frida Hagerton stared right at the three in the orb sphere as it descended toward her; she looked up at her parents. Frida took a step forward then, and her parents released their grip on her.

Melanie saw her body shimmer; she was changing, becoming corporeal again. She felt no different. A beep at her waist abruptly called her. She looked down and saw her lift/life belt reactivate its cocoon shield. She saw a similar field rise and wrap itself around Greg. The fields had been off since the two last deactivated them in the Mariner City museum.

"I think we're supposed to exit, now," Melanie whispered first to Greg and then to Ron Isley.

They both nodded, and with Melanie, stepped beyond the bubble shield contour, Greg and Melanie once again taking each other's hand. The three of them approached Frida, then.

"Mister Isley, hi," Frida told Ron, amiably.

"Hello, Miss Frida," he answered.

"You got my message; you're here. Are you coming with us?"

Isley glanced to the membrane. "You mean, go with all of you to Eighty-two Eridani?"

"Yes." Frida nodded and smiled at him.

"I'd like that, yes." He smiled and nodded. "Thank you for inviting me."

Frida shrugged. "Athena said to; she said you were okay; you weren't another Bill Saunders."

Ron laughed at that. "I consider that a compliment. Thank her for me."

Frida looked at Greg and Melanie, then. "My dad was furious with you when he found out you stole his viewwafer, but I'm glad you did. Athena thinks you both would make great additions to the group. Please say you'll come too. Athena and I are so hoping you will."

Frida seemed to react, then, as if someone was calling her. She faced back to the cavity membrane. They all did.

Athena was on the other side of the membrane, hovering like a wispy apparition of a beautiful female. She was waiting for Frida to let her out of that damn confinement zone.

Frida faced the three again. "She's impatient." She took a step forward then, to the Martian avatar orb, and Greg, Melanie and Ron Isley stepped back toward Keith and his group.

Kimberly held tight to Keith's arms as she watched their daughter deliberately step toward the orb. She entered it then, and suddenly it collapsed upon itself and possessed her. Like the other one before it, it caused all sorts of static charges to rise about Frida's hair and body. Each time of course, the force cocoon Frida wore got shorted out, no longer needed by the cocoon shield raised by the orb. Frida's body thus could appear to be unprotected in the Moon's vacuum.

She splayed her fingers as she stretched her hands down alongside her, and then slowly walked back to the membrane. Athena watched her, anxiously, and so full of what seemed sisterly love for Frida.

Frida stepped through the membrane and melted within Athena's presence.

Athena felt the surge of power within her, and reveled that she was at last complete. She turned then to the group out beyond the membrane. She gazed at them.

"Well, that's our cue," said Willard. "She's ready to leave that place, and she wants us in now."

A look of panic on her face, Melanie faced Greg, placing both her hands in his. "We're really going to do this?"

Kimberly went over to them, placing their hands in hers. "You won't regret it."

Keith joined in last, leaving his son and Willard to chat with Ron.

"Greg," he said, extending his hand, "good to see you again."

"You too," answered Greg.

Keith glanced to Melanie. "You married her, huh?"

Greg laughed. "Yeah."

Keith nodded. "I finally get to meet Melanie Richards."

She smiled shyly. "Don't be mad, Keith. Greg talked me into getting that code for your apartment. I was in love. I didn't know what I was doing."

Keith nodded. "I'm just sorry about what happened to your father, Greg."

Greg nodded. "I caused it; I involved him in all this. I wanted to prove to him that I too could be a part of something important . . . like him. If I hadn't went snooping around inside your apartment, found that viewwafer, he'd still be alive. . . . "

"Will all of you stop all that and please get in here?" pleaded Athena, suddenly. They glanced at one another.

Melanie glanced to Greg again. "Are we?"

He took her in his arms. "It's up to you, Mellie."

"On one condition," Melanie suddenly blurted, facing Athena. *"I want Samuel."*

"Who?" Keith asked.

Greg grinned. "Her cat."

"Is that allowed?" Melanie asked Athena.

Athena grinned. "You want me to swing by Earth and collect him? How will we explain his absence to your parents?"

"I miss him; he'll die of a broken heart if I never return."

Athena nodded. "All right. Anybody else?"

They all glanced to one another again, and grinned. As a group they walked then for the membrane. Each in their turn stepped through.

When they were all in, and their bodies all reposed upon slabs in the arena room, Athena descended to it, and with a single thought, whisked it all away. She reduced the entire room to memory pattern data and stored it in her thoughts.

She had the entire group—all three-hundred and three— within her, and gathering all her energy, literally pulling it from where it had resided within the energy modules of the cave, she charged the membrane. The pseudo-cave formations and the crystal array in the cavern's center all deteriorated into cosmic dust, and in seconds one would never believe that anything strange down here had ever occurred.

Like a purple-blue fireball Athena streaked through the cavern and funneled up the descent shaft, constricting herself just enough then to squeeze past the narrow fissure tunnel, and burst free of the mountain. She looked back toward Earth and willed herself toward it. In seconds she was inside New Allentown and the apartment of Melanie's parents. She made her way over to the living room's HoloView window where she found Samuel napping atop the sill.

Later that afternoon, the Richards would return to find a message stored in their recorder, a message from their daughter, a message about

Samuel's, Greg's and Melanie's whereabouts, a message the elderly couple would cherish, replay and keep a secret until the day they died.

Ascending once more into the sky, the magnificent facade of the North American continent behind her, Athena stared upon the starlight above old Earth. She sought out Eighty-two Eridani, and directed a thought impression to her people in faraway Elieutia.

"Mission complete," she said. "I'm returning for home."

The entire solar system was behind her in the wink of an eye.

EPILOGUE

Four years later

Alfred Winfry, now retired and former *InterWorld* chairman, lazily enjoyed the waning hours of daylight from a lounge chair in his Mariner City apartment. The terrace view before him overlooked the Mariner Valley trench, all in its red-rock splendor, topped by a sky also red-tinted.

"So much red," he thought. He missed the hues of Earth so far away in the night sky, and so much closer to the sun that its rays actually warmed the skin. Here on Mars the sun's light was but a feeble semblance, just a trifle. But if Earth was all blue sky, and Mars, red; what was life on Earth's moon like? "Like the crawl space under people's houses back when humanity still lived on Earth's surface," Winfry said in a low voice to himself. The Moon from its surface clearly resembled a room never actually meant to be visited, an anteroom, a place that needed to exist, but no place to seriously plan a vacation to visit.

There came a chime in the air above him. Someone had come calling and was out in the hall. He rose to answer the door, but heard his wife, Gina, leave the kitchen to do so as well.

He faced back to see her greet the man who had succeeded Alfred as *InterWorld* chairman. "Al?" Gina called. "It's James Bergan."

"Yeah," he answered, going over and greeting the man. "To what do we owe the pleasure, Jim?" he asked.

The man entered the apartment. "I guess you heard by now."

Alfred nodded. "The *Stellar Quest?*"

Bergan nodded.

"When?" asked Al.

Bergan glanced to Gina. "We lost the signal this morning."

Al smiled. "We can talk in front of Ginny, Jim."

"None of this is public knowledge as yet," said Bergan.

"But it will be eventually," said Al. "The *Saganites* have the transmission by now, you can be sure of it. . . .

(Saganites. The "We are not alone" amateur enthusiasts who regularly probed the stars for possible other-world radio transmissions, called themselves such in memory of *Doctor Carl Sagan*, the late twentieth century figure who first turned the quest to communicate with other life forms into a personal obsession all the way to the day he died.)

"In a few days," Alfred Winfry continued, "some bright, bored kid, somewhere, maybe on one of the out-worlds, with an advanced degree in applied mathematics, will figure out *InterWorld*'s decode algorithm." Alfred shook his head. "Wouldn't surprise me if the news hits the whole human population by nightfall."

"Or sooner than even that, perhaps," pursued Bergan, glancing again at Gina.

"Jim," sighed Gina, "quit worrying about me. I'm retired; I left the network. I'm not going to blab to the media outlets whatever *'secrets'* you're *'not here'* to share with my husband."

Her full name was Regina Myers-Winfry, and on Mars she up until recently hosted a local gab-fest talk show available as a live feed, available on Sensor Sphere home visual for distribution across the solar system. She even listed her last name as her husband's, Winfry, although why she would go by his last name and not her own even she could not explain. She thought it might be a past-life thing. She swore in a past life she was a top draw talk show celebrity, even owned her own broadcast network. A very famous woman, an actress even, she imagined, she was, in her former lifetime. A woman also known by the surname Winfry.

"Curious, isn't it though," Al said. "On Earth, it's late October by now, autumn. It was autumn then, four years ago when Randolph Phillips was found dead by that Cassini security guard, uh, Bill Saunders. His death was officially listed as an accident, a fall probably while cave exploring."

"What else could it have been?" barked an agitated Bergan.

"Not according to Saunders," said Al.

"Are you still giving serious thought to that fool's nonsense?" Bergan spat. "He's an idiot."

"I understand," smiled Al, "he's made much of that ordeal four years ago in the Lunar Alps. You've no doubt heard him." He glanced to Gina. "He's been on all the talk shows, published several books. He's done quite well for himself."

"Frankly, I wish he'd just *shut up!*"

"Like all the others did who were there back then? Funny, how most of them considered remaining mum to be in their best interests. I witnessed some strange events myself right here in the city. I guess reassignment wasn't an option for me."

"You *retired!*"

"Retired." Al grinned. "Of course."

Alfred Winfry over the years, since Ron Isley's abrupt departure from Cassini, had seen all the visuals that both Isley and Greg Phillips had sworn no longer existed. Alfred had literally grown fascinated by the subject. "I know what went down on the Moon and in Pennsylvania four years ago, Jim."

"You don't know what you know," Bergan replied.

"Fine. Are you here to make sure I don't make things worse? Don't worry. It's Saunders who's going to take the news of the *Stellar Quest*'s disappearance as vindication, proof of what he was told by that entity, Athena."

"We don't know the ship is lost."

Winfry smirked. "It all happened four years ago, remember. Four years is a long time."

"You're convinced they've been dead for four years? The ship encountered something which incinerated it instantly?"

"I haven't said anything," Winfry replied. "You sound like you pretty much have what happened up there all worked out in your head already. I've been expecting this news about the ship for some time now. I was told something up there had happened, back when it did. Have I ever told you that?"

"The Phillips's kid? Are you going on about that little piss-ant again? His father must be rolling in his grave with disappointment."

"Jim, what do you really want here?" asked Alfred Winfry, fatigued.

Jim Bergan glanced again to Winfry's wife.

"Ginny?" Al asked.

She nodded, and departed for another room.

"So?" Al asked after she'd gone.

"Do you have a viewing chamber?"

Al nodded and they retired to it. Once settled on the cushioned floor of the sound-proofed chamber, Bergan produced from his pocket a home visual viewwafer. Al reached over to the side storage nook and retrieved two headsets, visors and a playback unit.

"You still have important friends in high places," said Bergan to Winfry. "I've been asked to keep you informed."

"What is that?" Winfry asked of the recording.

"The final telemetry from the *Stellar Quest* before it quit. Even crew communiques. They'd sent us Intel hours earlier about strange occurrences aboard ship—"

"Really?" said Al, raising an eyebrow. He nodded. "So whatever happened in the last moments before you lost telemetry, you're telling me, was serious enough for the ship to wake up the crew."

Bergan shuffled uncomfortably on the cushions, but nodded. "That's correct. The crew was awakened. Something was seriously upsetting them. That was part of what they transmitted to us, their concern, hours before. They claimed they had intercepted transmissions they thought could only be real-time and of alien origin. Katill's crew in those last few hours were really rattled."

"I can imagine," said Winfry.

"They even claimed they were probed."

"Where from?"

"Eighty-two Eridani, at that time still sixteen light years away."

Al nodded. "Wow."

"But it's this last stuff you should see."

The program began and before Al Winfry came the *Stellar Quest*'s interior, the crew all assembled in the ship's bridge. An ethereal female "presence" all at once materialized before them, and the ghost-like specter of a little blond Earth girl eerily accompanied her.

Little Frida Hagerton, Winfry mused.

Captain Mitch Katill appeared to be conversing with the two spectral females, but there were no verbal responses from either, none that could be recorded by the vessel's electronics. Suddenly, the two females vanished; moments later, an explosion of light consumed the crew. The viewing chamber from that point on displayed only black.

"Unit off," requested Al of his viewing chamber. He removed his visor and headset. "My God."

"Uh huh," agreed Bergan.

"This is *For My Eyes Only,* I take it?" He fingered the visor glasses in his hand absently.

"I would think that went without saying," specified Jim Bergan. He nodded.

"Her name was Athena," uttered Al, ultimately. He nodded. "That's the name she went by."

"So I'm told you've mentioned before . . . *to others,*" Bergan replied.

He nodded. "She called herself an *Eleution.* They will be back, Jim. You can be sure of it. Back for the rest of us."

"Not any time soon, I hope," replied Bergan. "I hope to be long dead by the time they decide to return and do with us whatever the hell it is they've been planning all these long centuries. You'll be long gone yourself by then, I would imagine."

Winfry nodded.

***

After Bergan had gone, Al returned to the living room. Gina joined him, ultimately, as the last threads of daylight hung on the horizon. They sat down upon the sofa and pondered the terrace view.

"He looked terrible," said Gina of the new *InterWorld* chairman.

Al Winfry nodded. "You can guess why."

Regina Winfry had seen the Hagerton visuals herself in the past. "So, it's true? We're not alone out here in the galaxy?" "This isn't a galaxy, Ginny, or even a universe. It's a nursery. There may be many other worlds inhabited like ours out there among the stars. But until we're ready, we're here to stay in the home world solar system. We're all like caterpillars, not yet butterflies."

"I wouldn't mind being a butterfly," she mused.

"We'll get there," Al Winfry mused. "One of these days."

AUTHOR'S NOTE

The characters, Michael DeAngelo, Melinda Shepherd and Cynthia Bradshaw—mentioned in *The Stellar Quest* as earlier "captures" by Athena for her lunar membrane lair collection of captured human beings— reprise their roles from my novel, *Yesterday's Child: An Adventure Through Time* (currently available via **www.PaulFichera.com** as a Kindle e-book).

Chapter One of *The Stellar Quest* is also *Yesterday's Child's* "Epilogue chapter." And as such that novel's final chapter serves as a lead into *The Stellar Quest,* although in my opinion the two stories are best experienced reading *The Stellar Quest* first.

Paul Alexander Fichera
June 2020.

www.ingramcontent.com/pod-product-compliance
Lightning Source LLC
Chambersburg PA
CBHW030542260626
47157CB00006B/2154